The
Thunder
Of
Silence

By: Lynn Denay

Order this book online at www.trafford.com
or email orders@trafford.com

Most Trafford titles are also available at major online book retailers.

Printed in Victoria, BC, Canada.

ISBN: 978-1-4269-2811-6 (soft)
ISBN: 978-1-4269-2845-1 (hard)

Library of Congress Control Number: 2010902493

*Our mission is to efficiently provide the world's finest, most comprehensive book publishing
service, enabling every author to experience success. To find out how to publish your book, your
way, and have it available worldwide, visit us online at www.trafford.com*

Trafford rev. 5/28/2010

 www.trafford.com

North America & international
toll-free: 1 888 232 4444 (USA & Canada)
phone: 250 383 6864 ✦ fax: 812 355 4082

For Crystal, Jordan and Drew
You have been there through it all.
Always know that in this lifetime, no-one could love you more.
You gave and give me faith to find my dreams.

For Denise and Russell
You gave of yourself, shared your life and offer
support in too many ways to count.

For Roberta
You would come through a hurricane on a rector scale of 10 if
you thought I needed you and always reach into my weakest
moments and remind me that I'm strong.

You all believed when I didn't
and made me believe because you did.

For Hussh, you inspire me to look deep within myself and
not fear the known or the unknown and encourage me to
reach for the stars. With you, all things are possible.

For my family, I would not be here without your love
and support, the lengths you have gone to, to show
your love and support can never be repaid.

MY LOVE TO YOU ALL, FOR ALL ETERNITY!!

CHAPTER 1

It began in Algiers on the bayous of Louisiana. The families were fishermen by trade and worked their fishing lines on the bayou from sunup to sundown. No-one in the family would be excused from gathering the nets for any reason, except on school days and then, they surfed their lines after school until sundown.

In the sixties growing up in a family of ten or more was common, but for Michelle Monceret, it was an unspeakable nightmare. With a Mother like Marie it was next to impossible to find peace anywhere and at the tender age of twelve, Michelle made up her mind to find a way out of the darkness, no matter what the cost. She told herself nothing could ever be, as bad as, what she had lived through already. She would sacrifice anything to break the chains that kept her locked in the grips of Marie.

Michelle was the oldest of five girls and next to oldest of six boys and Marie kept an eye on Michelle at all times. She accused Michelle of things Michelle had no comprehension of and she was petrified of her mother with no-one to turn to. Michelle felt as if she never belonged in her family and grew up feeling as though she was an outcast.

Marie would lie in bed at night waiting until the wee hours of the morning and when the whole house was sound asleep, she eased out of bed, being quite as a mouse not to disturb her husband Charles from the deep sleep in which he had fallen. After she made it out the room and down the hall, she slipped quietly into the girl's room where Michelle laid, quietly crying and waiting for her visit from her Mother. Marie jerked the covers off Michelle and pulled her from the wall she had braced herself against while Michelle's sisters' Stacy and Cathy were on the top bunk pretending to be asleep.

Marie swore if Michelle cried out and woke her sisters, she would strangle her. Michelle would plead with her mother and swore to God she had not done anything, as Marie hit her with a closed fist in the face. Marie accused Michelle of sleeping with Charles her own father. Michelle swore to Marie she had not and would never, as Marie ripped off her panties and jammed her fist up inside Michelle, while covering her mouth with the covers to muffle the sound of Michelle's screams.

On a few occasions Cathy cried out begging her mother to stop, but Marie told Cathy to go back to sleep and not say a word to anyone, as she returned to Michelle and threatened to kill her if she ever said a word to a soul; all the while reminding her that know-one would ever believe her. Then she turned and disappeared down the hall. Marie slipped back in bed as if nothing had happened and off to sleep she would go.

Meanwhile, down the hall, Michelle crawled out of bed and to the bathroom with the help of Cathy. She sat on the bathroom floor while Cathy got a cold bath-cloth to help her wash the blood off her face and helped Michelle check the bleeding. This was almost an every night occurrence for Michelle. Although it wasn't always that bad and some nights it was worse and had been going on for as far back as Michelle could remember. After a while the pain stopped, as well as the bleeding and Michelle with Cathy's help crawled back to her bed and cried herself to sleep.

The next morning when Charles would see the bruises in her face, he would ask what happened. Michelle was scared to death for her father to hug, touch or acknowledge her at all, so she backed away and said the board on the bunk bed fell again and hit her in the face while she was sleeping. Then she ran down the hall with Marie watching from the kitchen.

Marie was a self centered women that had a jealous streak inside her know-one could have ever imagined. She dabbled here and there with the unknown, a little candle burning and a lot with an old woman known as Mamie that lived deep in the swamp. People all over the bayou knew Mamie and stayed clear of her at all cost. They knew she practiced voodoo with black magic and if they went in the swamp at sunset, they could hear a chanting in the air that made the hair on the back of their necks stand up.

The people on the Bayou also knew of a woman that lived in the city. She was an attractive woman that on one too many occasions, crossed Mamie's path. Mamie's husband was known to stray from home on his weekend binges and he enjoyed the company of beautiful women and soon the rumors of the affair traveled through the swamp like wild fire and it soon reached Mamie as well. On the next full moon rising, Mamie gathered the things she needed and went to her secret place in the swamp to perform her magic.

She waited until the clock's hand was almost midnight. Then she hurried along casting the circle she would do her bidding in. At half past midnight the bidding began. Mamie wrote a spell in blood on a virgin parchment, along with a picture of the women, placing it in a glass jar. Mamie then buried the container in the women's yard at sunrise.

Mamie then paid the women a visit and said her husband would soon be leaving on a journey never to return and Mamie told the woman, upon his departure, she would begin to find lesions and blisters on her legs that were from a spell she cast on her. Mamie then told the women, the jar had been buried on her property and if she could find the jar before the parchment began to rot she could break the spell. If not and the parchment began to rot nothing would break the spell or save her. The women of course became upset with Mamie and demanded she leave; so being the kind gracious woman Mamie was, she bid the women farewell and departed.

It wasn't long before things came to pass just as Mamie predicted. Mamie's husband's journey began and the women found a lesion on her ankle. She swore it was a coincidence until it began to grow. Then, she thought of Mamie's warning and started digging all over her yard trying to find the glass jar with the parchment. The whole bayou thought she had lost here mind as she began to tell them what Mamie had told her and begged for their help. That only scared the people of the bayou more so they left her alone to do her own searching. In a few weeks the lesions began to spread over her legs to the point she could know longer walk. She then had to hire a nurse to care for her at home and within a couple of months the women watched as her beauty disappeared before her eyes until she died. Mamie's husband never returned from the mysterious trip he took either.

All this only made the people on the bayou even more afraid of Mamie. No-one went deep in the swamp anymore, so that gave Marie a since of freedom, because she knew she would not be seen in her dealings with Mamie. Marie wanted to be the center of attention and wanted to possess Charles and make certain he would never leave her. She had Mamie cast many circles in which Mamie and Marie joined hands and performed the cast that conjured the sprits from the depths of hell that cursed the entire blood line for all eternity, because Marie didn't fully understand the consequences of her request and what would come for her and her family in the future would be unspeakable.

Meanwhile, Michelle turned fifteen and the nightly visits from Marie seemed slack off. David the oldest son; Michelle's brother started dating. In those days they had to have someone with them on their dates as a chaperone, so Charles made Michelle go with David. Michelle didn't mind; it was freedom from the house and her Mother. Michelle knew they would be stopping to pick up her cousin Linda and she would have an evening to do what ever she pleased.

After David picked up his date and Linda, he drove into town where he stopped at a gas station to let Michelle and Linda out after he gave the girls a few dollars and told them what time he would be back to pick them up. The girls stood in the station parking lot watching as David drove off. They looked at each other, laughed and ran to the ladies room to put on their makeup and do their hair for their night on the town.

When they finished dressing they walked down the street to the club where all the wild kids in town hung-out. Michelle walked in and looked around not really knowing what to expect. Linda on the other hand, was an old timer on the seen. Linda walked in and told Michelle it was time to scope the place out for some real fun. About that time, Darwin Breaux walked by and Michelle caught his eye. He stopped and asked her what her name was. Michelle looked up at him a little shy, but told him, her name was Michelle Monceret.

He held his hand out as if to shake her hand and told her it was a pleasure to meet her. He asked Michelle what she was doing there as Linda butted in and told Darwin she had seen him there a lot, but they just never seem to cross paths before. Then Dalton Cain, Darwin's friend walked up and introduced himself to Linda and asked if he could get her a drink. Linda said a drink would be a great start, so the two of them disappeared in the crowd as Darwin and Michelle stood there for a moment not really knowing what to say. Then, Darwin asked Michelle if she wanted a drink; thinking a drink would make her less anxious. Michelle said she would love one, so Darwin told her he would be right back and asked her if she would hold his pool stick while he was gone.

Linda walked back over when she saw Darwin going to the bar and told Michelle they had caught themselves two lives ones. Michelle asked what she meant by that and Linda told her those were the two wildest boys in the state of Louisiana and if they really wanted to have fun, those were the guys that could show them how. Darwin came back with the drinks and after a few games of pool and drinks, Linda and Dalton were getting really cozy at the table and suggested they all leave and go somewhere more private. They left the lounge and went to a hotel across the street from where David would be picking the girls up. Linda and Dalton got a room, but Darwin and Michelle stayed in the car talking. Michelle felt a strange peace with Darwin that she never felt before. She hoped he wasn't upset that she wasn't ready to go all the way and Darwin assured Michelle there would be plenty time and not to worry.

It would soon be time for David to pick them up, so Michelle asked Darwin if he would get Linda before her brother got there so they could get cleaned up. Darwin went to the room and a few minutes later Linda came out to the car and Darwin walked them across the street to the gas station. He asked Michelle if she wanted him to wait with her, but Michelle told him no, so he kissed her goodbye and went to get Dalton.

Linda and Michelle watched as they drove off. Then they ran in the ladies room to wash their make-up off and was combing their hair when they heard the horn from David's car blowing. They pulled their hair back in ponytails and out the door they went. When they got in the car, David asked what they had done with their evening and they said they had gone to the movies and seen double features.

A few months later, Michelle went all the way with Darwin. She felt as though that brought them closer together and she just knew in her heart that Darwin would be the one that would take her away from the horrifying life she had at home. After a few months of meeting Darwin in town on the weekends; Charles and Marie decided to drive in town one afternoon. David and Michelle had picked up his date and dropped the girls in their usual place. Only this time when the girls walked across the street to the club where their guys were waiting; Charles turned the corner in his car and Michelle caught his eye as she walked in the club. Charles being a Pentecostal preacher could not believe his eyes. He waited outside for a while debating if he should go inside or not, but the longer he waited the angrier he became. Charles was well known for his temper and just as Michelle leaned over and kissed Darwin her father came through the door and saw her.

Michelle didn't know what hit her when her father slapped her across the pool table from behind. She picked herself up stunned and looking through blurry eyes she couldn't believe what she was seeing. Charles had Darwin by the throat choking him. He told Darwin he was taking

5

Michelle to the doctor the next morning and if he had touched her, he was a dead man.

Michelle stood there not knowing what to do or say when her father grabbed her and threw her toward the door. Michelle looked back at Darwin with tears in her eyes and told him she was sorry. Darwin yelled back to her as she went through the door; that he loved her and everything would be all right. The ride home was a nightmare from hell. Charles was yelling and demanding answers Michelle knew she couldn't give him. He wanted to know, where the hell David was and how long it had been going on. Michelle just sat there not saying a word when Charles turned in his seat and slapped Michelle across the face. He demanded she answer him, but all Michelle could say was she didn't know where David was. Michelle tried to tell her father, that was the first time it had happened, but her father called her a liar and told her when he got her home she was in for the beating of her life, then he punched the dashboard and said he was going to kill David when he got his hands on him.

When they got home Charles told Michelle to go to her room and not come out for nothing until morning. As she walked down the hall he yelled he was taking her to the doctor the next morning and they would all see just what they were dealing with. Then, Charles called Michelle back to him and looked at her with tears in his eyes and asked her why she decided to live a life like that and where had he gone wrong. Michelle couldn't give him those answers, because she knew he would never believe her anyway, so she just told him she was sorry for everything and went down the hall to her room.

Back in town, Darwin and Dalton waited for David to come pick the girls up so they could let him know what had gone down in the club. When David drove up and saw Darwin standing there he blew his horn for Michelle and Linda like always. Darwin walked over to the car and told David they wouldn't be coming that time. David looked at him like he was crazy and asked him what the hell he meant by that when Darwin backed away from the car and told David that Mr. Monceret had been in town and seen Michelle and took her home with him. Darwin said Charles was mad as hell when he left with Michelle and David just sat in the car with Meg and said his life was over and he could never go home no matter what.

Meg asked David what he was going to do and told him if he planned on leaving she wanted to go with him. David said he was taking her home and was going to stay in town for a few days to figure out what to do.

David told Darwin that he had better stay away, because Charles would kill him; then drove away.

The next morning, a loud banging on the door woke Michelle. Her father told her to get out of bed and get dressed. Michelle got up and slipped on one of her old dresses from the closet and went to the kitchen where she thought her father would be waiting. As she walked down the hall she heard voices and remembered staying up until the wee hours of the morning waiting for David to come home and wondered if she could have slept through the fall out that would have followed. She looked around the kitchen and the living room for David; then walked outside to look for his car. As she stepped out the door she saw David's car wasn't there, but Charles and Marie were already in the car waiting for her and Charles yelled for Michelle to get in the car, they had a long ride back to town to see the doctor. Michelle climbed in the back seat and held her breath most of the way there. Then it hit Michelle; this was her way out. Michelle decided she would make everyone believe she was pregnant and thought Darwin would marry her and all her troubles would be over.

When they got to the doctor's office Charles went inside to talk to the doctor first. Then Michelle got out the car and waited in the front office for the doctor to call her. When she was called, she walked to the back with the nurse and sat on the table where the nurse asked her to have a seat and was told the doctor would be in to see her shortly. She sat there getting more anxious by the minute and the next few minutes felt like hours.

Then the door opened and the doctor walked in. He looked up from Michelle's file and asked her if she was ready for this and Michelle asked,

"Ready for what?"

Dr. Decody told Michelle Mr. Monceret, wanted to know if she had been sexually active and explained they we're going to do an examination to verify if she was still a virgin. Michelle looked up at the doctor and told him if her father really was going to go that far, she would just be honest and tell the truth about the whole thing. Dr. Decody looked at her a little surprised and asked her what she meant. Michelle admitted to him that she had been sexually active and already knew she was going to have a baby. Dr. Decody asked her how she knew she was pregnant, so Michelle told him she had sex three times and her period was two weeks late and she had been sick in the mornings for the last week. Dr. Decody agreed it sounded as if she was pregnant.

The doctor told Michelle, she could have saved herself a lot of embarrassment if she had told her father the truth from the start. He asked Michelle if she wanted to tell Mr. Monceret or did she want him to tell her father. Michelle said, she guessed he had better be the one to tell her father, because he might take it more calmly from him. Dr. Decody smiled at Michelle and told her he knew this was hard for her father and he would tell him. The doctor walked out the room forgetting he didn't examine Michelle and she waited until the nurse came back to the room to tell her she was free to go. Michelle walked to the car and got in the back seat. Charles started the motor and turned the car around to head for the bayou without saying a word. They passed the road for their house and Michelle asked if they were going somewhere besides home and Charles told Michelle he was taking her to her new home. Michelle asked,

"What new home?"

Charles told her, he was taking her to the Breaux's house. He said Darwin got her pregnant and he was going to marry her and take care of her from then on. Michelle just sat in the back seat thinking it was way too easy and asked herself why she had not thought of it before then.

As they pulled in the drive, Ms Allison Breaux came out to ask what they needed. Charles told her what a low life her son was because of what he had done and felt it was their responsibility to see to it that the right thing was done for all involved. Irvin Breaux came out to see what all the yelling was about. He too, couldn't believe his ears when he heard the news about Michelle being pregnant with his son's child. He told Charles he would talk to Darwin and if it was true his son would do the right thing in marring Michelle.

Charles walked over to the car and told Michelle to get out. As she stepped out of the car he told Irvin when he found his son to take care of everything quietly and if they needed him to sign anything; they knew where to find him. He left Michelle standing in the driveway when he drove off. The Breaux's stood there for a few minutes more in shock than anything else. Then, Ms Allison asked Michelle if she would like to go in the house and wait for Darwin. Michelle agreed and said she was sorry for any inconvenience she had caused. Ms Allison told her not to worry; they would get everything straight when Darwin got home.

Shortly before dark Darwin drove up in the driveway and was met at the door by his father. Irvin took Darwin outside to talk to him before he saw Michelle. After his father told him what was happening Darwin went in the house where Michelle was waiting. She could smell beer on Darwin's breath as always and he told her they would be married the next day. Michelle looked up at Darwin with tears in her eyes and asked if he was angry with her. Darwin told her he loved her and everything was going to be fine, then he took her by the hand and told her she could sleep in his room that night, he would sleep on the couch. Michelle laid in bed that night until the wee hours of morning thinking she would get pregnant right away and everything would be just fine.

The next morning, the Breaux's were up early. When everyone was dressed and fed, they headed to town. They stopped off at the Monceret's to get Charles to sign for Michelle to be married; then, they all went to the courthouse to finish the deed. That afternoon, Darwin and Michelle were married and settled in to live at the Breaux's.

Michelle learned quickly that married life with Darwin would be very different from dating him. He still went to town and drank with his buddies almost every night. He stayed out to all hours of the morning and told Michelle her place was at home, because she was pregnant. Darwin ran into David a few weeks after Michelle and he had gotten married and told David the news and told him he should go home because the worst was over as far as he and Michelle were concerned. David told Darwin to tell Michelle he loved her, but he had signed up with the Navy and would be gone for quite a while. David told Darwin to tell Michelle to take care of herself and the baby; when Darwin agreed to relay the message David just walked away. David married Meg after he enlisted in the Navy and was stationed in Italy for five years. Michelle was heart broken when Darwin told her the news, but knew there was nothing she could do then, but hope for the best for everyone involved at that point.

A couple of months went by and Michelle got her period right on time each month and she knew time was running out for her. Finally on the third month her period didn't come and knew at last she was finally pregnant. Michelle thought the whole world was going to fall in place until Ms Allison told her it was time to see the doctor to see how things were moving along. Michelle made up every excuse in the book, but Ms Allison made the appointment anyway.

Michelle admitted to Darwin that she wasn't pregnant when she married him. She told him she had to do something to get away from the claws of Marie, but she was pregnant then and stood there waiting for Darwin's response. What she got took her totally by surprise. Before she knew it, Darwin hit her in the mouth with a closed fist cursing her with every breath; he demanded to know why she would trap him, he was infuriated. From that day forward Michelle had traded one hell hole for another. She was beaten by Darwin and cursed almost on a daily basis.

Michelle just thought Marie was her worst nightmare. When the beatings started the Breaux's knew what was happening, but they were unable to do anything to stop it and Michelle knew she was on her own like all the other times in her life.

Michelle was three months pregnant when Charles came for a surprise visit to see how she was getting along. When he got out of the car and saw Michelle, he flew into a rage when he saw the bruises in her face. He told her to go inside and pack her things; she was going home and he was going to kill Darwin if he ever saw him again. Michelle looked up at her father scared and shaking as well as being so embarrassed it was hard to look him in the eye. She burst into tears and stood there crying. Charles walked over to her and tried to console her, but when Michelle hugged her father she saw Marie staring at her from the car and quickly pulled away and went inside to gather her things.

On the ride home she decided; she would never be put in that position again with anyone. Michelle swore she would stop anything Marie had in-store for her when she got home as well. She knew she had a child coming into the world and sat there thinking what kind of life the baby would really have and the price her child might have to pay in this life. Michelle decided no matter what; she was going to make it better for herself and her baby.

Much to her surprise the transformation in moving home went a lot better than Michelle had thought. There were no midnight visits from Marie, but even so, Michelle slept with the door locked and a chair behind it so she couldn't get in. The next few months went well and Michelle finally found herself letting her guard down and Marie's Mother, Ms Catharine came to visit. She spent a lot of time talking to Michelle about her life and what her future plans were now that she had a baby on the way. Catharine talked to her about all the abuse she had suffered and told her to be strong. Michelle's Grandmother also told her if she ever needed a friend to talk to she would always be there for her, but Michelle stared off in space as Catharine got up to walk away. Tears filled Michelle's eyes as she called after her Grandmother. She asked her not to go and then said she needed to tell her something, but made her promise she would never say anything to anyone about what she was going to tell her. Catherine turned and looked at Michelle, then walked back and hugged her while telling her she was safe and that she would never let anyone hurt her again. Michelle looked up at her Grandmother and told her about the things Marie had done to her all her life and told her Grandmother she was afraid of her mother.

Catherine looked at Michelle with a shocked expression. She told her she was going to get to the bottom of things no matter what it took. Michelle ran after her begging her to stop and reminding her that she had promised not to say a word, but Catharine stomped off anyway. When Catharine confronted Marie, Michelle was standing on the edge of the porch. Marie screamed all of it was a lie, but Michelle yelled it was true and her sister Cathy knew it was true too. Catharine called Cathy to the porch and asked her about what she had seen or heard when she was younger, but Cathy being scared half to death, took one look at Marie and said she never saw a thing and ran in the house crying. When Cathy ran, Marie walked over to Michelle and slapped her so hard she fell off the porch on her back. Marie screamed, she was lying, and told Michelle she would kill her and dove out in the yard on Michelle. Catharine pulled Marie off Michelle and told her she was going to kill the baby if she didn't stop, reminding her she was pregnant too. Marie just turned and walked in the house like nothing had happened. Catharine went inside with Marie leaving Michelle in the yard with a busted lip, bleeding.

Michelle ran in the back of the house looking for Cathy. When she found her hiding, she demanded to know why she lied for Marie and Cathy pleaded with her to forgive her, but she was too afraid of her mother to tell the truth. Michelle burst into tears again and hugged her sister. Michelle told her she was sorry she involved her at all and that everything would be all right, but from then on, Michelle kept her distance with Marie. Once again, Michelle swore that some day she would find a way out the hell hole if it was the last thing she would ever do.

CHAPTER 2

A few weeks later summer arrived. One morning that June Michelle was awakened in the middle of the night with a warm wet feeling underneath her. As she stood up trying to get out of bed she felt dizzy and fell back on the bed and screamed for help. Cathy was in the bed next to her and jumped out of bed and turned on the light. When Cathy turned to Michelle she was horrified at the sight of blood everywhere and she ran to get her parents. When Charles got to the room, Michelle was white as a sheet and had no color in her face. He screamed for Marie to get the car started and pull it around to the back door, as he was running down the hall.

Michelle's brother Mike helped Charles get Michelle to the car and Marie, Mike, Charles and Cathy took Michelle to the hospital. Dr. Decody met them and the staff went to work on Michelle to determine what was happening to her and the baby. After a while the doctor walked out and told Charles the afterbirth was pulling away from the wall and they didn't know if they could save Michelle or the baby. The Doctor told Charles it was going to be a long night and at that point, they couldn't take the baby, because of the position the baby was in. They started giving Michelle blood right away to try and get her stabilized for the time being. A while later in the waiting room, Marie's water broke and Charles went with Marie to the OB floor.

All the time in between Marie was beginning to reap what she had sowed as well. She wasn't sleeping nights, because the nightmares were horrid, as well as seeing sprits during the day and an ungodly presence followed her around and taunted her. When Marie found out she was pregnant again she was already going mad. Charles felt the presence and thought is was the devil trying to take his soul because he was a preacher and he tried to deal with the sprit, but it was too strong. Marie went into labor and since the baby was the thirteenth one for her, the labor was short, but the baby was stillborn and Marie stopped speaking. The sprits and entities were all around her and she was lost is a world of silence that no one could save her from. Again Marie thought of Mamie and wanted to reach out to her, for her to save her, but the curse of the blood line had already settled in and the god's of the underworld wanted their payment, their reward and Marie was lost in a room with what came to clam her soul.

Two days past, when Michelle opened her eyes again. She was in a great deal of pain, but the doctors wouldn't give her anything because her vital signs were unstable. On the sixth of June, the Doctors told Cathy, they had no hope of either Michelle or the baby living through the birth and they were not even sure if the baby was alive to help push its way out in the birth process. Michelle heard the conversation and laid there helpless as the doctor left the room. She screamed for Cathy to find a nurse to come help her and Cathy ran out the room not really knowing what was going on, but she was looking for anyone to help her sister. She ran across a nurse named Sherrie and told her what had been happening and pleaded with her to come help her sister. Sherry told her that it was time for her shift to end and she would send another nurse to check on Michelle in a little while, but Cathy burst into tears scared to death of everything that was happening and looked up at the nurse and asked if anyone really cared that her sister was going to die and the baby was already dead as she turned and walked away.

Sherrie watched as Cathy rounded the corner for the phones and glanced down at her watch to check the time. When she looked up she saw her replacement coming down the hall. Sherrie told her, she was going to check on a patient before report and as Sherrie walked toward the room where Michelle laid, she began to pray. She entered the room and walked over to the bed where Michelle laid lifeless and pale, she took Michelle's hand in hers and asked if she could do anything to help make her more comfortable. Michelle looked up at Sherrie and told her to please save her baby no matter what and pleaded with Sherrie not to let her baby be sent home with her Mother if she died.

When Sherrie looked at Michelle, she saw fear in her eyes. She touched Michelle's stomach and gave it a little push and the baby moved into the birth position. Sherrie told Michelle; she and the baby would be fine, but she had to be strong enough for the both of them and reassured Michelle she would not leave her until it was over. The next few hours seemed like years for Michelle and Cathy. Sherrie kept her hand on Michelle's stomach and when a contraction started, she and Cathy pushed from the top of Michelle's stomach while Michelle bared-down the best she could, to push the baby out.

Finally they could see the crown of the head and Sherrie told Cathy to go find the doctor, so they could finish the delivery. When Dr. Decody appeared in the doorway, Sherrie looked up and told him it was time to deliver the baby. He stood there in shock as the nurse moved to the bottom of the bed and pulled back the sheet for the doctor and turned and asked if he was ready to deliver the baby. He stumbled to the bed and asked the nurse to find some forceps so he could get a grip on the baby. When the nurse returned with all the supplies the doctor went to work. After an hour of working with the baby trying to pull it through and Michelle, being so weak she could know longer help and the pain so intense Michelle was going into shock. Dr. Decody said they were going to give it one more try and if it didn't work, there was nothing more he could do.

Sherrie literally got on top of Michelle and the doctor forced the forceps deep inside Michelle to get a good grip on the baby. With the next contraction the nurse pushed like she had never before and the doctor pulled a baby girl through the birth canal and into the world. Her little head was bruised from all the pulling and tugging, but she was alive, not only was she alive, this was a child born blessed with the gift of sight. A child of site born into a cursed blood line, a mixture of darkness and light and all that the two could imply in a lifetime if that was possible to comprehend, imagine or explain, but her life would touch many and change things as the family knew it. This was the beginning. Michelle was so out of it; she didn't know what she had. All Michelle remembered was looking at Cathy seeing her cry, the lights being so bright and everything going black.

When Michelle opened her eyes again, it was three days later and Cathy was sleeping on a cot next to her bed. Michelle was still so weak she couldn't sit up, so she called out to Cathy to wake up and asked, if the baby was dead or alive and what it was. Before Cathy could answer the door opened and Sherrie was standing there. When she saw Michelle awake, she walked in and gave her a kiss on the cheek and said,

"Girl you gave us all a terrible scare, but everything is going to be alright now."

Cathy walked over to the bed and said,

15

"It's a girl and she's beautiful, the baby is going to be fine."

Michelle burst into tears not believing her ears. She looked up at Sherrie and asked if she could see the baby, so Sherrie got up and went to the nursery. Michelle asked if anyone had been to see her or the baby and who knew the baby was born. Cathy told Michelle that her father Charles had been there and she told Michelle her little brother had died. Michelle felt bad, but was too exhausted for the news to fully sink in; she asked if the Breaux's had been called. When Cathy said they had not been notified, Michelle asked for the phone and asked Cathy to dial the number.

Ms Allison answered the phone and was glad to hear the news about her first grandchild. She told Darwin the news and hoped it would make a difference in his life, but he had no response and walked out the house, got in his car and drove away. As Michelle hung up the phone, Sherrie walked back in the room with the baby and told Michelle not to be scared of the bruises; they would go away in a few weeks. Michelle looked up at Sherrie and told her no matter what her baby looked like she wanted to hold her. When Sherrie laid the baby in Michelle's arms, she looked down at her daughter and began to cry when she saw all the bruises.

A few hours later they took the baby back to the nursery and Cathy told Michelle she was going down to the cafeteria to get her something to eat. Michelle was lying in bed half asleep when she heard a noise on the other side of the room. When she opened her eyes, she saw Darwin walking toward the door. Michelle was so weak she couldn't get out of bed to stop him. She pleaded with him to stop, but Darwin turned, looked at Michelle and told her, he hoped her and the kid had a nice life; then walked out the door and left the hospital without seeing his daughter.

A week went by and Michelle got a little stronger everyday and the time came for her to name the baby. She remembered earlier that year when things were better between Darwin and herself, a girl named Nicolette Mason had won the beauty pageant for Miss USA. Darwin had turned to Michelle and told her that one day his daughter would be that beautiful, so Michelle named the baby Nicolette Renee Breaux and planned to call her Nikki in hopes it would some day mean something to Darwin.

The next morning Charles came to visit and Michelle asked where Marie was. Tears weld up in his eyes as he told Cathy and Michelle that Marie went mad after the death of the baby. He could not explain what he saw or understand what happen, but she went mad, screaming,

"They were there and coming for her."

When Charles asked who are, "They," Marie ran through a plate glass window and into the swamp. They searched for two days and Marie was finally found in a tree in the swamp dead. Michelle could not believe what had happen; she felt bad for her father's loss, but as horrific as it was, it was no loss to Michelle.

What Charles didn't share was more horrific than one could imagine. When Marie died a presence, something evil appeared. Charles thought at the time it was the devil himself. He had never encountered something so evil in all his years as a preacher. Charles thought it was the devil coming to challenge him for his soul; he had no idea what Marie had unleashed on the family bloodline or the battle that laid ahead in his future at the time to save his family.

The following day Dr. Decody told Michelle she and the baby could go home. Again, Michelle couldn't believe her ears, but she turned to Cathy and said,

"Well what are you waiting for; call Daddy to come get us."

Dr. Decody told Michelle she had been through a very big ordeal and she needed lots of rest, that meant no heavy work for at least another month or two and he wanted to see her in his office in a few weeks to check her over to make sure all was well. When Charles came to pick them up from the hospital, Michelle was taken out in a wheel chair per hospital protocol, while Charles carried his granddaughter out of the hospital on a pillow. When he looked down at this tiny creature on the pillow, his eyes filled with tears when it hit him that he was holding his first grandchild. On the ride home Charles told Cathy and Michelle he had a surprise for them and announced they were moving to Georgia.

Michelle thought, a new place, a new home, and meeting new people might be the way to start a new life for her and Nikki. When they pulled up to the house, the truck was loaded and everyone was ready to leave. Mike made a pallet in the back of the car for Michelle to lay on for the ride while Mike drove and Charles sat in the front seat and held Nikki on a pillow.

The trip was long and hard for a newborn baby less than a few weeks old and a mother that almost died in childbirth. It was a rough ride in more ways than one, but everyone came through with a lot of hopes and dreams of what the move could do for all of them. A new beginning in more ways than one, new people, a new life; that was all Michelle could think of. Finally the car stopped and Michelle pulled herself up in the seat to see where they were and saw a, "For Rent" sign.

It stood next to a trailer park entrance where they were parked and Charles went in to talk to the owner while everyone else decided to stretch their legs and take a look around to see what they could find. The trailer park was next to a fruit-packing house were most of the people in the trailer park worked. Charles came out and announced they had a new home and it was time to get settled in.

While everyone was unpacking, Charles went next door to talk to the supervisor of the packing house to see if they could use a few extra hands. It turned out, that a number of people had headed home to other cities and they were short handed, so Charles got the job along with the kids too. Michelle started to work when Nikki was four weeks old, because money was tight and she knew she had to pull her own weight. It wasn't anyone's responsibility to raise Nikki, but her own.

It wasn't an easy life for Michelle or Nikki. Michelle laid awake at night thinking about the life she lived and wondered what kind of life Nikki would have. She thought about the price Nikki would have to pay for Michelle giving life to her; then she thought of how uncomfortable she was with Nikki. Michelle couldn't explain it, but Nikki was so self comforting and she never bonded with Michelle or Michelle with Nikki for that matter. Nikki was different and Michelle knew Nikki was different. Michelle couldn't put a finger on it and as she grew into a toddler Nikki played and spoke to the dead and argued that people where in the room when no one was there. Everyone told Michelle that kids had imaginary friends, but that answer only left Michelle with more questions and the answers could never be justified in her own mind.

Then Nikki was playing outside one day when a cousin dropped by. Mickey was a wild child and into drugs and ran with the wrong crowd, always wanting to a bad boy and leading Michelle's brother Mike down the same road. That afternoon when he got there to pick up Mike for their night out, Nikki was almost three. She walked over to Mike and whispered in his ear,

"Tonight walk home, don't ride in the car."

Mike hugged Nikki and laughed and asked her if she put another cat in the car. Nikki had found a stray wild cat and brought it home from the woods. When she couldn't calm it down she didn't want it to run away so she locked it Mike's car a few weeks back. When he got in and started driving down the road the cat jumped on his head and Mike had almost totaled his car. That would be a life experience that mike wouldn't soon forget. Nikki pushed him away and walked outside and stood on the porch. When they left Michelle walked outside and asked Nikki what she meant by what she said, Nikki looked at Michelle and told her Mickey would not be coming home anymore and if Mike got in the car he wouldn't make it home either, she said Mickey was a ghost among them and picked up her doll and went to bed.

Michelle couldn't believe what she heard come from Nikki's mouth and it was eerie how Nikki spoke as if she was in a trance. Nikki simply just went to bed and laid there staring at the ceiling. Michelle blew it off until the next morning when she woke up and Mike was sleeping on the floor in the living-room. She woke him up and asked him what happen that night. He said him and Mickey got into a fight at the club and he walked home because Mickey was to full of himself. Michelle asked where Mickey was then and Mike told her he didn't know and what was it to her. Michelle made Mike get up and wanted him to go look for Mickey. Michelle was sick to her stomach when she looked up and saw Nikki standing in the doorway. Nikki looked at Michelle and told her she told her Mickey was a ghost among them; then she turned and walked away. Mike sat up and reached for the phone. Just as his hand touched the phone to pick it up, it rang. When he answered it, it was their Aunt Patty wanting to know where Mickey was. She said he didn't come home the night before and his job was looking for him. Mike told her he would go find him and call her back. Mike hung up, ran to his car and burned rubber getting out on the highway.

He looked everywhere Mickey could be. When he got home he saw his Aunt's car in the drive way and was almost relieved when he saw Mickey's car across the street on a tow truck. When he walked in the house everyone was crying. Nikki was sitting in a little rocking chair staring out the window. Mickey was found with a bullet in the back of his head on the side of the road. His car had broken down and he had started walking. Someone had come up on him, tied his hands and feet behind his back, placed him face down on the ground and put a bullet in his head.

Michelle never looked at Nikki the same, she couldn't explain what happen or how or why it was possible for Nikki to have known what she did, but she knew it wasn't natural and it had to be evil. Michelle kept her distance from Nikki. That wasn't difficult since Nikki was so self reliant anyway. She tried to put it out her mind, but it ate at Michelle and eventually she became afraid of her daughter, because Nikki was something she didn't and couldn't understand.

Michelle decided she no longer wanted or could be a mother to Nikki, so she called Darwin to come to Georgia to pick Nikki up and take her home with him. Nikki cried when Darwin told her, she would be going home with him to live. Charles had gone to the dog tracks as usual, so it made it easy for Michelle to pack Nikki's things and tell her goodbye. As the car drove away Michelle stood in the driveway and watched as Nikki stared at her from the backseat window crying, pleading with her Mommy to keep her, but Michelle watched until Nikki faded out of sight, then walked back in the house with a since of relief, because it was finally over. It was, that is, until Charles got home and found Nikki gone. He told Michelle, come hell or high water he was getting his granddaughter back. He said Michelle could leave if she wanted to and he would raise Nikki.

CHAPTER 3

The ride back to Louisiana was a long one. Nikki was unsure being with Darwin and he was drinking as always, as was his friend Dalton. Nikki discovered early in life that she didn't like the smell of liquor. Nikki didn't like Darwin when he cried and tried to hug her and tell her he loved her either.

When they finally made it to the Breaux's house, Nikki's Maw-Maw, Ms Allison took her out the car. She embraced Nikki and took her inside. Nikki had a peaceful feeling with this woman even though she had not known her before. Her Grandmother told Nikki that everything would be all right and she was going to take care of her. Nikki asked where her Mommy was and when she would be coming to get her and her Grandmother looked down at her with tears in her eyes and told her, she didn't know where or when and if ever her Mommy would be back. Nikki started to cry and her Grandmother took her in her arms and held her until she cried herself to sleep.

Nikki woke up the next morning in bed with Gabrielle, Darwin's sister. She was staring at Nikki humming a song. When she realized Nikki was awake, she said,

"Good-morning sleepy-head, are you hungry?"

Nikki looked up at her and nodded yes, so Gabrielle took Nikki to the kitchen where her Maw-Maw was cooking breakfast for the family. One by one they meet Nikki then sat down and had breakfast together.

The next few months were difficult for Nikki. This was a whole new way of life that Nikki had not known before. She couldn't watch TV, because there wasn't one in the house. They only listened to gospel music and went to church five times a week. The Breaux's practiced a very strict religious belief and they lived by their religion.

The church was a fascinating experience for Nikki, at times she felt peace and at times her eyes were wide open when they prayed in tongues and cast demons out of people in the church. Nikki was supposed to be praying for the salvation of the soul when the church was performing the exorcisms, but Nikki watched with her eyes wide open. When they would make the demon speak and it was a lady, the voice was hoarse and male, it laughed at the preacher and told him his faith was weak and he couldn't make him leave; it took hours for the exorcisms and Nikki watched as they spoke in tongues being filled with the holy-ghost after the exorcisms. Nikki as small as she was admired the holy-ghost and wanted it with all her heart, but it didn't come when she asked for it like it did with all the others in the church.

Almost a year passed and Nikki was finally getting use to it all. Then one night while asleep on the floor in the back of the church, Michelle took her while know-one was looking. Michelle slid in the back door, took Nikki and out the door she went back to Georgia. Nikki woke up in the back seat of a car, when she looked up to see where she was, her Paw-Paw Monceret was driving and her Mommy was in the front seat. Nikki screamed,

"Mommy!"

Then she climbed in the front seat to hug her. Paw-Paw Monceret looked at Nikki with tears in his eyes and told her she was going home where she belonged and was never leaving again. Nikki was a little sad about leaving her Maw-Maw Breaux, because she had grown close to her, but she was happy to be home with her Mommy. When they got back to Georgia, Michelle introduced Nikki to a man named Jason from North Dakota. Nikki kind of liked him, but her Mommy liked him a lot more. Michelle told Nikki he was her new daddy and they would be going away with him soon to live as a real family. Jason and Michelle were married a month later and Michelle was packing their things to leave for North Dakota when Charles entered the room and told Michelle to pack only her things, because Nikki was staying with him.

Michelle told her father that she was taking Nikki with her, because Jason wanted to be a real daddy to her. Charles told her she had better take care of his grandbaby or he would never forgiver her. He then went to the eighteen-wheeler; looked up in the truck and told Jason if he ever laid a hand on Nikki he would hunt him down and kill him. Jason assured

Charles he didn't have anything to worry about while watching Nikki as she played on the side of the house. Lisa Nikki's favorite cousin came by and said she was going to the store and asked Nikki if she wanted to go get some candy. When Michelle said she could go, Nikki ran to the car with Lisa as Michelle yelled for them not to be gone long they had a lot to get done and she needed Nikki back for a bath because Jason was taking them to dinner that night. Lisa told her they wouldn't be long and she would give Nikki a bath when they got back from the store.

Nikki had always adored Lisa, she was the one that baby sat most of the time for Michelle when she worked and Lisa took Nikki to the store almost every-day for some sort of treat, usually candy. It didn't hurt that Nikki's great Aunt Blanch and Uncle Dillon owned the store on the corner and they made sure Nikki got what she wanted when she visited them. When Nikki got there that day she walked the candy isle as always and when her Aunt Blanch walked up and hugged Nikki, Nikki embraced her and held her tight. Her Aunt laughed and said,

"Auh you missed me huh?"

Nikki looked up at her and said,

"I'm gonna really miss you Aunt Blanch."

Her Aunt assured her she was only moving to North Dakota, but was sure Nikki would be back for visits, but Nikki just turned to the candy and starting picking her treats. Her Aunt left her alone to pick what she wanted and Lisa waited at the front of the store with Blanch and Dillon. When Nikki came to the front of the store her hands where full and she was dropping candy everywhere. Dillon walked over and laughed and asked if she wanted all the candy in the store because she was leaving for North Dakota. Nikki looked up at him with tears in her eyes and Dillon told her not to worry they would get a bag and every piece would go with her. Dillon bagged the candy and Nikki hugged her Aunt and Uncle and walked slowly out the door with Lisa. When they got to the car, Nikki was usually tearing into her candy, but she just sat in the seat with her bag of candy next to her. When Lisa got in on the driver's side she looked at Nikki and asked,

"What's wrong munchkin?"

Nikki looked and Lisa and said her Aunt and Uncle are ghost among them then and stared out the window. Lisa had heard the story of what happen with Mickey and Lisa questioned Nikki for an explanation. Nikki told her she couldn't talk about it, it was too horrifying and she didn't want to look anymore. Lisa asked her what she was looking at, but Nikki told her she felt sick and wanted to go home. When they got home Nikki went in the house and left the candy on the seat of the car. She went right to bed and lay there staring at the ceiling. Lisa went in the room and told Nikki she needed to start her bath, but Nikki said no, she didn't want to go out for dinner, she didn't want to eat; she just wanted to sleep. Lisa went to get Michelle to check on Nikki, after a few minutes she left Nikki alone and asked Lisa what happen at the store. Lisa told her that Nikki had gathered as much candy as she could when she came to the register. Lisa said it was if Nikki thought she was never going to get candy again. Then Lisa said Nikki told her that Aunt Blanch and Uncle Dillon were ghost among them. The hair on the back of Michelle's neck stood up and Michelle thought maybe the store might get robbed or something so, Michelle told Lisa to stay with Nikki she had to go out for while.

Michelle went to the store to see Dillon and asked him to close the store early that day as a favor to her, so her Aunt could help with her post wedding party before she left. Dillon agreed and said Blanch was already on her way home so Michelle could find her there. Michelle went back home, thinking all was alright because if the two were separated, nothing could happen in two different places. When Michelle got home Nikki wouldn't speak; she was in another trance like state, the same as when Mickey was murdered. Michelle tried to snap her out of it, but Nikki just laid there.

Meanwhile, when Blanch got home she went in her house as always and locked the doors as if she was in a Fort Knox boot camp. Blanch was a scardy cat when Dillon wasn't there, because Dillon didn't believe in banks and had a vault in their home where they kept all Blanch's jewelry and the money from the store. Only a few people knew that, but Blanch was terrified of that knowledge getting out and something bad happening. Dillon had installed cameras in the house and at the doors so blanch could see who was knocking, but if Dillon wasn't at home she wouldn't even allow family to visit.

Blanch and Dillon had two kids and one was the spawn of the devil himself. Dillon and Blanch tried all they could to save him from himself, to no avail. Dillon told him he was on his own and was going to be disinherited and was getting nothing when and if anything happen to them. Blanch being the loving sprit she was, always hoped for the best and tried to keep the peace between her son and her husband. Blanch opened the door that day to someone she trusted more than anything and when they entered her home they beat her unmercifully. Know-one will ever know if she opened the vault or Dillon did when he got home and they were waiting. Dillon too was beaten unmercifully and in the end the vault was opened and everything was cleaned out the vault. Killing them was not good enough for the perpetrators; they took Blanch and Dillon to the woods behind their house and gutted them like animals. The corner said they were still alive when they were hung by their own intestines in the trees. The corner and responding police said they had never seen anything so gruesome in all their careers. The door was left open to the house, the vault was left standing wide open, cleaned out of course, and the blood in the house looked as if someone or something had been slaughtered. The son was never a suspect; because the crime was too gruesome, know-one could do that to someone they knew or was related to according to the DA. One will never know, the crime would never be solved, and the protocol son died broke or money stolen a month later of an over dose.

The funeral was difficult; Nikki stared off into space and didn't speak for days. After the death of Jake the son of Blanch and Dillon, Michelle said it was time to leave. Paw-Paw Monceret hugged and kissed Nikki goodbye and helped her get up in the truck. The ride to North Dakota was also a long one, because they had to stop off in a number of towns for Jason to deliver the stuff in the back of his truck. Nikki slept in the cab of the truck with Michelle and Jason and woke up in the middle of the night screaming, because she could see her Mommy cut into pieces at her feet. Nikki struggled to tell herself to wake up, but she wasn't sleeping. Nikki saw this for three nights before she started screaming. She told them to look at the blood on the sheets and Nikki screamed that Jason had killed her Mommy. Jason told Nikki to wake up, because she was sleeping, but Nikki was wide-awake. Nikki just knew she couldn't be dreaming. Michelle sat up and slapped Nikki and told her to stop screaming and go back to sleep. She said, it was only a dream and they all needed to rest. Nikki laid down shaking and watched Jason's every move, because she was certain he was going to try and hurt her Mommy.

It snowed a lot in North Dakota, and Jason drank a lot just like Darwin. The schools were ok, but because of the snow and Nikki living half way up a mountain the bus couldn't get to her, so she had to wade through the snow to get home. Jason still drove his truck so he was gone most of the time and when he was home, sometimes he was really nice to Nikki, but sometimes when he was drinking he would be hatful to her as well. Nikki felt lonely all the time because; know-one was around to play with; so she continued to amuse herself. When Nikki was six, Michelle found out she was pregnant and told Nikki that soon she would be having a new playmate to run around with.

At first, Nikki was really excited. It wasn't long before Kirsten was born and came home from the hospital. Nikki thought Kirsten was really pretty and so little. She had never seen anything so little in all her life. She decided that she would always have to make sure Kirsten was ok, because she was the big sister and that's what big sisters did. At first, Nikki felt like everything was going to be great for them, until she noticed all the attention Kirsten was getting and how everybody just forgot about her. A few months later Michelle told Nikki she was having another baby, and Nikki felt like her whole world was ending. Shortly after, Ashley was born.

After Ashley was born, Michelle decided to go back to work, so she hired a lady named Sammy to sit. Sammy was mean to the kids and told Nikki she would cook her baby sisters in the oven if she did anything bad, or told anyone what she had said. She told Nikki that even if she said anything to anyone, know-one would believe her and then she would get her.

Day after day Nikki watched her every move. Nikki locked Kirsten in the back room with her, then would sneak to the front and watch until Sammy turned her back, then she grabbed Ashley out the play-pin, and ran to her room. Nikki locked the door behind her after her sisters were in her room safe. She stood by the door to listen to see if the sitter was coming down the hall or what she was doing and could hear the sitter on the other side of the door laughing. Nikki kept Kirsten and Ashley in the room with her everyday. They wouldn't come out the room, not even to eat while the sitter was there. Kirsten and Ashley cried, because they were either wet or hungry and when Nikki couldn't make them be quite so she could hear the sitter she would slap them or pull their hair. Some days Nikki would try to sneak out the room to get food from the kitchen for her sisters to eat. The only problem there was, if the sitter caught her, she chased Nikki back to her room with a knife.

The summer was winding down and the day came when the sitter told Nikki through the door that school would be starting soon and Nikki would be gone. She said she was going to get both Nikki's sisters and with her being gone there wasn't anything she would be able to do to stop her. While she was talking to Nikki through the door, Nikki was crying and asking her why when Nikki heard a car coming down the drive and ran to the window. She saw Michelle and her Aunt Selina, Jason's sister. The plant had shut down early that day because of an accident and they made it home early. When Nikki heard them come in the house, she watched for her Aunt Selina to leave to take the sitter home. When she knew the sitter had left the house Nikki ran screaming,

"Please don't let her come back, because she is going to kill me and bake Kirsten and Ashley in the oven."

Nikki told Michelle everything the sitter had told her she was going to do. Nikki also told Michelle the sitter had chased her with a knife to kill her because she was trying to get food for her sisters to eat. She thought all the threats didn't matter, she felt she had nothing to lose anymore and her only hope was to be able to convince Michelle that she wasn't lying. Michelle told Nikki the sitter wouldn't be coming back; she would find a new one. Nikki felt a since of relief, but she still had nightmares and would wake up during the night and go check on Kirsten and Ashley to make sure that they were breathing.

Michelle and Jason fought more because he was gone too much as far as Michelle was concerned. Jason was mean to Nikki more than he usually was and Nikki felt like she didn't belong anywhere and that no place was safe. All Nikki wanted to do was run away and find someone that cared, so she waited until Michelle put the kids down for a nap and when Michelle was a sleep, Nikki got up, packed a few things and snuck out the door. She was walking to the end of the street when the new baby sitter saw her. She called Nikki to come over and talk to her and tell her where she was going. Nikki told her, she was going to find her real Daddy and live with him. When the sitter asked where her real Daddy lived. Nikki told her she didn't know, but she was sure she could find him. Then she told Nikki all kinds of bad things happened to children that run away. A lot of kids were lost and never found or heard from ever again, but Nikki told her she didn't care, because it couldn't be as bad as staying there and she started walking back toward the street.

Nikki saw Jason coming down the road and turned to go back home. What Nikki didn't know was the sitter called Michelle and told her she had stopped Nikki from running away and she was on her way back. When Nikki opened the door to go inside, Michelle was waiting for her with a fly swatter. Michelle gave Nikki one of those beatings she gave her that left bruises all over her legs and back. She told Nikki if she ever tried to run-a-way again, that whipping would be lite compared to the one she would give her next time.

The next day the sitter asked Nikki what Michelle told her when she got home and Nikki showed the sitter the bruises on her legs and back, but before she could finish telling her what Michelle said the sitter told Nikki she deserved what she got and she had better never try anything like that again. Later that day she told Nikki it was naptime and she needed to go to sleep like all the rest of the kids. Nikki laid there wondering why life was so difficult, and felt like know-one loved or wanted her. She couldn't understand why Michelle was so upset that Nikki would want to leave, because all she did was yell, scream, and call Nikki names all the time.

The sitter came to the room to see if any of the kids were awake and told Nikki she was going to sleep wither she wanted to or not, but Nikki told her she wasn't sleepy. When the other kids woke up, the sitter took them to the kitchen and gave them all ice cream except Nikki. She made Nikki sit at the table and watch all the other kids eat theirs and the rage inside Nikki began to grow.

About six months later, Michelle woke Nikki up telling her they were packing their stuff to leave. They were supposedly moving home and Nikki asked where home was. When Michelle told Nikki Louisiana with Paw-Paw Monceret; Nikki jumped out of bed, helped Michelle load the truck with all of their things and they were finally on their way back to Louisiana. The move back with Paw-Paw Monceret was great, he always had a way of making everyone in his life feel wanted and welcome. Nikki would follow him on trails through the bayou and sometimes he knew Nikki was there and would call out for her to walk with him. He had a way with nature that was unreal to Nikki; it was as if he could speak to the animals. Nikki thought it was because her Paw-Paw was a full-blooded Indian and he mesmerized her.

The summer came and the fishing lines needed to be worked and Nikki was big enough to help so she joined in. They worked hard from sun-up till sundown every day except Sundays. On those days the Monceret kids Renee, Ricky, Mat, Chris, Kirsten, Ashley & Nikki took off down the bayou. Nikki would always remember having to walk home slowly, because they had to let their hair dry before they got home, because if Paw-Paw Monceret knew they had been swimming down the bayou, they would all get a lashing they would never forget. Paw-Paw Monceret was a strong man, he didn't give whippings very often, but when he did give one, a person knew they had one. He sometimes used a belt, but mostly switches, and the worst was when he used his hand. But know matter what Nikki loved her Paw-Paw Monceret, because he made her feel safe.

Nikki started school in Louisiana again and hated it, because she was one of the ugliest little girls anyone had ever seen. She had a pug nose, freckles, and short-short hair that stood up all over her head. She didn't fit in, so all the kids made fun of her. They teased Nikki all the time. When it was time for recess Nikki would hide out in the girls' bathroom to be left alone. Nikki did adore her teacher, she was young, pregnant and Nikki felt like she was the most beautiful person she had ever known. Her name was Ms Alisa. She noticed at recess Nikki was never around and told her she wanted to see her out on the playground with all the other kids. She said the kids would warm up to her if she just gave them a chance. So, the next day Nikki decided to take her up on her advice and go out on the playground to see what would happen.

Nikki walked around the playground and know-one said anything to her, so she thought Ms Alisa was right; things had really blown over, so she decided to play on one of the rides with a group of kids. Nikki was standing waiting for the merry go round to slow down so she could jump on when some kids ran up behind her yelling, telling her to get on if she was going to. Nikki was scared to move and started to back up, but someone pushed her from behind and she fell into the merry-go-round. The next thing Nikki knew, blood was running down her face. Nikki grabbed her eye and started running towards Ms Alisa. Her teacher was standing on the sidewalk talking to another teacher and a school aid saw Nikki and ran to help her. Ms Alisa stood there watching and Nikki saw her teacher laughing like some of the kids on the playground.

The next day Nikki's eye was swollen shut and black as could be. She had to go to school and listen to all the jokes about what had happened and know-one got in trouble for pushing her, so Nikki decided to stay on her own and stay away from everybody including Ms Alisa, because she felt that her teacher had lied to her and set her up to be humiliated and she was.

CHAPTER 4

In time, Michelle decided it was time for Nikki to see her real father again. She told Nikki she had called the Breaux's and they were excited about seeing her and she was going to spend the weekend with them. Nikki was six and didn't remember the Breaux family, but she went because she didn't have a choice.

When they pulled up in the driveway, Nikki saw kittens playing on the front porch, so she got out and went to play with the kittens, while Michelle spoke to Ms Alice. Darwin heard Nikki playing and went to see her. He grabbed her and was kissing and telling her how much he loved and missed her. Nikki remembered the smell of alcohol and hated it; she asked Darwin who he was and Darwin said,

"I'm your daddy."

Nikki looked up at him and screamed,

"NO!"

She ran to Michelle and started hitting Michelle in the stomach and begging her, to please tell her that was not her Daddy. Michelle grabbed Nikki by her arms and told her to calm down. She told Nikki that Darwin was her Daddy and she was staying there to get to know him. Michelle turned away from Nikki, got in her car as Nikki was begging her, not to leave her again, when Michelle drove away.

Grandma Breaux went over and picked Nikki up, carried her inside, and told her everything would be all right. Then she told Darwin to keep his distance for a while until Nikki was more comfortable with him. Again, Nikki met all kinds of people with her Grandmother. She went to church and liked it, because everyone was so nice to her there. The weekend ended of course and her Paw-Paw Monceret picked her up on his way back from the dog races. The next few weeks past kind of fast and as usual Nikki was always into something. She liked to experiment with stuff to see how far she could take things, so one day she was playing in the shed with some matches. Nikki sat down, lit a match and caught an old mattress on fire, then blew it out. Each time she lit the fire she let it get a little bigger and a little bigger until, she couldn't blow it out anymore. Nikki freaked; then ran out the shed. Nikki was too scared to tell anyone, so she ran in the house and sat down in front of the TV like nothing was wrong. Then she heard someone screaming "Fire," so she ran out the door to see what was happening. Ricky pulled the mattress out the shed and Chris ran for water. As the fire was put out Paw-Paw Monceret drove up. He jumped out the car and ran straight to Nikki, grabbed her up, and gave her a whipping of a lifetime. He told Nikki how upset he was and said she could have killed herself and made her promise to never play with fire again.

A few weeks later, Kirsten and Ashley's Daddy, Jason visited and Michelle told Nikki that Kirsten and Ashley was going to stay with their Dad for the rest of the summer. Nikki didn't want them to leave, but she knew she didn't have a say in the matter. She watched as Michelle packed their things and before long they were gone. It wasn't long after that, that Michelle was gone too. She left not telling anyone where she was going. Nikki thought it had to have something to do with her, because she was such a bad child or that Michelle was afraid of Nikki. Nikki was born with the gift of site and continued to tell Michelle certain things were going to happen. As time passed and Nikki's predictions became a reality, Michelle became more frighten of Nikki. Nikki promised to stop the dreams and thought if she was only better, prettier, something, or anything Michelle would have wanted to stay or would come back for her.

Nikki was alone again and Lisa her favorite cousin and sitter when Michelle wanted came to visit her. Nikki was so excited to see Lisa until she hugged her. Nikki back away and looked at Lisa. Lisa looked into Nikki's eyes and said you see it too or you feel it. Nikki looked at Lisa and Lisa said she had a dream and it was so real and it had been bothering her for days. She took Nikki by the hand and asked her to look deep inside herself and tell her what she saw. Nikki took Lisa's hands and they sat for a few minutes in silence, then Nikki said, bad people, you know will come for you. Lisa asked her if she knew when, Nikki said soon you will be a ghost among us; it will be night, when daylight is coming; you will know your death is imminent. Lisa looked at Nikki and told her she had seen the same thing and had hoped she could stop it. Nikki turned and walked away, she couldn't even look back at Lisa.

Nikki all, but shut down; when a week passed with nothing happening, Nikki started to come out her shell. Then the trance started, she saw Lisa alone at home in the dark, sitting in a rocking chair, she was calm, so calm, yet she knew she would die in minutes. Nikki went to bed and stared at the ceiling. Meanwhile, at Lisa's that night, Lisa went to bed and couldn't sleep, she tried to watch TV, but nothing could ease the feeling she had. The night had fallen and the wee hours of morning were approaching when Lisa went to the kitchen for water, she was so thirsty. When she filled her glass she heard a noise under the car port and knew they were there. She didn't run to the phone, she knew it would be no use. She walked into a small room just off the living-room, a sitting room she loved to read in. she sat in the big rocking chair and waited. She sat her water down and pulled out a pen from a crossword puzzle she was working and on the arms of the rocker she wrote,

"I can hear them, they are outside now; it won't be long until they will get in. Mom, I love you so much and I wish I would have had more time to be with you, to share more with you, to have been honest about so much. They are in the house now, I hear them, they are looking for me, it won't be, but a few more minutes now, know that I love you and my family, I know I am going to die here tonight and I'm so calm, I don't know why, bu….."

A scribbled line appeared at the end of the word she didn't finish. Again, another family member dies with no reason and no suspects, another case for the books of unsolved mysteries, another murder that would go unsolved. Nikki new Lisa was at peace when she died, Nikki couldn't see the face of the person that took Lisa's life, but she knew the last eyes Lisa looked into belonged to someone she knew. Nikki came to understand she was different and in going to church and listening to the preaching, Nikki began to think what she had was a curse and that she was evil, not anything blessed and she cursed what she had and wanted it to go away, she rebuked it like the preacher said, and it shall flee from you, only it didn't leave, so Nikki said she would ignore it and it would go away. She had so many questions about things she knew, why and how it worked, and so many questions about her questions, but no-one to talk to about them.

Nikki spent a lot of time between the Breaux's and the Monceret's, until the Breaux's told Nikki she was going to live with them. The Beaux's' filed a motion with the court for custody and Paw-Paw Monceret hired a private investigator to find Michelle in New Orleans. Then Nikki was playing in the grave yard while at the Monceret's and fell on top of a grave, when she looked up Nikki read,

"Michelle Monceret, Rest in Peace."

Nikki was horrified and ran to her Grandfather hysterical screaming,

"Why didn't you tell me my mom is dead?"

Charles tried to calm Nikki down and reassure her, but there was no calming Nikki, so he put her in the car and took her to the graveyard and told her to show him the grave. When Nikki took him to the grave, he explained to Nikki what dates on a tombstone meant. The lady with the same name had died ten years prior to then. Nikki accepted his answer and returned to the Breaux's. The next few months were strange; then Michelle showed up with the sheriff at the Breaux's. She told the sheriff she had custody and wanted him to go with her to get Nikki, but Maw-Maw Breaux had taken Nikki down the bayou and told her to stay there until she came for her. Nikki watched through the swamp. She could see the police looking for something, but was unaware; it was her they were searching for.

Nikki saw Michelle in the police car waiting and after a while they finally left and Maw-Maw Breaux came for her just as she promised. Nikki was then taken to Florida to stay with her Uncle Austin and Aunt Joan. She loved it there. Nikki went swimming every day in the pool at the clubhouse with her cousin Nancy and she was treated like she was one of the girls and for the first time she really felt like she was in a real family. Aunt Joan talked to Nikki all the time, she told her; she loved her and wanted her to live with them permanently. It was wonderful. Nikki thought all those people wanting her felt strange, but it felt good too. This was a new experience for her, for the first time she really felt like she belonged. At the end of the summer the Breaux's took Nikki back home with them to start school and her fairytale life ended.

The new school was like no-other Nikki had ever attended. It was a Christian school located in the back of the church the Breaux's attended. It was different, because there was no name-calling and the kids seemed to like Nikki and she liked being there, but she felt isolated and never felt like she belonged. The court battle between the families for Nikki went on and on. Nikki was sent back to the Monceret's, but still attended school at the church. That didn't work, so Nikki was sent back to the Breaux's.

The judges put Nikki's Paw Paw Breaux on the stand and ask him if he was seeking custody of Nikki for himself or his son Darwin and Paw Paw Breaux told the judge he wouldn't leave a dead dog in the presence of his son to take care of, little lone his granddaughter. He also said, in Nikki's life she had been shuffled around and he wanted to give her a stable environment to grow up in. After hearing all the testimonies, custody was granted to Nikki's Grandpa and Grandma Breaux.

Over the next couple years Nikki saw the Monceret's on the weekends from time to time. Her sisters got to come and spend one weekend with her at the Beaux's before they went to live with their Dad in North Dakota and Nikki didn't see Michelle anymore either; she too disappeared.

Nikki continued to go to the Monceret's for the weekend every now and then and while there, she played with David, Mike and Chris. Nikki had egg fights at Easter and a couple of years of going to look for a Christmas tree before Christmas. She played cops and robbers with the boys and Nikki was placed on the handle bars of the bicycle and was the siren. Nikki was screaming like a siren when they hit a pot hole and her foot came down and got caught in the spokes and it chewed the skin off to the bone on her ankle. The boys would pick her up and take her in the house and tell the adults to fix her so she could go play some more. Nikki swung from vines in the trees, playing in the woods and sliding down hills on boxes. It was great, she was such a tomboy, she fit right in with the rest of the guys; that was until David wanted to play house, and play house they did.

Nikki was the wife of course and David the husband. David was fifteen; Nikki was ten. He told Nikki in real life husbands and wives did things to each other that felt good and in time he was going to teach her all about those things. That day was a lot sooner than one would have thought.

David performed oral sex on Nikki and asked her how it felt. Nikki told him it was weird and she wasn't sure she wanted to do it again. He told Nikki, that at first it was suppose to be weird, but she would get use to it after a couple of times. The other two boys saw what David was doing and decided they wanted in on it too. One by one, they took turns touching Nikki, fondling her, performing oral sex on her, and rubbing their penises between her legs until they had orgasms.

Parts of this for Nikki felt nasty and she hated it, but she didn't want to lose them as friends, so she did what they wanted and promised that she would never say anything to anyone about their game. The first time

Nikki had an orgasm, she was eleven and it was the strangest feeling she had ever had. She thought that must be what David was telling her, when he said that one day it would be great, then Nikki began to like the things David did to her on her weekend visits.

A short time later, one night at church the preacher was preaching on fornication. Nikki got the message that what she had been doing with David, Mike and Chris was wrong and she would burn in hell for it. She prayed for forgiveness and promised she would never do it again. Nikki thought it was ok, because they never put their penis inside her and she thought that God would punish them for what they had done, but knew she couldn't go see them anymore.

On Nikki's last visit she was sitting in the yard watching Ricky work on his car and the boys were running around as always. Ricky was rebuilding an old car from scratch and had it broken down and stripped to the shell of the car. He had only one seat in the car under the steering wheel. He got the car started and was driving it in circles cursing cause it wouldn't go fast. He said he was heading out for a little drive and asked the boys and Nikki if they wanted to ride. Everybody knew Ricky was crazy as could be, but Chris said it couldn't be that bad cause Ricky was cursing cause the car wouldn't go fast, so everybody including Nikki jumped in. Ricky punched the gas and hit the pasture, it was full of vines and Ricky was doing donuts and laughing at the top of his lungs while the boys and Nikki were hanging on for dear life. Nikki was holding on by placing her fingers in holes where screws was missing in the frame so she wouldn't be thrown out the car and they all knew the ride wasn't stopping till somebody was hurt, dead or thrown out the car. Finally Mike fell off the back of the car and Ricky stopped laughing his ass off. Nikki jumped out the car and walked back to the house.

Nikki thought of how many times she saw her life flash before her eyes, like when Ricky screamed

"Oh God, No Breaks!!

Going down a gravel road with a sharp curve at the bottom and Ricky screaming we're gonna crash and praying out loud for God to help him. Everybody jumped out the truck on the gravel road and got skinned up pretty bad. When Ricky got to the end of the hill, he stopped the truck and fell out on the ground laughing. Nikki laughed when she thought how crazy he was and knew she was also going to miss them because she wouldn't be seeing them anymore either. She went home that afternoon and knew a part of her world was closed off and she would never be the same because a part of her was gone; her innocence and it could never return.

Nikki went to bed that night after church and was visited by her Grandfather Monceret in her dreams. He was holding his chest and said he couldn't stay, but he wanted Nikki to know he loved her and would always be there for her. Nikki begged him not to go, but he said he had no choice it was his time; her Grandfather told her to remind Michelle of the watch and what to do. Nikki sat up in bed with sweat running down her face as she tried to tell herself it was just a bad dream. Nikki knew it wouldn't matter what she tried to tell herself she knew her Grandpa Monceret was going to die. She ran to the phone and called her Aunt Sissy whom was married to Michelle's brother. Nikki told her she had to find Michelle it was urgent she speak to her, so Sissy gave Nikki the last number she had for Michelle. Nikki called Michelle thinking, hoping, and praying she could stop what was going to happen. When Nikki told Michelle her Grandpa Monceret was going to die, Michelle became angry with Nikki and told her she was evil and never call her again; it was a lie. Nikki hung the phone up not knowing what to do or say, but she knew her Grandpa Monceret was leaving this world and she could do nothing to stop it.

Nikki tried to tell herself again it was only a bad dream and to let it go. She understood Michelle's reaction, because she knew she didn't want her Father to go either. Nikki wondered again if she was evil and why she was the one chosen to know the things she knew. Nikki went back to bed, but couldn't sleep. She refused breakfast and sat in her room by the window all morning. Nikki thought if she didn't tell anyone else and remained quiet it wouldn't make it so. Nikki had her back to the door when her Grandmother Breaux walked in the room and embraced her from behind. She kissed Nikki on the top of the head, but Nikki continued to stare out the window. Nikki's Grandmother Breaux whispered in her ear she was sorry, but her Grandfather Monceret died of a heart attack that morning. Nikki said in a low voice staring out the window she knew and wanted to be alone. Her Grandmother left the room and Nikki vowed to never dream again. Life from then on at the Breaux's was different from anything one could ever imagine. It was like Nikki stepped off into another world never to be heard from again, she became someone else.

Nikki thought she needed to find friends in the church to spend time with, so she made friends with the girls in her class: Annie, Dolly, Becky, Candy and Katie. They all went to school and church together and got along well most of the time. They spent weekends together and almost every night Nikki had a friend at the house after school. They played games and of course they played house and told dirty jokes, all the things little girls do.

This life was strange for Nikki, because she got crushes on girls and boys, but never would confess those feelings, not even to God, because she was taught it was a mortal sin to even think it. Amazingly some of these friends had some of the same experiences as Nikki with brothers or cousins. They knew it was wrong, but those confessions brought the girls together and bonded some of them for life. Nikki knew that two of these girls would not live long lives. She knew one would die in an auto accident in the next couple years and one with her whole family would die suddenly and tragically with no warning, but Nikki refused to acknowledge the information.

As time passed Nikki became close to her Grandpa Breaux as well. She followed him around like a shadow all the time. They fed the cows together every evening, went fishing together on the weekends, and would sneak off to a café his brother owned to get a hamburger and watch whatever sport was on TV. This was their private time and they never told anyone. Nikki knew her Grandpa Breaux wouldn't tell on her for watching TV. She trusted him to keep her secret and she kept his. Her Grandma Breaux was a religious woman and Grandpa Breaux respected his wife's beliefs, even though they were not his own, so to watch TV, he went to the café and while at home he honored her wishes.

Nikki felt as though she was so close to her Pawpaw Breaux that nothing else mattered. Other people in the family began to tease her about being his shadow. To Nikki it didn't matter, she was as happy as could be to have someone that wanted to be with her as much as she wanted to be with them.

Nikki was a child with a vivid imagination. She made up stories that were out of this world, like when she was in a public school a Brahma bull chased her through the school and the principal almost got killed trying to save her. She thought it was great, because the other girls laughed, so she made up more stories. Then one day a new family moved to the church with two girls, Stacy and Kelly. They were like Nikki, they had been out in the world and seen the same things Nikki had seen and probably done some of the same things as well and soon, Stacy and Nikki became really good friends. They had a lot in common, their backgrounds and just stuff in general. All the other girls were born and raised in the religion, so acceptance for them was easy, because that was all they had ever known.

Stacy and Nikki on the other hand, knew what it was like to play with boys, watch TV, listen to the radio and dance. One will never miss those things until they are taken away.

One by one, all the other girls stopped playing with the two girls and Nikki found herself being alone again. Nikki thought the parents were afraid she would teach their kids about the world, so they told them to stay away from her and Stacy. Nikki also had a very special friendship with Dana as well. Her family didn't really care what anyone else in the church thought. One afternoon, Nikki was going to go play at Dana's. She got up early so she could help her Grandpa with the feeding and help do all the errands they normally did on the weekends. Her Grandma Breaux left for town to do her shopping and the house was empty.

When all the chores were done, Nikki told her Grandpa she was going to change, so she could go to Dana's for a while and he told her he would miss her at the café that day. Nikki was sitting on her bed putting on her shoes when her Grandfather walked in her room. She looked up, smiled at him and asked if he needed something. Her Grandfather turned and closed the door behind him. He walked over to Nikki and pushed her back on the bed. He told her he wasn't going to hurt her and slipped his hand up her dress and started to pull her panties down. He pushed his body against her leg and Nikki could feel his erection on her knee. He told her that she wanted it as much as he did and everyone was gone so that could be their last chance and started trying to push his fingers inside Nikki.

Nikki screamed out in pain and told him to stop, it wasn't right and she managed to sit up and thought she was going to get away. He pushed her down on the bed, hard that time, and told her to shut up, because he didn't want to hurt her, but he would if she made him. He unzipped his pants and just as he started to push himself inside Nikki, she heard a voice yelling,

"Anyone home?"

Her Grandpa put his hand over her mouth and told her if she spoke a word when he had the chance again he would really make it hurt. Then he turned, pulled his pants up, and left her room closing the door behind him.

Nikki got up and got dressed in a hurry and ran out her room. Her Uncle Sam was in the living room with her Grandpa and she said hi while passing through. Nikki said she was suppose to already be at Dana's as her Grandpa Breaux stood up and told her he would drive her, but Nikki told him, she was riding her bike and would be home later. Nikki peddled as hard as she could to Dana's house. When she got there, Dana's sister asked her, what was wrong with her; she was white as a sheet. Nikki told her that her Grandpa Breaux had played a mean joke on her and it really scared her, or maybe it was because, she had just paddled her bike all the way there. Nikki knew in her mind with all the stories she had created, that everyone would think this was one too, and of course she would be the one to get in trouble, so she decided she would never tell anyone and would have to stay away from her Grandpa Breaux from then on as well.

The next few months were strange for Nikki. She stayed to herself a lot and kept her guard up for her Grandpa. Making sure she was never alone with him at anytime. The strange part, was thinking how everyone teased her about being her Grandpa's shadow, but not one person noticed that she know longer did anything with him.

Nikki started spending a lot of time with the girls from church again. Stacy and Nikki started to go their separate ways from the rest of the girls again. They started to experiment with everything they could find. They found cigarettes in Darwin's room, so they lit one and took a couple drags off it. Later, Stacy felt guilty and confessed what they had done at school. She and Nikki were punished and had to write the whole science book, word for word. They weren't allowed to go out at recess, they had to stay in and write. Then, in the summer they had to turn in so much a week at church. It was a grueling summer, but it too ended.

The next school year, Nikki spent the night with Stacy, Kelly and two other girls from Seattle. They were having a slumber party, and did all the things little girls do. They stayed up almost the whole night, told stories and they started telling dirty jokes that they had known from their past life before church. Sex was a big issue to each one of them. They were all approaching puberty and they all wanted to grow up so bad they couldn't stand it.

The next day, however Kelly and Stacy confessed to the principal at school, once again, but this time, they said it was only Nikki that was telling the jokes. Nikki was called out in the hall by the principal. They had told Brother Grant the school principal the joke Nikki had told. He asked Nikki if she was demon possessed and needed to have them cast out. Nikki told him, she wasn't the only one, telling jokes, but Kelly and Stacy swore they hadn't. Nikki then got to go up to the big church and have a talk with Brother Jones the pastor of the church.

This talk was just what Nikki needed. He stood there in all his glory demanding she tell him what her problem was and telling her; she was going to burn in hell for all her sins. He also told Nikki he was sure she was demon possessed and needed an exorcism. So, Nikki went back to her class and told everybody that they didn't have to talk to her anymore, because she was demon possessed and was going to hell. They all looked at her and told her they were going to pray for her to live right and get the demons out of her soul.

Brother Grant, believe it or not, gave Nikki's Grandmother the option of punishing her or the school punishing her. She chose to do it herself. Days went by without anything happening to Nikki and she could hear Gabrielle her Aunt and her Grandma Breaux argue, because Gabrielle wanted to give Nikki the whipping she thought she deserved. Her Grandma had assured the church Nikki would get what she deserved for punishment. Unfortunately, Gabrielle and Nikki hated each other, because Gabrielle was always trying to act like she was Nikki's mother and tried to tell her what to do and tried to spank Nikki when she didn't listen to her. Nikki's Grandma was always on Gabrielle, telling her to leave Nikki alone and let her do what she wanted. Nikki's Grandmother said if Nikki needed correcting she would do it. Of course, that wasn't good enough for Gabrielle she loved to fuss at Nikki in front of her company and try and whip her in front of them as well. She got a rude awakening when Nikki started to fight back. Nikki had gotten enough of Gabrielle pushing her around all the time.

The day did come when her Grandma Breaux told Nikki; she had to get her spanking for the jokes she told. She took Nikki to her room and gave her five licks on her behind. After she was finished, she left the room and closed the door. Nikki heard Gabrielle tell her Grandmother she didn't think the whipping was severe enough for what she had done, but Nikki's Grandma told her to mind her own business. That night after dinner, Grandma Breaux and Nikki were setting in the living room. Her Grandmother was reading and Nikki was just lying around killing time. She walked over to her Grandmother's chair and sat down in front of it. Nikki told her, she had whippings from her before and they hurt, but that one didn't. Her Grandmother looked down at Nikki and smiled. She told her it didn't, because she knew Nikki wasn't the only one telling dirty jokes. Nikki jumped up and hugged her Grandmother's neck. She told her Grandmother that she loved her more than breathing. Her Grandmother hugged her tight and told her it was time for bed, so she kissed her Grandmother goodnight and turned in.

Nikki laid in bed thinking, it was strange that know matter what happened, her Grandma Breaux was always there, and she always knew the truth even when know-one else did. Nikki also thought how she listened to her and understood her for her. It was like her Grandmother knew she had a rebellious streak, but she accepted Nikki know matter what. Nikki knew that know matter what happened or would happen in the future, she knew she would always have someone to turn to that she could believe in.

CHAPTER 5

Michelle showed up again to see if Nikki wanted to live with her, her new husband and her sisters. Nikki told her she would have to talk to her Grandma Breaux and if she said she could go, she would. Nikki sat down and told her Grandmother she wanted to go for her sisters. It was important to Nikki that she knew them and they knew her. Her Grandma told her that she hoped that everything would work out like she wanted. She agreed to let Nikki go, but she also told her, she was a big girl and she knew her way home if it didn't turn out like she hoped it would.

When Nikki met Mavis, Michelle's new husband, she took an immediate disliking to him. She didn't feel comfortable at all being around him, but wanted to know her sisters, so she moved to the west bank in New Orleans. Then Michelle, her new husband Mavis, Michelle's brother David and Nikki left for North Dakota to get Nikki's sisters. On the way there Nikki had know idea what they had in mind. She was excited about seeing Kristen and Ashley that nothing else mattered. They pulled up to the school where her sisters attended and Michelle and David watched each bus to see which one they were on.

When they got off the bus at school, Michelle and David ran up to them, picked them up, and started running up the street with them. Nikki jumped out the car and started running toward them because she was so excited to see them. Michelle was screaming at Nikki to get back in the car. She and David jumped in as Mavis peeled out. Ashley was crying and Kristen was asking who everyone was. Michelle told her, she was her Mama and they were going to live with her and they drove back to Louisiana where everybody was waiting to see them. Everybody made such a fuss about how beautiful Kristen and Ashley were and how big they had gotten.

Everyone was so excited to see them, but know-one asked how Nikki had been or even noticed her there.

Nikki then, went back and forth from the Breaux's to Michelle's a few times within the next year. She hated being at the Breaux's, it was so boring and nothing to do. She hated being at Michelle's, because all she did was baby-sit and get yelled at for everything Kristen and Ashley did.

She couldn't go make new friends at Michelle's, because she was too busy watching her sisters. She had to clean house all the time and get her sisters ready for school, get them to their bus stop and then get herself to school. Nikki became resentful and started to beat Kristen and Ashley every chance she got. Nikki made them take off their cloths and she beat them with a paddle. Sometimes Kristen would try to fight back, but Nikki hit her in the head to make her stop. Ashley stood there with no cloths on and begged Kristen to make Nikki stop and Kristen would tell Ashley she couldn't. After the beatings were over, Nikki told them if they told on her the next time would be worse than that time and it gave her a sick since authority to know she had them scared of her. Nikki made their lives a living hell. She took all of her anger and resentment out on them every chance she got.

The school Nikki attended was the worst she had experienced. None of the girls wanted to be friends with Nikki she wasn't one of the pretty girls and all the boys called her a dog, because her nose was pug, and she was covered with freckles. They made Nikki's life a living hell at school. She hated every part of her life and felt she had know-one to turn to. Mavis also hated Nikki and made her life at home a living hell. He went out of his way to help Kristen and Ashley, and told them all the time how much they were loved and wanted. The more he did that, the more Nikki resented her sisters and lashed out at them. Although when Nikki turned thirteen, she decided it was time to change and stop making her sister's lives so miserable and protect them. Nikki came to realize that she would always have to watch after her sisters and take care of them; because it was obvious to her that know-one else was going to. Physically Nikki changed too, her hair was longer, her skin smoother, and boys started to look at her differently, but by then, Nikki hated them so there gestures of friendship were quickly dismissed.

Then one Sunday night, before school, all their cloths were dirty because, their washing machine had broken. Nikki told Michelle that she would go do the cloths at the laundry mat if she would take her. Michelle and Mavis got up, loaded the cloths and dropped Ashley and Nikki off at the laundry mat and Michelle told Nikki to call her when they were finished. On Mavis's way out the door a scruffy man entered and shook Mavis's hand and introduced himself. Mavis stood there for a few minutes talking to him, then yelled,

"See you girls later."

An older lady was in the laundry mat doing her cloths as well. Nikki thought somehow she made it safe. Then, Nikki was standing at the end of a table folding cloths and Ashley was playing a video game, when all of a sudden a hand-covered Nikki's mouth. The man kissed Nikki on the check as she looked up at him, then he let Nikki go and told her he was sorry, he thought she was someone else and turned and walked away. Nikki stood there stunned not really knowing what to do as the stranger walked over to a chair and sat down. Nikki watched him to see if he was washing cloths. After a while she realized he wasn't there to doing cloths. Nikki walked out the laundry mat to go to the pay phone. She called Michelle and was trying to tell her what had happened, but she couldn't get it out, the words just froze in her throat as another vision started.

Nikki saw a dark room, a bed with something white hanging all around it, she was in such pain, she couldn't see, she was terrified and bound by ropes, her arms were in more pain than one could think possible. Nikki made herself look away and denied the existence of the vision or the possibility of that being something waiting for her. She told herself if she made herself wake up, she wouldn't see it and that would make it not so.

Nikki looked up and saw Ashley with the old women running out of the laundry mat screaming. All Nikki could do, was scream at the top of her lungs,

"RAPE!"

A man from the store started running in her direction. The phone went dead as the stranger ran out of the laundry mat, jumped the fence and disappeared in the trailer park by the shopping center they were in. Mavis got there, jumped out of his truck and took off after the guy on foot to try and catch him. While, Michelle went to Nikki and asked her what happened. Nikki couldn't tell her, she was too upset, because Ashley was hysterical and she ran and heed under a car in the parking lot. All Nikki could think about was her sister. Nikki wanted Ashley to be ok, so she knew she had to pull herself together, so Ashley would know that everything would be all right. Mavis came back without the guy and Michelle started laughing at him, because he still had shaving cream on his face. The police were called to the scene, but Nikki was so shaken, she couldn't remember what the man looked like, so the officer made a report and Nikki went home.

Nikki felt uncomfortable with Mavis trying to make her talk to him about what had happened. Nikki didn't want to talk to Mavis about anything, she hardly knew him. Michelle was in her own world, one that at the time Nikki couldn't understand, so Nikki went back to her life style. All the kids Nikki's age were doing their own thing, going skating or spending the night with friends or just hanging out with each other. Nikki, on the other hand, was at home baby-sitting or cleaning house. Nikki didn't feel like she fit in at school or at home.

Nikki tried to act like she was a bad girl. Making people think she was tougher than she really was. Nikki talked bad, but backed down when she was confronted. She hated school, she hated her life, and she felt like nothing was ever going to be all right. Nikki wondered how her life would be when she grew up. She cursed, drank and smoked cigarettes and thought the world would have to learn to live with her sooner or later, not her learning to live in this world. Nikki didn't know what she was trying to hide, cover up, run from, or what she was so afraid of, but she knew she wasn't normal and wondered how she could be from this earth at all. She didn't feel real, she knew she had a body, but it didn't feel like hers, it belonged to someone else. She closed her eyes and her dreams became reality. Nikki knew there was a presence with her, but she was not sure what it was or why it remained. In time Nikki began to think the presence was evil, because she had been taught by religion that knowing the future was evil and of the devil. Nikki remembered the shadows of people that danced on her wall at night while she slept. Nikki tried to tell herself it was just her imagination until her Uncle Chris went in her room one night and saw the images on the wall and almost killed himself running down the hall screaming. He screamed in Nikki's face that the devil was dancing on the wall in her room and she was evil. In time Nikki too began to believe she was evil.

Nikki didn't understand Michelle at the time, but she knew Michelle was scared of something. Michelle was not sleeping well and she wanted the lights on all the time, Michelle was terrified of the dark. Michelle was one of the most unbelieving persons that ever walked the face of the earth in God, so when she asked Nikki where her bible was Nikki couldn't believe it. Nikki gave her bible to Michelle and Michelle carried it with her wherever she went. If she went to the bath room to pee, she took Nikki's bible with her. Nikki entered the house on a few occasions and heard

Michelle talking to herself and went to check on her. When Nikki walked in the room, the room was cold as ice and Michelle would be standing with the bible open reading scripture out loud. Nikki backed out the room a couple times because she didn't understand what she saw, but she knew what ever was in that room with Michelle was not of this world and was more evil than the demons that were exorcized during exorcisms at the church she grew up in and she also knew Michelle was terrified of it.

A few weeks past and they went home for a gathering of Michelle's family. During dinner the woman started talking and Michelle burst out in tears. Nikki was sitting in the living room and heard the conversation and was amazed by what she heard. Michelle told her sisters she felt like she was losing her mind. She said something was coming to her and it was evil and she didn't know what to do. Cathy admitted something was coming to her as well and it was in the form of a black panther. Cathy said it came out the woods at night and would sit on her back porch and cry like a baby. Cathy was terrified of it and told her husband Ret about it. Ret worked nights and was gone after sundown and on the nights Ret was home this thing would not come. Ret told Cathy she was seeing and imagining things because she was scared to be at home after dark by herself, so she never talked to him about it again, but then the presence changed forms and would come to her in her sleep.

Cathy said it would paralyze her in her sleep with Ret sleeping next to her and it would talk to her. It said things like go ahead and scream, he can't hear you. Cathy said it told her it could jerk her out the bed and through the window and the window would never break and Ret would never know she was gone. Cathy said she couldn't breathe and then it started to come to her during the day and when it entered the room, Cathy said she would go into a trance.

Michelle said she tried to pray, but it would laugh at her. She went to a priest and he eventually told her, it was something attached to the family, there to collect their souls. He told Michelle to pray. She said she tried that, but it laughed at her. Then the priest told her to get a bible and when it came to her for her to let the bible fall open and to start reading out loud. He said for her to keep reading and the louder it got she needed to read louder and tune it out until it left her. Cathy asked if the bible was helping. Michelle said it made it leave, but it took a while before it would go. Michelle said it was always a shadow to her, it never had a true form, but the room would always get so cold just before it would appear. Cathy said the temperature changed for her too when it appeared.

Cathy started crying because she was scared and Michelle too because they didn't understand it and they didn't know what to do to get rid of it either. Mike one of their brothers' was standing in the hall way listening to their conversation and went in the kitchen and was laughing at them, he told them they had lost their minds and nothing like that was real. Cathy told him to shut up and not challenge the presence because it may make its presence known. Mike was laughing and started screaming,

"Hey you, Mr. Ghost come on out the wood-work, show yourself; if you think your big and bad enough to scare my sisters come see me."

A shadow appeared on the wall and Cathy screamed; Nikki stood in the living room because the whole house was then freezing cold. Michelle looked at Cathy and Cathy screamed

"Oh God!"

Mike laughed again and a shadow filled the entire kitchen and Mike grabbed his throat because he could breath. He was turning blue when Michelle reached in her purse and started reading the bible and Mike broke and ran in the yard. Michelle continued to walk through the house reading the bible out loud. The presence left and Mike got his composure back. Michelle decided it was time for a sit down when she realized this thing was showing itself to not only to her, but others and would appear if challenged. Michelle made it clear to never challenge the entity again until they knew what it was and how to deal with it. They packed their belongings and returned to their lives. They tried to put what they saw out of their minds, but that was just the beginning of what was to come.

As time went on, Michelle was more distant and Nikki started using drugs at school and met a wild child by the pool one afternoon. He had deep blue eyes and said all the things Nikki needed to hear and asked her to go to a party in the neighborhood that night. Nikki told him she wasn't allowed to date, but he could ask her Stepfather Mavis. When Cid asked Mavis, he said Nikki could go as long as she was home by midnight. As Nikki got dressed Michelle went in and helped her fix her hair and told her to have a great time, but remember to always be a lady and remember she was being trusted to make the right decisions. Michelle said she had to be home on time and not make Mavis regret letting her go. Nikki told her not to worry, she would be on time. Just as the words left her lips the doorbell rang. Nikki knew it was Cid, so she hurried out the bathroom and found Cid standing in the living room with Mavis.

Cid gave Nikki flowers and told her, she looked beautiful. He asked if she was ready, because they didn't want to be late. Nikki bid Michelle and

Mavis goodnight and out the door they went. The night was magic, Nikki danced and laughed, for the first time, she felt alive. She never wanted to loose that feeling. There were a lot of kids there, and most were high on drugs. They were passing joints around like it was candy. Nikki took a few, "Hits," as they called it and after a few minutes, Nikki too felt no pain. Nikki didn't want it to end, but she knew she had to be home on time if she ever expected to be allowed out again, so Cid walked Nikki home. As they approached the door he turned and pulled Nikki close to him. He looked in Nikki's eyes and kissed her. Nikki melted in his arms and knew, at that moment her first love was born. Nikki pulled away and said goodnight. Cid asked if he could call her the next day as she was getting ready to open the door, laughing she turned and said

"You better."

Cid called her to come back to him and told her she should go inside and go straight to bed. He said she would be better off if she didn't talk to her parents, because they might know she was stoned. Nikki told him not to worry; she would be careful and would talk to him the next day then watched as he walked away. She slowly opened the door and saw Mavis and Michelle waiting at the kitchen table for her. Nikki walked in and said she was really tired and all she wanted to do was go to sleep. Mavis, of course wouldn't hear of it. He had a million questions that Nikki had to answer with the best lies she could think of, on short notice. He seemed to buy the story, so Nikki rushed off to bed at the first given opportunity.

A few weeks later, there was a barge on the river that collided with a ferryboat. Mavis was the next in line to get on the ferry; in fact he was on the ferry and was told he had to back off because the load was too full. Mavis stood there waiting for the ferry to return and witnessed the accident. He went home that night in tears and told his family this fascinating story. When Nikki went to school the next day, everyone was talking about the accident. So Nikki started telling them about the story Mavis had told them the night before. Nikki said he was actually on the ferry, but before she could finish telling them he had to get off the ferry, everyone started asking if he was dead, because there had been no survivors. The questions were coming so fast and the kids just got louder and louder, so Nikki gave up trying to answer their questions and walked away. That night her teacher called Mavis and told him, Nikki had told everyone at school he was on the ferry and had died. She also said she thought Nikki was withdrawn and she would like to help if she could. Mavis told her he would handle the situation and thanked her for the call. After he got off the phone Nikki got another one of his famous whippings and was punished for a month. Nikki tried to explain to him what happened, but with all his yelling and screaming at her about how dare she wish him dead, she gave up again and just stopped trying.

The next week at school, Nikki's teacher took her out in the hall and asked her how her home life was. She said if Nikki felt she was abused in anyway, she could help. Nikki thought she could trust her, because all she wanted to do was help right. Nikki started crying and told her how alone she felt, and that she never had freedom to make friends, because she was always taking care of her two sisters, or cleaning house, and that Mavis was mean to her. She said that even when her sisters got in trouble; she still got a whipping, because Mavis and her mother thought she should have taught them better. Nikki placed her trust in this teacher's word and promise of help. That night, the teacher called Mavis. She told him everything that Nikki had entrusted in her. Nikki only thought her life was a living hell until that phone call. Mavis made her life the rest of the year unbearable. Cid slowly, but surely fell off the face of the earth, except for an occasional card or letter in her locker at school. Nikki tried to talk to Michelle about the problem, but when she approached Michelle, she slapped Nikki across the face and told her how ungrateful she was. She told Nikki she should be happy to live in the house with Mavis, especially with him not being her real dad and that he was so much more of a man than her real dad would ever be. Michelle never missed the opportunity to tell Nikki what a low life her dad was and how he would never be anything to anyone. Michelle told Nikki, she was just like her father by not liking Mavis and not being the prefect kid she should be.

The summer finally came and they moved, because Mavis said Nikki caused him enough embarrassment at school. They moved to the other side of the city for a fresh start. Mavis told Nikki if she ever told anyone she was unhappy at home again he would beat the living hell out of her. The move was all right, the apartment was small, two bedrooms, so all three girls had to share a room as usual. Nikki knew that she could never trust anyone again, so she decided that at all cost she was going to find a way out one day, but until that opportunity came, she had to walk a fine line.

Mavis was an undercover cop and he wanted Nikki to go make friends in the apartment complex so she could help him bust all the kids that used drugs. When Nikki refused to get involved, he told Michelle that Nikki was on drugs and needed to be put in the state reform school, known as LTI to make her straighten up. Mavis made arrangements for him to take

Nikki to LTI for a tour of the correctional facility for teens. He walked her through the building and sat her in a room where she was visited by some of her soon to be cellmates. They came in the room all tough looking, talking tough and cursing mostly. They told Nikki they couldn't wait until she arrived; they scared the hell out of her.

Mavis told Nikki that she was going to do everything he told her from that moment on, or on the next screw up she would be placed in the locked down unit at LTI and assured her all the arrangements had already been made. Nikki went home to think things through, and decided to go to Michelle and beg her to stop Mavis. Nikki told Michelle, that Mavis was a crazy man and pleaded with her not to let him send her to LTI. Michelle looked at Nikki as if she couldn't see her and told her she was headed for LTI and she would not put a stop to it. So Nikki told Michelle she wanted to move back with her Maw-Maw Breaux. Michelle said she had spoke to Ms Alice and she had told her, she didn't want Nikki to come back there, she was on her own, so Nikki waited until Michelle and Mavis went to sleep then slipped in the living room to call her Maw-Maw Breaux. When Nikki reached her, she told Nikki that Michelle had never spoke to her and it was time for Nikki to come home. Ms Alice told Nikki her Dad had remarried and was putting his life together for the first time and maybe after a while she could live with her Dad and his new wife if he continued to prove he was on track. The next morning Nikki was awakened by her Grandmother's voice in the living room and Nikki went home with her Grandmother.

A few months later, Nikki went to live with her Dad and his new wife Sheila. Life for Nikki once again became incredible. She finally was in a school she loved and made several friends, one of the best parts, was for the first time, Nikki was one of the most popular girls in school. She tried out for cheerleading and made the team. Jeff Daniels the captain of the football team was crazy about Nikki and they became the couple that everyone envied.

Nikki thought her life was going to be fine, she thought she was cool and started smoking cigarettes. When her Dad found them in her room, he made her smoke a whole pack in front of him making her sick as a dog and Nikki experienced her first panic attack, not a big one just enough to make her heart race, her palms sweat, and feel faint. She refused to smoke anymore, because she thought the smoking was what triggered it.

Nikki had freedom like she had never had before and was enjoying her life to the fullest. Then Sheila told Nikki that she would need to move to the smaller bedroom, because her daughter would be moving home with them as well. Katie, Nikki's stepsister, moved in and told Nikki to leave her things in the bedroom with her, because their room was bigger than their parents and they could get to know each other better if they were together. Katie was great and they bonded like know one could have ever imagined.

They were inseparable and did everything together. The fact that Katie was older, seventeen and driving was a great benefit to them both. There were no limits to them at that point. Her friends and Nikki's friends just went hand in hand. They all ran the roads together, hung out together, and Katie taught Nikki how to drive. Katie attended all Nikki's school games and cheered as loud as she did; Nikki on the field of course and Katie in the stands. They talked, shared their souls and thought life could never be better.

Nikki's friends were the best in the world and her first Christmas with her Dad, Sheila and Katie was a-dream-come-true. It was an incredible family celebration; Nikki met Sheila's whole family and hit it off great. Sheila's sister Susan became Nikki's favorite Aunt and Shelia's parents became another set of Grandparents for Nikki. All of them were a perfect fit and they became a close nit family. That is of course until Darwin, started slipping away drinking again. Darwin started getting home later and later, then not going home at all some nights.

Katie met Rick and fell in love and she too started spending more and more time away from home and Nikki stayed away with friends or with Jeff to avoid listening to the fighting when Darwin did decide to make it home. Nikki hated that part of her life, but it only happened once a month or so and she told herself it would pass. She prayed to God it would all be all right, but the frequency of course grew and Nikki knew her beautiful family was falling apart and she couldn't stop it. Katie moved back to North Carolina and Nikki felt lost without her soul mate and confidant, but she understood that Katie had to go.

Some of Nikki's friends were also struggling in their unhappy home lives and decided to run away together and see the world. Nikki, of course was invited to tag along. She wasn't totally unhappy with where she was, but she was mad at Darwin for destroying their life. Nikki thought if she tagged along she could shake Darwin up and he would see what they had, was worth having. Nikki had never thought about running away before, so she followed instructions from her friends and took notes. She made a list of what to take when she left, but she lost her list one day. She didn't think much about it at the time, but then Darwin started asking some strange questions. Nikki didn't really pay attention to the questions at the time, until the weekend before she was to leave and Darwin asked her what she was doing that weekend. Nikki told him she didn't have any plans, and then he asked if she was planning a trip for the weekend. Nikki told him she wasn't, then Darwin got angry and threw the list in her face, and gave her the beating of her life.

Nikki was covered in bruises on her back, her buttocks and legs. Darwin screamed that Nikki would never lie to him again. Darwin became so angry he threw the belt down curled up his fist and grabbed Nikki's collar. He almost started to punch Nikki, but she looked in his eyes and closed hers anticipating the blow when Darwin threw her on her bed and left the room.

After a while, Darwin went to Nikki's room and asked why she had planned to leave, she told him she didn't think it mattered, because he was throwing their family away anyway and she didn't want to sit around and watch it die. Darwin said her thoughts were absurd and she was grounded for a month as he left her room. Nikki called Nancy to tell her, her Dad knew about the plans, because he found her list, and might call the other parents to warn them. Nancy didn't waste any time, she was on the phone with Mike and they took off before her parents got home from work.

Katie came back that weekend for a visit and Sheila and Katie got into an argument. Nikki heard Sheila screaming, what a low life Katie's Dad was, and Katie not being too pleased, started cursing back at Sheila. Then Nikki heard Sheila tell Katie she wasn't too big to get her ass whipped. Katie said, she never said she was, when Sheila grabbed a belt and starting hitting Katie. After a while of hearing the licks passed, Nikki went to the living room as Katie started to hit Sheila back. Nikki ran next door to Sheila's parents to get Roman, Shelia's dad to help. Roman ran to the house and put Sheila in a chair and told her to chill out for a while.

Katie had tears streaming down her face when she told Sheila she was going back to her Dad's and would never come home again and walked out the door and went to her Grandparent's, next door for a few days. Each day after school, Nikki went to see Katie and begged her to move back home, but Katie told her she couldn't.

Katie picked Nikki up from school the next day and told her she was leaving for good. She told Nikki she loved her as if she was her sister and that she would miss her, but if she ever needed her for anything, she would always know how to find her. Katie knew one day Nikki would understand her reasons. Katie kissed Nikki's cheek and let her out in the driveway. Nikki stood there and watched her go as the tears rolled down her face.

Life was definitely a little boring with Katie gone and her best friend Nancy too. Then the police starting hounding the "In crowd," about any contact from Nancy or Mike or where they thought the two could be. The click of friends separated and kept to themselves.

Then, Nikki came home from school one Friday afternoon thinking it was just another day and found Sheila cooking dinner as usual. The house was spotless and Sheila was excited about their shopping trip that weekend. Then, Darwin didn't come home that evening. The later it got the angrier Sheila became. When Darwin walked through the door Sheila was waiting. They had one of the worst screaming matches Nikki had ever heard. Nikki was so scared she called her Maw-Maw Alice to get her Dad, because she thought he had completely lost his mind.

When her Grandparents arrived, Darwin jumped Sheila and starting beating her in the face in front of Nikki's Grandparents. Nikki ran out the door screaming,

"Get that crazy son-of-a-bitch out of here!"

Then Nikki heard Darwin going after her, but Paw-Paw Breaux grabbed Darwin and told him he wasn't going to touch Nikki. Darwin told his Father that Nikki called her Grandma a bitch and he wasn't going to stand for it. Grandma Breaux pushed him across the room and Darwin landed on the sofa as Grandma Breaux told him it was a figure of speech and she knew Nikki never intended any harm to her.

Nikki stepped back in the door and saw her Maw-Maw Alice walk over to Darwin and smack him in the nose with her fist. She heard her Grandmother tell Darwin that he had better get himself together and said he was going home with her for the night and get his-self straight. Darwin told his Mom to get Nikki's stuff together and take her as well, but Grandma Breaux told him Nikki was staying with Sheila. Grandpa Breaux grabbed Darwin and dragged him to the car by the ear and they took him home with them.

Shelia asked Nikki if she was all right. She said she was fine and asked how she was. Shelia said she was fine, but she couldn't live like that anymore. They hugged and the two sat and watched TV for a while. Then Shelia got up and walked down the hall to the back of the house. After a while, Nikki heard whimpering from down the hall. When she looked, she saw Shelia standing with her back to Nikki, leaned over the washing machine with her arm swinging back and forth. Each time her arm came back, Nikki heard Shelia cry out. Nikki called Shelia and asked if she was all right, but Shelia screamed for Nikki to stay in the living room. Nikki was worried and walked down the hall to see what was wrong. As Nikki approached Shelia, she asked her if she was sure she was all right. Then Nikki saw Shelia with a knife hacking away at her wrist, blood shooting everywhere. Nikki froze for a moment, she couldn't think. Nikki couldn't remember anybody's phone number except Katie's, and she was in North Carolina.

When Nikki got Katie on the phone, she told Nikki to get Roman her Grandfather next door. Nikki threw the phone down and ran out the door, it was dark, so Nikki ran into bushes and a tree on the way next door. She couldn't think, she couldn't see, as she moved through the night air, she felt cold and clammy physically, but she couldn't feel her skin or any sensation. It was as if, time stood still and she thought she was never going to reach Shelia's parent's house next door. As Nikki turned the corner of their house, she saw the lights on. Nikki was banging on the door, but when Roman opened the door, Nikki couldn't speak. Roman could see Nikki was terrified, and he took off running to the house when she couldn't answer him; Nikki followed behind. Roman ran in the house and Nikki pointed down the hall where Shelia stood in the same position she left her in, still hacking away at her wrist. Roman grabbed Shelia and wrestled her to the floor. Roman screamed for Nikki to get a towel and call 911. Nikki ran through the house to her bathroom to get a towel and grabbed the phone on the way. Nikki dialed 911 and told the operator they needed help, because her Mom was hurt. Then Nikki dropped the phone and ran down the hall to get the towel to Roman. Nikki helped wrap Shelia's hand in the towel and applied pressure to stop the bleeding. By that time, Shelia passed out on the floor. Roman was trying to get Shelia to come around as Nikki sat on the floor holding her wrist and praying to God Shelia was going to be all right. Nikki realized she had blood all over her and as she looked around the hallway, all she could see was blood dripping down the walls and it covered the floor.

Shelia was white as a ghost and wasn't coming around. Nikki heard the sirens and knew help was almost there, but she wondered if it was too late. The EMS attendants loaded Shelia up in the ambulance and Roman got in the back with her. Nikki stood in the driveway as the ambulance started up and turned on the sirens. As they drove away, Nikki sat motionless on the steps for a while and finally gathered enough strength to move back in the house.

Nikki sat on the sofa thinking how crazy things were. She knew her life there was over. Nikki loved her Grandmother Breaux with all her heart, but she also knew she couldn't conform to her religion after living, what she finally called a normal life. Nikki knew she wouldn't be happy at her Grandmother's, so she had no other options for a life that was not consumed in religion except with Michelle, so she called her. Michelle told Nikki to gather her things she would be there the next morning to get her. Nikki fell asleep on the sofa that night wondering how her life was going to change, wondering if Mavis would lighten up or would she go back to the same thing she ran from. Nikki drifted off to a relaxed state and just as she started to drift off in a dream state, she heard Michelle's voice calling her name.

Michelle said if there was anything in the house Nikki wanted, she should take it. Nikki told Michelle she liked the stereo, but it wasn't hers. Michelle said; she could have it, because that was the least Darwin could give her for all the crap he pulled, so Nikki packed her cloths while Michelle loaded the stereo. Nikki stood in the door taking one last look around. Even though it was not the greatest looking place in the world, she knew she had never been happier anywhere else and her fairytale life again, was over. Nikki walked toward the car, but she knew in her heart, she was walking away from the remnants of the only home she ever really had.

Standing on the edge of the bayou Nikki thought, life on the bayou would never change. The swamps would be there forever and the alligators would lie on the banks until the end of time. The next few days were an adjustment, and things seamed to be all right. That is until the cops knocked on the door looking for Michelle. They read Michelle her rights and placed handcuffs on her when Mavis walked in and stopped them. He worked in the narcotic division and told them he would bring Michelle in for questioning. When Mavis asked what the charges were, Nikki heard the officer tell him, Michelle was being charged with felony theft, because she stole a stereo. Mavis told the officer there was way more to the story than he was willing to go into at the house, but he would take Michelle to the station and clear everything up. Nikki felt bad for Michelle, because Nikki thought what was happening was her fault, Michelle was just trying to let her have something she wanted and Michelle was in big trouble, because of her.

After a while, Michelle showed up with some other officers. Michelle called Nikki to her room with Mavis and told Nikki, she had to press charges against Darwin for rape or the police were going to put Michelle in jail for twenty years. Michelle knew Nikki still had bruises between her legs from the last whipping Darwin had given her and Michelle had told the police she thought Darwin had raped Nikki.

Nikki started crying, she was scared and not sure what to do, but Mavis grabbed her arm and told her she was going to tell the police that Darwin raped her to save Michelle or else, and Nikki knew what the else meant, so she agreed. Mavis and Michelle told Nikki what to say and then let the police officers in to take her statement. They took pictures of the bruises between her legs from the belt Darwin used to whip her. The bruises did look like she had fought someone off in a sexual assault, so they finished the paper work and left.

It turned into a huge ordeal. Nikki had to go to court to testify against Darwin. Nikki told Michelle before the trial she couldn't go through with it, because she was scared she would mess up and she just wanted to go home and forget the mess. Mavis grabbed her again and asked if she wanted to see her Mother go to jail for twenty years, because of her and told her she had nothing to fear, except him, if she didn't do what she was told. Nikki went in the courtroom and told them exactly what Mavis told her to and stared at the floor the entire time she spoke.

Nikki cried when she spoke, not because of the emotion that goes along with telling the truth in regards to being raped, but because she knew she was lying and there was know way out. The Breaux family was politically connected and had already made arrangements for the ordeal not to go any further. The charges were dropped in the end, but Darwin was so mad at Nikki, he wanted to press charges against her for stealing the stereo, but the judge told him the stereo was returned, so let it go. The judge told Darwin it would be in his best interest not to press the issue and let Nikki leave with Michelle without any problems.

Nikki sat in the back seat looking out the back window of the car. She could see her Grandmother Breaux watching the car until they were out of site. Nikki was so embarrassed and humiliated there were know words to describe. She felt as if her Grandmother Breaux would never forgive her. Nikki really didn't care how Darwin felt, and she didn't care how her Grandfather felt, but she wanted to die when she thought how her Maw-Maw Alice felt. Nikki cried all the way back to Algiers.

CHAPTER 6

When they got back Mavis reminded Nikki of LTI and started in again on the drugs and wanting her to help him bust people. Nikki knew her Maw-Maw Alice would never forgive her and knew she could never go home again. Nikki also knew she would have to find her own way, so Nikki told Mavis she would do what he wanted. In the mean time, Nikki vowed to start looking for her own way out from anybody that knew her at all. Nikki vowed, she would get out somehow and never look back. She knew know-one really wanted her and all Michelle would do was listen to Mavis and not hear a word from her. Nikki knew she would be called a liar and Michelle would take Mavis's side. Nikki also knew Michelle was still in a world of her own walking around carrying the bible with her through the house. She felt she had know other choice, because know matter what happened Nikki would be put in LTI.

Nikki started hanging out on the bayou and met some people that were into the drug seen and had some major connections. Nikki fit right in with Mavis pushing her to do drugs and Michelle oblivious to what was going on. Nikki began to like the feeling of being high, because life sure didn't seem bad when she was stoned. Nikki had a crush on Leonard the mysterious guy that lived in the swamp that surfaced from time to time in his Piero at the edge of the bayou for supplies and whatever else he could find. He had a reputation as a playboy and being a wild man so to speak, but Nikki thought he hung the moon. Nikki heard wild parties happened at Leonard's and major drugs were also distributed there. Even though, she was madly in-love with him and laid in bed at night dreaming of Leonard making love to her, she was only fourteen and Leonard had never noticed her before. In the long run, however Nikki was more afraid of Mavis than she was in-love with Leonard, so she knew she had to find a way in that crowd.

Nikki knew Leonard came in for supplies on Fridays, so she hung out on the bayou just to get a glimpse of him passing. She was sitting on the pier one Thursday afternoon reading, not really paying attention to anything. When she looked up and saw Leonard and some other guy docked at the end of the pier.

Leonard looked up and saw Nikki sitting there and asked if she'd like to blow a jay with them. Her heart sank to her knees, but Nikki replied graciously with,

"That's cool."

She walked over and Leonard introduced her to his friend Cid and Nikki asked Leonard how he knew her name. He laughed and said, all the boys on the bayou knew her name and when she disappeared for extended periods of time they held their breath awaiting her return. Nikki laughed, then realized Cid was her first love. Cid recognized her as well and asked if he could call her sometime. Nikki gave him her number and headed for home. When she walked in the door Mavis was waiting for her, he started in, wanting to know who she met that day and what contacts she had formed. Nikki told him, she had met some people at the end of the bayou and gave them her number. She said she would wait and see if they called and where it would lead. Mavis said to keep him informed, he wanted first and last names, so he could run background checks on them, to see if they already had an arrest record. Nikki told Mavis, if they called, she would get a chance to spend some time with them, and find out what they were into and get their names as well. Mavis left the room and Nikki fell on the bed and cried herself to sleep.

A couple of days went by and Nikki began to think she wouldn't hear from Cid again, and actually stopped tensing up every time the phone rang. Then, she was called to the phone, to hear Cid's voice on the other end. He asked if she wanted to go to a party that weekend and Nikki told him she'd love to. Mavis was all too pleased to hear about the party.

Mavis went to Nikki's room while she was getting ready and told her, that was the night. Nikki told him she would do the best she could to get the info, but that wasn't what Mavis wanted to hear. Mavis grabbed her and told her, he knew there was going to be drugs there and that she had better get him some hard evidence to bust the punks. Nikki told him again she would, and she would call him if there was anything to report. Mavis told her, she had better call within the hour and if there weren't any drugs there, she had better have her ass home by nine; which was only an hour away.

Nikki went to the living room with Mavis at her side. She greeted Cid with a hello when Cid walked across the room and kissed her on the cheek and Nikki told him they should go. Mavis called out to have a good time; of course Michelle was nowhere to be found. Walking to the party Cid asked Nikki if she had been dating. She told him no and Cid acted a little surprised and told her it was a little hard to believe. He said, after all she was fourteen and when he had told her Dad he was eighteen; he never blinked an eye or acted like he might think he was too old for her. Cid kept pushing for answers and Nikki finally broke. She burst into tears and told him about Mavis and how he wanted her to bust people. She told Cid that Mavis wanted his ass served on a silver plate.

Cid stood there, Nikki thought in shock; then said he wanted to get the story straight. He said,

"You mean to tell me that Mavis would sell out his own daughter to bust someone."

Nikki told Cid if she had to die it wouldn't matter to Mavis. Nikki said all she wanted to do was to get the hell out of there and away from Mavis. She was scared of Mavis and if she didn't give him something he was going to have her put in LTI.

They walked along the bayou and talked for a while. Nikki told Cid she needed to go, so she could be home for nine. She assured him, he didn't have anything to worry about, she would tell Mavis there were know drugs at the party, and she would take the consequences. Cid reached out and grabbed her to pull her closer to him. As Cid hugged Nikki and held her in his arms, he whispered that everything was going to be all right, because he was going to make it that way. Nikki pulled away and asked what he meant by that and he told her, she didn't have to go home at all. She could live with him. Cid said he would protect her and that Mavis would never have the chance to hurt her or threaten her again. Nikki told Cid that Mavis would kill him first, but before she could say anything else, Cid kissed her and asked if she really wanted out.

Cid wrote his phone number on a piece of paper and tucked it in her pants and told her when she was ready or if she needed him to call the number and he would be there. Nikki turned to go, so she wouldn't be late and she felt she could face almost anything.

When Nikki walked in the house, Mavis was standing in the kitchen, he yelled

"Why didn't you call?"

Nikki told him there weren't any drugs, so she didn't call. Mavis called her a lair, because he claimed to have had another inside man at the party. He turned to Michelle and told her the phone call he received was his man, and he told him, he saw Nikki blowing grass at the party. Nikki said that was a lie, but Mavis told Michelle it was his worst nightmare, and in the morning he was taking Nikki to LTI and they would straighten her ass out once and for all. Nikki ran to her room and closed the door. Michelle went to Nikki's room yelling and screaming. She woke Kirsten and Ashley, so Nikki went to the bathroom and said out loud what a bitch she thought Michelle was. Michelle went in the bathroom and slapped Nikki in the mouth and told her if she thought it was bad there, she had know idea what bad was really going to be like until she got to her new home. Michelle told Nikki to pack her bags, but not much, she wouldn't need a lot where she was going.

Nikki turned to her and told her she was evil and the presence that came for her knew it, that's why it laughed at her when she prayed. Nikki told her if she thought carrying that bible around was going to save her she had another thing coming. Michelle sat on the floor and asked Nikki for the first time what she knew about the presence. Nikki told her she knew it was evil and was brought to the family and the why she didn't know, but she knew it was there for her sanity. Nikki said when her grandfather appeared to her before his death he said to remind Michelle of the watch. Michelle looked up at Nikki and tears came to her eyes. Michelle got up and walked away.

Nikki didn't know that was the reminder of the talk she had with Charles before his death. He went to Michelle and told her he knew he was dying and soon he would be gone. He told Michelle she was the first born daughter and it would come for her first, he told her it would make it's rounds to all his children and they had to unite as one in battle and go to his grave site together and his last born son needed to take his watch and all the kids needed to read a certain scripture out-loud and his youngest son needed to bury the watch at the grave site then leave. He instructed them to go and never look back and never return to his grave. He said this would bond the entity to him at his grave, it could extend to the outer family possibly, but not to his children. He told Michelle if it extended itself to other family and she went to visit it would show it's self and if she entered the house it could leave with her again and then there would be no hope of making it leave. Michelle thought her father was having a mental breakdown and she put the conversation out of her mind; that is until Nikki spoke the words she knew she could not dismiss or shrug off any longer. When Michelle left the bathroom, Nikki shrugged it off and decided Michelle could give in and or give up, but she had, had enough.

Nikki went to bed and waited until she knew everyone was asleep; then she got up packed a few cloths and kissed Kirsten and Ashley on the check and wished them well. She cried hoping their life would be different from hers and somehow knew it would be. Nikki snuck out the window and made it to the store where she called Cid. When Nikki told him what happened. He said for Nikki not to worry, he was on his way to get her. The next few days were wonderful as far as Nikki was concerned. They laughed, talked and Cid held Nikki when she was scared. He made her believe that everything was going to be all right.

Then, Cid ran in the door and told Nikki the cops was there looking for her. Cid said she had to hide or they would put him in jail and take her back to Mavis. Cid went out the door to try and stall the cops and Nikki hid in a stereo cabinet. She could see the cops searching for her through the fabric that covered the speaker and could hear them asking Cid questions. Cid didn't think they would search the house, but Nikki knew they would. Cid must have thought she was just in the back, because when they started searching Cid's face got pale. When the officers came from the back of the house, Cid stood putting his hands out to have the handcuffs placed, but the officer shook his hand and told him he was sorry for the interruption and left. Cid fell on the couch. When Nikki got out the stereo cabinet he busted out laughing and asked her how she fit in there. Nikki laughed and told him she had the hiding place picked out days before, because she knew one day they would come.

Nikki spent months in the house hiding, afraid to go outside. She hid in the oven, under the sink in the bathroom. If it was a small place and Nikki thought they wouldn't look for her there, she jumped in. Nikki was petite with an exceptionally small frame, which made it easy to hide in small places. The cops never thought to look in places that small, so they never found her.

A couple months later, Nikki went out with the crowd of people they were hanging with. They went to roller city and Nikki heard the DJ page her name over the intercom system, so they left. One night a cop stopped Nikki, showed her a picture of herself and asked if she had seen the girl.

Nikki knew she couldn't always live on the run for the rest of her life, so Anita one of the girls that hung out with them and Nikki decided to hitchhike to find Darwin. Nikki thought if she could get in touch with him that things would be different and he would help her talk to her Maw-

Maw Alice. Nikki planned a goodbye evening with Cid and that night she lost her virginity to him, Nikki thought she owed him that much for all he had done for her till then.

The next day Anita and Nikki started hitchhiking and a car stopped to give them a ride. It was two baseball players that had just finished a game. They won, so they were drinking and offered Anita and Nikki a beer. Anita took one and told them they were headed for the interstate going to the West Bank. The guys said they would be happy to take them to the interstate, in fact if they didn't mind letting them make a stop on the way, they could even take them as far as the West Bank.

Anita agreed and they climbed in. They seamed like nice guys and Nikki felt safe with Anita, because Anita wasn't worried about a thing. The stop was the park where they had played that night. There wasn't a soul in sight and the guy driving asked Anita to take a walk with him. As she walked away, Nikki grabbed her arm and told her not to leave her, but Anita said,

"Everything is cool, these are nice guys, you don't have anything to worry about, but scream, I'll hear you and I'll come running if you need me."

Then she disappeared.

Nikki was standing by the car when the other guy walked over to her and asked if she was all right, Nikki said she was fine, just a little worried about where Anita was and what was taking so long. He put his arm around Nikki and told her everything was fine and call him Bill. Then said it was time to go find their friends, so they could get the hell out of there. Nikki told him he could go and she left walking back towards the interstate. Nikki didn't know what she was going to do, but she knew she wasn't walking into the woods with that guy either.

When Nikki got to the interstate she walked to the next exit and down to the store, she got a coke and was sitting on the side walk when a van drove up and a guy got out and went in the store, when he came out and saw Nikki he asked her what she was doing sitting there all alone. Nikki talked with him a few minutes and he seemed to put her at ease and he asked if she wanted him to take her anywhere and drop her off because it was getting late. Nikki asked if he could give her ride back to the other side of town and he agreed. Nikki got in the van and everything went black.

When Nikki woke up her hands were bound and she was hanging by them from a hook in a dark room. Her feet were bound, but they could touch the floor, so she tried to stand to take the weight off her arms, because they were killing her. She tried to focus, but her vision wouldn't clear, but she could hear someone in the room with her. She tried to speak, but the words wouldn't come. The more she tried to stand her weight fell of her wrist pulling her arms more and the pain was excruciating. The man that gave her a ride and introduced himself as Allen walked over and took her hair and pulled her head up. He kissed her hard on the lips and told her she was going to live like she had never before and not to worry, his face would be the last she saw in this world too, but in the mean time, enjoy the ride, he blew a powder in Nikki's face and forced a pill in her mouth.

Nikki was beaten into submission, and the torture was anyone's worst night mare. He cut her loose and Nikki thought he was going to let her go. He opened a door and told her to run if she wanted to live. Nikki sat on the floor, she was too scared to run, but he walked over and kicked her in the stomach and screamed he would kill her if she stayed; Nikki pulled herself up and made it to the door. When she got to the edge of the trees, he grabbed her and started kissing her. His grip was tight, so she couldn't scream, but she still had the strength at that point to fight, so she kneed him between the legs and he fell to the ground. Nikki started running in the woods to get away from him. She was screaming at the top of her lungs for help, but no-one came.

Allen was right behind Nikki, hot on her trail. She stepped in a hole and fell, when she looked up Allen was standing over her. He told Nikki he was going to get a piece of ass for the ride, if he had to take it, so be it. Nikki was screaming, but he punched her in the stomach and told her, she could make it hard or easy. The more she screamed the harder he punched. Nikki stopped screaming and told him she was still a virgin and begged him not to. He laughed and told her, virgins were his specialty and he would show her what a real man could do. Allen stood up, pulled down his pants and kept his foot on Nikki's stomach so she couldn't move. Nikki was crying and begging him to stop; then he took a knife out his pocket and put it to her throat. He told her, she was going to say what he wanted her to say, and was going to fuck him the way he wanted to be fucked or he was going to rip her apart.

Nikki went numb inside, she could feel what he was doing and she could hear his words. She could hear her say the words he wanted her to say, but it was like she was watching a bad movie, because this wasn't happening to her, but it was. Nikki told him she would do what he wanted and begged for her life. He stood her up and told her to take off her pants, she did. It was freezing, but she couldn't feel the cold. Allen spread out his jacket and told her to lay down on it, she did. He told her to close her eyes and get ready to feel what he had to give her, but her eyes were open and her body was numb. She closed her eyes and started praying for God to help her live; then she felt his tongue sliding along the edge of her leg. He told Nikki to spread her legs and she begged him again to stop. He stood up and kicked her in the side and told her to open her legs. When she caught her breath, he was back on top of her. He told Nikki, she must want to make it hard, and must want it to hurt and he was willing. Nikki told him she didn't want to make it hard and begged him not to hurt her, but he put the knife back to her throat and told her, she was going to be his sweet little girl and fuck big daddy the way he like it or she was going to get cut, one time for every mistake she made from that point on.

He ran the knife down her stomach and told her to open her legs, she did. Allen knelt between Nikki's legs and told her he was putting the knife at her feet. He told her, she had better not try anything, and if she tried to hurt him while doing anything he told her to do or if he had to pick the knife up again he would slit her throat and asked if she understood. She told him she did. He told her to close her eyes and know matter what happened; she was not to open them again for anything; she closed her eyes and he tied a blind fold tight around her eyes. He stood her up and turned her in circles until Nikki fell to the ground with her head spinning. Nikki felt him pulling her into a sitting position, so she sat up. He tied another handkerchief around her eyes, so even if she wanted to open them she couldn't. He put a bottle up to her lips and told her to drink. Nikki tried to ask what it was, but he slapped her and told her to drink or he was picking up the knife, she drank. It was strong liquor and it took her breath, she choked. While she was coughing, she could hear him laughing.

Then he said for her to take a deep breath. While breathing in, Nikki could smell that he was blowing her a shotgun from a joint. He told her to lie back and not move, so she laid on the ground. For the next few minutes all she could hear was the wind in the trees and suddenly she felt like she was floating. He asked how she felt. She told him she felt strange, that the earth was moving and she was scared. He told her to do what he said from then on and she would be fine. Nikki was mad and scared, but this torment was agony. She told him, she would do what he wanted, but just get on with it, and get it over, just do it and stop waiting.

He grabbed her and said,

"Fine, you're ready to be fucked, I'll fuck you."

Nikki was pleading with him not to hurt her, that, that was not what she meant. She could feel him trying to put himself inside her and started crying. He was cursing, because he couldn't get an erection and backed away. Nikki thought it was over, and then she felt him moving back between her legs again. Her head was spinning, but she was trying to remain calm. She felt his tongue on her and she felt sick to her stomach, because it also felt good. Nikki had so many emotions raging in her mind and yet she laid there like a zombie unable to express them or to stop what was happening. He told her to tell him it felt good, she told him what he wanted to hear. He told her if she didn't let go and let him make her have her first orgasm he was going to kill her.

Nikki laid there and decided she wanted to live and told herself it wasn't really that bad, that part, that is, wasn't that bad and she tried to relax. Nikki thought if she made him think she was into it, she could figure a way out or to get loose from him again. She started to let her muscles go and really feel his tongue sliding up and down and all around the outside of her. It felt good, but then he slid his tongue deep inside her. She cried out because it hurt and at the same time it felt good. She heard him laugh and told her to tell him she wanted more; she told him what he wanted to hear again and again. She felt him moving back up her body. His face was then next to hers, and she felt his penis pressing against her body, then he had an erection.

She could feel his size on her stomach and thought how large he felt. Then suddenly, he pulled back and placed himself at the opening of her vagina and told her to tell him she wanted it, she told him she did, as the tears streamed down her face. He forced himself inside Nikki. The pain ripped through her entire body. She was screaming before she knew it. He stuffed her underwear in her mouth and kept thrusting himself inside her harder and harder. He was cursing, because he couldn't come and told her she was going to get him off know matter what it took. He pulled out, grabbed Nikki and forced her on her stomach. He grabbed her hips and pulled her up to him on her knees. He told her if she pulled away or tried to lay down, it would be the last move she ever made.

He put himself back inside her, holding her hips. He was thrusting himself in and out. Nikki could hear his moans over her screaming. He grabbed her hair with one hand and kept the other hand on her hip. He pounded like a wild animal until he exploded inside Nikki, then fell on top of her and told her,

"You did good."

Then said she could get dressed, but if she tried to run he would catch her and she would die. She got dressed and sat down by a tree. He walked over to Nikki and told her that they were going back to the van and he would drop her off where she wanted. Nikki walked back to the van in silence only it wasn't the van he took her to. Nikki still had the blindfold on and was taken back to the cellar and he bound her hands again. Nikki tried to resist, but he told her the fun had just begun as he hung her back on the hook he had originally placed her on.

He left the room and Nikki could hear running water and him singing. She tried so hard to focus, but the blind folds were so tight. She rubbed her head on the side of her arm trying to displace the blindfold so she could see where she was. Finally a tiny glimpse of a light came through and Nikki could see a bed, ropes, chains and locks, with candles burning. Cob webs and dust everywhere, but the bed had crisp white sheets, with lace flowing from the ceiling. Nikki was so confused she couldn't imagine how this could be possible. The singing stopped and the water stopped running and then there was quite until Nikki past out hanging from her wrist.

Nikki woke up in excruciating pain and she was freezing, water was hitting her so hard and it was freezing cold, Allen was back in the room with her and cutting her clothes off with a knife and hosing her down at the same time. He told her she had to be spotless for his bed and when he thought she was clean enough he dried her naked body with a towel then picked her up and carried her to the bed. Again he bound her wrist and ankle to the four posts in the bed with chains and locked them. Her position was changed often and she was beaten and raped repeatedly until there was nothing left, not even a will to live.

Then the chains were released and Nikki laid there, she didn't fight, she didn't speak even when spoken to. She was wrapped in a blanket and taken to the van and laid in the back on the floor. She felt the van moving and the next thing she felt was herself flying in the air when she was thrown from a bridge into the bayou. Nikki hit hard on a limb and as the water hit her skin her world went black.

When Nikki opened her eyes, it was two months later in an ICU bed, she was found by a fisherman and barley alive. Know-one knew who she was and her face was so swollen she had slits for eyes and two tiny holes where her nose was. It took some time before they figured out she was a run-a-way. Michelle and Mavis were notified and they visited from time to time, but Nikki was un-responsive. When she woke up all Nikki wanted was her grandmother, but the worst was yet to come.

Allen's next victim was stronger and he was not as prepared for her as he had been with Nikki and she was lucky enough to get away when she picked up a branch and knocked him out when he came after her. He was in police custody at that point and Mavis getting the attention he got being a police officer and his daughter being brutally raped and beaten within an inch of her life paid Allen a visit. The desk sergeant just happen to need coffee when Mavis arrived and let himself in the cell with Allen. Mavis broke his nose, his arm and four ribs, before three other officers acknowledged the disturbance and went to see what was going on with a man placed in a private cell. They rushed in and pulled Mavis off him before he killed him. Mavis was brought up on assault charges and lost his job in the process.

Allen was given a speedy trial and sentenced to life in Angola State Prison with Nikki's testimony. When he was sentenced Mavis leaned over and whispered in Nikki's ear not to worry he would never see the outside walls or leave Angola alive, he promised her that. Nikki just looked at Mavis and turned away, she didn't know why he was so upset about anything he had made her life a living hell and if it had not been for him in the first place Nikki would have never ran-a-way. Two weeks later Allen hung himself in his cell in prison. After his death, the police wanted to speak to Nikki and asked her if she felt remorse for a man that hung himself in jail. Nikki was infuriated and screamed at the officer to go fuck himself and her only regret was she wasn't there to see it and told him to get the fuck out. He told her Allen's death was under mysterious circumstances and a formal investigation was going to happen. Nikki told him to investigate away she didn't give a shit that he was dead, then told the officer maybe he needed to go look at the photos of the five other women that died in Allen's hands, look at the pictures of what she looked like when they were trying to identify who she was and what his last victim that survived looked like and ask us all if we really give a fuck if he is dead or alive. The Detective stood and told Nikki he was leaving, but he would be in touch. Mavis told him he wouldn't be in touch if he had any further questions he could call his attorney and he handed him a card to the attorney. Mavis made it clear Nikki would not be answering anymore questions.

Four and a half months from the attack Nikki told Michelle she wanted to go home. Michelle told Nikki that Mavis was leaving and they would be getting a divorce, but Nikki told Michelle she didn't care, she wanted to go back to live with her Maw-Maw Alice.

CHAPTER 7

When Nikki got home she wasn't eating much those days. The more someone tried to make her eat, the more she resisted. Nikki really didn't know why food became such an ordeal. All she knew, was she meant know-one was going to tell her when or what to eat anymore. She knew she felt helpless and if she couldn't control anything in her life, her thoughts or her feelings. She could control what she put in her mouth. Things were sprawling out of control for Nikki and she stuffed her feelings deep inside a chest within herself never to surface again.

If anyone was a strong force, she vowed to break them before they could break her. She respected people until there was a confrontation, then instead of giving in or compromising, it became a form of submission to Nikki. She vowed; she would never be forced into any form of submission again, so the battles began. Nikki's childhood friend was killed in an automobile accident, and Nikki was numb to the world, she refused to see, hear, or feel anything.

Nikki felt sick all the time and soon the nausea was overwhelming, so Nikki went to town with her Grandmother to see a doctor. Nikki sat in the lobby waiting in a daydream until, she heard,

"Nicolette Breaux."

She snapped out of her daydream and walked down the hall to see the doctor. The nurse asked for a urine sample and placed her in a room. When the doctor walked in, he talked to Nikki about the exam and what she could expect. He asked questions about how sexually active she was and the last time she had intercourse as well as when her last period was. Nikki told him about the rape almost five months prior and that she had sex with Cid once, a couple days before and she hadn't missed a period.

Dr Lanks told her it wasn't uncommon to have the first couple of periods in the first few months.

He asked Nikki to lay down on the table, put her feet in the stirrups and relax. Nikki was embarrassed, but the nurse held her hand and told her, it was all right and would be over before she really knew it. The exam was uncomfortable, but not unbearable. It lasted only a few moments, but it felt like hours. He gave Nikki his hand and pulled her up in a sitting position and told her she was pregnant and measured about five months.

Dr Lanks told Nikki there was still time to terminate the pregnancy, but he would have to schedule the procedure that week. Nikki asked him, what he was talking about; was he suggesting she have an abortion. Nikki hopped off the table and said there would be no abortion. She was having the baby and nothing was going to stop her no matter what happened. Dr Lanks stood there in shock; Nikki didn't think he really knew what to say. He asked if he could do anything else for her before she left and Nikki said she didn't need a thing as she walked out the door. She felt numb inside; reality had not hit her that she was really pregnant. Nikki was so busy fighting with the doctor on the abortion issue, that the outcome was to far gone for her to even think about at that point. She went down the long hall to the end of the building where the waiting room was to find her Grandmother. As Nikki walked, the longer the hall seemed to get.

When she finally reached the end and she saw her Grandmother, she walked over to her. Her Grandmother stood up and asked Nikki if she was all right because Nikki had no color in her face. Nikki turned around just as her head started spinning, and fell on the chair. The whole room swarmed around her like she had nothing to grab on to. When it finally started to slow down, her Grandmother stood there with the nurse. They told Nikki to say something, to let them know she was all right and Nikki looked up and said,

"I am going to have a baby; I am really going to have a baby."

Her Grandmother stood there with tears in her eyes and said,

"Well let's go home and face the music."

In the car Maw-Maw Alice asked how far along Nikki was. When Nikki told her five months, her Grandmother looked at her and said,

"Oh my, that means we don't know if this is from the ra----."

But before she could finish, Nikki covered her lips and told her she was to never repeat that to anyone. Nikki said know-one in the family was to know about that. Nikki didn't want people looking at her baby or treating it different. Nikki made her promise that she would never say a word and her Grandmother promised; it would only be between the two of them.

Her Grandmother accepted the news as fast as Nikki did and Nikki felt like she had a true friend in her Grandmother. The rest of the family didn't take the news so well. Nikki's uncles told her what a disgrace to the Breaux name she was and Darwin had himself a nine-day drunk. Darwin cursed her for everything he could think of. Her Aunt Gabrielle told her she hoped her and the baby died and her Grandmother slapped Gabrielle and told her she was going to have to beg God to forgive her for those words. Her Aunt Joy slapped Darwin in the mouth when he was yelling, and told him if he had been half a person and given Nikki to her and his brother Jake, when Nikki was little, she would have been raised better and it wouldn't have happened. She also said, as far as Nikki being a disgrace to the Breaux name, he had better take a long look in the mirror before he ever passed judgment on her again.

Everyone was yelling and having themselves' a fit; it was a mess. Nikki couldn't take the outbursts and retreated to her room to hide out and hoped the tornado that she had let loose on her family would settle down, but she knew, she was in for a long ride before it was going to pass.

Nikki's Grandmother went to her room to check on her and Nikki thanked her for not saying anything to anyone and for supporting her. Her Grandmother just sat there while everyone else was having a fit and just calmly said Nikki was pregnant and nothing was going to change, the fact that Nikki was pregnant, so they just might-as-well get use to the idea.

Darwin wanted Nikki to abort, but her Grandmother told him that was not an option and he needed to leave her house and not return, until he sobered up and came to his senses. Nikki told her Grandmother, she knew she couldn't stay there and she didn't know what else to do. Her Grandmother sat on the bed with her and took Nikki in her arms and hugged her. She told Nikki that everything would be all right, and she would find a way through it for them know matter what.

CHAPTER 8

The following week Nikki went to Cross-creek in Montana, a home for unwed mothers.

Getting settled in her room was an experience. A couple of girls asked Nikki if the father of her baby was black or white. Nikki told them he was white and asked why they wanted to know. Dana, one of the girls in the welcoming party, told Nikki three white girls there, was having black guys' babies. In those days, that wasn't the typical norm, but then again nothing in Nikki's life was the norm anyway, so she shrugged them off and finished unpacking.

All her meetings with the housemothers and social workers went well. They all had one goal, for Nikki to give the baby up for adoption. She let them know from the start, she was only there to get away from her family. She made it clear she was not giving up her baby. Then, she was informed that she would have to pay for her stay, if she wasn't going to give the baby up for adoption. Nikki asked about the girls that stayed there and kept their babies and asked if they had to pay. Ms James told her,

"Of course not, it is a decision process."

Nikki's Grandmother stood up and asked how much Nikki's stay would be and wrote a check. Nikki was to stay there until her due date; then return home. Nikki was a tiny girl even five months pregnant; she didn't have a tummy. Everyone told her to eat, eat, eat or the baby would never live as small as she was, so Nikki sat with a spoon of peanut butter and glass of water between meals.

The first time Nikki heard the heart beat, she was so excited; she didn't know what to do. Every move, every kick was so special. Nikki talked to the baby everyday, although Nikki just knew it was a he. Nikki told her that she loved her and it didn't matter to her why she was there, it just was meant to be. She told her that she was always going to love her, take good care of her, and nothing would ever come between them.

The girls in the home were from all walks of life. Nikki had Dana as her roommate and formed some strong friendships with the other girls. They had pajama parties, talked about their lives, what they hoped they would become; their boyfriends, their mothers, sex, you name it, it was a subject discussed. They promised each other they would always keep in touch, knowing they would all go their own separate ways. Know-one there would want to remember those relationships; because that was a time in all their lives they would want to forget. Nikki was the only one planning to keep her baby.

Nikki wrote Cid and called his mother to let him know where she was. She got several letters from him and they talked on the phone a few times. Michelle showed up to see Nikki and told her she was remarrying. Nikki told her congratulations, but didn't know why she would want her to know. Michelle told Nikki she came to see her to tell her to her face, she was different. Nikki asked what she was talking about; different. Michelle said she called a family meeting and all the kids talked about the presence that was with them and the sheer terror they all felt. She said a couple of the boys were not so open, but the rest that were having some bad encounters told them they were going to the grave site and recite the scripture and they reluctantly agreed. Michelle said they went at almost midnight and gathered at Charles's grave.

She said at midnight they joined hands and recited the scripture and Nikki's youngest uncle buried her grandfather's watch as instructed in his grave. Then they turned and walked away. She said it was going to be hard not to be able to go back to his grave to pay her respects, but she went to see her aunt a few weeks after the gravesite ceremony and when she stepped out the car she saw the shadow appear under the carport. Michelle said she couldn't believe her eyes as it glared at her. She said she told her aunt she forgot something at her brother's house down the road, got back in her car and left. She said she felt free for the first time in years. She assured Nikki she was really pulling her life together and wanted all her kids with her, but Nikki told her she could forget it; she was staying where she was and going home when the baby was born. She told Nikki if she ever changed her mind to call her, but Nikki told her to go home and sit by the phone to see how long it would take for it to ring.

Nikki returned to her life at the home for unwed mothers when Michelle left. A couple of the girls in the home were from that area and was scared to go out in public, so a couple of the local restaurants and one theater would let the girls go after hours to a closed theater to see movies or eat out. The girls were all dying to see the new movie "Up in Smoke," with Cheech and Chong.

They were all little rolie polies, but they waddled in the theater and watched the movie. They laughed until they hurt and some of the girls actually had false labor pains when they got back to the house that night and the house-mother, forbid them to go back to the theater.

One of the girls had her boyfriend come to see her and they ran away together to get married and kept their baby. She wrote the girls a month later to say she was married and was settling in back home. She said in the letter, she knew her life would not be what she had hoped for, but she was in love with the father of her baby and wanted to keep the baby. She was happy and the girls were happy for her.

Another girl, Stacy had a visit from her boyfriend and he brought a joint. She told Nikki, Dana and Josie to meet her after dinner and they walked to the lake to feed the ducks; which was another pass time for the girls. When they got to the lake she pulled out the joint. They got stoned together and sat on the bank of the lake laughing. They made it back to the house and crashed like good little girls, just in time for curfew.

Then one afternoon Nikki was sleeping and was awakened by a rolling thunder and lightening. It wasn't like any other storm she had ever heard. Nikki thought the end of the world was happening. She jumped out of bed and ran down the hall to find someone to help her. Help her do what; she wasn't sure, but to help her. Nikki ran into the social worker, Ms Brenda in the hall. She saw how terrified Nikki was and pulled her in a room to calm her down. That was Nikki's second panic attack, but much worse than when she had to smoke a pack of cigarettes.

Things soon seemed to settle down for a few weeks and Nikki saw girls come and go at the end of their pregnancies with ages that ranged from twelve to nineteen. They all talked about where their babies came from, some from boyfriends, some from rapes and some from incest. Then one night, around three in the morning Nikki heard screaming coming from down the hall. She got up to go see what was happening. It was Keri a mentally retarded girl that was pregnant from her stepbrother. She was screaming at the top of her lungs and the housemother was freaking out, because Keri didn't know she was in labor and didn't tell anyone

77

she was hurting. She was delivering the baby when she finally started to scream. Nikki stood in the doorway with the rest of the girls watching, not believing their eyes. Keri was scared out of her mind and in so much pain at the same time. The housemother was screaming for her to lie down and breath, but Keri was crying. It was difficult for her to be reasoned with, but they finally settled her down and the baby was delivered. The housemother turned and saw all the girls standing in the door and told them to go back to their room the show was over. On the way back to their room some of the girls were crying and Nikki thought,

"Oh my God, I am going to die, I know that I'll never live through something like that."

She was scared to death and panic attack number three hit.

A few weeks later a girl from LTI was brought to the home. She had gotten pregnant by a guard there and the facility wanted to keep it quite, so they shipped her off to Montana. The girl was resentful and she didn't like Nikki from the start. Nikki thought the girl felt like she was still in prison and had to defend herself all the time. She was aggressive and standoffish, so Nikki kept her distance. Then one night going down the hall a month before her due date, this girl jumped Nikki from behind and told her she was going to kill her and her baby. Nikki fell into the double doors of the laundry room. Everyone heard a sonic boom and heard Nikki yell,

"Bitch your gonna get it now!"

All the girls came out of their rooms to see what was happening and the housemother pulled Nikki off the girl, Nikki told Ms James what had happened and everyone said what they heard, but because Nikki was keeping her baby and the girl was giving her baby up for adoption, they thought it would be best if Nikki went home.

Nikki called her Grandmother and told her what happened. Her Grandmother told Ms James if anything was wrong with Nikki or her baby, she was going to be held accountable and she would come for Nikki the next morning. Nikki hated the idea of going home, but it was time for her and the rest of the family to get ready for the baby, her due date was less than four weeks away.

Settling in back at home was an experience. Nikki would sit and make up erotic stories about Cid to tell her Grandmother just because, she knew Gabrielle was listening; pretty much just to piss her off. Nikki thought Gabrielle was jealous about her being pregnant because she was still a virgin at the age of twenty-four. Nikki could hear Gabrielle and her Grandmother argue about their talks. Gabrielle telling her Grandmother,

Nikki was know good and asking her why she couldn't see that from everything Nikki was saying in their conversations. Her Grandmother told Gabrielle,

"That's all talk and I let her talk. There is nothing wrong with that." And Nikki would hear Gabrielle storm off to her room as always.

Nikki knew she would have to face everyone now that she was home. She wasn't too worried about it at that point. Nikki thought they could either accept her and the baby or kiss off and she really didn't care which they chose.

On Nikki's return, Darwin was so concerned for Nikki's soul that he paid Brother Jones, the church pastor a visit and begged him to save Nikki's soul. Darwin told Brother Jones it was too late for him, but not for Nikki and to do what he had to, to save her. That night in church Brother Jones was preaching hell-fire and brim stone. He called Nikki out and told her to pray and get her heart right with God or she would never have another chance. Nikki thought, it was a true message from God and wasn't sure what she had done, but she went to the alter and was begging God to forgive her for all her transgressions. Nikki prayed harder than ever before and asked God to have mercy and forgive her sins. She asked God to save her soul and the soul of her unborn child. As Nikki was praying and pleading with God, Brother Jones went to her, pulled her head up off the alter, and told her to pray for forgiveness, because she was sorry, not because she got caught. Nikki said,

"What?"

Bro Jones repeated what he said,

"Pray for forgiveness because you are sorry, not because you got caught."

Nikki stared at him as he said those words to her again. Everything Nikki had believed in as child until then, to her became a lie and her faith in religion in any form left her. She new God himself, her and her Grandmother knew how her child was conceived, and she knew God would have never sent her a message like that. Nikki stood and turned around; the whole church was kneeled with hands on each other's backs reaching for Nikki praying for her salvation. She turned and walked out the church doors never to return again as far as she was concerned. Nikki walked home that night to find her Grandmother in the living room sleeping in the rocking chair. She told her what happened and her Grandmother held Nikki while she cried. When Gabrielle got home from church she was raving. She told Nikki's Grandmother that Nikki turned her back on God that night and she would burn in hell for it. Nikki's Grandmother told Gabrielle to be more concerned with her own soul right then and let Nikki worry about hers.

Gabrielle was enraged with her Mother for defending Nikki and Nikki felt bad for all the slack her Grandmother took in keeping her secret, but her Grandmother never betrayed Nikki's trust, or shared their secret with a soul.

CHAPTER 9

Nikki's due date was June 28th. The doctors said everything was progressing well and told Nikki to come back the next week; she was two weeks away from her due date. On the way home her Grandmother decided to stop at a store. She was in the other person's lane when they rounded a corner, and had a head on collision. Nikki had looked up, just in time to see the car coming. She turned sideways in the seat to help decrease the blow on her tummy. On impact, Nikki was thrown in the floor of the car. She wasn't hurt, but she was pinned in the vehicle and had to be cut out, she was scared, because she started having labor pains, but they stopped a couple hours after the accident.

Her Grandmother got some cuts and bruises, but over all she was all right too. The man driving the other car was angry, but he too was fine. Darwin was the first to arrive on the scene after Nikki's Grandma called him. He stood in the doorway of the car and talked to Nikki until the police and the fire department could get there to cut her out. They were all lucky that time, but Darwin and Nikki's Grandfather insisted her Grandmother give up her driving privileges. That in itself was a fight. Her Grandmother was a very independent woman and liked her space and her freedom. Driving to her; was freedom, but she admitted she was getting up in age and her sight was not as good. She was unwilling, however to surrender her driving privileges. The fight ended, because know-one ever won a fight with Nikki's Grandmother. She stood her ground until the end of time, so her Grandfather and Darwin stormed out the house and her Grandmother went to the kitchen to start dinner.

Nikki walked for exercise, went swimming with the girls and was diving off a diving board at the pool by the church on her due date.

Everyone told her she was crazy and was hurting the baby, but Nikki cleared everything she did with her doctor. He said they were healthy as a horse. Her appointments with Dr Lanks came and went, she was going every week and her due date was a month over. She was told by Dr Lanks, her body just liked being pregnant and that she was not going to go into labor on her own, so he was admitting her to the hospital to induce labor the next morning. Nikki was scared to death again, but went to the hospital to get settled in her room.

That night she laid in bed rubbing her tummy. She told the baby, that would be their last night together like that, and by that time the next day, she would be in Nikki's arms and she couldn't wait. At five o'clock the next morning the nurse transferred Nikki to labor and delivery. As she rolled down the hall Nikki tried to be brave, but inside she was freaking. She knew the baby had to be born, but she wondered if she would survive the delivery. Nikki tried to pray, but she had no God to pray to at that time, just wishful thinking. That without a true faith didn't get her far. Dr Lanks examined her and told the nurse to start an IV and give her some medication to start her labor. In his examination Nikki heard the doctor ask the nurse to hand him a wick. Nikki wasn't sure what he said, but she felt something warm running up her back. Dr Lanks stepped away from the bed and Nikki's stomach knotted up and she doubled over in pain. Nikki screamed,

"What did you do?"

Dr Lanks said,

"You are four-and-a-half-centimeters dilated, so I broke your water, which will start your labor."

And boy was he right; her labor pains started five minutes apart. After a while, they let her Grandmother in the room to see her. When she went to Nikki's bedside, she took Nikki's hand just as another contraction was hitting. She squeezed her Grandmother's hand as tight as she could. Her Grandmother held on and never tried to get loose. When the contraction was peaking, her Grandmother asked the nurse, why Nikki's labor was so intense, if it was just starting.

The nurse told her Grandmother that she was already dilated four-and-a-half-centimeters so when Dr Lanks broke her water, she went into hard labor, because her body just needed a little push to get started. Four minutes passed and the next contraction started.

Her Grandmother told Nikki to breath and she talked her through four hours of breathing and panting, but Nikki was growing weary and wanted it to end. She was getting weak and her Grandmother said she looked pale. The nurse was checking Nikki more often and adding one machine after another. First it was the baby monitor, then a probe on the head of the baby vaginally, then oxygen by a nasal cannula through her nose with a pulse ox on her second toe of her right foot. Then came the heart monitor for Nikki and the second IV in her right hand.

Then Michelle walked in the room. Nikki's Grandmother stood as she entered. Nikki was resting bracing for the next contraction, so she had her eyes closed. She heard Michelle speak to her Grandmother and opened her eyes. Michelle walked to her bed and acted like she was bending down to hug Nikki. As she embraced Nikki, she whispered in her ear,

"Die God Dam you, because you don't deserve to live."

Nikki pushed her away and asked her what she said, just as the monitors started alarming. The nurse ran in, Nikki's heart started with premature ventricular contractions, followed by tachycardia. The nurse screamed for help and told her Grandmother and Michelle to leave the room. Nikki remembered several people standing over her trying to talk to her, telling her to wake up, but she couldn't, she heard the doctor scream.

"We're losing her!"

She felt her life slipping away from her as she lay there under the lights and all those blankets. She had been so cold before, but then she was warm. She felt safe and at peace.

Her blood pressure elevated to 260/170. She was passed stroke level. They pushed several drugs to try and control what was happening, but Nikki wasn't responding. Nikki heard the doctor walk outside her door, and tell her Grandmother that she wasn't going to make it. It would be her or the baby. He was pretty sure the baby might have a chance, but he didn't think Nikki was going to come through. He told her Grandmother if there was anyone she wanted to call she needed to do it then, because he couldn't say how long she would be there.

Michelle said she was going outside to smoke as Nikki's Grandmother headed for the phone. She called the church were a revival was going on and requested prayer by the whole church. Brother Jones stopped the service and told the church that Nikki's Grandmother called and said Nikki was dying and they needed to pray for a miracle from God to deliver her.

Gabrielle ran to the alter and fell to her knees praying harder than anyone in the church, the tears streamed down her face as she begged God to spare Nikki's life. Something happened in the room Nikki laid in as they prayed. The bright lights that had surrounded her were fading.

She could hear the doctor talking and could feel two nurses, one on each side pushing down on her stomach as if they were trying to push the baby out without her help. Nikki realized, she was in the delivery room and the doctor was trying to get the baby out the birth canal. She heard him say wait for the monitor to show another contraction and for the nurses to push as hard as they could. Then he said,

"If this baby does not move on this next contraction we are going to have to cut her to get the baby out."

Nikki could feel a tear rolling down her cheek and she begged God for strength. She began to feel her body again. Then she felt the beginning of a contraction. Nikki gripped the bars and started pushing with the help of the two nurses. Nikki thought she scared the doctor, because he backed away from the table when she gripped the bars and came too pushing. Nikki pushed for an hour before she delivered a six pound ten ounce girl. After she was born and they laid her on Nikki's stomach, she looked down at the baby. The baby looked up at Nikki as if she knew or could see her very soul. Her eyes were the bluest Nikki had ever seen, she was warm and tiny, and Nikki knew she would be fine, because she came from her and that in it-self made her a survivor.

The nurse pried Nikki's hand off the bars of the bed to get her to hold her baby. Nikki had gripped the bars for so long and so hard, the inside of her hands were a solid bruise. When Nikki looked at her baby, she realized God had answered her prayers. Nikki had prayed throughout her pregnancy that God would let the baby look like her. God truly answered her prayers; it was scary how much this baby looked like Nikki at birth, and every distinguishing Breaux feature, the baby had.

Nikki's vital signs became unstable again, so they took the baby to the nursery and she was sent to recovery in hopes of being stabilized. Most women stay in recovery anywhere from thirty minutes to two hours, but Nikki was kept for twelve hours. She was given dose after dose of IV push drugs for her heart and her blood pressure. She stabilized finally, after eight hours, but they kept her another four hours to be sure the danger had passed before she was sent back to her room.

As the nurse rolled Nikki in the door of her room, she saw Michelle in the room with her Grandmother, a couple of Aunts, and some friends of Michelle's that she had never met. Michelle also had her new husband Kevin; number six, with her. Nikki's eyes were swollen shut from pushing and because she was still in cardiac overload with the fluid shift in her body. She could hardly open her eyes and felt like she had been ran over by a freight train. Kevin went to Nikki's bedside and introduced himself, but Nikki wasn't in the mood for visitors. The nurse walked in with the baby, but before she could turn and walk out with her, Kevin took the baby out of the nurse's arms.

Then the nurse started fusing about all the people and said they had to leave. Her aunts started to say goodbye as Michelle went to Nikki's bedside. Nikki asked Michelle, why she said what she said, but Michelle acted like she didn't know what Nikki was talking about. Nikki asked Michelle why she said,

"Die God-dam you, because you don't deserve to live."

The room grew quit and all eyes fell on Michelle and Nikki waited for an answer. Michelle brushed Nikki's cheek with her hand and told Nikki she never said anything like that to her. Michelle answered her by saying,

"Nikki you were so messed up on all those drugs, you were hallucinating."

The only problem, Nikki hadn't had any drugs at that point. Nikki looked at her Grandmother and asked if she could hold her baby as the nurse burst in the door insisting they all leave.

Her grandmother stayed, as Nikki held the baby, but she was so weak she couldn't hold her, but a few minutes. The baby was crying when they laid her in Nikki's arms, but just like in the delivery room she looked up at her Mother and stopped crying. They had a connection from the start; Nikki felt it and so did she. Her Grandmother walked over and told her she was one of the most beautiful babies she had seen and said she had never seen a baby at birth look so much like one of its parents. Nikki told her Grandmother about the prayer; she prayed throughout her pregnancy, that the baby would look like her. They both cried together as her Grandmother, thanked God for his mercy and blessings and she asked Nikki what she was going to name her. Nikki smiled and said she would be named Tricia Renee Breaux. Nikki then handed Tricia to her Grandmother and drifted off to sleep.

CHAPTER 10

The next day in the hospital, was a day of visitors for Nikki. The nurses went in early to get Nikki up and dressed so she could start walking the hall. She felt like a train wreck, but there was no arguing with the nurses, they had a mission and it was going to be accomplished. Nikki's Aunts on Michelle's side of the family Cathy and Stacy visited for quite a while that day. They both held the baby and told Nikki how beautiful Tricia was and how blessed Nikki was to have her. It was a nice visit until Michelle showed up with her new husband Kevin in tow. When Michelle got there, Stacy and Cathy said it was time for them to go. Cathy was standing in the doorway with Michelle as Stacy leaned over and hugged Nikki to say goodbye. When Stacy leaned over and embraced Nikki she whispered in her ear,

"Don't you let your Mama get her hands on that baby, do you hear me."

When she pulled away, she had her fingers to her lips as if she was shushing Nikki and squeezed Nikki's hand before she walked to the door. Cathy hugged Nikki and said her goodbyes as well. They both said they would see Nikki later and asked where she was going when she left the hospital. Before Nikki could answer, Michelle said Nikki was going back with her, but Nikki said she was going home with her Grandmother Breaux. Cathy told Nikki to take care and she would call later.

Nikki's Grandmother Breaux couldn't stand to be in the same room with Michelle, so she said she was going down to the cafeteria to eat and asked if she could bring Nikki anything. Nikki told her she was fine and she didn't have to go, but she said she wouldn't be long. When Grandma Breaux left, Michelle pulled up a chair and told Nikki she wanted Nikki and the baby to go live with her and Kevin because things would be different. She said Nikki's sisters were excited about the baby and she knew she could help Nikki get on with her life. Nikki told her she would think about it, but she was going home with her Grandmother.

Nikki was discharged a couple days later and she took Tricia to her Grandmother Breaux's to start her life. Nikki took Tricia to church and had her baptized; Nikki dedicated Tricia to the lord. She wanted Tricia to be blessed always and in Nikki's heart, she knew if she baptized her that God would always keep her safe. Grandmother Breaux bought Tricia about twenty little dresses and her Aunt May made Tricia a twig-light blue dress that she was baptized in. Several ladies from the church brought cloths and diapers, but Nikki's friends shunned her as if she were a disease in the church. It really didn't bother Nikki, because she had Tricia and her Grandmother Breaux's love, but Nikki knew Tricia would need more and one day she would too.

Michelle called Nikki again and told her she could have a knew life there with her and she would help Nikki get started. She said neither Tricia nor Nikki would ever be accepted in the church, and they deserved better than that. Nikki thought they did too, so she agreed to go back to Allergies in New Orleans with Michelle. Nikki wrote Cid and told him about Tricia and was shocked when he wrote back and said he wanted to marry her and be Tricia's Dad. Nikki wrote him back to let him know she would call him when they got back to New Orleans.

Cid was excited to see Nikki and Tricia when they arrived. He told Nikki he still wanted to marry her and raise the baby. Nikki wanted a family of her own and wanted Tricia to have more than she could have offered her alone. There was nothing in this life Nikki didn't want Tricia to have and nothing she would not have sacrificed to see that Tricia got it.

Cid had his own trailer and was working on a local construction contract. He asked Nikki to bring the baby over and check out the trailer, so Nikki gathered the diaper bag and went for a visit. It was shocking, when Cid asked her to move in and Michelle agreed. Nikki thought Michelle was trying to keep her word in allowing her to build a life with Tricia, so Nikki moved in with Cid and worked for cash at a sandwich shop around the corner from where they lived. While Nikki worked, a lady in the trailer park kept Tricia for a dollar an hour and things seemed to be going well the first few weeks.

Then, Nikki got in from work one Friday and asked Cid if he could keep Tricia for a little while, so she could go to the store for diapers and formula. Cid agreed, but told Nikki she needed to hurry back, because he was expecting some friends. When Nikki asked him who was coming, he told her a few new friends she needed to meet and some old friends that were glad to hear she was back in town.

Nikki walked to the grocery store for the things she needed. When she returned several people were there already and Cid asked Nikki, what was wrong with Tricia? Nikki told him that nothing was wrong with her when she left and asked why he thought something was wrong. He said Tricia's face looked swollen and she wouldn't stop crying. Nikki asked him where Tricia was and Cid pointed to the back room and said he left her in her carrier on the bed. When Nikki entered the room, Tricia was in her carrier with her back to the door. Nikki was putting the bags on the floor while saying,

"Hey my little munchkin what's going on?"

When Nikki got to the bed and turned the carrier around to see Tricia, she was horrified. Tricia was black and blue, her face was swollen and her eyes were black and blue. Her lips were swollen to the point they almost looked like they were going to burst. Tricia had thrush and had a purple liquid medicine that someone placed in her mouth, so Nikki couldn't tell if Tricia was bleeding or it was the medicine. Nikki turned the carrier around and Tricia reached for her. Nikki picked Tricia up to try and examine her, to see how bad she was hurt, but Tricia was clinging to Nikki's neck. Nikki had to pry her away to look at her.

Nikki was hysterical when she got a really good look at Tricia. She ran out the bedroom with Tricia asking what had happened. Cid said, he didn't know, he was lifting weights and didn't know if a weight hit her or not, he said Tricia looked like that when he got out the shower. The people that had gathered in the trailer were leaving as Nikki ran out the door with Tricia in her arms, running down the street to get her to a hospital.

Nikki saw the lady that kept Tricia and screamed for help. Ms Daisy stopped and took Nikki to the hospital. When Nikki ran in the doors of the hospital emergency room she was screaming,

"Look what somebody did to my baby!"

The nurse took Nikki to the back and called the doctor. Nikki told them what Cid said, that he might have hit her with a weight when he was exercising. The doctor ordered x-rays and called child protection. The X-Ray showed knuckle prints in Tricia's skull. The doctor went back in the room with Nikki and asked who would do such a thing and told Nikki about the knuckle prints in Tricia's skull. Nikki broke down and started crying, she told the doctor, she couldn't imagine who would have done such as thing, but she wanted to know if Tricia was going to be all right. The doctor said it was too soon to say at that point; they were admitting Tricia and the police were on the way.

Nikki called Michelle and she said she would be there in about thirty minutes. Michelle showed up with Kevin in tow of course. Nikki was hysterical and Kevin was supportive. Kevin held Nikki as she cried. Everyone there cried, even more when the doctor let them in to see Tricia. Tricia was screaming at the top of her lungs when they entered the room. Michelle tried to talk to her and Kevin tried to pick her up, but Tricia only screamed louder.

Nikki sat on the chair by the door when they entered the room sobbing as Kevin and Michelle went to the crib to see Tricia. The doctor entered the room with a nurse and told them the nurse had to stay until the police arrived. Nikki stood up and went to Tricia's bedside to try and calm her. Tricia reached for Nikki, even as tiny as she was at two-an-a-half months, she knew her Mommy. Nikki picked her up, as the doctor was saying she shouldn't touch her until the police arrived, then Tricia stop crying when she snuggled up to Nikki. Nikki walked to the rocker in the room and rocked Tricia to sleep in the presents of Michelle, Kevin, the doctor and nurse.

Ms Davis from child protection arrived. She asked Nikki about the living conditions at the trailer and what kind of job Cid had. She said she was going to the trailer to talk with Cid and she would have her report complete and turned into the District Attorney's office before Tricia was discharged. The Emergency room doctor spoke on Nikki's behalf. He told, Ms Davis he didn't think Nikki had been the one to abuse Tricia for several reasons. He stated the fact that Tricia could only be consoled by Nikki was his first clue, the second, Tricia reached and cried for her Mother and last Nikki's hands were not big enough to leave the knuckle prints that were left in Tricia's skull. Ms Davis said time would tell and departed.

Ms Davis got to the trailer, but know-one was there or they wouldn't open the door. She returned to the hospital and told Nikki she had reason to believe, someone was there, but had refused to answer the door. She told Nikki, those were actions of a guilty individual and wanted to know who lived in the trailer. Nikki told her know-one else lived there and Cid had to be home. She advised Nikki to remove Tricia's and her things from the trailer while they were completing the admission process at the hospital.

Kevin agreed to take Nikki to the trailer to get their things when Nikki asked him. The ride was quite, Nikki never spoke a word and Kevin just drove the car with his eyes on the road never looking at Nikki or saying a word either. When they arrived at the trailer the door was locked. Nikki knocked and then started banging on the door. When know-one answered the door, Nikki went to the back door, which was unlocked and went in. She walked through the trailer to the front door and opened it for Kevin. When she opened the door, she told Kevin she guessed Cid had left and started to gather her things.

Kevin stood in the living room while Nikki packed the baby's things, then Nikki dropped one of Tricia's bottles. It sounded like a sonic boom when it hit the floor and broke into a million pieces. Nikki started to clean it up, when she saw Cid stumbling down the hall. When Nikki saw him she asked why he didn't open the door. Cid told her he was sleeping. She asked him again what happened to Tricia. Nikki said to tell her every detail he could remember like who was alone with Tricia and where Tricia was at all times when she left her with him.

Cid told Nikki he couldn't remember all the details and he needed to go back to sleep, because he needed to get up the next morning. He was walking passed Nikki, as he told her what he said and pushed her out of his way while passing. Nikki turned into a tiger and said to him,

"You did this didn't you?"

Cid laughed as he got to the hallway. Nikki tore down the hall and attacked him like a wild animal, Cid was screaming for Kevin to get her off him and Nikki was screaming,

"I'll kill you, you son-of-a-bitch. You think you can beat the shit out of a baby and get away with it, what the fuck where you thinking? Why did you do this?"

Cid screamed louder and started to fight back. He thought he would hurt Nikki, but he was no match for a mother enraged over her child. Kevin stepped in, but had difficulty-getting Nikki off Cid. Kevin told Nikki to let the police handle it, but Nikki screamed,

"Fuck the police; I'll kill that son-of-a-bitch for what he did to my baby!"

Kevin drug Nikki out the trailer and told her he would bring her the next day when Cid was gone to get her stuff. Nikki cried all the way back to the hospital and Kevin didn't speak a word. At the hospital, Nikki was videoed with Tricia over the next week during their hospital stay, without Nikki's knowledge. Nikki rocked Tricia, fed her, and played with her throughout the time there. She never left Tricia's side. When they discharged Tricia, the doctors were still adamant that Nikki had not been the abuser. Dr Gremillion told Ms Davis, with Child Protection, that he supported the decision to release Tricia to Nikki when she was discharged. Ms Davis told Nikki that Tricia would be released to her custody with the understanding that Tricia would never be brought back to the trailer. Nikki agreed it would never happen and she took Tricia with her back to Michelle's.

Nikki was enraged that Child Protection was not filing charges. Ms Davis told her, they would continue the investigation, but unless someone saw the person do it, there was nothing more she could do. Ms Davis sat beside Nikki with her briefcase in tow. She pulled out papers and told Nikki she was closing the case; there was nothing she could find to prove who had abused Tricia. Nikki was angry, but there was nothing more that could be done, but Nikki was also relieved, because Tricia was fine and she was taking her home to be with her.

Nikki vowed she was going to get a job and raise Tricia without a father. She thought she had grown up without both parents and didn't turn out half bad. Nikki knew the road would be a hard one, but also knew she would do what ever it took to give Tricia what she needed.

Michelle was distant at home and Nikki never knew how to take Michelle. Kevin worked all the time and Nikki's two sisters Kristen and Ashley fought over Tricia constantly. Nikki was extremely protective of Tricia and fussed at the girls to be careful. She told them to hold Tricia a certain way and not to walk when they were holding the baby. Michelle got angry with Nikki and said Nikki would make people hate Tricia, because she was so fussy over Tricia, but Nikki couldn't lighten up.

A few days passed, when Michelle told Nikki she was going to the grocery store for milk and diapers. Michelle told Nikki that diapers were expensive and asked her if she knew how she was going to support Tricia. Nikki asked if she could go to the grocery store with her and maybe put in an application for a job, if Michelle was willing to keep Tricia while Nikki worked. Michelle agreed, so Nikki thought that was the beginning of a real relationship with Michelle.

The grocery store wasn't hiring, so Michelle shopped while Nikki went to the stores next door to put in applications. When Nikki walked in Shoe Gallery and asked for an application, the store manager saw Nikki filling out the application and introduced herself to Nikki as Ms Bobby. She told Nikki that her friends called her Peewee. Nikki laughed and said

"Yea, I am usually called half-pint or little-bit sometimes."

Peewee asked Nikki how old she was and Nikki told her, she was fifteen. Peewee asked whose baby she had and Nikki told her she was her daughter. Peewee told Nikki by law she couldn't hire anyone under sixteen, so Nikki, thanked her for her time, and apologized, she just really needed a job to raise her kid.

Nikki turned to walk away, but Peewee called her to come back. Peewee told her to lie about her age and she would give her the job. Nikki asked for another application and on the date of birth, she made herself a year older. Michelle seemed pleased when Nikki told her she had a job. Kevin worked in the grocery store next door, so Nikki would get dropped off on his way to work. Kevin also brought her home and on the nights Nikki had to work late, Peewee took her home. Peewee and Nikki became close friends. They talked about life and every subject known to man. Peewee became someone that Nikki respected and admired, she was like another big sister to Nikki and Michelle seemed to be fine keeping Tricia while Nikki worked. It all seemed well for a couple weeks. That is, until Michelle called Nikki at work to tell her Ms Davis called from Child Protection to say they were going to take Tricia.

Michelle said; Ms Davis had proof that Nikki was the abuser and was coming to take Tricia. Nikki was hysterical and swore there was know way they had proof, because it didn't exist. Michelle agreed with Nikki and said she knew Nikki had not hurt Tricia, but they had to find a way to stop them from taking her. Nikki said she would take Tricia and go home to her Grandmother's, but Michelle said they would find her there too. Nikki burst into tears she couldn't loose Tricia and wouldn't let them take get her either.

Michelle said she knew a way to stop them, when Nikki asked how. Michelle told Nikki she had called an attorney after Ms Davis called to ask what to do. The attorney advised Nikki to sign Tricia over to Michelle and when the mess got straightened out; Michelle could sign Tricia back over to Nikki. Michelle said Kevin was going to pick her up and take her to the Judge's chambers and the attorney would have the papers waiting for her when she got there.

Nikki told Peewee what was happening and said she had to leave when he got there to sign the papers. Peewee told Nikki she could go, but she wanted to call a friend of hers that was an attorney to see if he could help. Nikki thanked her, but told her Michelle had already taken care of everything and she would call her when it was done. Peewee made her promise to call her right away and asked Nikki if she really trusted Michelle. Nikki told her not until recently but Michelle was really trying to help her out raising Tricia, so Peewee hugged Nikki and told her,

"Take care kid."

Nikki left with Kevin when he got there. She tried to talk to Kevin on the way, but he was completely silent. Nikki asked him if he was mad at her or something, but Kevin only said he was looking out for Tricia's best interest and that was all that mattered. Nikki told Kevin she knew this was going to cost a lot of money and she would pay him and Michelle back every penny when it was over. Nikki promised she would give them her paycheck, or what was left after she bought diapers and formula for Tricia, but Kevin told her not to worry about it.

When they got to the Judges' chamber, it was a friend of Kevin's that was handling the paperwork. He slid the papers across a big oval table they were sitting at. Nikki sat on one side of the table alone and Kevin sat on the other side with his lawyer. The judge was sitting at the center of the table and handed Nikki the papers and Michelle's signature was already on the papers. When Nikki started to read the papers; they were not custody papers; they were adoption papers. Nikki said she thought the papers were for temporary custody, but Kevin told her they were taking a different route. Nikki said, she didn't want to sign adoption papers, but the judge told her he didn't see that she had a choice. Nikki looked at Kevin and he said for her to remember what Michelle told her and sign the papers. Then he asked Nikki if she wanted to loose Tricia forever. Nikki said she didn't, so he told her to sign the papers and they could keep her.

Tears streamed down Nikki's face as she signed the papers. She looked at Kevin and said,

"You're giving her back right."

Kevin said, that everything Michelle had told her was true, but that was the only way it could be done. After signing the papers, Kevin took Nikki to the house. Michelle was waiting and told Nikki, she had to leave for the weekend, so when Child Protection got there, she could show them, the papers and tell them that Nikki was gone and she would be raising the baby. Nikki told Michelle she didn't know anyone she could stay with, but Michelle told her, she couldn't be there when Child Protection showed up.

Nikki called Peewee and was to spend the weekend with her and Kevin waited while Nikki packed a bag for the weekend. Nikki held Tricia and cried as she kissed her bye on the cheek. Nikki told Tricia she loved her and she would see her Monday after work, it was Friday so it would be three days and she would be back.

Michelle told Nikki it would be over in three days and they could tear up the adoption papers and it would be behind them. Nikki cried and hugged Michelle, she told her she was scared of leaving, but she would go, because she didn't want to loose Tricia. Nikki walked out the door, to find Kevin waiting in the car with the motor running. Nikki got in the car and Kevin drove her to her job where Peewee was waiting. Kevin never spoke a word on the ride there and Nikki cried all the way. When they arrived at the store Nikki got out and took her bag out the back seat. She told Kevin she would see him Monday after work and Kevin looked straight ahead and said,

"See ya then."

Nikki went in the store where she worked. Peewee had called a couple employees in to relieve her and told Nikki she knew she would be to upset to stay, so they were leaving to go to her house. The weekend felt like it would never pass. Nikki tried to call Michelle several times to check on Tricia, but the phone rang and rang, know answer and know answering machine. Peewee told Nikki the answering machine must be broken; hers broke all the time or they had it turned off for whatever reason. Nikki had a sick feeling in her gut she couldn't explain, but she thought it was just because she was missing Tricia.

Monday came and the day dragged, five o'clock finally got there, but Kevin didn't show up to get Nikki. She sat in the parking lot thinking he was working late, but it was getting dark, so Nikki started to look for his car and couldn't find it. Nikki went in the grocery store where Kevin worked and asked the manager when Kevin got off, but Nikki was told, Kevin didn't work there anymore, his last day was Friday.

Nikki was blown away; she ran out the store and started walking to the house where Tricia was. It was well after dark when Nikki arrived. The house was dark with no lights on. Nikki walked up to the door by the garage and turned the doorknob; the door was unlocked. Nikki entered the house to look for Michelle or wait for them to come home, but when Nikki walked in and turned on the light switch, it almost blinded Nikki. She blinked her eyes and was frantic as she looked around, she ran room to room looking and seeing nothing, not a trace of anything, the furniture was gone, the cloths were gone, not a stitch of food in the cabinets, Tricia was gone, no phone was in the house, no sign of life, not even a note.

Nikki went to the neighbor's and asked if they knew where Michelle and Kevin had moved and the neighbor told Nikki she saw them packing up and they told her they were leaving the state, but didn't say where they were going. Nikki asked when they left and was told,

"A big truck, eighteen-wheeler, got there Friday night and they packed most of the night, all day Saturday and Saturday night and pulled out Sunday morning."

Nikki went back to the house, looked in all the closets, the attic, and the storage room again hoping, praying for a trace of something anything, but nothing. Nikki sat in the dark in the living room that night in total shock. She was scared out of her mind and felt lost and unsure of what was happening. She couldn't believe; Michelle would take Tricia and leave without telling her anything. Nikki had left the phone number where she could be reached at Peewee's, so Nikki thought if Michelle had Peewee's phone number why she didn't call. Nikki thought something had to have really gone wrong on the house visit from Child Protection, so Michelle took Tricia and ran with her. Nikki told herself that Michelle would call her at work the next day to tell her where to meet them.

Nikki went to work the next day and waited close by the phone. Peewee was blown away at the story and asked Nikki if she had heard from Child Protection herself. Nikki told Peewee she hadn't, that they had contacted Michelle. Peewee was convinced that there was something Nikki didn't know all along, but Nikki couldn't hear it. Later that afternoon the corporate office showed up for a surprise inspection of the store. In reviewing Nikki's employment records they noted there was not a picture ID of Nikki in her folder. When Nikki didn't have one on her they told her she had to go get one and bring it back. Nikki knew she was in trouble and Peewee was terminated for hiring Nikki, but said it didn't matter. She told Nikki to call her Grandmother to come get her, so she could go home and get help to straighten out the mess. Peewee told Nikki she was moving to South Carolina where she had family and would be leaving in the next couple of days. She said Nikki could stay with her, until her Grandmother got there to get her if she wanted. Nikki told Peewee over and over how sorry she was, because she got fired for helping her, but Peewee said she was ready to go back home anyway and it was their loss, not hers.

Nikki called Child Protection and spoke with Ms Davis. She told her she wanted to come to the office and see the evidence she had, that proved Nikki had beat Tricia. Ms Davis was shocked and asked Nikki what she was talking about. Nikki told Ms Davis not to act stupid, she had called

Michelle and told her that she had evidence that proved that Nikki had beaten Tricia and was going to get the baby. Ms Davis told Nikki she never made such a call, the case was closed when Nikki left the hospital with Tricia to return to her parents and raise the baby.

Nikki was in total shock. She told Ms Davis what had happened, the adoption and Michelle leaving and asked what she could do. Ms Davis told Nikki, it was probably for the best and said, she couldn't help Nikki and hung up the phone.

Nikki told Peewee that Child Protection had never called Michelle. Peewee said she was afraid that was going to be the ending of the story, she said,

"Nikki it was too smooth, the call, the papers already prepared, the judge and the attorney being friends with Kevin. Nikki going in that room without a lawyer and sitting on the side of the table without representation; all that was too convenient."

Peewee told Nikki she was leaving the next day and asked her what she wanted to do, go with her, or call her Grandmother. Nikki told Peewee her Grandmother was coming to get her the next day, so Peewee told her she could wait until that evening to leave. Nikki told her not to worry, that she knew she could always and forever depend on her Grandmother. Nikki laid awake that night wanting to kill Michelle if she could find her. One minute screaming in her mind,

"I'll kill the bitch!"

The next minute crying in her mind thinking,

"What if I don't find her?"

It was a long night, but morning surely came as it always did. Nikki got up before Peewee and left her a note to say she was going to meet her Grandmother. Nikki thanked her for all her help, and told her to have a safe trip back home. Nikki said she hated goodbyes, so she left a note instead of waiting for her to wake up.

She walked back to the shopping center where she worked to get her last paycheck. She went next door, where the store manager knew her through Kevin to get her check cashed as always. Then she walked outside to the pay phone to call her Grandmother. When Nikki's Grandmother answered the phone, Nikki burst into tears; it was so hard to contain her emotions, so her Grandmother waited for her to compose herself. After a few minutes Nikki could finally speak. She told her Grandmother she missed her. Her Grandmother said she loved her and missed her as well, then said,

"Honey they let you make phone calls in there,"

Nikki asked her what she was talking about. Her Grandmother said Michelle called and said Nikki was strung out on drugs, had beaten the baby half to death, and she had to put Nikki in a place to dry her out and take the baby and leave the state.

Nikki was mortified, she told her Grandmother; she was not doing drugs and would take a drug test to prove it. Nikki told her Grandmother the truth about what happened and said,

"I'm standing at a pay phone on the streets in New Orleans, my Mother has stolen my baby and I don't have any place to go."

Her Grandmother told Nikki to tell her where she was and she would come get her, but Nikki was so embarrassed and didn't want to be another source of embarrassment for her Grandmother, she said,

"Maw-Maw, I want you to know that I love you, I have always loved you and I always will, I don't want you to worry about me, because I'll be fine, I will be fine, I'll talk to you later."

Nikki hung the phone up as she heard her Grandmother calling after her to wait. Nikki knew her Grandmother would come to her rescue, but at what cost. Nikki was sure the whole family was told what Michelle had said, and Nikki knew the fall out in going back, would be more than her Grandmother could take. She also knew her Grandmother would have fought like a tiger for her, but she couldn't put her though anything else.

Nikki hung up the phone and sat down on the sidewalk. She had one hundred on two dollars; know place to live and know job. She couldn't go home, she had no place to stay, she had the cloths on her back and two changes of cloths in her bag. Nikki was fifteen, no way to get a job and no friends except Cid's. Nikki wanted to die were she sat, but her heart kept beating.

Nikki's money lasted four weeks; she only used it to eat. She slept behind shopping centers behind the dumpsters so they would break the wind. It was winter and quite cold that time of year in Louisiana. When it rained Nikki huddled up in the corners to try and stay dry, not too successfully most of the time. She bathed in the sink at gas stations mostly or where ever she bought her food that day. She walked the streets aimlessly, as if she were a zombie, no course, no purpose, no nothing.

Something inside Nikki died and she knew she would never be the same. She also knew if a person couldn't trust their own parents, who could they trust, NO-ONE. Nikki went back to the area of town were Cid lived. She didn't know what to do or why she went, but she had no money, no food, nowhere to live and no other place to turn. Cid welcomed her back with open arms, but the rules of the relationship changed. Cid was possessive, jealous and angry. One night Nikki looked at Cid and asked him why he did what he did to Tricia and he became so enraged he beat Nikki until she almost couldn't breath. Nikki thought he was going to kill her, but he stopped before she lost consciousness. Cid told Nikki she better never bring up the subject again and she didn't.

Nikki was trying to survive the relationship and live in the process, but she got slapped for little things like, the coffee wasn't hot enough, or the kitchen wasn't clean enough, or dinner was five minute late. Nikki's life became a bigger nightmare than she ever thought could or would happen. She was scared to stand up to Cid and scared to leave him too.

One evening driving down the road, Cid stopped at a red light and a guy in a car pulled up along side Cid and Nikki. The guy looked over and smiled at Nikki sitting in the passenger seat. Nikki turned her head without responding, but Cid saw the man smile at her. When the light turned green the man pulled off slowly, but Cid stayed parked and he turned to Nikki and asked,

"Where have you fucked him before?"

Nikki told Cid she had never even seen the guy before, but Cid slapped her and called her a liar. Nikki was crying and told Cid she had never seen the guy before and had not had sex with anyone, but Cid wasn't buying. He turned the car around took Nikki home and beat her half to death again. After the beating, Cid went in the kitchen, got a beer and sat on the sofa. He told Nikki she was never leaving the house again for anything. If they needed groceries, he would go get them, but Nikki was not to leave the house. Nikki went to the bedroom and sat on the bed crying. Cid went to the room and called Nikki a slut and a whore. Nikki tried to tell Cid, she had not been with any other man, but he was drunk and angry and wouldn't hear her.

Nikki got up and started putting cloths in the draws from the wash she had done during the day. She had learned not to argue with Cid, because the beating would be worse and last longer. Nikki hoped he would just go to bed and pass out, but as those thoughts ran through her head, Cid grabbed her from behind, slung her on the bed and told her it was time she learned how to make her man happy.

Nikki tried to crawl to the other side of the bed to get up and leave the room, but Cid grabbed her, pulled her pants down and ripped her panties off. Nikki was trying to get away, but he was too strong. Cid entered Nikki from behind with a death grip on her hair. She couldn't move, the louder she screamed the harder he pounded inside her until he exploded.

Cid told Nikki if she got pregnant, he would kill her because he didn't want any kids running around. He also told Nikki if she tried to leave, he would hunt her down and kill her. Nikki was afraid to sleep, eat or move. She was afraid to leave the house and afraid of staying there too.

Then, Cid got a contract for a job in Texas he had to go do. Nikki thought she would stay at home while he was gone, but Cid told her she was going with him. Nikki asked what she would do, while he worked and he said she would work with him. Cid's boss hired Nikki on Cid's word. They worked construction, so Nikki became the clean up girl, hauling out the trash and sweeping up. The guys picked at Nikki and joked with her, but she was too afraid to joke back or even smile for that matter.

One night after work Nikki was in the shower and Cid came in the bathroom and told Nikki to get out he wanted to talk to her. Nikki got out, dried off and wrapped a towel around her. Cid was waiting in the room sitting on the edge of the bed. When Nikki entered the room Cid was holding a small jar of Vaseline that Nikki used on her legs after she shaved sometimes. Cid asked her what the jar of Vaseline was for so Nikki told him it was for her legs and he asked her if she shaved while she was in the shower. Nikki said she had; then he told her to come to him. Nikki walked across the room slowly. When she got to the bed where he sat he lifted the towel with one hand and started to rub the ointment on her leg. Nikki told him she could do that; then Cid slapped her. He told her, he saw the way other men looked at her, wanting her, and he knew she wanted them. Nikki said she didn't, but Cid reached in the jar and smeared a handful of Vaseline in Nikki's face.

As Cid rubbed the Vaseline in Nikki's' face, he told her he would see her dead before he allowed another man to touch her ever. Nikki told Cid she couldn't see; then he slapped her and asked if she could see then. When she said she couldn't, he went to the bathroom for a towel and Nikki bolted out the door and ran to the office screaming for help. The desk clerk didn't speak English, so Nikki was standing there screaming for help with Vaseline smeared all over her face in a towel. The clerk told her to go get cloths. Nikki was screaming that Cid was going to kill her, please help. Then Cid showed up and grabbed Nikki, and told the clerk his wife was ill, he would take care of her and picked Nikki up and carried her back to the room.

When he got her back to the room Cid ripped the towel off her, grabbed her hair twisted it up in his hand and pulled Nikki up to his face. Nikki was on her tiptoes trying to release the pull on her hair, but it was know use. Cid had his death grip on her and he wasn't letting go.

He told her, she could never get away from him and she would well remember that night for the rest of her life. He said if she ever tried to run again, it would be the last. Cid punched, kicked, bit, choked, and beat Nikki with his belt; she was covered in bruises. Cid dared Nikki to scream; when she made a sound he hit her harder. Cid knocked the breath out of Nikki on several occasions and she thought for sure he would kill her that night. Nikki waited for the police, thinking the clerk would have called, but know-one ever came. When the beating stopped, Cid sat on the edge of the bed, he looked at her and asked why she made him do that to her. He asked why couldn't she see how much he loved her and why she made him hurt her.

Nikki apologized over and over again like she did over and over in the past, but it did no good, Cid wouldn't hear her. Nikki stood there with both her eyes black, the whites of her eyes blood red from being strangled, her ribs bruised, and eighty percent of her body black and blue. Just when Nikki thought it was over Cid stood up took off his cloths and told Nikki to come to him. Nikki crying and terrified, but she crawled to him. He pulled her up off the floor to him, held her and kissed her. He turned off the lights and pulled Nikki on the bed with him. Nikki thought he was going to sleep, but Cid intended to ride Nikki as he had never before and he did. When it was over he refused to let her go to the bathroom to clean up that time. He kept a death grip on her and fell asleep. Nikki laid still, because she didn't want to disturb him. She cried most of the night, not from emotional pain, but from physical pain. Emotionally, Nikki was already dead. She was a zombie in a body nothing more, nothing less.

CHAPTER 11

The next morning when Nikki turned on the lights, the sheets were covered in blood where she laid. She stumbled to the bathroom and Cid told her she looked a mess and wouldn't be going to work with him that day. He also said he was putting a button on the door, so if it open he would no. He said, if the door opened he would be on the other side waiting and what she got the night before would be just a taste of what was to come. Nikki said she wouldn't leave the room, she wouldn't even look out the window and she didn't. She sat on the bed in silence, no food, no water, no nothing.

That night when Cid got back to the room, he told Nikki they were going home the next day and he had a surprise for her. Nikki's seventeenth birthday was three weeks away and Cid said,

"You have just enough time for all your little spots to be gone. You know, that in Louisiana you can get married at seventeen and you don't need anyone's permission, you can sign for yourself."

Nikki looked at Cid with no response, she thought about the last two years of her life with Cid, the beatings, the rapings, and she knew if she married him her fate was sealed, but she knew she couldn't say no, because what would he do then.

When they got back to New Orleans Cid called his friends and told them about the wedding. He seemed happy and loving even tender at times, but all Nikki could think; was how to get out of the wedding. One of Cid's best friends visited and saw Nikki covered in bruises and asked what the hell had happened to her. Nikki and Dave were also friends, but she told him not to say a word to Cid, because he would kill her. Nikki told Dave she didn't want to marry Cid, but was too afraid to tell him and Dave said he would take care of it, not to worry.

On their wedding day, Dave showed up and told Cid it was not cool to be married and why would he want to marry Nikki when he got all he wanted anyway, but Cid wouldn't hear of it. Dave told him Nikki didn't want to marry him and he shouldn't force her; then Cid went crazy. He attacked Dave in the front yard and Nikki tried to break it up and got punched in the face. She called for the neighbors to help and the two guys next door pulled Dave and Cid apart. Cid yelled at Nikki and told her to tell him right there in front of Dave she didn't want to marry him, but Nikki was too afraid. Cid told Dave he must have misunderstood what she said. Cid told him they were going to the justice of the peace that afternoon and if Dave valued their friendship he would be there too.

Sure enough that afternoon, Nikki stood in front of the justice of the peace and said the vows that she knew would seal her fate in this life. Her knees were shaking and she was sick to her stomach, but she said,

"I Do."

Nikki became Ms Nicolette Renee Decker. Cid was happy for a few months and the beatings weren't as bad as before. Nikki couldn't hold things in her hands, because she trembled all the time. If she dropped something, she got slapped, if the wind blew, she got slapped. Nikki was dead, but something inside her yearned for life for something anything, but what she had.

Nikki woke up one morning and knew something inside her was different, she wasn't afraid anymore. She got out of bed fixed Cid's breakfast and walked him to the door. She kissed him goodbye and told him she would see him that night. Cid looked at her with a puzzled look on his face, then he left for work. When his car was out of site; Nikki packed a suitcase and left walking not knowing where she was going, but she was gone. Nikki had apologized for the last time and she was taking her freedom no matter what the cost. Nikki had said she was sorry so many times the words became something she screamed in her sleep. She vowed she would never say those words again, because the thought and the sound made something sour in the pit of her stomach. Every time she got hit she apologized for making him hit her, when Cid raped her over and over again, he made her apologize for not being good enough or something in the fight was her fault. When Nikki asked Cid what he wanted, he replied,

"I want an angel to come home to and a whore in the bedroom."

Nikki would never forget those words either. An angel and a whore, what a combination, one she swore she would never be for any man. Nikki kept her emotions to herself, even when she was alone she stayed busy; so she wouldn't think, music playing; the TV on; something in the background, but never silence. Nikki couldn't stand the silence. At that point in her life, Nikki was numb to her own feelings, but had a glimpse of a life in her dreams. Nikki could hear the sound of thunder in the distance during her brief moments of silence and knew a tornado was on the horizon. She knew one day the thunder would catch up to her and the storm would rage until the tornado she contained within her soul completed its course, but that day, she became determined to out run.

Nikki hitched a ride to Lafayette, Louisiana. She hid her suitcase in a ditch and went to fill out applications at the fast food joints. She went to work at Burger king and slept behind the nearest shopping center bathing in the bathroom before work once again. She could eat free at her job and lived on one meal a day, until her first check. Then she rented a travel trailer about a half-mile from her job. She walked everywhere she went and didn't mind.

Then, Nikki met a streetwalker named Candy one day while walking to the grocery store and struck up a conversation with her. She told Nikki about all the money she made and how easy it was. Nikki wanted to know how she could sleep with all those men and not know them and Candy said,

"Baby its thirty minutes of my time in their car and I've got one hundred bucks and I'll bet you make a hundred bucks a week."

Nikki told her,

"Yea, that was about right and asked how she got customers."

Candy was all too helpful. She told Nikki all she did was put on some sexy cloths, show some skin with some hills and walk the street the rest was history. She told Nikki when she got a few regulars it wasn't so bad. Nikki was numb inside anyway so she decided instead of going to the grocery store she would go shopping for an outfit and give it a try. Candy was right in the first day Nikki made two hundred dollars. Nikki kept her job at Burger King during the day and walked the street at night. On day two Nikki met a guy rolling in money. His name was Nick Calais.

Nick told Nikki she didn't have to walk the street and he would give her anything her heart desired, and did. Nikki furnished her little trailer, bought a TV, a stereo, and everything else one could imagine. One afternoon when she got home from work Nick had bought her a car as a surprise. Nick had the car sitting in her driveway with a big pink bow wrapped around it. Nikki had given Nick a key to the trailer and he was waiting inside for her.

Nikki thought; he pretty much furnished the place, so Nick might as well have a key. Nick was kind and gentle with Nikki. He told her, he had fallen madly in love with her and the next purchase was a house for Nikki. He was married, had grown kids, and didn't want to break up the so-called happy home, but told Nikki he couldn't live without her either.

Nikki took it with a grain of salt, one because Candy told her,

"Don't ever believe a man with his pants off, they'll tell you anything to get what they want and keep coming back for more as long as it feels good."

Nikki cared about Nick, but she never loved him, he was a source of survival and nothing more. Nikki still worked at Burger King which made Nick crazy, but Nikki was determined to maintain some sense of her own independence. Nikki thought if Nick went, at least she would still have her job.

Nikki worked the morning shift and was off at two o'clock everyday. She worked every other weekend, so she was pretty accommodating to Nick's schedule. Nick loved to snort coke and gamble. Nikki thought it was pretty great, because when Nick was loaded he couldn't perform sexually, so Nikki thought she was getting paid a lot of money for a lot of nothing.

Nikki's boss Lucas at Burger King was attracted to Nikki and asked if they could spend some time together. Nikki liked Lucas and thought he was an attractive man, so they spent some afternoons together when Nikki knew Nick was out of town. She shared her bed a couple of times with Lucas and he feel in love with her, but Nikki was in like and left feeling empty when she had sex with Lucas, so she ended the relationship, but they remained friends. Lucas cried when Nikki told him she couldn't see him anymore and he told her, she would always be held dear to him. Lucas said, no matter when, where or how much time passed, if she ever needed a thing, money, lunch or a tank of gas, to always no she could call him for it and he promised he would see to it that she got it.

Nikki thought there was no such thing as true love and decided she was better off on her own taking money from Nick. She decided to start saving money to move away and start a new life somewhere else when the ride was over. The only problem, Nick sidetracked Nikki by talking her into snorting snow with him, and she liked it too much. Nick planned trips away so he and Nikki could sit in a room for days blowing snow. One day turned into a week and the weeks into 4 months. Then one day Nikki was waiting for Nick after work, but he didn't show up. Nikki read in the paper that a very prominent citizen had passed away of a massive heart attack on his ranch in Palm Springs, Florida. Nikki was devastated at first and wondered what she was going to do with her life, she knew she was going to have to move and see if she could start a real life on the other side of town.

A couple of weeks passed after Nick's death and Nikki was trying to put some money away for her move. Nikki pulled up in her driveway after work one afternoon and a man in a blue suit got out of a four door black Crown Victorian and called out to Nikki. She froze when he called her by her name and asked if she was Nicolette Renee Breaux. Nikki turned to him and asked,

"Who wants to know?"

The man approached her and said he was an attorney handling the estate for Nick and he was a very close personal friend of his as well. Nikki told him she knew who he was and asked what he wanted with her. He told Nikki he was given very strict instructions by Nick to handle something for him personally and quietly if anything ever happened to him. He handed Nikki a box that was sealed with tape and Nick's signature across it, so if the seal had been broken someone would know. Under Nick's signature was a note that said for your eyes only. The man told Nikki he didn't know what was in the package, but was told whom Nikki was and where to deliver the package. He also said he had the package in his safe for the last six months per Nick's instructions. He turned and started to walk away, but turned back to Nikki and told her that Nick really loved her and she always made him smile.

Nikki just stared at the man as he turned and got in his car and drove away. She stood in the driveway for a minute still shell-shocked that Nick actually told someone else about their relationship. They traveled out of town, to go out in public and never went out in public in the city. As she stood there she couldn't believe what had just happened, but she thought it would fit Nick's character to pull something out of the ordinary. Nikki went inside and laid the package on the kitchen table, it was heavy and she wondered what could be inside, but she was also afraid of what could be inside. She wondered if Nick sent her documents of some of his shady deals he told her about, was it a goodbye note, or did Nick's wife find out about her and was she sending her a package to let her know she knew.

Nikki wasn't ready to open the package, so she put it in the closet in the living room and went to take a bath.

Nikki stayed in the bathtub for two hours letting out the cold water and turning on the hot water to keep the water warm. She finally decided she couldn't live in the tub, so she got out and cooked dinner. She called Candy and invited her to eat, but she said she was going out to work and told Nikki she needed a new John. Nikki didn't tell Candy about the package, but she did tell her, that part of her life was over. Candy laughed and told her she thought she was better than her, because Nikki lucked up on Nick the second day she was out there and he took her in. Candy said, Nikki took his money the same and it didn't make her any better. Nikki told Candy she never said or thought it did, she was grateful Nick came along when he did, but he changed the circumstances for her and gave her what she needed. Candy told her,

"Good-luck honey, but you've got a lot to learn about life sweetie and I just don't have the time to teach you."

Nikki hung up and knew she wouldn't see or speak to Candy again. She was angry, because she knew Candy was right. She took Nick's money and he furnished her home, bought her the car she drove and gave her, her independence, but it was in exchange for his money. Nikki knew Nick was in love with her and tears came to her eyes, because she knew she cared for Nick, but she was never in-love with him.

Nikki turned on the TV and watched a movie until she felt sleepy and went to bed. As she crawled between her sheets she stared at the ceiling and couldn't go to sleep. The thought of the package consumed her. She tossed and turned and finally after two hours of restlessness, Nikki told herself to open the package. She went in the living room and took the package out the closet. She laid it on the table and lit a cigarette. She stood in the kitchen smoking staring at the package. When Nikki put the cigarette out, she walked to the table and broke the seal. There was a tape and several tan envelopes inside the package. The tape said play first before you open the other packages.

Nikki put the tape in the VCR and hit play. It was Nick sitting on a balcony with the beach in the background. He had a drink in his hand and was sitting in a white whicker chair. He started by saying hello to the love of his life. He said if Nikki was playing the tape that something had happened to him, but he needed to know he had said a few words and took care of a few things after the fact. He told Nikki he knew he had a ninety percent blockage in his heart and his heart muscle was too weak to withstand surgery and his life style didn't make him a good candidate for surgery either.

He knew he was living on borrowed time, but the time he had shared with Nikki was the best times of his life. He told her he wished he could do more than what he had done, but his wife would have found anything more and he didn't want to bring embarrassment to his family. He was torn between his family and her, but he knew with certainty his family would be more than fine. He wanted Nikki to know she was the one that had his heart when he left this world and asked her to please destroy the tape and open the other packages and put them to good use and know he wished her the best from heaven. Nick's last words were,

"Goodbye my love."

Nikki sat there with tears streaming down her face; she walked to the VCR pulled the tape out, took it to the sink, broke it, pulled the film out and put the outer shell in the trash. Nikki took the film outside and burned it. She went back in the house and smoked another cigarette before she opened the rest of the packages, by that time Nikki had figured out, one was money and decided her move could then come sooner than later.

When Nikki opened the second package it was the deed to the house and the title to her car, both was in her name, with a note that said, you'll never be homeless again, it's yours free and clear. Nikki was in shock when she reached for the other envelopes. She never imagined she would find what she did, all one hundred dollar bills, one hundred thousand dollars worth. She was freaked out about the money and scared that someone would miss it somehow, she thought,

"Hell how could someone married make a hundred thousand dollars disappear and the spouse not know it."

Nikki couldn't sleep the rest of the night. She made up her mind that the next day was moving day, it was time to move in another direction and the money Nick left her would give her a fresh start. Nikki also thought what Nick tried to do was too much and someone sooner or later would show up to take it from her. Nikki put the house up for sale and in four months Nikki returned to New Orleans to find another place to live. She went back to New Orleans, because Dana, a girl she had became friends with at work was moving back to New Orleans as well. Dana told Nikki, she had to move back and meet her neighbor, but Nikki said maybe one day, but then she needed some time on her own. Nikki got a small apartment in the quarter and found a job at Waffle House as a waitress. The pay sucked, but the tips were really good and Nicks' money came in handy with the sale of the house. Nikki decorated her apartment and bought a new car. She checked into going back to school, but since she never finished school she would have to get a GED and take her SAT to get in. She wasn't afraid of getting her GED, but thought she wasn't smart enough to score a good enough number on the SAT to get accepted, so she settled for her job as a waitress and enrolled in beauty school. Nikki made excellent grades in beauty school. The school had a program that allowed Nikki to get her GED in the process. She completed the first year in beauty school making excellent grades, but failed the GED and gave up.

Nikki settled for her job at Waffle House where she met Mike and Lisa Thomas whom ran the waffle house where she worked. Nikki hit it off well with both of them. They worked the day shift together and was off in the afternoons. Mike and Lisa had a nice condo and it was the hang out for wayward souls and sure enough, Nikki found her way there as well; by invitation of course, but she found herself there. Nikki and Lisa became tight friends and bonded like nothing Nikki had experienced before, as time went on the bond became tighter and tighter.

Lisa and Nikki spent an enormous amount of time together, watching movies, shopping, and reading books. It was nothing for Mike to get home and find Nikki and Lisa snuggled together on the couch sleeping. The two girls were like close sisters in the beginning. Nikki and Lisa would sit up at night playing backgammon and shooting shots of Crown until they passed out.

About six months into the friendship, one weekend Nikki and Lisa was playing backgammon and shooting Crown as usual and Lisa told Nikki, Mike was attracted to her. Lisa said he thought Nikki was erotic and sensual and wanted to have sex with her. Nikki assured Lisa she loved her too much to ever mess up their friendship and she didn't have a thing in the world to worry about. Lisa laughed and told her she knew more than anything she trusted Nikki. Lisa said she didn't mind if Nikki wanted to sleep with Mike and asked Nikki if she was attracted to Mike. Nikki of course was, Mike was tall, dark complected, had medium brown hair full of curls, big brown eyes, and the finest ass she thought she had ever seen. Nikki and Lisa laughed together when Nikki admitted her thoughts. Lisa encouraged Nikki to go up stairs and crawl in bed with Mike and wake him up. She said she would come in and join them a little later. Nikki asked, what she meant by, join them and Lisa laughed and said Nikki needed to live a little. Nikki stumbled upstairs to the bedroom where Mike was sleeping. She crawled under the covers and kissed him on the shoulder.

Mike had his back to Nikki, but he reached up with his hand and cupped Nikki's face. When Mike turned over, Nikki wondered what he would do and was surprised when he embraced and kissed her passionately. His tongue, teased her tongue. Their lips met and she could feel him growing hard against her thigh. Nikki wanted him like she had never wanted another man before and she felt a throbbing sensation between her legs that she had never experienced before either. As Mike kissed her, she melted into the soft oversize bed they were in and thought she never wanted that moment to end.

Then Nikki thought of Lisa and asked Mike if he was sure Lisa was all right and said she should go check on her. Mike told her Lisa was fine and would come in to check on them soon enough. Nikki was too caught up in what was happening and Mike was more than ready to take Nikki when Nikki heard the door open. Lisa entered the room and Mike got up and kissed Lisa standing in the door. Nikki wasn't sure what to expect next and was a little shocked when Lisa came and got in bed with her and left Mike standing in the doorway. Mike lit a joint and offered Nikki a drag. He leaned over the bed and blew a shotgun into Nikki's mouth. When Nikki exhaled, she felt Lisa touching her inner thighs, stroking her with her fingertips. Lisa went up to Nikki's face and kissed her softly on the lips, it felt strange at first, but then Nikki really liked the feeling; it was one she had never experienced before. The kiss was soft, tender, not rough, or rigged. Nikki kissed Lisa back again and again. The two girls touched, caressed, and kissed each other until Nikki thought she was going to explode. Then, Lisa started kissing Nikki again. First on the lips, then the neck, to the breast, then to the stomach, and ran her tongue down along the side of Nikki's thigh. She had separated Nikki's legs with her own leg placed between Nikki's. She kissed and softly bit Nikki's inner thigh. It was soft, tender and erotic Nikki screamed out engrossed in the excitement and pleasure. Lisa brought Nikki to an orgasm that pulsated to her very soul. Just when Nikki thought it was over, Lisa brought her back to the edge of the universe on the verge of another orgasm, when Mike got back in bed with them. Mike kissed Nikki softly as he went back up Nikki's body kissing her softly. He noticed Nikki was trembling from the sensations her body was experiencing. Mike entered Nikki and brought her to another orgasm. As Nikki heard Mike moan in ecstasy, she became more and more aroused. Lisa was Kissing Nikki while Mike was having his way with her, until he too exploded inside Nikki and fell on top of her and Lisa. The three of them couldn't move that night; they readjusted themselves on the bed and fell asleep until the next morning.

When Nikki woke up, she was still in bed with both Mike and Lisa. She remembered the night with a smile on her face, but wondered how things would be when the two awakened and wondered if this would be the end of their friendship. The thought of never seeing Lisa again brought tears to her eyes. Nikki got up and went to the bathroom. She showered and went back to the room. Mike was lying in bed, but Lisa had gone down stairs to cook breakfast. Mike told Nikki to come back to bed; Lisa would be up in a minute with breakfast. Nikki got back in bed and Mike made love to her again. Lisa came back in the room in the middle of Mike and Nikki having their morning delight and said; she was going to get jealous if Nikki didn't share her husband with her. Nikki laughed when Lisa put the breakfast tray on the dresser and dove head first in the bed. Mike kissed his wife and told her, he loved her. Nikki thought, what a relationship, that the two of them together were beautiful. Mike pulled his wife to him as Nikki went for the breakfast tray feeling hung over. Nikki sat in the chair bedside the bed eating toast slowly as she watched Mike make love to Lisa.

Nikki watched in amazement. She thought this was truly how a man should touch a woman. She watched as Lisa kissed her husband and laughed when Lisa told her to come over there and let her show Nikki the way to a man's soul.

Lisa taught Nikki how to give a proper blowjob. Nikki almost vomited when Lisa took Mike in her mouth and he orgasmed. Nikki told Lisa if that was the way to a man's soul, she would never get there and they both laughed.

That day turned into another and weeks turned into six months, Nikki learned more about herself sexually than she could have ever thought possible. Nikki saw very little of Dana or anyone else for that matter. Her world revolved around Mike and Lisa. That was until the company they worked for promoted Mike to regional manager and was placing him in Atlanta. Lisa begged Nikki to go with them, but she didn't want to be that far away. Nikki thought if Michelle settled down again it would be in New Orleans and she wanted to stay close, so she could get Tricia back again. Nikki helped Mike and Lisa pack, had their fair-well party and wished them well. She promised to stay in touch and go visit now and then.

When Mike and Lisa left, Nikki went wild, partying every night in the local clubs; she met another girl her age, Lane who was just as wild as she was. They did the town. Lane and Nikki became roommates for a while and were close friends. Lane was the wild woman-bringing guy after guy home, but Nikki had a crush on the lead guitar player in the band where she and Lane hung out, so Nikki didn't chase other men. Nikki liked Jake they snorted coke like is was going out of style. Jake always had it and Nikki was always willing to blow it with him.

Nikki's partying days was numbered and she knew it, she quit her job as a waitress and found another one working in a shoe store again. She didn't make as much money as before, but she like it. She started seeing more and more of Dana, her friend from Lafayette again. After a couple months Dana started nagging Nikki again, about meeting her neighbor, but Nikki wasn't ready to meet anyone else at that time. She told Dana, she wasn't interested in another relationship right then, but Dana wouldn't let it go. Dana told Nikki there was something about his eyes she couldn't explain and Nikki just had to meet him to see his eyes; then she would leave her alone. Nikki told her maybe one day, just not then.

Of course, eventually Nikki let her guard down. She felt safe at her new apartment and new job. Then after the store closed one night she was walking to her car and something hit her from behind. When Nikki turned around; it was Cid. As he grabbed her, Nikki became enraged and turned on him like never before; she was like a caged animal again. Cid was astounded; he didn't know what hit him. Cid hobbled off, but Nikki knew the worse was yet to come. She also knew he would come back and he did.

Nikki could be in a grocery store, out in a club, getting off work, it didn't matter where she was. Just when she thought she made it to her car safely, like a thief in the night, out of know where, Cid appeared. Nikki carried several more bruises, but Cid carried a few too. He told Nikki he was going to kill her and she told him, he would have to before she would go back. Nikki meant, if it cost her, her life, she would not run from him again and she didn't.

Nikki was lonely and called home for the first time in five years to speak to her Grandmother. Her Grandmother wanted her to come home, but she said she couldn't, but promised she would visit soon and her Grandmother told her Michelle was back in New Orleans and where she was living. Nikki thought this could be her chance to get Tricia back and drove to the apartments to see if she could find Michelle. Michelle was happy to see Nikki and told her Tricia was in California with Kevin, but he was bringing her there in a couple of weeks, so Nikki hung out at

Michelle's waiting. Nikki went to work and partied at night in the clubs with Michelle. A few times Nikki was leaving in front of Michelle and Cid jumped her in the parking lot. Cid almost killed Nikki before Michelle could get him off her one night and Michelle called Kevin and told him he needed to come sooner than they had planned, so he got there the next day.

Tricia was five years old and a spitting image of Nikki. Nikki thought that Kevin was going to live with Michelle, but he was only in town to get her two sisters Kirsten and Ashley. Michelle and Kevin had divorced, but he agreed to help take care of Nikki's younger sisters, even though the girls were not his.

Nikki left to go to the store for sandwich stuff, because the kids were hungry. When she got back, she made it through the parking lot and thought she was home free. Then she entered the hallway to the apartment and Cid was waiting under the stairs. He grabbed Nikki by the throat and told her he was going to kill her. He hit her head against the wall so hard it made a sonic boom; Nikki was losing consciousness when the door swung open and Kevin stepped outside to see what was happening. When he saw Cid with Nikki pinned against the wall choking her. Kevin went crazy and grabbed Cid, he asked him, if he wanted to hit a real man and beat the crap out of Cid, he told him he was living there then and Nikki would be moving in with them as well. He said if a hair on Nikki's head got parted wrong from that moment forward he would find him and he would die for it.

The police was called and charges were pressed against Cid, but Nikki too was asked to go down town for a bench warrant. Nikki asked what it was for, and was told for issuing worthless checks and Cid was laughing when they were putting him in the car. Nikki went down town and was finger printed and pictured. The judge let Nikki sign herself out on her own when Nikki told them she had written the check to an auto shop to have Cid's car fixed just before she had left. Cid closed the account and the check bounced, but Nikki didn't know he had closed the account.

The judge called the bank to verify the account balance on the day the check was written; the funds were there. The account was closed two days after the check was written. Nikki paid the check and all charges were dismissed, but she had endured the experience of being booked. At least the police officer had let Kevin drive her downtown instead of handcuffing her and taking her in. Nikki never saw Cid again after that night. She fell asleep on Michelle's couch when she got home that night. When Nikki got up the next morning Kevin had taken Tricia, Kirsten, and Ashley with him back to California.

When Nikki opened her eyes, she was sore all over, had bruises on her throat, and scratches everywhere. She looked in the mirror after walking through the apartment and realizing everyone was gone again. She thought she would have liked to thank Kevin for helping get Cid off her, and at the same time, wanted to kill him for taking Tricia. She also thought Kevin could give Tricia a better home than she could, but he couldn't love Tricia more. Nikki was closer however, to getting Tricia back, because she then knew Kevin was in California. She also knew the last name of his family, "Thompson."

Michelle walked in the door and was putting her purse down in the kitchen when Nikki walked in. Nikki asked where everyone was and Michelle told her they were gone. Nikki sat down and told Michelle they needed to talk. Nikki said she had avoided confronting her because, one she knew Michelle didn't want to discuss it and she didn't want to blow her chance of seeing Tricia again. Michelle looked at Nikki and told her she had done nothing wrong. Tricia was with a wealthy family that could give her a better life and Nikki screamed at her what gave her the right to make that decision for her. Michelle told her she was her mother. Nikki jumped up out the chair and went to Michelle and stood in her face and told her she better think of a much dam better reason than that. Michelle backed away and told Nikki she didn't want to talk anymore and thought it would be best if she left.

Nikki turned to her and told her if once in her life, just once Michelle could have acknowledged she made some really bad choices and just once said she was sorry just one time, maybe they could have had a starting place some kind of a beginning. Nikki said never again would she ever walk around the room and see this huge white elephant in the room and act like there was nothing between them. Nikki told Michelle she would never forgive her for what she took from her and for what, so she could go off and loose her too. She said she was leaving because if she stayed she would end her life and she had better pray she never saw her again. Nikki turned and walked to the door. As Nikki reached for the door, Michelle said,

"I'm sorry."

Nikki turned and looked at her. Michelle said,

"It didn't work did it?"

Nikki looked at her and said,

"No, I guess it didn't, words never will ease or take away what you did, so I hope you're happy with yourself, you sat out to destroy, and you destroyed."

Nikki opened the door and walked away. Nikki was enraged at losing Tricia again, but had know one to voice her feelings to, so once again Nikki remained silent and the thunder in the distance rolled closer and Nikki ran harder.

CHAPTER 12

Nikki returned to her own apartment, she took a bath, got dressed and went to work. Nikki spent the next few months alone in her apartment watching TV or listening to music. She talked with Dana on the phone, but didn't venture out, except for work.

After a few months Nikki called Dana and told her she was going for a visit. Dana had bought her parents house and was getting settled when Nikki arrived. They had coffee in the kitchen that night and sat on the front porch waiting for Todd to come home. When Dana introduced Todd to Nikki she thought he was attractive and a nice guy. Todd and Nikki then started hanging out together almost every night. Todd was infatuated with Nikki, but Nikki was in like with Todd.

Nikki thought Todd's eyes were strange; they were gray. Todd wore glasses and would take his glasses off and tell Nikki to look into his eyes when he asked her to move in with him after a month of seeing each other. Nikki looked in those eyes and melted like butter, the next day she started packing and two days later on her day off she moved her things in and her life with Todd began.

Todd was an engineer with a local firm and part owner. He was tall six feet two inches, weighing two hundred and fifteen pounds. He had sandy blond hair down to his shoulders and a killer tan. Todd was a muscle man with perfect skin. Nikki was in lust more than love at the time. Todd introduced Nikki to his friends and family, which loved and adored Nikki from the start. Their first Christmas together Nikki got more presents than Todd; she thought it was hilarious.

Every Sunday they had dinner at Todd's parents, Mr. and Mrs. Bankston. Nikki thought the Bankston's were incredible people. Mr.

Bankston adored Nikki and they became quite close. Nikki looked at him like the father figure that had always been missing for her and Mr. Bankston was all to please to fill that roll. Ms Bankston was sweet and friendly; Nikki and her shared recipes and luncheons during the week, but Ms Bankston came from money and seemed to Nikki a little too high class at times. Todd of course was the black sheep of the family, being an engineer. Todd's little sister Clara was in college studying to become a doctor and his older sister Gay was a CPA and married to a professional football player that played for the Miami Dolphins and Todd's oldest brother worked at NASA and married a Chemist.

Although Nikki was truly loved, she never felt like she could measure up to that family, because she was a high school drop out working in a shoe store making minimum wage. Mr. Bankston told Nikki his son was in love and that was all he needed to know, so Nikki joked around, acting like, she felt like part of the family, but she didn't.

Her sex life with Todd was incredible; Todd knew his way around the bedroom and Nikki felt safe and protected with him. She was tiny weighing about ninety pounds soaking wet and Todd adored her body. He told her, she never had to wear cloths around him; he loved to just look at her.

Their life together involved several friends from Todd's work mostly. Nikki's friends became the wives of the guys Todd worked with. They all hung out, bar-b-qued, watched sports and had too many crawfish boils to even count. Their lives together were full and Nikki thought she had finally arrived in the place she had wanted to be and had longed for all her life. A few of Todd's friends wives were jealous of Nikki, because she could eat like a horse and never gain a pound, but also of Todd and Nikki's relationship, because they never fought. They seemed to rock along enjoying life and each other.

Nikki enjoyed entertaining at home, it fact Nikki and Todd hosted most of the gatherings for their group of friends. Nikki and Todd bought a two story house and settled in their life together. Nikki adored Randy, Todd's boss, his girlfriend Mika was sort of stuck-up, but Nikki tolerated her for Todd's sake. Jamie was Todd's coworker with his wife Brenda and last, but not least, David and his wife Candice. Of the three couples, David and Candice were the most entertaining for a period of time. David was an incredibly good-looking man and Candice couldn't keep him home. Nikki spent most of her time with Candice, listening while Candice cried on her shoulder. The day finally came when Candice left

David, because he told Candice he didn't want children and he didn't want a committed relationship. The only problem with that, Candice was six months pregnant. Nikki didn't have much respect for David after that.

Randy was a nut case, always joking, laughing and carrying on. He told joke after joke and kept everyone around him in stitches. It also didn't hurt, that he too was drop dead gorgeous. Mika and Nikki had tension between them that was obvious to the others. When asked, Nikki just told Debbie she had an experience with Mika a couple years back that she would like to forget, but Mika wasn't likely to admit the truth or let it go. Mika took pot shots at Nikki when she could, and Nikki let them slide for a while. Randy had, had enough of the tension and remarks long before Nikki. Then Todd came home one day and told Nikki that Randy and Mika were breaking up. Nikki was relieved, but also sad for Randy, because he really seamed to be in-love with Mika.

Then, Randy showed up at the house to talk to Nikki. He asked what the tension between Mika and her was all about. Nikki told him, he needed to discuss it with Mika, but Randy said he had spoke to Mika about it at length, and was told that Nikki owed Mika money for staying at her apartment once and she never collected the money Nikki owed her. Nikki laughed and asked Randy, if Mika had really told him that. Randy said Mika was adamant about it. Nikki said if Mika thought she owed her money and that was the real problem, why not ask for the money or remind her of it, let her pay it back and move on. Randy had told Mika the same thing, but Mika wanted Nikki to go to her and not make a big deal out of it. Nikki laughed even louder and said,

"Not make a big deal out of it, hell the tension was so thick it could have been cut with a knife."

Randy asked Nikki again for the truth. He told her, he knew he would never get the truth from Mika, so he was asking for the truth from her. Then Todd came in on the tail end of the conversation and told Nikki she should tell Randy what she had told him the night she met Mika. Randy looked at Todd and asked, if he had known the whole time. Todd of course did, and played stupid, because Nikki swore him to secrecy.

Randy then demanded to know. Nikki told him it happened a few years ago before Mika and him were together, but Randy didn't care he wanted to know the truth. Nikki told Randy that she and Mika were friends a few years back. Nikki had her own apartment and spent some weekends with Mika partying. Mika had called Nikki at work one day and asked her to drive her to a clinic for a pregnancy test, so Nikki agreed to take her. When they arrived at the clinic, Mika asked Nikki to wait with her. Sitting in the lobby, Mika told Nikki she thought she was pregnant and didn't know what she was going to do if she was. She told her she might be crying when she came out and asked, if Nikki could spend the night with her. Nikki agreed, and told her if she was pregnant, she would help her as much as she could. Mika thanked her with tears in her eyes, then the nurse called Mika and she told Nikki she would be back shortly, so Nikki sat in the abortion clinic waiting patiently for Mika to come out with the news.

The wait went from minutes to an hour, Nikki thought,

"How long does it take to complete a pregnancy test?"

Nikki was antsy and went to the desk to ask what was taking so long. The nurse told her, that Mika had not seen the doctor yet, but it shouldn't be much longer. Nikki sat back down in the waiting room. Nikki was sure Mika was pregnant and was waiting to see the doctor to see how far along she was. She was thumbing through a magazine when a nurse burst through the door asking for the party there with Mika. Nikki stood-up and the nurse took Nikki by the arm and led her to the back. When they got behind the door away from the lobby the nurse turned to Nikki and told her she needed to go in the room with Mika and calm her down. Nikki asked how far along Mika was, so the nurse told her she was pretty far, if she waited one more day, they wouldn't have been able to terminate the pregnancy. Nikki asked the nurse to repeat what she said again, but the nurse told Nikki that Mika had, had the procedure and was upset and she needed Nikki's help to calm Mika down. Nikki was in shock and asked,

"What procedure?"

The nurse told Nikki, Mika had terminated her pregnancy. Nikki asked her what she meant again and said,

"I just brought her here for a pregnancy test."

The nurse told Nikki again,

"Mika terminated her pregnancy and was upset. The appointment was scheduled for a week in advanced and Mika had done fine with her counseling visit the day before."

Nikki was lead to the room by the nurse where Mika was laying on a stretcher still sedated. Nikki walked over to her and asked her if she was all right. Mika told her, she was burning inside and felt something warm running out of her. She asked Nikki to look under the sheet to see what was wrong. When Nikki pulled the sheet back, she saw Mika lying in a puddle of blood and jerked the sheet back down. As the sheet was put back in place Nikki had looked away so she wouldn't see all the blood. Nikki was looking over the end of the bed and saw the machine they used to terminate the pregnancy, as Nikki stared at the machine, she saw the glass jar attached to the machine with blood and tissue floating in the jar, Nikki blinked her eyes to clear her vision and saw a tiny hand float into view in the jar. Nikki looked at Mika and said,

"Oh God, what have you done."

Mika was waking up and the room got really hot for Nikki. She started sweating and felt cold. Nikki started walking toward the door; she had to get out of there. As she opened the door the nurse saw her and Nikki told her she was passing out, just as she hit the floor.

Nikki woke up in the physicians lounge with a nurse popping an ammonia pill under her nose and Mika setting in a chair by the couch Nikki was laid on. Mika asked her, if she was ok and Nikki moaned and told her she wanted to leave. When they got home, Mika tried to tell Nikki she didn't want anyone to know what she had done and thought she could have kept that from her too. Mika thought she could go in get the procedure over with, walk out and know one would ever have to know.

Mika said, it took her some time to save the money, so the procedure was more difficult than she or the doctors had anticipated, but Nikki told her to shut-up. Nikki said she was her friend and deserved the truth and not be made a part of something like that.

She told Mika that she too, was pregnant and probably from a rape and could not terminate the pregnancy. She said, she had tremendous female problems, because of her choice to give birth, but said she would have never terminated the pregnancy. Mika was angry with Nikki and told her she had no right to judge her. Nikki told her, she was right, but Mika had no right to rope her into a situation like that without her knowledge either and Nikki left. Nikki returned to her own apartment and never saw Mika again, until she showed up with Randy.

Nikki looked at Randy and said they never tried to talk or contact each other again. When Nikki saw her with Randy and he seemed in-love with her, she tried to be cordiale to Mika, but Mika was defensive and guarded. Randy had tears in his eyes and was speechless for the moment. He turned to Todd and told him, he should've told him what happened instead of letting it linger on. Todd told him, he couldn't do that out of respect for Nikki and that Nikki never intended to tell him. Nikki had hoped that Mika and she could be civil, because of the guys working relationship and friendship outside the job. Mika chose to drag the situation out and lie about it. Nikki sat back to see how far she would go and Mika ran it in the ground.

Randy went home and called Mika. When he confronted her about the situation, she denied it at first, but then confessed. She told Randy, she didn't want to be in a relationship with anyone that knew. Mika had told Randy, he was the second man she had been with and had played the game of appearing innocent and sweet without anything to confess. She figured he wouldn't see her in that way again, so she finalized the ending of the relationship.

Randy hung up and called Todd to meet him for drinks. Todd went and the next few months, the two other couples with Randy met out at clubs for drinks and carried on their friendships. Mika was seen on multiple occasions hanging all over different guys and Randy attacked one guy one night and bet the crap out of him before Todd and David could get him off the poor guy. Randy was dying inside and Nikki felt responsible. Randy started blowing snow like it was going out of style. He was an engineer and part owner of the firm too, so he made killer money; which made it easy to support his habit. Randy started throwing parties at his house and their little group of friends became snow blowers every weekend.

Nikki's money finished disappearing with snow and Todd was blowing his money too. Randy and Todd were blowing snow during the day at work extending it into the night. The eye opener for Nikki was when needles came into the picture. One night at one of Randy's famous parties, Todd and Nikki were the only ones that showed up. Randy wanted to use needles to hit the snow, so Todd showed him how to melt it down. Randy couldn't find his vein and Nikki was in snow heaven and told him she would look. Nikki found his vein and shot him up, then Todd shot himself up. They both had their own needles and tried to coach Nikki into trying it. They told her if she felt it once it would be the greatest thing she could ever imagine, but Nikki was already in snow heaven and refused to participate.

The days turned into weeks and the weeks into months. Nikki wanted something more and knew something was missing, but she was so loaded on snow she didn't care anymore. Her days were spent snorting snow and watching Todd snort or hit himself up. He always used clean needles and swore he would never put himself in any danger and Nikki was too loaded to care.

Then Todd's supplier Jason showed up at the house early before Todd got home one afternoon. Jason sat on the couch while Nikki was in the kitchen making tea. He sat a three-inch vial filled with white powder on the coffee table and asked Nikki for a mirror. Nikki gave him the mirror and told him that Todd would be home any minute. Jason said he was going to start the party without him and Nikki laughed and told him a few lines wouldn't hurt. Jason had a second vial the same size he placed on the table and said the second vial was for Todd. The teakettle whistled in the kitchen, so Nikki left to finish making her tea. Nikki loved hot tea in a cup, it could be a hundred degrees outside, but she still loved her tea.

When Nikki returned to the room, Jason had laid out three lines and went to the bathroom. Nikki thought,

"I'll show him, laying out lines and walking away."

She sat her cup of tea down and pulled out a straw from the drawer by the sofa and snorted all three lines. When Jason walked back in the room, he saw the lines gone and became frantic. He asked Nikki what happened to the lines he laid out and Nikki told him she did them. When Nikki saw the look on his face, she knew something was wrong. She stood up and asked what was wrong, but when Nikki stood up, she felt like someone poured hot water from her head to her toes and her whole body went numb.

She looked at Jason and asked,

"What was that?"

She remembered him telling her,

"It's PCP."

He told Nikki he was going to offer her and Todd a taste of something wild, but she only was suppose to have half a line not three whole ones. The room was spinning for Nikki when Dana walked in from next door to see her. Nikki's face was white as snow; she had no color what so ever. Dana was sitting next to Nikki on the sofa and Nikki would ask,

"Where is Dana?"

Dana told Jason, Todd was on his way home and would be ferrous, but before he could reply, Todd walked in. When he saw Nikki he was frantic, Jason ran to him and told him Nikki snorted three lines before he could stop her.

Todd asked,

"How the hell did that happen to happen?"

Jason told him he had pulled out the two vials, one his own and the other for Todd. Jason said; he had laid out three lines, because Nikki said Todd would be home any minute and he was going to offer to treat the two of them to a new experience. Then after laying out the lines, he said, he went to the bathroom, while Nikki was in the Kitchen, and when he got back, she had already snorted them.

Todd punched Jason in the mouth and told him, he was an idiot for laying it out and leaving it, without telling Nikki what it was. Todd said if anything happened to Nikki he was going to kill him.

Todd went to Nikki and took her in his arms. Nikki smiled at him and asked where Dana was again. Dana told her she was right beside her and everything was going to be all right. Nikki laughed and said,

"Everything is alright."

Nikki tripped for three solid days, the first day was a great high, everything was funny and felt good, although she really couldn't feel her body; the second day things were scary. Although Nikki knew she was in the world, she knew she couldn't come down off the high she was on and still couldn't feel her body. Todd never left her side and Dana was in and out checking on Nikki. The third day was total terror. Nikki was pacing the floor, pulling her hair, pinching herself, and stomping on the floor trying to feel her feet, because she still couldn't feel her body, but was fully aware of the nightmare and sheer paranoia sat in.

Nikki prayed and promised God if he would let her come down off the high, she would never touch drugs again. On the fourth day, Nikki opened her eyes and realized she had fallen asleep; she had not slept in three days. When she looked around the room, Randy was sleeping in the chair by her bed. Dana was sleeping across the foot of the bed and Todd had her in his arms past out from shear exhaustion, because he hadn't slept in three days either.

Nikki didn't remember much about the three days, except the intense paranoid felling. She woke up exhausted. As she stirred in bed, Todd woke up and asked how she was doing. She said, she was fine, but she had just taken her last trip on drugs. Randy sat up in the chair and said,

"We all have, this was enough to scare the shit out of me too. I thought you were going to OD and my whole life flashed before my eyes too."

Nikki smiled at Randy and he walked over to her and said his life too was spinning out of control and he realized they were all spending all their time, money and energy on parting and they needed to get a grip. Todd said,

"A-man brother."

The next few months were getting back to normal without the drugs and Nikki and Todd spent more time with Todd's family. It was back to dinner on Sundays and conversation. Back to the football games that Joe played in and life seemed great. Nikki was close to Mr. Bankston, Todd's dad and he asked what had happened in their lives that kept them so distant for several months. Nikki told him everything was fine, that her and Todd had been busy fixing up the house they bought and settling into their relationship. Mr. Bankston asked if their relationship was all right and Nikki smiled and assured him, all was well. Mr. Bankston told Nikki he was proud of Todd and was thrilled to have her as part of the family and asked why the two of them had not set a wedding date. Nikki smiled again and said; it just wasn't time to do that yet, but maybe soon.

What Nikki didn't tell Mr. Bankston, was the endeavor with the drugs and how she suspected Todd was still using and lying to her about it. Nikki begged Todd to stop using and live a normal life, he agreed because Nikki was the most important thing in his life, but he still could not lay the drugs down.

Within a few months, Nikki knew when Todd walked in the door he was high on snow and the fights continued. Todd denied it, but after arguing he'd admit he had blown a few lines that day, but swore that was all. Eventually, Todd drained his savings and started selling things to support his habit. Nikki would come home from work and find things missing. Todd of course, denied he sold the things. Todd told Nikki the things had been gone for a while and at times Nikki thought she was losing her mind. Nikki stopped going to the family dinners and football games or any other socials the family had.

Mr. Bankston paid Nikki a visit while Todd was gone and asked Nikki what was going on. He noticed Todd looked bad and was losing weight and wanted answers. Nikki broke down and told his Dad that Todd had a problem. Mr. Bankston was ferrous and waited for Todd to get home. He confronted him, but he told his Dad he had only tried drugs a few times and Nikki found out about it and freaked. Todd assured his Dad he didn't have a drug problem, but was having some stomach problems and was seeing a doctor so he didn't want him to worry. Mr. Bankston went in the living room where Nikki waited and told her everything was going to be fine, he had a talk with Todd and got it straight. Nikki was thrilled. That is until three days later when Todd came home and Nikki found his stash with his needles again. Todd flushed his stash and broke his needles to show Nikki he was stopping. Once again Nikki hoped it was true, but didn't hold her breath.

CHAPTER 13

Nikki felt it was time to reconnect with her own family and called her Grandmother again. Her Grandmother was always happy to hear from Nikki and begged her to come home for a visit. Nikki made plans to leave the next weekend for the bayou, but Todd had already made plans to play golf with Randy. Nikki told Todd it was better if he didn't go, because under the circumstances her first trip home should be alone. Todd told her he understood, kissed her bye, told her to be careful, and hurry home.

As Nikki entered the bayou, her Grandmother sat on the porch waiting. Nikki thought nothing would ever change. She laughed out loud and said she could be gone fifty years and return and nothing would change. The alligators would still be laying on the river bend, the lightening bugs would still light up the night, and the crickets and frogs would scream forever. Her Grandmother's arms were still as big as always and she smelled just the way Nikki remembered when she hugged her. Nikki was smiling as she remembered all the things about home and broke into tears when her Grandmother embraced her. Nikki sobbed in her Grandmothers arms while her Grandmother stroked her hair and told her she loved her. Nikki felt disrespectful, because she went home in jeans and had on makeup, but her Grandmother told her, it didn't matter, she knew Nikki was a child of God, blessed with a gift, and as long as she embraced that gift she would never go wrong. Nikki hugged her Grandmother tighter, but didn't tell her she had not felt the gift in quite some time.

She sat for six hours talking with her Grandmother, while several other family members and members of the church stopped in to see Nikki. It was nice to see the rest of the family and some old friends from school, but she really only needed to be near her Grandmother. Nikki was told one of her childhood girlfriends was killed in a storm with her husband and her baby. Nikki was speechless and she remembered the vision as a child playing and spending time with her friends, that one would die in an auto accident and the other suddenly and tragically. Nikki never told the girls what she saw and when she heard the news she wondered if she would have warned them all those years ago, could it have turned out different. Nikki couldn't think about it anymore, she closed her mind off to the possibilities and focused on her visit. Nikki told her Grandmother she had started beauty school and dropped out, because she failed her GED. Her Grandmother assured Nikki, she could do anything she was determined to, if she wanted it bad enough. Nikki told her she was thinking of going back, but wasn't sure what to study and finances were tight, but she knew she could get grants and student loans to cover the expenses.

Nikki gave her Grandmother her address, phone number, promised to stay in-touch and come home more often. When Nikki left, she did so with such an overwhelming sense of peace. As Nikki was leaving the bayou, she spotted the church she grew-up in and stopped to go inside to see if it too, was just as she remembered, it was. It too smelled the same, looked the same and gave her the same feeling every time she walked in the door as a child, a sense of excitement and peace. As Nikki turned to leave for the first time in many years the gift returned. Nikki saw Todd moaning, calling out her name, he needed her, but Nikki couldn't tell why, his skin color was bad and he struggled to breath. Nikki snapped out of it; she refused to see anymore and high-tailed it home to make sure Todd was all right.

Todd expected Nikki to spend the night on the bayou, but Nikki couldn't stay, not being part of the religion anymore. When Nikki got home Todd was out and didn't come home that night. When he walked in the door Nikki knew he had been somewhere blowing snow the whole night. She demanded to see his arms to search for needle marks. Nikki had already stopped having sex with Todd months before, because of him using needles and lying about the drugs. Nikki thought if he would lie about the drugs, what else he would lie about. Todd begged Nikki for sex, but she wouldn't have any part of it, until she knew he was off the drugs and she was safe.

A few weeks later Nikki was home with Todd when Darwin called and said he was in the city to bring something to Nikki from her Grandmother. Teddy, a friend of Todd's was over and both got really nervous about Nikki's Dad showing up. Nikki laughed, because she thought, Todd was nervous about meeting her Dad. Nikki opened the door when Darwin drove up and he visited a while; then gave Nikki a check from her Grandmother to start school. He told Nikki her Grandmother made him drive all the way there to give it to her so she could start school. He said if she needed anything more, all she had to do was ask. Nikki cried and Darwin tried to hug her, but hugs from Darwin were always cold and stiff to Nikki so she just said her goodbye. Darwin told Nikki he needed to use the bathroom before he got back on the road and of course, Darwin was drunker than Cutter-Brown as always. When Darwin came out the bathroom he didn't say goodbye to Nikki, he walked right passed her. Nikki said,

"Bye Darwin,"

As he was walking out the door; he turned to her and told her she was pissing her life away and if her Grandmother new what she was doing there, it would kill her. He told Nikki to use the money for school and nothing else or he would never forgive her for betraying her Grandmother. Nikki told Darwin she didn't ask for the money to begin with and how dare he judge her for living with Todd after the life he lead and that her Grandmother already knew about her life with Todd. Darwin said,

"Like hell she does,"

and walked out and slammed the door.

Todd and Teddy had excused themselves when Darwin got there and disappeared in the back yard. Todd came in after Darwin left and went to the bathroom and immediately called Teddy to come there. Nikki heard them arguing in the hall, so she went to see what the problem was. Todd was panicked when Nikki walked in the bathroom and asked what the hell was going on. Todd started apologizing to Nikki and swore it was the last time. Nikki looked at him stunned and asked,

"The last time for what?"

Todd asked Nikki, if she moved the towels and Nikki asked why the hell she would need to move the towels and Todd grabbed Teddy and asked if he was screwing with him. Teddy was a lot smaller than Todd and was assuring him he didn't touch anything and didn't know where Todd put the stuff, as Nikki asked,

"What stuff?"

Todd turned to her and tried to hug her, but Nikki pushed him off her and demanded to know what stuff. Todd told Nikki, he and teddy was going in the bathroom hitting themselves up and they hid the needle in the towels, but it was gone. Todd thought Nikki's Dad found it, but Nikki said,

"There was no way Darwin found that shit and left there without killing somebody."

Then, Nikki realized, what Darwin was saying to her and thought he might go home and tell her Grandmother she was strung out on drugs and Nikki became ferrous with Todd and told him to get his shit and get out. Todd told her he was sorry, but he wasn't leaving, he loved her and they were going to work it out. The more upset Nikki became, the more upset Todd became. Teddy went to the living room and sat down while Nikki and Todd were in a screaming match in the hall. Nikki said, if he wasn't leaving, she sure as hell was and started packing her things.

Todd was begging her not to leave and said he didn't feel right something was wrong. Nikki told him he was dam right something was wrong, she was getting the hell out, then Todd grabbed the dresser. As Nikki turned to him, he hit the floor. Nikki ran to Todd and screamed for Teddy. Teddy ran in the room as Todd started jerking in a grandmal seizure. He stopped breathing and then started foaming at the mouth; Nikki called 911 for assistance; then called Todd's parents. Mr. Bankston got there a few minutes after the ambulance.

When Todd started coming out of the seizure he screamed Nikki's name at the top of his lungs. Nikki went to him and told him everything was going to be all right, she was there. Todd was taken to the emergency room and his Dad asked Nikki what happened; due to the circumstances Nikki told him. Mr. Bankston was ferrous, but contained his emotions; Mrs. Bankston was ferrous and screamed at Nikki she should have gone to them before then and Nikki told her, she did tell Mr. Bankston and Todd lied to him, what else was she suppose to do. Todd's was positive for cocaine and they administered IV Valium to stop any further seizure activity. Todd was told by the emergency room physician the seizure was drug induced. He said if Todd wanted any quality of life, he had better not touch drugs again.

Todd promised Nikki, if she stayed, he wouldn't do drugs again and they would rebuild their life. Todd refused to answer any questions from his parents, so his Mom left the hospital angry and Mr. Bankston told Nikki, he would come to the house the next day for a heart to heart with Todd and he wanted her in the room with him for the conversation; when Nikki agreed, Todd's Dad left. Nikki returned to Todd's room and slept in the chair at his bedside. The next morning the doctors told Todd again why he had the seizure. He assured everyone, he learned his lesson and was going home to be a good boy, so he was released and Nikki drove him home.

Todd's Dad was waiting in the driveway when they got there. Todd turned to Nikki and told her, he didn't want to talk to his Dad about the situation, but Nikki told him, he no longer had a choice if he wanted their relationship. Todd got out the car and started walking towards his Dad's car. Mr. Bankston got out and told him, he was there for a talk and they needed to get a few things ironed out. Todd agreed, so they all three went inside.

The tension was thick as Nikki sat on the sofa; she decided to let Mr. Bankston do the talking. He asked Todd how bad the drug problem was. Once again, Todd denied it. Mr. Bankston looked to Nikki for answers. Nikki said times were difficult and she knew Todd had lied to her about how much he was using and even used in the house under her nose.

Nikki looked at Mr. Bankston and told him she too had used in the beginning and told Mr. Bankston about her trip on PCP. She said she was too afraid to use anymore and Todd had promised, he too would stop and they would put their life back on track. Nikki looked at Todd and told him he had to come clean and admit how bad things were. She reminded him of all the fights they had, because she had busted him using and he tried to lie his way out. Todd sat on the sofa with his head in his hands and admitted to his father that things had gotten way out of control, but said the last episode scared the shit out of him, just like what happened to Nikki and was certain it would not happen again. Mr. Bankston asked him if he needed help to stop using, but Todd said he could put it down and walk away.

Nikki asked him if he could put it down and walk away, why hadn't he done it by then. Todd told her it was hard, because his friends used. Nikki told him his new set of friends, not the old ones, because he didn't see them anymore. He stopped playing golf with Randy on the weekends and lied about being with Randy, because Randy would call for Todd during the time Todd was suppose to be with him.

Todd told Nikki he wanted to reconnect with his old friends and he would cut his ties to the ones he bought drugs from and begged her not to give up on him. Nikki told Todd she loved him, but she wanted a life and not one that included drugs to have fun, Todd agreed and his Dad left thinking things would be all right. Todd went to Nikki and asked if they could start putting their life back together, because he wanted that more than anything in the world. Todd kissed Nikki and picked her up and carried her to the bedroom to make love to her, but Nikki stopped him and told him he had to wear a condom, because she didn't fell safe at that point without one. Todd told her he never shared needles and was clean as a whistle, but Nikki refused to believe him and the conversation escalated into another fight, so Nikki left the bedroom.

A few weeks past and Todd's behavior didn't improve. Mr. Bankston called Nikki to check in, but Nikki told him if he wanted any more questions answered he needed to talk to Todd. The family dinners on the weekend were tense; Ms Bankston was so pissed at Todd she couldn't even look at him. She was cordial to Nikki, but Nikki knew the feelings weren't the same.

Todd started missing a lot of work, calling in a couple times a week and Nikki told him he was being careless and his partners would soon start to question his behavior. Todd told her he owned part of the dam company and it was his right to take off when he dam well pleased, so Nikki never brought it up again.

Nikki and Todd stopped seeing any friends or family for a period of time, of course Mr. Bankston checked in on occasion to make sure all was well. Nikki thought slowly, but surely they were rebuilding their life. Todd was putting back on the weight he lost and was looking pretty dam good, but Nikki still wouldn't sleep with him, until he consented to a HIV test. He completed the test, but Nikki told him they would have to use protection until six months passed and he tested clean again and Todd was ferrous, he told Nikki he wanted to feel her, not a piece of rubber between the two, he needed to feel her, but Nikki refused.

Todd came home from work the next day and Nikki knew he had used again. Nikki just looked at him and knew. Todd wanted to no how she could just no, but Nikki refused to talk to him. She told him he had to leave, but Todd told her, she would have to kill him to get rid of him. Nikki went to bed and locked the bedroom door so Todd had to sleep on the couch. When Nikki got up the next morning, she walked in the kitchen where Todd was making coffee. He said,

"Good-morning baby,"

and tried to hug Nikki from behind, but Nikki pushed him away. As Nikki was leaving the kitchen, Todd hit the floor with another seizure, Nikki called 911 again, and Mr. Bankston. When Todd's Dad got there, Nikki got in her car and went to work. Mr. Bankston called after her, but she turned and said she was threw with the shit and walked away. Todd came out of the seizure and refused to go to the hospital. He got in his bed and fell asleep. The EMS attendant told Mr. Bankston, Todd would sleep most of the day, but advised him to see a neurologist for possible medication to control the seizures. When Nikki got home, Mr. Bankston was watching TV in the living room. Todd heard her come in and went to talk to her and Nikki asked him if the night before was worth it. Todd told her it wasn't, but he was going out of his mind, because he wanted her so bad he couldn't breathe. Nikki told Todd the only way she was going to agree to stay was if he agreed to do drug screens for her on a regular basis for a while and if he tested dirty one time she was packing her things and moving out. Todd agreed to Nikki's conditions and Mr. Bankston thought Nikki was going to get a handle on the situation. Mr. Bankston told Nikki he loved her and he knew why Nikki wouldn't set the date, but he hoped all this would blow over soon and all their lives could get back to where it was. Nikki had tears in her eyes when she told Mr. Bankston she had hoped for the same and walked him to the door.

When she closed the door, she turned and saw Todd waiting for her. He said he couldn't stand not touching her and needed to feel her more than he needed to breathe. Nikki felt guilty and thought for a moment that maybe the reason he went out the night before and turned to drugs was, because of her own depravation she placed on him, so Nikki went to Todd and kissed him passionately. Todd embraced her and before Nikki could even think about saying no or wait, Todd picked her up in his arms and carried her to their bedroom. Todd never let his lips leave Nikki's as he pulled her cloths off. Nikki started to resist, because she wanted to still use a condom, but Todd was a different person at that moment and so strong, he over powered Nikki. The more she tried to pull away the tighter his grip became. Todd tore at Nikki's cloths and ripped her panties off and buried his tongue between her thighs. Nikki moaned with pleasure and then pulled herself up on the bed out of Todd's reach. Nikki reached in the drawer beside the bed for a condom, but Todd pulled her to him and entered her without it. Nikki was screaming for him to stop. The louder she screamed the louder Todd screamed with pleasure until he exploded inside Nikki and fell on top of her limp.

Todd realized what he had done, and tried to console Nikki, but she wanted no part of him. Nikki crawled out of bed and went to the bathroom. Todd tried to go in the bathroom, but Nikki locked the door. Todd screamed through the door he was sorry, but he couldn't wait for her anymore, he craved her, she consumed his mind and he had to have her. Todd sat on the floor outside the bathroom crying. Nikki opened the door and told him if he ever touched her like that again she would kill him and she meant it. Todd grabbed her and sobbed uncontrollably.

The next few weeks were the same, no emotions. Nikki was just a shell of a person. She didn't no what she was felling, but she knew she wasn't happy. She got up on a Saturday morning, cleaned house and took a bath and told

Todd she was going to the grocery store for groceries. Todd sat on the couch as if he was in a daze or something, so Nikki finished dressing and left for the store. Nikki walked the isles of the grocery store, picked out her items and went through the checkout line. When the cashier finished ringing up her groceries and gave Nikki her total, Nikki opened her wallet to get her money, but the money was gone. Nikki searched frantically, but it was gone. Nikki was totally embarrassed and told the cashier, she must have left her money on the kitchen table and would go get it and come right back.

Nikki left the store crying walking to her car. She told herself that was the last straw. When Nikki got home, Todd was on the phone with his Dad. Nikki asked who he was talking too and Todd told her he called his Dad. Nikki yelled

"Are you telling him what you did?"

Todd said

"Yes."

Nikki yelled

"I sure as hell hoped so,"

and yelled loud enough for him to hear that he had better come get his son, because one way or another he was leaving.

Nikki went in the bedroom and opened the balcony doors and started throwing Todd's things over the balcony. Todd went to the room and tried to stop her, but there she was no stopping her. Todd told her his father was on his way and he was so sorry for what he had done. Nikki asked him, how he could let her take a bath, get dressed and leave for the grocery store knowing he had taken her money. Todd said he was sorry again, but Nikki wanted to no why he needed the money and where it went. Todd admitted he bought snow with it, but snorted it instead of shooting it. Nikki screamed,

"Do you think it makes a difference how the hell you do it?"

Mr. Bankston pulled up and saw most of Todd's things on the lawn. He went in the house to try and talk to Nikki, but there was no more talking for her. Nikki told Mr. Bankston Todd had a serious problem and she was tired of dealing with it. She told him to take his son home with him and then he would get a taste of what life had been like for her. Mr. Bankston said maybe the two of them needed a break, but they seemed to really love each other and surely they could work it out. Nikki told Mr. Bankston that if Todd was in love with her and not the drugs they could have worked it out, but the only thing Todd was in-love with was the drugs and she wasn't sharing him with that any more. Nikki continued to through Todd's things over the balcony and Mr. Bankston went to the living room and told Todd to get in the yard and load his things in his truck. His Dad told him, he hoped all those highs were worth what he had probably lost and Nikki could hear Todd crying, but she kept throwing his stuff over the balcony until she had unloaded everything Todd had upstairs. Mr. Bankston and Todd was on the ground picking up and putting in the car as fast as they could with Todd crying and begging Nikki not to end their relationship, but Nikki wouldn't acknowledge him. When Nikki finished throwing his things out, she closed the doors, locked them and went downstairs.

Nikki was so angry with Todd, she couldn't see straight, but she refused to cry. The next morning Nikki called a realtor to put the house up for sale and started looking for an apartment on the other side of town. She changed the locks and had the phone number changed to an unpublished number, then moved into her own apartment the next weekend. When the house sold Nikki called Todd at his parent's to attend the closing. Todd refused thinking it would hold Nikki in the relationship or keep a tie, but Nikki told him she had already moved out of the house and it could rot as far as she was concerned. She said, if he didn't want his credit affected he would be at the closing, because that would be the last time he would see her.

The house was listed in both their names, so Nikki had already arranged for the profits from the house to be paid at closing in two checks, half to her and half to Todd. Todd showed up and signed the papers. Then he slid them across the table to Nikki and begged her not to sign. Nikki signed and handed the papers back to the attorney. The couple buying the house sat there stunned, because Todd actually cried during the closing. When the process was finished and the checks were disbursed, Nikki got up to leave with the couple; they walked out in front of her and Todd grabbed Nikki's arm to keep her in the room and said,

"Nikki please."

Nikki stood there; she didn't want more of a scene than there had been already. Todd told her he loved her and couldn't imagine his life without her. Nikki laughed and said,

"You mean you can't imagine your life without the blow."

Todd told her he was clean and would drug screen everyday for the rest of his life if that was what it took to keep her. Nikki told Todd she knew it wouldn't be one week, before he would test positive again. Nikki told him, he could have died when he had a seizure and yet he still did it again and again even after the second seizure. Todd told her he stopped shooting after the second seizure and never touched another needle again. Nikki said,

"Well praise God for something, now you just blow the piss out of it and I guess that is ok right?"

Todd told her if she would give him one more chance he would test everyday to prove he had been off the drugs and was staying off. He said all he wanted was; what he had with her and nothing would ever be more important to him than saving their relationship. Nikki asked how long had it been since he blew snow and Todd said he had not touched it since she threw him out three months ago. Nikki told Todd to swear on his life and Todd said,

"I swear on my life and the lives of our unborn children."

That sentence brought tears to Nikki's eyes and she said,

"OK Todd come with me."

Todd asked where they were going and Nikki said,

"To the nearest lab, if you test clean you got another chance if you test positive you'll never see me again."

Todd went willingly with Nikki to the hospital lab. The ER doctor wrote an order for the screen after Todd signed consents to release the information to Nikki. Todd went in the lab with the lab tech and gave his sample willingly. Nikki waited in the waiting area and thought,

"My God, maybe he is clean or he would have never agreed to come here and if he came, he surely wouldn't go through with the test."

Todd walked out with a smile on his face. The tech said the results would be ready in about an hour, so, Todd asked Nikki if she wanted to go get lunch and come back. Lunch was great, Nikki felt her love for Todd re-igniting in her heart and thought they would go home together that night and that night would be the first night of the rest of their lives.

In the restaurant Todd had signed the back of the check he got at closing and handed it to Nikki. He told her to deposit it, in her account and they would start looking for another dream home. Nikki took the check and put it in her purse. The hour was up, so it was time to head back to the lab.

When they returned, Todd had to give his code for the results and they were asked to wait in a small room by the emergency room. The doctor that wrote the order came in and sat down. He looked at Todd and asked if there was anything he would like to say before he talked about the results. Todd said no, so the ER doctor asked Todd to consent to a blood test. Nikki was confused; supposedly, Todd was too. Todd asked why he needed a blood test, was there something wrong with the urine results. The doctor looked at Todd and told him the tests were based on numbers and he had reason to believe that Todd had used a substance in the last twelve hours to clear his urinary tract of any residual drugs. Todd laughed when Nikki stared at him and said,

"You're joking right!"

The doctor told Todd, it wasn't a joking matter. That certain substances should have been present in the urine sample and they weren't, so a simple blood test would clear the whole matter up. Nikki looked at Todd and told him to give the sample and stop wasting time. Todd took Nikki's hand with tears in his eyes and said he couldn't. Nikki was blown away again, she looked at him and asked if he had taken something to flush his system and he admitted he had. Nikki was ferrous and pulled away. Todd started begging Nikki to give him another chance and he would test clean and stay clean she would see. Nikki reached in her purse and pulled out the check he sighed and threw it at him. She told him to blow that up his nose, in his arm; it didn't matter and stormed out. Todd ran after her, but Nikki requested security to help her to her car. She drove away and swore she would never believe another man again, especially if he said he loved her, because he would be a dam lie, if his lips were moving, he would be lying.

As Nikki hit the gas another vision hit her. Nikki saw Todd in a hospital bed and he looked so bad. There were machines all around him and his mother was at his bedside. Todd was dyeing; Nikki snapped out of it again, she didn't want to see. She knew all along that's why she refused to sleep with Todd, because she was terrified of contracting HIV. She knew the vision would become a certainty in Todd life and also knew she couldn't change or stop what was coming. She was ferrous she was given the information. She couldn't understand if she couldn't stop or change the bad things she saw; what was the point in knowing. She didn't want to know anymore, she just wanted to be left alone.

CHAPTER 14

Nikki went home to find a way to rebuild her life on her own. Once again, she was alone, no family, no friends, and no life partner. Nikki was scared, but refused to show it, lonely, but denied it, angry, but refused to feel it. She absolutely refused to morn for Todd. She was determined there would be no looking back.

In the apartment complex where Nikki lived she met her two neighbors. Debbie lived across from her and Laura beside her. Laura had three kids and Nikki would bring home candy to pass out to the kids almost everyday and she and Laura became pretty close friends. Laura was struggling raising her kids and Nikki was always alone, so she offered to get a bigger apartment and split the bills with Laura. Nikki was content to go home and have Laura and the kids there. Nikki played with the kids and took them swimming in the pool. Laura stayed up half the night and slept half the day. She had a government check coming in for support of the two boys and didn't have any ambition to go climb a corporate ladder.

Laura used Nikki's second car and stayed in the roads as much as she could. One night Nikki got home from work at midnight and found the two boys sleeping in bed and the little girl sleeping on the floor in the hall. Laura was nowhere to be found. Nikki put Amy to bed and waited for Laura. Nikki was ferrous when Laura got home and told Nikki it was none of her business how she raised her kids. She said she knew they were ok, because she put them to bed before she left. Nikki told Laura that Amy crawled out of bed and was sleeping on the floor in the hall and God only knew what she could have gotten into.

Laura told Nikki, she was moving in with Willis, Amy's Dad; they were going to try and make a life together. Nikki told her that was fine with her and she helped Laura pack her things and move to Willis's house. Nikki didn't talk to Laura much for a few months, but did maintain the contact, mainly because Nikki didn't have many friends and wanted some sort of companionship more than anything else. Nikki also, spent a lot of time with Debbie and moved back into her smaller apartment across the way from Debbie. Debbie and Nikki shared the cooking duties, laid out by the pool together and played tennis in the park next door to the apartment complex. Nikki enjoyed her friendship with Debbie, because she was alone most of the time too, because her husband's job required him to travel all the time. If CeCe was home four days a month it was a miracle.

Nikki had some meaningful talks with Debbie about her life and enjoyed the companionship. Debbie too, was unfaithful to her husband every chance she got. Nikki watched man after man come and go across the walkway and couldn't imagine how or why Debbie stayed married to CeCe. Debbie didn't work and enjoyed the freedom she had with her husband gone. She told Nikki about CeCe's infidelities before they left their hometown and how they owned their own grocery store and the girl CeCe was seeing robbed them blind and caused them to file bankruptcy. They lost everything. Debbie said she was too embarrassed to stay there in her hometown and too pissed at CeCe for putting his trust in that girl and blindly sacrificed their life and their relationship.

They moved to Louisiana to make a new start and CeCe had to travel with the job he found. Debbie realized she wasn't in-love with her husband anymore, but wouldn't divorce him because of their son Devin. Nikki asked how she lived with the infidelities, so Debbie told her, she told CeCe what she was doing and knew he did the same on the road. Nikki thought that kind of relationship sucked, but she didn't end her friendship with Debbie.

Laura visited from time to time and they hung out by the pool or cooked dinner and let the kids play. Debbie wouldn't come over when Laura was there, because she didn't like Laura and told Nikki the girl was trouble and would wind up dragging her down, but Nikki didn't listen. Then, Laura showed up one morning about three bagging on the door. When Nikki answered, Laura was standing there covered in bruises from head to toe. She was crying and told Nikki that Willis beat her, because he thought she was unfaithful.

Laura asked Nikki to help her get her things the next day and Nikki agreed to go later that day before Willis got home from work to get Laura's things. Nikki went to bed and Laura fell asleep on the couch. Laura told

Nikki the kids were staying with her mother for a little while so she could find a job and get on her feet. Nikki was relieved because she really didn't have room in her one bedroom apartment for three kids and another adult.

That morning about eleven Nikki got dressed and took Laura to Willis's house to collect her things, but Laura's things were gone. Nikki took Laura back to the apartment and headed for work. When Nikki got home that night Laura was waiting. She took Nikki to a storage and told Nikki a friend told her that Willis had put her things in storage. Nikki saw the lock on the shed and asked Laura if she had a key, but she didn't. Laura tried to pick the lock with a bobby pin and after fifteen minutes Nikki looked in the trunk of her car, took out a crowbar and broke the lock.

The storage shed was packed from top to bottom with all kinds of things: TV's stereos, cloths, dishes, and boxes. Nikki told Laura to get her cloths so they could get out of there before someone, namely Willis showed up. Laura went through boxes and pulled out her cloths while Nikki loaded them in the car. Laura said she knew Nikki collected wine glasses and she had gotten Nikki some as a surprise. She said the glasses were from Germany and was searching for the box she had put them in when Nikki asked her when she packed the glasses. Laura told her that everything she had was in that storage so she knew they had to be there too, and opened the box that had the glasses in it.

Laura pulled out one of the glasses and Nikki had to admit they were unusual and beautiful as well. Nikki asked where she had gotten the glasses and Laura said they came from her Aunt that visited from Germany. Nikki asked her if she was sure she wanted to give the glasses to her, because they could be a family air-loom, but Laura insisted Nikki take the glasses for her trouble. She really wanted Nikki to have them in-addition to saying she really didn't care for the glasses. Nikki laughed and said,

"Well, since you put it that way. I guess I'll take the glasses."

Laura knew she would and handed the glasses to Nikki and asked if she was ready to go, so they loaded the boxes sitting by the car and headed back to Nikki's apartment.

A few days later Laura packed her things, called Willis and left without saying goodbye. Nikki wasn't upset that Laura left without saying goodbye. She was too relieved that the situation was over. Nikki wanted more out of life, but wasn't sure how to get it, but didn't think she was smart enough to make it better. She felt like she was stuck to a degree, but she knew one day she would find a way to complete something.

A few weeks later the phone rang at two O'clock in the morning, Laura was on the other end screaming that Willis was dead. Nikki asked her what happened, but Laura was too frantic to speak. Nikki was still half a sleep and really didn't care if Willis was dead or alive, but she tried to calm Laura down. Laura told Nikki that Willis had gotten the flu and was running a high fever. He wanted to go to work the next day and told Laura to go get him something that would help him sleep and relieve the flu symptoms, so Laura went the drug store and got Nyquil. Willis told Laura to take the kids and go to her mothers, because he was going to take the medicine and turn up the heater in the waterbed and see if he could sweat the fever off.

Willis aggravated the situation with the heat and taking so much cold medicine it knocked him out. His fever rose in his sleep, causing a seizure that caused his death. Willis was twenty-nine years old. It was a tragedy, but not one for Nikki, that was until the police arrived.

When Laura called Willis in the middle of the night; he didn't answer the phone, so Laura went to the house to check on him. She called the emergency system for assistance. When the ambulance arrived they pronounced Willis at the scene and told Laura the corner would have to come to the scene to investigate. The police got there and was standing around with nothing to do and an officer noticed some items in the house fit a description of some items that had recently been reported stolen. When they asked Laura about the items, she said they were Willis's and he had bought them from a guy in the neighborhood. The police told Laura they had reason to believe that certain items in the house were stolen and asked her permission to search the house and verify ownership of the items in question or they would call for a search warrant and take her down town. Laura told the cops to search and take what they wanted.

In the search the police found the German dishes and questioned Laura about the remainder of the dishes. Laura told them she had given the wine glasses to Nikki. Then, of course they wanted to talk to Nikki. Nikki got on the phone with the officer to answer his questions, but he wanted Nikki's address to question her in person. Nikki gave her address and got out of bed, got dressed and called Debbie across the hall to tell her what was going on. She said she couldn't imagine why the cops wanted to talk to her, but Debbie told her she was getting dressed and coming over. Debbie didn't think it would be a good idea for Nikki to be alone when they got there. Debbie started to say she told Nikki to stay away from

Laura; she was trouble, but Nikki told her it wasn't time for a lecture and she just wanted to get though the officer's questions.

Debbie got to Nikki's and a few minutes later the knock at the door startled both Nikki and Debbie. Nikki let two plain cloths officers in and they asked Nikki how she had gotten the glasses. She told them about the night Laura and Willis had gotten into their fight and she went with Laura to a storage where Willis had taken Laura's things. Nikki said Laura pulled the box of glasses out and said her Aunt from Germany gave her the glasses. She said Laura told her, she didn't like them and since she knew Nikki collected wine glasses she could have them, so she took them. The officer asked Nikki how they got in the storage if Willis took Laura's things there. She said Laura didn't have a key that Laura had tried to pick the lock and when that didn't work, Nikki pulled a crowbar from her trunk and broke the lock to get Laura's things.

The officer asked Nikki if she remembered where the storage was and what else she saw in the storage. Nikki said she did and she had seen TV's and stereos with boxes. The officer yelled,

"TV's, stereos and boxes and you never question how Willis got all those things!"

Nikki said she didn't know much about Willis and what she did know about him was enough to know she didn't want to know anymore. The officer told Nikki she would need to take them to the storage and show them where she broke the locked. Nikki said she would, but Debbie told her she didn't think Nikki should go. She asked her to wait and call an attorney and let the attorney handle it, but Nikki said she hadn't done anything wrong, so she would take them to the storage and be done with it. Debbie told her she was ridding with her, but the officer told Debbie she could follow, but Nikki would be riding with them. Nikki got her coat and headed to the door.

When they arrived at the storage, Nikki showed them the storage where she helped Laura get her things. There was another lock on the door, so the officer called in a request for a search warrant with the probability of recovering stolen items. They waited an hour before another officer and team showed up with the search warrant and called the owner to come down to the facility. They broke the lock and open the door. Sure enough, the items in the storage were stolen and the serial numbers matched the ones reported stolen. Nikki was standing at the police officers car when he came back. She asked if they found what they thought they would and he told Nikki they had recovered stolen items in the storage and started reading Nikki her rights. Debbie was screaming,

"What are you arresting her for?"

Nikki was sick to her stomach and couldn't breathe. The officer told Nikki she was being booked for breaking and entering, felony theft and possession of stolen goods.

Nikki was taken downtown, fingerprinted, photographed and placed behind bars. Debbie called a bell bondsman to help get Nikki out of jail, but didn't have five hundred dollars to pay him to get Nikki out. Laura was booked and charged with the same charges as Nikki. Laura tried to tell Nikki how sorry she was. She said she didn't know what Willis had been doing and had no idea where he got his stuff. Nikki reminded Laura that she had told her the glasses came from her Aunt. Laura said it was Willis's Aunt. Nikki screamed,

"You told me it was your Aunt!"

Nikki said for her to just get away from her and leave her alone; she didn't want anything more to do with her. All Nikki wanted was her freedom and to figure a way out of the mess she found herself in. Then, about four in the morning a girl was booked for fighting with her man. When she got to the cell she was drunker than Cudder-Brown. She spotted Nikki right away and walked over to her and asked her what the hell a fine thing like her was doing there. Nikki said she was in the wrong place at the wrong time and the girl sat beside Nikki and asked her if she thought she was too good to be in jail with her pretty blond hair and flawless skin and started touching Nikki's face. Nikki pushed her away and told her to leave her alone and the girl bowed up and told Nikki she would mop her little white ass all over the floor if she didn't give her what she wanted and she wanted Nikki's companionship. Nikki looked at her and told her she would have to wipe her little ass all over the floor before that would ever happen and the girl reached for Nikki as Laura jumped in and stopped her. The two of them tied into a fight in the middle of the cell. The girl screamed she was going to fuck Laura up and then she was going to fuck up her friends' pretty face too. The cops rushed in and took the girl to the solitary confinement for the night. Laura's nose was bleeding and she had some scratches on her face, but Nikki just turned her face to the wall and laid back down on the cold cement slab. The next morning Nikki called Lucas, her old boss she had an affair with for help, because she didn't know where else to turn. Lucas told her not to worry; he would be there in less than an hour.

Nikki was placed back in the cell after her phone call. She tried hard not to panic, but it took every ounce of her being to stay calm. Her heart was beating out of her chest and she thought she would never have her freedom again. She also knew she was facing felony charges that if convicted, she could serve years in prison. Nikki thought she would kill herself before she would go behind bars again or serve time for something she didn't do. The Desk Clerk passed the cell doors and told the ladies anyone not bailed out by ten o'clock that morning was going to be shipped to parish prison. One of the girls started screaming, she would be killed if she went back and the officer told her she should've thought about that before she did what she did to get her there in the first place. The girl went to the corner and sobbed uncontrollably as the other ladies were throwing toilet paper at her and screaming to shut up, but she couldn't contain her emotions. Nikki realized real quick what parish prison must be like. She was a tiny girl, Nikki thought; if Lucas didn't come through for her, her life too would probably be over.

Nikki looked up when the doors to the cell opened and the girl from the night before walked back in. Laura was sleeping and Nikki thought,

"Oh well, I might not even make it to parish prison, because if this girl sits on me, my life is over here and now."

The girl came through the door laughing. She asked what honky she wanted a piece of last night and of course the rest of the girls quickly pointed Nikki out. When Nikki and her eyes met, the girl burst out laughing and went over to Nikki and sat beside her. She said,

"The police officer told me, I did all kinds of things last night when I came in and told me I beat the shit out your friend too."

Nikki said,

"Yea, you were pretty loaded last night and yea I think you hurt my friend pretty bad."

The girl grabbed Nikki, hugged her tight, and said,

"My old man gave me some really bad shit and fucked me all up."

She didn't even remember her name laughing with every-word. She said her man fucked her mind up, so she fucked him up with a knife and he would think twice, before he fucked again, if he did.

Nikki said,

"Yea, men can fuck your head all up, if you let them."

The woman told Nikki she was a pretty white girl and if they had to go to parish prison she would look out for her. Nikki thanked her, but prayed she got out before then. The girl said yea what ever works and asked if anyone had a cigarette and a girl on the other side of the cell gave her a one, so the woman stood at the door and smoked.

The desk officer was mean as a snake and seemed to get off on tormenting the woman about being shipped to parish prison. She kept giving them the countdown to when they would be transferred, if they didn't bond out. Of course ten O'clock came and she took great pleasure in getting the women to line up outside the cell to prepare them for transport. They were lined up outside the office in central booking and an officer opened the door to go into the locked down area. Nikki saw Lucas standing beside the window and screamed for him to find Debbie she was out there in the waiting area somewhere. The desk officer had a fit and told Nikki she could not speak to anyone on the outside; it was against policy and the rules. Nikki said it might be their rules, but not hers. The officer got in Nikki's face and told her, she was being shipped to parish prison and she would know what hell was when she got there and promised she would see to it. The transport van pulled around and the double doors opened. The desk officer said it was time to load and pushed the girl in front of the line towards the van. The girl stumbled, but caught herself and started the precession toward the van. The officer sitting in the window where Lucas was standing opened the door and said

"Nikki Breaux is bonding out."

The desk officer said Nikki Breaux hasn't bonded out yet and she was transferring her to parish. The front desk officer told her Nikki Breaux was not going anywhere they were processing her release as they spoke. The desk officer walked over to Nikki and told her she got lucky that time, but she couldn't wait to see her again. Nikki told her to go fuck herself and dared her to hit her.

Nikki was released after the paperwork process was completed. She walked through the doors to freedom with Debbie and Lucas sitting on the other side waiting. Lucas asked Nikki what happened and Nikki told him what she knew at that point. Debbie was still spitting bullets over the whole mess and couldn't believe they even arrested Nikki. Lucas told Nikki she was going to need a really good attorney and he would help her get one. Nikki said she would be appointed a lawyer by the courts, but Lucas wouldn't hear of it. He said the surest way for Nikki to wind up serving time would be to show up with a public defender that was too eager to bargain and go eat lunch.

All Nikki could think about was going home and taking a bath. Lucas hugged her bye and told her he was going to make some calls. He made

Nikki promise to call him the next day by noon. Nikki agreed and thanked him for coming to her rescue and promised to pay back every penny. Lucas told Nikki not to worry about a thing, because she had no dept to him.

Nikki went home and showered while Debbie cooked Nikki something to eat, but Nikki said she couldn't eat. Debbie told her to sit her butt down at the table and eat, so she did. The next day Nikki called Lucas. He had already located an attorney that said the charges were bogus and said he could get them dropped. Nikki went to see the attorney and asked what his fee would be to take the case. He said, his fees were paid in full and was given instructions not to discuss fees with Nikki. Nikki told the attorney she really needed to pay her own bill and if he didn't quote her his fee, she would seek counseling elsewhere and he would need to give Lucas his money back. The attorney gave Nikki his fee promptly of a thousand dollars if the case never went to court. She asked if she could give him half that day and the rest in a couple weeks; he agreed.

Nikki wouldn't speak to Laura, mainly because she didn't have anything to say to her, but also under advice of council. All the charges against Nikki were dismissed before her court date. Nikki called and thanked Lucas again for his help. She sent a check to his job, for the money he put out, to get her out of jail, but Lucas sent the check back torn-up with a note that said,

"Friends for life and I'll always be here for you, know questions asked, ever."

CHAPTER 15

Nikki wanted to reconnect with some old friends, so she called Jamie and Brenda. When Nikki was with Todd she and Brenda had a close friendship, so she wanted to see if the friendship was just because of her relationship with Todd or if they really bonded like Nikki thought. Brenda was all too excited to hear from Nikki. Jamie welcomed Nikki back into their lives with open arms as well. Brenda said she had so much to tell Nikki she didn't know where to start. Jamie still worked at the company as an engineer and told Nikki the partners bought Todd out at his request. She said Todd found out he was HIV positive and wasted the money on drugs and refused to get out of the whole he dug for himself. Brenda said Todd also stole his Mothers checkbook and wrote checks all over town to support his habit. Nikki was sorry, but thought Todd's Mom had held Nikki responsible for Todd's drug habit and thought since she wasn't around to blame anymore; she wondered who she wanted to put it off on then. Brenda said she wasn't putting it off on anyone anymore, because the entire family cut Todd off after settling the debt for the checks he wrote.

Brenda was strange or gave Nikki a strange feeling when she was around her. Nikki thought it was just that it had been a long time since she spent time with her, but she didn't remember Brenda being so dramatic. Nikki worked days and spent most of her evenings with Debbie or either Jamie and Brenda. She moved to another apartment, down the street from the complex she lived in, because her neighbors stared at her when she passed and Nikki was embarrassed, because her neighbors had seen her escorted out by the police. She still waitressed, but searched for something more from time to time, but nothing else seem to pan out. Nikki went back to work at Dana's Shoe store and somehow felt better selling shoes.

Jamie and Brenda had problems of their own, just like when Nikki was with Todd, but then Brenda didn't want to appear vulnerable in-front of Nikki, so she wouldn't talk about their problems, except for the subject of Jamie's ex-wife Zema. Brenda hated Zema with a passion. Jamie and Zema were married for four years and out the blue, Jamie got home after work and found Zema's bags packed and waiting. She told Jamie, she wasn't in-love with him anymore, was leaving, and she wasn't taking Tiffany their two-year-old daughter. Zema walked out and never returned not even for a visit. Nikki knew the story when she was with Todd and knew Jamie was heart-broken when Brenda moved in with her son and got pregnant right away. Jamie married Brenda to do the right thing and a year later, came another pregnancy. Brenda didn't work; she stayed home to take care of the kids, while Jamie worked.

Zema had returned to fight for visitation rights to see her daughter. Brenda however, was just as determine to keep Zema away. Brenda told Nikki that Zema was strung out on drugs, had sex parties, just name it; Zema did it. Zema was supposedly busted for drugs over and over again and screwed the district attorney to get the charges dropped. She said Zema was in with drug people that had shootouts with guns and Brenda would die, before she saw Tiffany go into that kind of situation. Nikki told her, she agreed with her, but she had to calm down over the situation or she would give herself a heart attack. Brenda said Zema had threatened Nikki, because she knew Nikki was friends with Brenda. Nikki was appalled and started to hate Zema too, based on what she was told. Then Brenda had her confidant back again, because she and Nikki would sit around bashing Zema.

One weekend, when Nikki and Brenda were out shopping, Brenda wanted to go back to Nikki's apartment and have lunch. It was a girl's day out, as they called it, which meant Jamie had the kids and Brenda and Nikki ran the roads that day either shopping, going to see a movie or dinner out. When they got to Nikki's apartment the door looked like someone had broken in. Brenda was bold and didn't show one sign of fear. Nikki on the other hand was terrified. They entered slowly and searched everywhere, but nothing looked disturbed and no one seemed to be in the apartment, so they both relaxed and thought it was a figment of their imagination. Nikki took her bags in the bedroom and put them on the bed when Todd came out from behind the bedroom door and closed himself and Nikki in the room. Nikki screamed and Brenda ran down the hall to get to Nikki. Brenda heard Todd tell Nikki if he couldn't have her no one else was going to have her either. Brenda screamed through the door she was calling the cops if he didn't open the door. Nikki told him to open the door and they could talk. Todd opened the door and told Brenda she needed to leave that it was between him and Nikki. Nikki tried to run out the room, but he grabbed her and told her she wasn't going anywhere as he fell on the bed with Nikki in his arms. The next thing Nikki knew, Brenda had pulled a forty-four from her purse and stuck it in Todd's face. Todd let Nikki go and she jumped up and called Jamie to come over to her apartment and get Todd. While Nikki was on the phone with Jamie Brenda was backing Todd down the hall. Todd was thinking about taking the gun from Brenda and evidently Brenda knew what he was thinking and said,

"Go a-head, make my day."

Brenda backed Todd out the apartment and told him if he came back, she would shoot him or he would go to jail. Jamie wanted to talk to Brenda, so Nikki gave her the phone. Jamie asked her if she had lost her mind and who the hell did she think she was, Clint Eastwood with that statement. Brenda told Jamie she wasn't going to stand by and watch Todd hurt Nikki, so she pulled the gun and it had gotten him off Nikki and out the apartment. Jamie said for Nikki to pack a few things and for both them to get their butt's to the house.

Nikki stayed with Jamie and Brenda's a few days and asked Jamie if he would help her move. Nikki found another apartment and got settled in, but she never felt secure alone again. The shadows in the apartment seemed to move. Every noise made Nikki think someone was in the apartment with her and she started sleeping on the floor with her pillow at the front door, so if anyone opened the door she would no or if she needed to get out she would be by the door.

Brenda's stories of Zema continued to grow and she kept telling Nikki that Zema wanted to kick her ass, just for the sake of kicking it. One night while Brenda was cooking, Nikki asked Jamie what kind of person Zema was and wanted to no why she was the object of Zema being so upset. Jamie asked her why she thought she was the object of Zema's anger and Nikki told Jamie all the threats Brenda had told her. Jamie knew Nikki was already scared out her mind after what happened with Todd and knew she was sleeping on the floor in-front of the door except the nights she slept at his house, so he said, Nikki under his breath, so Brenda couldn't hear, that he never heard Zema say anything about her, and as far as he knew, Zema didn't even no who Nikki was. Nikki asked Jamie why Brenda would tell her those things about Zema if they weren't true and Jamie said Brenda was obsessively jealous of Zema, because she knew, he never really got over her and when she came back in the picture it was more than Brenda could handle.

Nikki changed the subject when Brenda brought up Zema, but that didn't last. Brenda said Zema was out looking for Nikki, or she was going to send a friend of hers to pay Nikki a visit so Nikki asked where Zema lived. Brenda told her, but told her to stay away from that part of town, because she didn't want her to get hurt. Nikki on the other hand had enough and was going to pay Zema a visit. Brenda was frantic and told Nikki if she went there, she wouldn't come out alive, but that wasn't stopping Nikki. She drove to Zema's house and knocked on the door. When Zema opened the door, Nikki told her if she wanted a piece of her ass to walk out in the street and take it.

Zema stood there for a minute then asked her, who she was.

Nikki said,

"The friend of Brenda's that you've been threatening for the last six months."

Zema laughed and asked Nikki inside for a drink and conversation. Nikki accepted and they shared a bottle of wine and talked for hours. They hit it off as if; they had been friends all their life. There were very few people in this world that Nikki hit it off with from the start and Zema was one of them.

When Nikki got home that night she had a message on her answering machine from Brenda saying if she really did go to Zema's, not to ever call her again. Nikki wanted to get to the bottom of why Brenda felt the need to involve her, when she wasn't part of any of it, but Brenda wouldn't take her calls. Nikki waited the next day to make sure Jamie was at work and thought Brenda would be more inclined to talk about the situation if Jamie wasn't around. When Nikki knocked on the door, Brenda opened it and told Nikki to wait out front, she was going to get her cigarettes and they could talk outside, because she had just put the kids down for a nap. Nikki went to her car to get her cigarettes and lit one waiting for Brenda. The next thing Nikki knew, she saw four cop cars pull up with screeching tires and guns pulled, telling her to step away from the car with her hands in the air. Nikki asked what the hell was going on and an officer said, they received a call from the lady of the house that told them, someone was at her door with a gun and she needed immediate assistance. Nikki started laughing and told the officer he must be joking. The cop assured Nikki it was no joking matter and sent his partner to the door. When Brenda came out she said Nikki came to the door with a gun in her hand. The cop asked if he could search Nikki's car and she gave him permission. It was clean, so the officer asked Nikki what the problem was. She told him the story about Zema and said she wanted to talk to Brenda about the situation and see if they could iron things out, but she could see that Brenda needed more help than she could offer.

The cop told Brenda she had better be real careful about falsifying police reports, because that was a felony offense and next time she called the station and said there was a person at her door with a gun and they were waiting for her in the front yard, there had better be someone with a gun. Brenda went inside and closed the door. The officer walked Nikki back to her car and told her it would probably be best if she wrote that friendship off and Nikki told him not to worry after that day it was written off. That night Jamie called Nikki at home and asked her what the hell she was trying to do. Nikki asked him what the hell he meant, so Jamie said,

"You scared the hell out of Brenda coming here with bullet holes in your car, she thought you were strung out on drugs and had to call the cops to get you to leave. Why would you do this?"

Nikki told Jamie his wife version was ludicrous, there were no dam bullet holes in her car and she would be happy to meet him anywhere to prove it, she wasn't on drugs and would piss in a cup to prove that too. She told Jamie what Brenda did and what the police officer told her. She also gave him the phone number of the police officer that responded to the call to verify what he told Brenda. Nikki then told Jamie his wife had some serious issues and it was way beyond anything he could imagine. Jamie told her he was sorry for the call and wished Nikki well. Nikki told him she wished him well, because at that point, he needed it more than she did and hung up the phone.

Nikki lived in her one bedroom apartment still sleeping at the door with her pillow and blanket. There were very few people she socialized with and she spent most of her time alone. She had lost her friendship with Brenda and Jamie and would never know the real answers or reasons behind, why Brenda said the things she did and wanted or tried to involve Nikki the way she had. Nikki thought Brenda was too jealous of Zema and wanted someone to share in that jealously with her, but Nikki had no reason to be jealous of Zema. Nikki guessed Brenda made up everything, just to make her hate someone she didn't know hoping Nikki would sit around bashing Zema too. It just didn't turn out that way.

Zema called Nikki to tell her, it was her birthday, and said Rick her boyfriend was taking her out on the town for drinks and a good time. She invited Nikki to tag along because Zema wanted to introduce Nikki to her friends. Nikki was excited about a night out with the possibility of starting a new friendship. She really liked Zema, so she put on her blue jeans, fixed her hair and out the door she went.

Nikki met Rick and Zema at the club that night; when she got there they were already playing pool. There was a small group of people with them, so Zema introduced Nikki as,

"Her new best friend in the world."

Nikki laughed and ordered a drink. They played pool half the night while Nikki drank with Zema toasting with shots and mixing alcohol. Zema couldn't hold her liquor quite as well as Nikki, so she got sick and started crying. Rick was upset; because it spoiled their night and all Zema could do was cry and through up. Nikki took her to the bathroom to help her clean up and washed her face with paper-towels from the basin. Zema hugged Nikki, kissed her on the cheek, and asked her not to leave her. She told Nikki she thought she had known her all her life and wanted their friendship to grow. Nikki hugged her and said, she wouldn't leave her and their friendship would grow. Nikki helped Zema out the bathroom and Rick was waiting to take her home. He asked Nikki to follow and help get Zema to bed. He told Nikki, Zema had taken X and knew she shouldn't drink on it. Nikki asked,

"What's X?"

Rick laughed and said,

"Boy you really have been out of circulation for a while haven't you?"

Nikki said,

"Yea, I guess I have, so what's X."

Rick laughed even louder and said,

"A drug that makes you feel better than you ever imagined you could, everything feels perfect and everything is totally erotic, you can have an orgasm from thoughts and never be touched."

Nikki laughed and said,

"An orgasm from thoughts and never be touched, I really need some of that shit."

Rick laughed and asked Nikki to help him get Zema to the car. She followed Rick to their house and helped get Zema out the car. Zema vomited all over Nikki when she stood up to walk in the house and almost fell on top of Nikki. Rick was upset screaming at Zema, telling her he had told her not to drink; she didn't need any alcohol. Zema was crying again, so Nikki told Rick to help her get Zema to the bathroom, so she could clean her up and clean herself up too. Rick picked Zema up, took her to the bathroom and sat her in the tub. He asked if she needed him to do anything else and Nikki told him she could handle it from there, but asked if Zema had some jogging pants and a T-shirt she could borrow so she could take a shower and clean up too. Rick told her, he was going to the kitchen to fix a drink for the both of them and he would get Nikki something to wear when she got Zema settled.

Nikki helped Zema out of her cloths and rinsed her off. Zema cried most of the time when she wasn't in a semi-unconscious state. She took her to bed and tucked her in. Zema pulled Nikki down on the bed with her and hugged her. Nikki told her she was going to take a shower, but she would be back to check on her as soon as she got cleaned up. Rick met Nikki in the hall and handed her a drink. He said bottoms up girlfriend and asked how Zema was. Nikki said she was resting and would probably be asleep by the time she finished her shower. Rick told Nikki she could put on the robe in the bathroom and he would look for some cloths while she showered. Nikki went to the bathroom, took off her cloths and downed her drink. She let the hot water run on her face and trickle down her back. The water felt different, it was alive and refreshing. Nikki soaped her body up, just as she had done a million times before, but this time it felt funny, strange, it almost tingled as well. She got out the shower and put the robe on and went to the living room where Rick had a fire going in the fireplace. The fire memorized Nikki. It was so bright, so warm; the popping sounds made Nikki's skin tingle.

Rick asked if she had finished the drink he brought her. Nikki had almost forgotten about the drink, the room was strange, funny, warm and erotic all at the same time. Nikki handed Rick the empty glass and said,

"One more of those please."

Rick took her glass and laughed as he headed toward the kitchen. Nikki went to the fire place, she couldn't take her eyes off the fire from the moment she entered the room, even when Rick asked her questions she stared at the fire when she responded. She was standing in front of the fireplace when she felt Rick from behind. He had embraced her and kissed her on the neck. Nikki wanted to say,

"Stop!"

But, the feeling was so intense. Rick kissed her and ran his tongue down her neck and down her back as he pulled the robe from her body.

Nikki felt the warmth from the fire on her body. It seemed as if her skin was on fire and every touch from Rick made her body scream with desire. Rick was tender, yet aggressive, he lead Nikki into a night of ecstasy before she knew what hit her. She woke up thinking she had a wet dream, but was sleeping in front of the fireplace, wrapped in a blanket. Nikki jumped up and thought,

"How could she have let something like that happen? My God, Zema was in the bedroom passed out, this would surely be the end of their friendship; dead before it could even begin."

Nikki wanted to leave before she saw Zema, because she didn't no how she could face her. She scrambled to the bathroom in search of her cloths. While she was dressing, Zema went in the bathroom and hugged her. She told her what a great person she was for taking care of her and could never thank her enough and said she was excited they had found each other. Zema said she missed her friendships with females and desperately needed that in her life. Nikki had tears in her eyes, when she told Zema she needed it way more that she did, but she wasn't that great of a person. Zema laughed and said,

"Cut the shit, you're great."

Zema said she was dazed and it took her a few minutes to get back in reality the morning after X. Then she looked at Nikki and asked her how she liked it. Nikki was speechless, but asked,

"How she liked what?

Zema said,

"X, how did you like the X? Rick told me he gave you some with your drink last night and you looked pretty happy staring at the fire place when you passed out."

Nikki said,

"Was that, what I was feeling?"

Zema laughed even louder and told Nikki to take off those smelly cloths she had something she could put on, then for her to come to the kitchen so she could fix her a huge breakfast. Nikki asked where Rick was that morning and Zema said he left early to meet a friend, but would be back later that day, so they had the morning to spend together for just girl talk. Nikki followed Zema to the bedroom and put on a pair of Zema's jogging pants and a T-Shirt. Zema fixed breakfast while Nikki smoked a cigarette outside. She thought she should tell Zema what she did, but she didn't want to hurt her and she didn't want to loose her friendship either. Nikki went in the house when Zema called her for breakfast. She ate slowly thinking about the night before wondering if she sent Rick clues or any signs she wanted him. Did she smile too much; did she laugh too much at his jokes, what did she do. She thought she had to have done something or what happened would have never happened, it was her fault, but how was she going to handle it.

Rick walked in the door just as Nikki decided it was time to tell Zema what happened. Nikki's eyes met Rick's and he smiled warmly at her. Nikki told Zema she had to go and would call her later to see what was going on. Nikki walked to her car and Zema followed her out and hugged Nikki and told her their friendship had just begun and if she needed anything at all anytime to call her. Nikki hugged her back squeezing Zema tight. Zema laughed, pulled back and told Nikki she didn't have to go, but Nikki told her she had too. As Nikki pulled away, she watched Zema in her rear view mirror and thought she would never see her again.

CHAPTER 16

When Nikki got home she cleaned her apartment and was gathering her cloths to wash when there was a knock at the door. When she answered, Rick was standing there and asked if he could have five minutes of her time. Rick sat on the sofa and said he was sorry in one way for what happened, but not in another, because he would never forget the night before. Nikki sat there; she didn't speak. Rick said he was attracted to her when he saw her that night. The way she moved, the way she spoke and there was some kind of mystery that surrounded her that intrigued him. He too, was already on X and he lost site of Zema. He loved Zema and would never want to hurt her, but he was intoxicated on X and when Nikki stood in front of the fireplace he lost it. He told Nikki when he touched her, his skin felt as if it was on fire and he had never experienced that before with anyone. He said he would never forget that night, but he loved Zema and didn't want to loose her. Nikki too cared about Zema and wanted their friendship. Rick asked if they could be friends and put that night out of their minds and let it be history. Nikki said she could, because unlike what she heard, she only remembered bits and pieces of the night. It seemed more like a dream than reality to her, but she wanted Rick to know the comment, she made was only a comment, not asking to be drugged or given a drug. Nikki said if she wanted the drug or anymore in the future she would ask for it. Rick told her again, he was sorry if he misunderstood and it wouldn't happen again.

Nikki told Rick she had a lot to do that day, because it was her only day off before returning to work as she was walking to open the door. On the way out Rick told Nikki Zema really needed a close girlfriend and Nikki said,

"Me too."

When she closed the door. Nikki felt strange, but decided to put it in the past and move on. She hoped Rick meant what he said, but knew time would tell.

Nikki spent a lot of time with Zema over the next couple of months, their friendship grew and the bond between Nikki and Zema made them inseparable. They cooked together, slept together, showered together and hug out in the bedroom watching TV. They were closer than sisters and most husbands and wives. Nikki kept her apartment, but spent almost every night at Zema's. They were as close as intimate lovers, although they never made love; they kissed on the lips, held each other and stroked each other's back while watching TV. Rick was gone most of the time and all hours of the night. When he made it home, he would find Nikki sleeping with Zema, so he slept on the couch. He made a few comments about Zema sleeping with Nikki more than him and asked if he should be jealous. Zema laughed and replied,

"Dam right, you should be, while winking at Nikki."

Nikki never commented too much, except to say, he should be home more and Rick respected Nikki and said the comments were well deserved. Nikki asked Zema what Rick did for a living, but her answers were always vague. Nikki saw people come and go and money passing hands. She pretty much put, two and two together that Rick was dealing. Nikki kept her nose clean and Zema did the same. They smoked an occasional joint now and then, but it wasn't on a daily basis or even weekly for that matter. Nikki told Zema if Rick was dealing he shouldn't do it in their house, because if the cops busted the place, everybody including her would go to jail. Nikki told Zema, if Rick was dealing and continued to do it in the house Zema would have to see her, at her apartment, because she wasn't going back to jail for nobody. Zema promised she would talk to Rick and make sure he cut the stuff out or keep it from the house.

The traffic at the house stopped, but Rick was gone more. Nikki still worked during the day at Dana's Shoes and was struggling to make ends meet. Nikki really liked her job, but it just didn't pay for any extra stuff Nikki wanted or needed. Nikki's boss Tammy was also great. She was single and dating and had a great relationship with her ex-husband Bret that she sat up from time to time and when Bret spotted Nikki, it was love at first site. Nikki thought he was attractive, but a little too sure of himself.

He sent Nikki flowers at work and called several times to get her to go out with him and Tammy said Bret was a great guy; she just wanted to party more than he did and was totally cool if Nikki wanted to go have dinner with him. Nikki told Zema about Bret and she encouraged Nikki to go have dinner and bring him back to meet her or make him pick her up at her house and drop her off there too. Nikki said she would feel better about going if Bret picked her up at Zema's and dropped her off there as well, so Nikki accepted Bret's dinner invitation.

Zema helped Nikki get dressed and seemed more excited about the date than Nikki. When the doorbell rang, Zema ran to the door, while Nikki finished touching up her make-up. Bret was a body builder, a gorgeous man to say the least. Zema fell in love at first site, most women did. Nikki however didn't. She liked Bret, but he was too sure of himself for Nikki. Bret was courteous and sweet, he kissed Zema's hand while telling her the pleasure of meeting her was all his. Bret said they had reservations so they needed to get going, but he needed to get something out of his car first. Bret told Nikki she had to close her eyes and wait until he told her to open them. When Bret got to the door he looked back to make sure Nikki had her eyes closed. Of course she didn't, so he told her again to close her eyes. Nikki closed her eyes, but opened them when she heard the door close. Zema was rolling in the kitchen when Nikki asked her if she ever heard anything so corny in all her life, but Zema thought Bret was sweet. Bret opened the door slowly just as Nikki closed her eyes again. He told Nikki she could open her eyes when she was ready. When Nikki opened her eyes, she saw Bret standing in front of her with a box of candy and a dozen of red roses. Nikki smiled and thanked Bret for the flowers; then asked Zema to put them in water for her. Zema took the flowers and told Nikki she would wait up for her.

Dinner was nice and the conversation dragged at times, but Nikki kept a smile on her face. Nikki relaxed after a while and actually enjoyed Bret's company. Nikki told Bret she didn't date much and their date; was actually the first date she had been on in a couple of years. Bret said he was honored and hoped he would be the last man she ever dated, because he was intrigued. Nikki smiled, it was getting late and she had an early appointment the next day, so Bret paid the tap and took Nikki to Zema's.

Over the next couple of weeks, Zema's house started looking like a funeral pallor from all the flowers Bret sent. Bret sent flowers to Zema's and to her job; Nikki was flowered out. She talked to Bret everyday on the phone and saw him almost everyday, either at work or in the evening. Bret was in management at an Exxon plant and made killer money, but that didn't impress Nikki much either.

Bret took Nikki to his house and introduced her to his son Danny. Nikki got along great with Danny, but the bond between her and Bret was not solid. Bret wanted Nikki and tried to seduce her on multiple occasions without success. Nikki stopped him dead in his tracks every time. Bret said she didn't know what she was missing, he was great in bed, but Nikki told him she would have to take his word for it; she wasn't ready to go there. Nikki continued to see Bret a couple of months, but told him she wasn't ready to have a long-term relationship, but Bret continued to send flowers, called her at work and Zema's all hours of the night.

Rick joked about the situation and asked Nikki if she had sex with Bret and blew his mind or what. Nikki laughed and said she never let him touch her except to kiss her and Rick replied,

"Good thing you didn't fuck him, you'd never get rid of him."

Nikki laughed, but she knew she didn't want Bret in that way; know matter how dam good-looking he was or how much money he had; he wasn't the one. Nikki went back to spending all her free time with Zema, hanging out watching movies or reading in bed curled up beside her. Then one night at four O'clock in the morning the phone rang, it was Mona the wife of Santos a well-known drug runner. Mona told Zema, Rick was busted and the cops were on the way to search her house and she needed to get out. Zema jumped out of bed and told Nikki to get dressed they had to leave right away. Nikki was dressing asking; what was wrong, but Zema was too busy dressing and grabbing cloths to answer. Nikki got in her car with Zema and pulled away, just as the cops pulled in the driveway. They searched the house and found fifty thousand dollars with two pounds of cocaine. Rick was in big trouble.

Nikki took Zema to her apartment and waited for a call from Mona that never came. Zema called the police station and found Bret was busted and charged with possession with intent to distribute narcotics and Bret was placed under a five hundred thousand dollar bond. Nikki and Zema both knew there was no way Rick was getting out of jail and all Zema could do, was sit and cry. Nothing Nikki did consoled her. Zema had cops on the force as friends and they helped her make arrangements to see Rick. During her visit Rick told Zema, that Santos sat him up, because he owed him a hundred thousand dollars. Rick said a major deal fell through and Santos wouldn't take the dope back, it was the money or his ass. Since he didn't have the money, he guessed it was his ass. He said the only way he was going to get out was to turn state evidence on Santos, but he knew he couldn't get close enough again to Santos to do that.

He said he had to find out where the stuff was coming in and when the next deal was going down. Zema was crying, because she felt hopeless, then Rick told Zema to find Nikki and get her to come down to the police station and talk with the cops that busted him, because she could help and Zema asked how the hell Nikki could help. Rick said, Santos was infatuated with Nikki and his dick would rule his head. If Nikki could get close enough to him, she could find out everything the cops wanted to no. Rick said it could be dangerous, but he thought Nikki could do it. Zema said, she would talk to Nikki, but Nikki had to decide for herself, because if something happened to her, she didn't know what she would do. Rick agreed, but assured Zema, Santos would play it cool with Nikki.

Zema called Nikki at work and told her she had to see her right away and Nikki agreed she would see her after work. Zema waited on the front steps for Nikki and told Nikki what Rick wanted her to do. Nikki told her, they had lost their minds; she knew Santos's reputation and knew he had taken some people out. They were never found of course, but to say the least they were gone. Nikki asked Zema why the hell Rick was still breathing, why would Santos let him get busted and not take his life. Zema said, Santos loved Rick like a son and couldn't take him out that way, but would let him serve hard time to teach him to be loyal. Nikki said,

"Loyal, my ass, what a friend."

Zema cried and begged for Nikki's help, she said she couldn't imagine her life without Rick. She had to find a way to get him out of jail or she would go set Santos up herself. Nikki told Zema she would sure as shit get herself killed, because Santos would know what she was up the minute she walked in the door. Zema said she had to do something, so Nikki broke down and told Zema she would go down town and meet with the cops to see what they had to say.

The next morning Zema took Nikki to the police station. Detective Ricco and Detective Dustin told Nikki if she would arrange the bust, Rick would go free. All charges would be dropped, with his testimony and hers if needed, to sentence Santos. Nikki told the detectives she would see what she could find out about Santos and try to arrange the bust, but she sure as shit wasn't walking in an open court room to testify against him. After arguing back and forth a few minutes they realized Nikki wasn't going to be swayed about testifying, so they agreed for her to get as much information as she could, and set the bust up.

Rick told Zema to move to the other side of town and brake off all contact with anyone knowing Santos. Zema had a friend that worked in the plants named West that had a three bed room condo and wanted some room-mates, so she packed her things and moved to West's. The cops told

Zema and Nikki to brake contact as well so Santos would think, Zema left town, because Rick was going down, leaving Nikki alone and vulnerable. Sure enough, Nikki went in a convince store where Santos hung out to buy cigarettes and the chase was on. He asked Nikki where Zema was and she told him, Zema went back somewhere east to her family, since Rick was in jail and she couldn't support herself. Santos seemed to buy it, but Nikki was leery. He asked her what she did with her time now that her friend was gone and Nikki said she was looking for another friend to spend time with. Santos leaned over and told Nikki he could be that friend. Nikki said,

"Yea, Santos you could, but I just need a friend nothing more, could you handle that?"

Santos told her; sure they could, start as friends and see where it lead and offered to take Nikki to lunch and promised to behave himself by offering good conversation. Nikki had lunch with Santos and he kept his promise. He was charming and tried his best to be a gentleman. That is of course for the first fifteen minutes; then Santos told Nikki he could and would give her the world if she would let him. Nikki told Santos the world sounded good, but could they just get through lunch for the moment. Santos asked what would happen after lunch and Nikki responded with,

"Time would tell."

Santos said he liked mystery and time would tell. Nikki told him that she was seeing someone else at the time, but that didn't sway Santos from his mark. Nikki agreed to see Santos the next day after she got off work. Santos on the other hand told her she would never have to work again if she was his lady and Nikki reminded him he was married at the time, but Santos laughed and said,

"Married, yes, but not dead."

When Nikki told him she didn't date married men, Santos told her that could be easily rectified. Nikki left the restaurant freaked; she knew she was in way over her head, but the guilt she felt in having sex with Rick the night she first met him, made her think, that was a way to make things right with Zema for her karma. Zema never knew what happened with Rick, but Nikki did. Keeping Santos at arm's length was difficult and he showed up at her apartment in the middle of the night quite determined to possess Nikki. Nikki thanked God she had agreed to have dinner with Bret that night and because he had too much to drink she let him stay. Bret was passed out in the bedroom and never heard the knock at the door. Nikki told Santos he was out of his mind when she opened the door and found him standing there. Santos told her he had to have her, but Nikki was determined she wasn't sleeping with him for nothing.

Nikki insisted he leave before he woke Bret. Santos agreed, but told her he wanted her to go with him on a trip the next day. He told her he would open his world to her and show her how much he could give her. He said she needed to see his power then she would want him like no other. Nikki told Santos she would go, if he left right then, so Santos walked to the door, but tuned and grabbed Nikki to try and kiss her. She pulled away and told him to go right then and Santos told her to be ready at ten O'clock the next morning and be prepared for the wild side of life, because he knew that she liked the wild side of life. Nikki asked what he meant by that and Santos told her he knew about the night she shared with Rick, but that night wouldn't hold a candle to the evening he planned for her. Nikki closed the door and sat on the couch crying. She called Ricco and Dustin, because they had talked her into this situation.

They were insistent that Nikki go the next day. Somehow they had gotten word on the streets of a major deal going down soon. That meant Santos would be involved somehow and she was to find out the how. Nikki woke Bret up the next morning and told him he had to go. Bret said he wanted to take the day off and spend it with Nikki since he passed out on her the night before, but Nikki told Bret he had to go to work. He wanted to see Nikki that evening, but Nikki told him she meant what she told him the night before, when she said she wasn't attracted to him in that way. Bret told her again she didn't know what she was missing, but Nikki didn't care, she wanted him to go. Ricco and Dustin arrived as Bret was leaving, he wanted to know what the hell was going on, but Nikki told him, it was best if he didn't know. Bret said if she was in trouble he could help, but Nikki assured him she wasn't, she was helping a friend and pushed him out the door.

The officers put a bug in Nikki's purse. It looked like a make-up compact and told Nikki even if he searched her purse he wouldn't know what it was if he found it. She waited in the parking lot, so Santos wouldn't go to her door and wondered how he knew where she lived in the first place. She also knew she was in too deep to turn back. When Santos pulled up Nikki got in his car and asked where they were going when she spotted the detectives and knew she wasn't alone, she felt safer knowing they were close, but not close enough, as far as Nikki was concerned. Santos said,

"You like the wild side of life, so let me show you how wild life can be. Today you'll meet the under world and tomorrow you'll never be the same, you will become my princess and the world will know, I possess you."

Nikki stared out the window with no response, but thought that day would probably be her last day on the earth. When they arrived at a small villa in the countryside, Santos told her to get out and follow close behind him. He told her to stay behind him and if anything went down she would be protected. They went in a small, a frame house where three men were waiting inside with suitcases and a man bound by ropes on the floor. Santos turned to Nikki and asked her what she thought should happen to traders that betrayed him. Nikki was pale and flushed, she thought she was going to faint, but said,

"Let him go?"

Santos looked at the big guy standing by the door and told him to cut him loose. He looked at Santos like he had lost his mind, but

Santos yelled,

"You heard the lady, cut him loose."

The man walked over and took a hunting knife out a holster on the side of his leg and cut the man's hands and feet free. He got up, took off the gag and sat on a dirty sofa in the room. Santos lead Nikki by the hand to the sofa and sat her about two feet from the man. The man sat on the sofa trembling, he spoke nervously and told Santos he was sorry, he had gotten in trouble and the pigs; but Santos raised his hand and asked him if he was confessing, but before he could finish speaking. Nikki's ears were ringing, she couldn't hear and something warm was running down the side of her face. She lifted her hand to wipe her face and turned to the man on the side of her. She couldn't hear; then realized the man standing by the door had pulled his gun and shot the man before he finished his confession. Nikki also realized the warm wet feeling on her face was the man's blood that sprayed her face on impact. She looked at Santos and saw his lips moving, but she couldn't hear a word he was saying. It was like everything was going in slow motion, a warped slow motion. Santos stood up just as the swat team burst through the door. The man by the door raised his Uzi and was taken out by the first officer that entered the room. Nikki hit the floor and covered her head. The other man and Santos were detained face down on the floor when Nikki looked up. Nikki was in shock when Ricco entered; hand cuffed her, read her, her rights, and dragged her out the door.

On the way to the car, Ricco told Nikki not to speak. Nikki was placed in a cop car and driven downtown. Ricco and Dustin told Nikki on the way she was going to central booking and lock up, so Santos wouldn't know she sat him up. The other man in the room with Santos was a drug lord from Mexico. The cops knew Santos was bringing in drugs from

Mexico through Texas, they didn't know how he was getting it passed the border, but that day they confiscated one-million dollars in cash and two suitcases packed with the purest cocaine money could buy.

Nikki was in shock, it was like a really bad nightmare, the kind you have when you know you're having a nightmare, but you can't wake up. Nikki was taken to central lock up where she was processed with Santos at the same time. As the shock wore off, Nikki started crying. To Santos, it looked like Nikki was scared and crying, because she was facing hard time. He yelled across the room for her not to worry that both of them would be out before the morning. Nikki stood and screamed,

"Fuck you, Santos."

as the officer dragged her to lock up. Nikki spent another night in jail for show. Ricco sent a female officer to tell Nikki she had an attorney there to see her and Nikki was taken to an interrogation room where the arresting detectives Ricco and Dustin were waiting. She was told they didn't think Santos knew or even suspected her, but for her own safety, they suggested she move and start her life over somewhere else. They assured Nikki Santos would not be released on bail and Rick had tied several loose ends up to nail him. Nikki demanded to know why they arrested her and asked how much trouble was she in at the time. Ricco told her she was booked for her own safety, so Santos wouldn't suspect her of anything. Ricco told her it was a good thing she was in shock and on the floor when they entered the room; they didn't know who they would find dead. They also told Nikki the man executed was an informant Santos made. Then Nikki was told she was free and the records of the booking would be destroyed with her photograph in time. They had everything on tape and if they absolutely needed her in court they would find her. Nikki said'

"Fuck you, and fuck court, I am not going in a open court to testify against him, do you not realize, I saw a man blown the fuck away last night, I've been booked, photographed and fingerprinted again, for what, for nothing, and your dam right it could have been me that could have gotten the fuck blown away, so find me, mother fucker, I won't be opening my mouth."

Nikki walked to the door and started sobbing before she could get out the door. She wanted to appear tough, but she was terrified. Ricco reached for Nikki, but she pulled away and walked out the door. When she got out the station Zema was waiting. Nikki ran to her and collapsed in her arms and sobbed uncontrollably. Nikki got in the car and Rick drove them home. Nikki told Rick if he ever even looked at drugs again, or even thought about dealing again, she would kill him herself, he wouldn't have to worry about anybody, but her, because she would kill him. Rick told her he knew what she was saying and swore he wouldn't forget the second chance she had given him.

Rick drove Nikki to the condo they shared with West. Zema drew Nikki a bath and got her a glass of wine. She bathed Nikki and held her while she cried herself to sleep. Nikki and Zema stayed in bed for three days and never left the room. Rick brought them breakfast, lunch, and dinner in bed and slept on the couch. The following week, Nikki moved into another apartment across town and looked for another job. Nikki called Debbie to touch base with an old friend and spent a few days with Debbie, but never told a soul what she did or what she witnessed.

Nikki spent more time with Debbie and hung out with Zema less frequently, because she felt guarded when she was with Zema and couldn't understand why. Then Debbie called to ask Nikki if she knew a Bret Presley. Nikki laughed and said she did, but more importantly, wanted to know how Debbie knew about Bret. Debbie said, Bret had taken out an ad in the newspaper, asking anyone knowing the where a bouts of Nicolette Breaux to call a number for him. Nikki said, she had to be kidding and wanted to see the paper. When Debbie brought the paper to Nikki; sure enough the ad was Bret searching for Nikki. Of all things in the world he could have tried, that was the least expected from Nikki. She called the number and Bret answered. She agreed to meet him for dinner and he asked again if Nikki had a change of heart, but Nikki had not. Bret said, he thought he would always be in-love with her, but Nikki told him they had not had that serious of a relationship, so he couldn't be in-love. Nikki told him, she thought he was just heart broken, because he found someone that didn't melt at his feet. Bret was offended, but said he was glad to know Nikki was doing well. She assured, him she was fine, even though her core was shaken, she would survive. When Bret left that night Nikki hoped he would find someone to give him what he was looking for, she also knew she was not that someone.

CHAPTER 17

A few weeks later, Nikki started to worry if it was possible to be traced through her job. She had changed stores, but not companies. Nikki talked with Zema about the situation, because Ricco had notified Nikki that Santos was out on bond and asked Nikki if she ever had sex with Santos. Nikki was appalled by the question; Ricco told Nikki he didn't mean to upset her or invade her privacy. It was just that while Santos was in jail he had gotten sick, so they transferred him to the infirmary and while testing, he tested positive for AIDS. Nikki calmed down and thanked him for the call, but told him, she had not had that kind of a relationship with Santos. Nikki asked if his wife had been notified of the results, because when Santos went to jail, Mona was pregnant. Ricco told Nikki Mona was notified, but had not been tested to his knowledge.

Nikki thanked her lucky stars; she escaped that situation with her life. Then she thanked her lucky stars, she also escaped with her health. She also thanked the internal voice that told her to steer clear of Santos because she knew something was wrong with him. She almost called Bret to say thanks for getting drunk and passing out at her apartment that night, but she chalked it up to a lesson learned and moved on.

Zema agreed because Santos being out on bond, it would be a good thing to change jobs altogether, so Nikki started looking for employment elsewhere, but not soon enough. When Nikki went to work a few days later, she looked up while unpacking shoes from a shipment and there Santos stood in the flesh. Nikki's heart sank to her toes, she lost all color in her face, but knew she had to pull herself together or she would die right there, if he suspected her.

Santos walked up to Nikki and asked if she thought he was going to let her get away that easy, but Nikki played the pissed off game with Santos. She was scared to death, but bold too. She told him there was nothing to get away from, she didn't have a relationship with him and all she got from her day that was suppose to be unforgettable; which it would be a day burned in her memory for all time, was busted and facing time. He told her not to worry about a thing, because he would take care of everything for her as soon as he finished taking care of his arrangements. Nikki told Santos not to worry about her, she would probably jump bond, leave the state and run for the rest of her life. Santos leaned in towards Nikki and said, she wouldn't run anywhere without him. Nikki told Santos he had to leave or it would cost her, her job. He agreed, but told Nikki, he would be back. Nikki watched through the glass window as he pulled out of the parking lot then she picked up the phone and called the narcotic division for Ricco. She reamed Ricco before she told him Santos found her and had come in the store where she worked. She said she didn't give a shit what it took, but she had to know he couldn't get to her. Ricco told Nikki they would give her some money to leave the state and start over if she wanted that kind of help, but that was all they could offer her unless she agreed to testify. Nikki told him she needed the money, because she was walking out the store and wasn't planning to return to get her last check and sure wouldn't be leaving a forwarding address.

Ricco told her to go downtown to the narcotic division to meet with him and Captain Rimy. Nikki didn't give an explanation to her boss; she picked up her purse, said she had to go, and walked out. She drove downtown and met Captain Rimy and Ricco. Nikki was livid when she got there. She told them, they had promised her she was safe and Santos would not be released. They assured her, he would not go free and they were pushing for a speedy trial. Nikki told them speedy trial or not, she wasn't stupid, she knew Santos found her to let her know, he knew where she was and could take her out any time he wanted. She also knew he was playing her.

Ricco told Nikki that Santos knew if anything happened to her, he would be the first person they would go after. Nikki looked at Ricco and asked if he really thought, she would give a shit, if she was six foot under, if he really got Santos or not.

The Captain offered Nikki five thousand dollars to move and get settled. He also told her, if she testified he could give her more and get her placed in the witness protection program. Nikki said she wasn't walking in a courtroom, because it wouldn't matter if Santos was sentenced to death, the day of her testimony, she wouldn't live the next twenty-four hours. The Captain looked at Nikki and asked if she really thought Santos was that powerful. Nikki looked at him and said,

"If he's not, how the hell did he get out on bond after killing a cop, when you said, you had a iron tight case, and why the hell would he be, the first person you would go after, if I came up missing."

The Captain was a bit speechless, but Nikki just put her hand in the air to end the conversation. She looked at the Captain and asked for a police escort to her apartment to get her things. The Captain told Ricco and Dustin to accompany Nikki.

She took their money and went to get her personal belongings; she packed her cloths and took her make-up. She called the landlord and told him he could sale the furniture to pay for breaking the lease, but she had to leave and couldn't return to move her things. Nikki rented another apartment and bought used furniture. Only the bare essentials from Goodwill; she was comfortable, but scared, in fear for her life and couldn't sleep. Every shadow that moved on the wall at night terrified her.

Nikki bought a gun, but didn't know how to shoot it and didn't know where to go to learn to use it either. So, one night Nikki was sitting on her couch and thought if someone did break in on her, she hadn't shot a gun in her life and didn't know if she could pull the trigger. Nikki got in her car with the gun and drove down the interstate. It was about four o'clock in the morning and the road was deserted. Nikki thought, if she could just shoot the gun, she would feel safer with it, if she knew what it would feel like or what to expect if she had to shoot it.

Nikki reached for the gun on the seat next to her and pulled the car on the side of the interstate. She slid to the passenger seat and rolled down the window. She took the gun in her hands and pointed it toward the sky, she looked for oncoming traffic, it was clear. Nikki closed her eyes and pulled the trigger. Her heart raced as the gun kicked, but her grip was tight and she was able to hold on to the forty-four. She put the gun on the floor of the car and got back in the drivers seat and drove home.

Shooting the gun actually gave Nikki a since of protection, she knew she could pull the trigger. She might not be able to do it with her eyes open, but she knew she could pull the trigger if she needed to.

Nikki told Zema what she had done on the side of the interstate and Zema asked; if Nikki was sure know one saw her. Nikki said she didn't think so, but she couldn't swear to it. Zema told Nikki she could be charged with discharging a firearm inside the city limits if she had gotten caught, but Nikki said it was worth the risk, because she knew she could use the gun if she had too. Zema told her if she ever had to pull the gun out, just pull it out and use it, not to hold it on anyone, because the chance of them taking it and using it on her would increase. Zema made it clear if it ever had to do with Santos, shoot to kill, because she thought the same as Nikki, that Santos had figured out Nikki had something to do with his bust. He may not have gotten all the details as to how, but he knew. Zema was afraid too, but wouldn't admit it.

The trial date was closing in and Rick was still expected to testify. Rick would be held in protective custody during the trial and would not be released until sentencing. Nikki was glad for herself that her part was over and she was getting ready to leave when Zema told her; she needed to talk to her about something. When Nikki asked about what, Zema was hesitate, but asked Nikki to tell her the truth about her and Rick. Nikki almost fell off the couch, but asked what she wanted to know and why. Zema told her that Mona had told some of their friends that Rick and Nikki had sex in the living room the night she got drunk and passed out. Nikki was just about to come clean, when Rick walked in the door. He walked straight to Nikki and told her he was sorry for lying about her. Nikki looked at him strange and asked what he was talking about. Rick said he told Santos and some of the guys that he had screwed her, because they were all turned on by her and he wanted to look like the big macho man.

Nikki didn't know what to say when Zema walked over to the couch and sat down beside Nikki and told Rick he was a piece of shit for lying like that and he should have never said what he said and lead those people to think what they thought. Rick said he was sorry, he just wanted to be macho; his ego had gotten the best of him. Nikki never responded, she said she had to go, because she was trying to set up interviews the next day. Zema hugged her and told her she missed her and wished she would stay or come back. Zema missed spending time with Nikki like they use to and needed her support, especially when the trial started the next month. Nikki assured her she would be there for her, but she wouldn't be going to the courthouse. Zema said she wasn't going to the courthouse either, she would know from afar what was going on and that would be good enough for her.

Nikki found another job, but making ends meet was difficult. She struggled as always and continued to look for alternate employment. The trial came and went, Rick testified against Santos and the audiotape of the night of the shooting was played. The photographs from the shooting were displayed with the drugs and money; under heavy security of course and Santos was sentenced to death for the execution of a police officer. The drugs were ordered to be destroyed by insemination. The money collected went to state programs and disbursed as needed and Santos was taken into custody immediately.

Rick was released from protective custody and life actually started settling down for all of them. Nikki, however, still slept at the door with her pillow and blanket and a forty-four under her pillow. Then Nikki woke up one morning and reached for the gun under the pillow, but it was gone. She freaked because she thought someone was in the apartment with her. She got up slowly and looked around the room. She wondered how someone could have gotten in without her hearing them. If they hadn't come through the front door, she knew they would have had to break a window. She stepped away from the door after checking the locks; they were still intact. Nikki turned to face the living room and spotted the gun on the sofa. She ran and grabbed the gun and held it pointed outward ready to shoot. She walked the entire apartment, kicking open doors, searching room to room. When she was satisfied that know one was in the apartment she went back to the living room.

Nikki told herself, she had to have been sleep walking and carried a loaded gun through the house with her. She also told herself, she had to find a place for the gun that was safe, but accessible if she needed it, so she placed the gun in top of her closet with a box in front hoping if she reached for the gun in her sleep the box would fall; hit her and wake her up.

That afternoon Nikki went to the mall shopping and ran into Ms. Bankston. She embraced Nikki and told her she knew how hard she tried to get her son to stop using drugs. Nikki tried to change the subject and asked about Mr. Bankston. She told Nikki he had past-away several years back from a heart attack. Nikki expressed how sorry she was for her lose. Ms. Bankston told Nikki Mr. Bankston adored her and she was sorry things turned out the way they did. Nikki said she was sorry too and was trying to say goodbye when Ms. Bankston asked her if she was coming to the funeral. Nikki looked at her a little surprised and asked her what funeral. Ms. Bankston said the final arrangements for Todd's funeral the following day and the wake that evening. She had tried to reach Nikki to talk to her about the arrangements, but couldn't locate her. Nikki told her she didn't know Todd had died. She had no contact with anyone that knew him anymore. Ms. Bankston told Nikki Todd never got over her and in all that time that past when he died he still carried her photograph in his wallet.

Nikki was speechless; she didn't know what to say. Ms. Bankston said they cremated Todd and they would have the wake that afternoon and the funeral the following day. Nikki asked her if Todd had been sick for a long time or did he have an accident. Ms. Bankston told her Todd died of complications with his health. She said there were so many machines and they tried to save him, but he was too sick and she was at his bedside when he past and he seemed at peace when he left this world. Nikki had tears in her eyes as she thought about the vision she had when she saw him the last time. Ms Bankston asked if she would come see her, she would love to just sit and talk for a while sometimes.

Nikki agreed she would and told her she would go to the wake, but she couldn't attend the funeral. Ms. Bankston agreed and told Nikki she hoped she would not be offended when she came to the wake. Nikki asked her why she thought she might be offended by something there and Ms. Bankston told her she had tried to reach her because they did a video of Todd and his favorite things to play at the wake and she knew Nikki was the love of his life and she had included some photos of her and Todd in the video. Nikki was touched and told Ms. Bankston she would not be offended in the least and would see her that afternoon. They embraced and Nikki walked away.

Nikki attended the wake and saw so many of her old friends and the video brought tears to her eyes as she saw the reminders of the days they shared before the drugs took over their life. Nikki had a private moment with Todd's ashes and she told him she hoped with everything inside her he was finally at peace. Nikki gave her condolences to the family and said her goodbyes to her old friends and departed. Nikki went home, numb and tried to rebuild her life and wanted to try and figure out what the meaning of life was. She needed a purpose, she needed answers, she needed something; she just didn't know what that something was.

Nikki still craved a better life, a better job, and peace of mind. She thought she might never feel safe again and wondered at times, if she had ever really felt safe in her life. She continued to look for another job and responded to an ad that sounded too good to be true, but she was intrigued and willing to chase a rainbow and bet on a long shot, so she went on the interview. When Nikki walked in an incredibly good-looking man greeted her. He introduced himself as Desmond Stewart and told Nikki to take a seat. It was a group interview setting and he was waiting for the rest of the people to show up. He was tall, blue eyes, blond hair, funny, and had an incredibly nice butt. He told Nikki to have a seat and he would tell her when to start the application on top of her desk. Nikki on the other hand, turned the application up and started to fill in the blanks.

Desmond embarrassed Nikki, by calling her out in front of everyone in the room. He made a remark about the in-ability to follow instructions and Nikki thought,

"Oh well, I just blew the interview and it hadn't even started yet."

She put the pin down and turned the paper face down, she watched Desmond as he walked across the room talking about making big bucks, taking chances in life and believing in your future. Then he said,

"If you're not an independent thinker, have the ability to follow instructions, and you don't see yourself in the future reaching your full potential you are dismissed at this point."

Nikki sat there; a couple of people got up and walked out. Then Desmond told the rest that remained to complete the application with the test on their desk. Nikki finished the paper work and handed it in. Desmond thanked her for her time and said he would be calling back for second interviews in the next few days or by the next week. When Nikki turned in her paperwork, Desmond was friendly, but not too friendly. She left thinking she blew it.

Nikki drove to Zema's to tell her about Desmond and how attractive he was. She told Zema she had never just met someone and felt something like that before. Nikki said she had made a complete ass out of herself in the process. Zema laughed and bet her twenty bucks he'd call. Nikki said she was on, but she wouldn't hold her breath.

Sure enough, the phone rang with Desmond on the other line. He offered her the opportunity to come to work for the company and Nikki accepted. She thought she was going to get rich selling air filter systems door to door. The company had a referral system and a lead generating system that required cold calling to generate appointments for the opportunity to sale their equipment. Desmond did most of the training sessions and cracked jokes most of the day. He seemed to get off on telling dirty jokes and embarrassing Nikki. Nikki was the only female in the training session. About half way through the training session Desmond asked Nikki if she new the difference between an exotic lover and a kinky lover. Nikki looked up and realized all the guys were staring at her. Nikki decided it was passed time to shut Desmond up and thought, if she didn't shut him up then, she would never live that moment down, so Nikki looked at Desmond and said,

"Well Desmond, I really don't know the answer to that question, but if you give me one of each, I'll be happy to let you know when I'm done."

The guys in the room rolled, Nikki thought Desmond for the first time in his life, was speechless; it was a priceless moment. After work Desmond asked Nikki if she wanted to meet at the club down the street for drinks and maybe a round of pool. Nikki knew Desmond was engaged to the secretary in the office, the boss's daughter, but Nikki didn't think about it. She enjoyed the classroom time and wondered what Desmond would be like outside the classroom setting, so she went.

Nikki sat at the bar waiting for Desmond. When he got there, he ordered his crown and water at the bar and headed to the pool tables. Nikki laughed and joked with Desmond half the night. She was unusually comfortable with this man, more laid back and at ease than she had ever been. She thought it was as if she had known Desmond all her life. One drink led to another and another. Needless to say neither Nikki nor Desmond was feeling any pain.

The night started winding down when Desmond rounded the pool table and entered Nikki's personal space. Nikki looked into Desmond's eyes and when his lips touched Nikki's she felt the earth move. That kiss lead to another and Desmond following Nikki to her apartment that night. On the drive to Nikki's apartment she was calm, excited, and totally at ease. When they got to her apartment she offered Desmond another drink. He accepted, so Nikki fixed his drink and invited Desmond to her bedroom. They walked together to the bed and had intercourse. It wasn't erotic or passionate, just sex and Nikki walked Desmond to the door and kissed him goodbye. She went back to bed and slept a couple hours, got up, got dressed and headed to the office. When she got there, Desmond greeted her warmly, but his fiancée was in the office, so things had to be kept quite and private. Nikki didn't think Desmond was too interested in another evening with her because they had, had a great time playing pool and joking around, but the sex wasn't that great. Much to her surprise Desmond asked if she wanted to meet for a game of pool later, so again she accepted. Meeting after work at the club two blocks from the office, became a nightly ritual. Desmond would stay with Nikki until three or four O'clock in the morning and go home to shower for work. The sex between the two became more and more erotic and passionate every time they met.

Nikki of course told Zema everything and had to pay the twenty-buck bet she lost, but chalked it up to a well-spent twenty bucks. After training was complete, Nikki hit the streets selling air filter systems, it was difficult. She was only paid for machines sold, so money in the beginning was tight. She didn't have the money for her rent when it was due, so Zema told Nikki to move in with her and Rick. West had his own bedroom, Zema and Rick had theirs and they had an extra room and Zema said they too were struggling and if they split the rent three ways they would all be happy people. Nikki packed her things, put her furniture in storage and moved her personal belongings in her new bedroom. Nikki sold her furniture and gave Zema six months rent. Nikki's car was paid for, it wasn't much of a vehicle, but it ran. She thought if she only had to worry about gas money and eating for a while she could build herself up in the business and go from there.

Nikki could sell the air filter systems and moved up the ladder of making more money with each sale. The company put her in the office on a part time basis to help Marcy the secretary; which was Desmond's fiancée. Nikki filed, ran errands and Marcy tried to teach Nikki how to type, that was a joke in itself.

Nikki worked in the field part time and in the office half the time. Nikki got to know Marcy and really liked her, but Nikki was also in-love with Desmond. Although they all worked together in the office know one knew about the affair between Desmond and Nikki. Marcy was sweet and innocent for the most part, but Nikki thought how naive she was too, because every night, Desmond was with her until three or four in the morning. Desmond told Nikki he was completely in-love with her, but he couldn't back out of the marriage to Marcy. He swore to Nikki, he wasn't having sex with Marcy and promised her if she would trust him, he assured Nikki the marriage wouldn't last. Nikki was so in-love with Desmond she would have taken him any way she could get him, so she agreed to see what would happen. At the same time though, she really liked Marcy and felt guilty about what she was doing to her behind her back, but she loved Desmond more than she cared about hurting Marcy.

Zema adored Desmond, she laughed and joked around with him and made him feel at home when he was there. Desmond spent most of his time with Nikki and their bond grew into something that made them inseparable in this lifetime.

Nikki as well as Desmond craved the other. She could be taken to multiple orgasms time after time with Desmond. Nikki had never experienced sex in that manner before. She thought since it had never happened before with anyone else, it would never happen again with anyone else. Even in Nikki's relationship with Todd, her sex life was a good one, but this one touched Nikki on a totally different level. Nikki knew for the first time she was totally and completely in-love with another human being. She didn't want to imagine her life with anyone else, but this man. Nikki also knew the circumstances of that relationship were not under the best pretenses, but she was too far-gone to turn back at that point.

Life seemed pretty good. Then Nikki got a call from Kirsten one of her half sisters. Michelle was married to another man in California, that was filthy rich of course and he and Michelle had gotten into a knock down drag out fight and Michelle started crashing and breaking things in his mansion so he had her taken away and admitted to a psych ward and the doctor wanted to talk to Nikki. Kirsten begged Nikki to go to California and help Michelle. Nikki didn't know how she felt about hearing from her sister, but she agreed to go and see what she could do. When Nikki got to California, Michelle's husband Brock let her in and asked if she would pack Michelle's things. He wanted her to go with him to the hospital that night because he wanted to tell Michelle she was moving out, but he would help her financially until she was settled elsewhere. For Nikki's sister's sake, Nikki agreed. Nikki and Zema packed most of the day and cleaned up more glass than one could ever imagine. Brock was nice and thanked Nikki for helping get the house back in order. The staff left when the escapade started and had not returned at that point. Nikki looked around the house and was mesmerized by the way Michelle was living; it was a three story house that over looked the beach in Malibu and had a glass elevator in the center of the house to take you to each story. There was a pool on the roof that went to the edge of the house that seemed to drop off into the ocean. It was a spectacular view.

The visit that night to the mental hospital was something Nikki could have never prepared herself for. When Michelle saw Nikki she ran to her and told her the doctors there had told her she was eaten up inside with guilt over the way she had done her children and asked Nikki if she could believe he said that to her. Nikki just stared at Michelle, she couldn't even speak when Brock walked up and Michelle ran to him, he hugged her and told her he missed her and it wasn't hard to see Michelle was going home with him after all.

Brock told Nikki she and her girlfriend Zema was more than welcome to stay at the house and he offered to repay her the money it cost her to come there and her gas money to go home as well. Zema accepted his offer before Nikki could speak and Nikki found herself on her way back to the mansion on the beach for a few days. When they got home that night Nikki went for a swim in the pool and a walk on the beach and thought how at peace she was. That night when she went to bed Nikki fell in a deep relaxed sleep until she woke up with a blood curling scream at ten minutes after two. Zema said the hair on the back of her neck stood up the scream was so terrifying and said Nikki just laid back down on the pillow and went back to sleep. Every night for four nights at ten after two Nikki woke up screaming and would lay back down and go back to sleep. Nikki called Desmond and he told her he was flying out there that day to see her and he would pay for a suite at the hotel that evening so Nikki and Zema went to the hotel that night and Nikki slept through the night without so much as a whisper.

Nikki told Desmond the next morning she was fine and he left to return home and Nikki went back to Michelle's for two more days only to wake up again both nights with a blood curling scream at ten after two. The morning Nikki was preparing to leave she was in the kitchen with Michelle and she told herself she was going to speak up and it didn't matter to her how Michelle felt about it. Nikki told Michelle she had something to say and she knew she was not going to like it, but she knew she could not leave there until she said what was on her mind. Michelle took her coffee to the table and asked Nikki what she wanted to say. Nikki told her that something really bad had happen there or something really bad was going to happen in that house at ten after two in the morning. Michelle asked her how she would know that and Zema asked how she could not have heard the screams from Nikki every night at that time that she slept in the house.

Brock entered the room and said he heard the screams and wanted to know what was happening. Nikki told him she knew things sometimes and sometimes things came to her in her sleep and she couldn't explain it and she knew Michelle was uncomfortable with it from the time she was born. Brock asked her to explain the feeling and Nikki said she couldn't, all she knew was it was bad, really bad and because of it hitting her in that way, a way it had never come to her before and always at ten after two she felt the time meant something and it was horrific because of her reaction to it. Michelle said to drop it and Nikki said she would, but she couldn't leave there without telling her. Nikki said what she did with the information was her choice and Nikki got up from the table to leave.

Brock reached out and took Nikki's hand. He told Nikki three years prior his mother lived with him and the room Nikki slept in was her room. He said he was away on a trip and someone broke into the house to rob it and found his mother there. Brock said his mother was beaten and strangled to death in that room and the corner called her time of death at ten after two in the morning. Brock said he never said a word to anyone because you don't tell people someone was murdered in your home and he tried to put it out his head.

Nikki told him she was so sorry and never intended to hurt him by making him relive anything that bought so much pain, but she sensed what happen in that room and if it had not happen it was coming and she couldn't leave without saying be careful. Brock thanked her and Michelle took her coffee cup back to the kitchen and Nikki said her goodbye and went home with Zema. Zema had a million questions for Nikki that Nikki was not prepared to answer because she didn't have answers herself. It just was what it was sometimes. Nikki couldn't understand how she just knew things sometimes with certainty and sometimes when she wanted to know things it didn't work like that, but she had no answers and she didn't want to talk about it so Zema dropped it.

Nikki was settling in at home again and a few months past when Brock decided Michelle could stay, but her kids had to go. He threw both Nikki's sisters out at two o'clock in the morning in their t-shirts. Kirsten was standing on a street corner at a pay phone with Ashley, no money and no cloths. Nikki didn't know what to do so she called Darwin and told him what had happened to the girls. He was upset and said it sounded like something Michelle would let happen. Nikki didn't have any money to send her sisters and definitely not dependable transportation to go get them either, so Darwin called the girls and said he would send them some money or go get them. Kirsten told Darwin they could call a friend and maybe go there if he would send some money to get them through a few days. Darwin told her to call the friend and call him back with an address to send the money. Both the girls were still in school and didn't want to change schools at that point, so they stayed in California with Darwin's help. Kirsten moved in with an older man and was forced to have sex with him for room and board and Ashley's best friend went to her parents and they agreed to take Ashley in, if she agreed to stay in school. Their lives were not easy ones, but they did what they had to, to survive at that point. Nikki didn't know where they were and assumed they returned to live with Michelle when they didn't call her again.

Then, Kirsten got pregnant and Michelle said she would pay for an abortion. After the abortion Kirsten didn't have any where to go, because she had drank and fist fought every person she knew. She had gotten drunk on several occasions and showed up where Ashley was staying to beat the crap out of her for nothing, so Kirsten was forbidden to return, as well as half the town businesses and residents didn't want her around either. So with this in mind and the fact she hated the man she was forced to sleep with, she called Nikki out of desperation. Nikki bought Kirsten a bus ticket after clearing it with Zema that she could stay there with them for a while. When Kirsten showed up, Nikki opened her heart to her. Kirsten cried a lot about the abortion and told Nikki how miserable her life was. Nikki tried to console her, the best she could and talked to her boss about a job for Kirsten. They hired Kirsten and put her in the telemarketing department. Kirsten set the appointments, and Nikki would go for the show. Nikki told Kirsten about Desmond and made her promise to keep their secret if she got her a job and Kirsten agreed.

Nikki spent as much time with Desmond as she could at that point, but wedding planning and other things made their time less and less frequent. Kirsten set her own agenda and became friends with the telemarketing supervisor and her husband, which was Marcy's stepbrother. Nikki and Kirsten grew apart again as always and started arguing more and more so Kirsten moved in with Janie and Crosby her supervisor. Of course Nikki warned Desmond that it would only be a matter of time before Kirsten would air their secret and expose them to hurt Nikki.

Desmond decided to go to Marcy and tell her that he had been friends with Nikki and had met both Nikki and Kirsten at the club down the street to play pool. He told her that Kirsten was mad at Nikki for asking her to leave and would try and get her fired, so she might say things that weren't true, so Marcy would be prepared. Marcy went to her Dad to talk about the situation and just when he decided to terminate Kirsten, Crosby requested his meeting. He told his Step-Dad that Kirsten had told him about the affair and he had followed Desmond and Nikki and knew it was not a lie. Crosby demanded Kirsten stay, because she was his best marketer in the phone room.

The boss Mr. Austin decided to call Nikki in his office and told her, he knew she was fucking his daughter's fiancée and it was going to stop. He told her he wasn't taking her job from her, but she was not to see Desmond again. Nikki denied what was said, but he was very adamant that it was true and it would end. When Nikki walked out the office, Marcy looked up from her desk. Nikki looked at her and said she was sorry for all the crap she heard and she didn't do anything to intestinally hurt her. Marcy told Nikki she had already spoken to Desmond and she knew it was all a crock. She told Nikki that Desmond told her he met her to play pool and they had a friendship and nothing more. She knew her step-brother was an ass and needed something to make himself look better in her father's eyes, so he used something with Kirsten's help to de-fame Desmond. Nikki was speechless, but said she was glad she was so secure in her relationship with Desmond that it wouldn't affect her. Nikki knew this was the beginning of the end of her job and most probably her relationship with Desmond too.

Nikki saw less and less of Desmond and Bret showed up with flowers again at Zema's. Desmond acted like he didn't care when he saw the flowers, but Nikki thought it did. Nikki didn't have any feelings for Bret and Desmond knew it, so he wasn't intimidated in the least. In fact he encouraged Nikki to date, just not to have sex with anyone. Nikki thought Desmond was out of his mind when he made the suggestion, so they fought. One fight turned into another and another; then at the office Desmond was a total ass to Nikki. Nothing she did was right and he made her cry more than he ever knew. Marcy told Nikki that Desmond was upset about the Kirsten deal, but he would get over it. Nikki told Marcy he could go fuck himself over the Kirsten deal.

Marcy said to give it time and it would pass, but Nikki resigned and got another job. Nikki also told Marcy everything Kristen had said was true. She admitted to the affair with Desmond and told her she was sorry. Marcy on the other hand, asked Nikki for proof that she had, had sex with Desmond. Nikki asked her if she was joking, but Marcy was serious. Marcy told Nikki that Desmond had already warned her that Nikki would try to start some crap, so she wanted Nikki to prove she had sex with Desmond. Nikki laughed and told her if she was that stupid and naive she deserved him, so she wished her well and left the office and started her life elsewhere.

Rick started disappearing again at night, so Zema and Nikki were back spending time with just the two of them again. Nikki told Zema if Rick was dealing drugs again she was moving out and they were on their own. Zema assured Nikki, Rick was spending time with some special friends of his and he didn't think Nikki would be too comfortable meeting them, so Nikki asked, what was wrong with them. Zema laughed and told her nothing was wrong with them; they were just gay men that dressed in drag. Rick loved the gay bar scene at the time, so him having friends like that, didn't surprise Nikki.

Rick and Zema were going out with a group of Rick's friends to the gay bars and invited Nikki to go with them. She declined, but told Zema to ask, if Rick's friends wanted to get dressed there at the house before they went out, because Nikki was intrigued by the thought of seeing these people in person. When the invitation was offered the guys accepted. While they were in route to come there and get dressed Desmond called and asked if Nikki wanted to talk. He wanted to apologize for being an ass and Nikki accepted his offer to come, but told him he needed to make it later in the evening, because Rick and Zema were having some friends over before they went out and Desmond told her he would see her that evening.

The guys came in wearing hip hugger jeans, t-shirts and hills and their hair was longer than Nikki's. They looked pretty feminine to Nikki and she thought they were prettier than most girls she had seen. Nikki watched them do their hair and makeup and watched as they rolled out their dresses and waited in the living room with Zema for their grand entrance. Nikki was blown away when they entered the room. They looked better than she did when she dressed to go out and then thought she couldn't remember the last time she had gone out. She was snapped out her trance by a knock on the door and Zema opened the door to find Desmond standing there. She invited him in and told him to have a seat and Desmond said,

"I think, I will, I'll just sit right here between these two beautiful women."

Nikki just watched Desmond as he made his way to the couch and sat down with a big smile on his face. Nikki told him to let her introduce him to everybody before they left, so Nikki said,

"You already know Zema, and Rick, remember West, I know you haven't seen him much, but he does live here. Of course this is Jamie, Mark, and Steve," while pointing to the two ladies Desmond had gotten comfortable sitting between.

Desmond said,

"Mark and Steve."

Mark said,

"You heard her right darling, but when I am dressed like this I am usually called Mia and Steve is usually called Chris."

Chris extended her hand to greet Desmond, but before you could blink an eye Desmond stood and stepped over the coffee table towards Nikki to kiss her. Zema was grinning from ear to ear and made the announcement, that it was time for them to go, so they headed towards the door. Mark and

Steve hugged Nikki on the way and told her they would catch up with their new friend later. Mark told Nikki she might wanna educate her man in the living room about some facts of life and told Nikki he would bring her some of the conditioner he used the next day. Nikki told him she couldn't wait to see him as he walked out the door. When they were gone, Nikki burst out laughing. Desmond; however was not that amused. He told Nikki she should have warned him or something, but Nikki told him, he was the one so eager to plop down between two beautiful women and burst out laughing again. Desmond sat down and lit a cigarette. They talked for a while and Desmond told Nikki he couldn't and didn't want to imagine his life without her, but Nikki said she wasn't staying in a relationship with a married man. Desmond asked Nikki to trust him that it wouldn't last long; that he already had a plan in motion, but Nikki needed to trust him. Nikki told Desmond she would try, but she didn't know how long she would or could deal with him being married to someone else and Desmond held Nikki again and they made love as passionately as ever and fell asleep in each other's arms.

A few days later Nikki was getting ready for work and was looking for her favorite sweater. She couldn't find it in her closet or the laundry room, so she went in Zema's room to look in her closet. When Nikki was shuffling the cloths around she saw a box in the corner of the closet. Sitting on top of the box was a plate with a bag of weed and a pipe. Nikki pulled the box out and opened it. The box was full of individually wrapped bags of marijuana and several one-ounce bags of cocaine. Nikki was livid. She took a couple bags of pot and a bag of cocaine in the living room and waited for Zema and Rick to get home. When they walked in the door, Nikki threw the drugs at Rick and asked him what the hell was he doing bringing that shit in the house again. He said he had lost his job and needed to make some quick money, so he hooked up with some old friends and started moving some stuff.

Nikki screamed,

"Old friends! Do they happen to know Santos?"

Rick told her they didn't, but Nikki told Rick he had lost his fucking mind. He would be dead and soon she would be too. Rick told her not to worry, because Santos had died in prison from AIDS complications. Nikki told Zema and Rick she didn't care, if he was dead, he still had friends that respected him and would off the both of them just for the principle. Nikki started packing her things to move out and Zema begged Nikki not to go, but there was no stopping her. She told Zema that Rick promised her, he would never deal drugs again and asked, if she remembered that she could have been exposed to HIV, and she almost lost her life. She asked if she knew that everyday Nikki looked over her shoulder to see if anyone was following her and if a stranger looked at her too long she wondered if they were friends of the drug-cortile.

Zema said, she did remember what Nikki went through, but this was something that Rick had to do right then to meet bills and said Rick would stop again in another month when he got another job. Nikki looked at her, because she realized Zema knew about the drugs being in the house and told Zema she had lost her mind, but maybe if she was sitting in a room when someone sitting next to her was blown away and their brains splattered on her face, she too might take it a little more personal. Zema told her she was way too upset and needed to calm down. Nikki told her she was crazy and asked what if the cops had been watching like they had Santos. She asked if she knew that if they busted the house, if she understood they all would go to jail. Then Nikki thought about Desmond. She asked Zema what if the cops would have busted in the door when he would have been there, he too would be gone.

Zema sat on the bed and started crying. Nikki told her she could cry if she wanted too, and stay in that life, but she sure a hell wasn't, and said if Rick got busted again, not to call her, because she wasn't getting involved ever again. Zema asked Nikki, if she ever intended to see her again, but before she could finish the question Nikki told her when hell froze over as long as she stayed with Rick. She said Zema was stupid if she thought Rick would only deal for another month. She said if he really wanted to make a living he could find a real job. The trouble was, Rick wanted to party all night and sleep all day and that life style would interfere with a real job and asked when the last time Rick went on an interview. Zema didn't answer, so Nikki told her she was gone.

Nikki called Desmond and told him she needed to look for another place to stay, because Rick and Zema were losing the condo. Nikki didn't tell Desmond the truth about what she had done with busting Santos and or how ugly it had gotten. She was afraid to tell him that she even walked close to that path in life. Desmond got her a hotel room for a few days until Nikki got a new apartment and Desmond started staying with Nikki as always leaving around three or four. Nikki got a small one-bedroom apartment again across from Debbie. She furnished it, the best she could and Desmond helped get her a beautiful L-shaped couch with two ottomans. The couch was soft and comfortable; with the two ottomans in front of the couch it looked almost like a king size bed. When Desmond wasn't there, Nikki slept on the couch in the living room. To her it was an improvement from sleeping in front of the door.

Nikki spent time with Debbie again catching up, playing tennis at the park again and hanging out by the pool. Nikki wanted Desmond and missed him terribly, but he had to account for his time a little more carefully and attend all the pre-wedding parties. Nikki told Desmond she was pregnant to see if he would turn away from the marriage, but he didn't. He acted happy about the news and told Nikki that baby would bond them to each other for life, but Desmond married Marcy as planned. He swore to Nikki he didn't want to, but he couldn't back out. Nikki couldn't understand why and all he could offer her was that too many people were involved in the arrangement and he had to up hold his end to honor his family. Nikki tried to accept that explanation, but she couldn't. The day of Desmond's wedding he had spent the night with Nikki. He made love to her before she fell asleep in his arms and when she woke up that time he was still there. Desmond made love to Nikki again before he left. Nikki was invited to the wedding, but she knew she wasn't going.

When Desmond returned from his honeymoon, Nikki was beside herself. She told him she didn't want to see him anymore, because she couldn't stand the idea of him being married. Desmond told Nikki that he may have married Marcy and he hadn't seen her in a week, but he had not touched his wife sexually. Nikki told Desmond there was no need for him to stay, because she had lost the baby. Nikki told him he was free to go to his wife, but Desmond couldn't leave her. He told Nikki he craved her smell, her taste, and her body. He didn't want anyone else and he couldn't loose her. Nikki cried and pushed Desmond away, they struggled with each other, but then they made love as passionately as ever. Nikki saw Desmond several times a week, but only for a few hours. There was no more seeing him every night, except a few. Nikki was lonely and told Desmond how she felt. Once again, Desmond told her if she wanted to see other people for company, he would understand. He said it would be just until he could settle things with his marriage, but she did not have his permission to have sex with anyone. Nikki was angry with Desmond for suggesting she date again. Then asked him how he could make an offer like that to the woman he claimed to be in-love with, if he was planning on being there himself. Desmond told her he loved her enough to let her have a life that he couldn't give her at that moment in time, but wasn't telling her it was ok to have sex with other people.

Nikki had opened her soul to Desmond. She admitted she was bisexual. She told him about her relationships with men and women. There was so much she shared, but so much she kept to herself, because she thought Desmond wanted money and fame and not a poor country girl from the bayou with a shady history. He wanted sweet, innocent, a well to do family, and all that that implied. Nikki knew she wasn't those things and couldn't give him that.

CHAPTER 18

While playing tennis in the park with Debbie, Nikki met a coach jogging. He stopped outside the gate and introduced himself as Terri Brooks. He lived about a block away and had noticed her playing tennis on a few occasions. He coached at a private school around the corner and lived across the street. Nikki told him, it was nice to meet him and admitted she was horrible with names, so she would just call him Coach. He smiled and said that would be fine with him if, she agreed to have dinner with him, so Nikki accepted his offer.

Coach was tall, brown hair, and hazel eyes, a very attractive man in great shape. Debbie was in lust of course, but Nikki's heart belonged to Desmond. Nikki had dinner with Coach and invited him in when he took her home. Nikki had sex with the Coach that night, not because she wanted him, but because she wanted a life. One that she had given up on with Desmond, but her heart still ached for something.

Nikki told Desmond, she had a date and that she brought him home with her and had sex with him. Desmond was crushed and cried in front of Nikki, but Nikki had hurt so much, from missing Desmond all the time, his pain didn't touch her. He demanded Nikki not see him any more, but Coach was more persistent than Nikki thought he would be. Nikki listened to Coach talk, he told her he could offer her so much in life if she would let him give her that. Nikki wanted Desmond, but knew she probably wouldn't have him, so she slept with Coach again. When he touched her, she didn't feel a thing, she was numb inside, after sex, Nikki told Coach he had to go and she didn't want to see him anymore. He was upset, but Nikki didn't care she wanted him gone.

Slowly, but surely, Desmond and Nikki drifted apart. Nikki didn't know where Desmond and Marcy lived and thought she would never see him again. A few weeks later, Desmond was sitting outside Nikki's apartment smoking cigarettes, thumping his butts at her bedroom window. Nikki told Desmond to get the hell out of her life and run his ass back to his wife. Desmond looked at Nikki and told her he was.

The next year Nikki stayed to herself again. She spent time with Debbie and made a few friends through work. Nikki started selling air filter systems for another company and was doing well. She took a few trips she won for in-services and additional training. Nikki met Lynn at the office and was invited to the local clubs with the girls, so she went. Lynn and Nikki hit it off so Lynn asked if Nikki wanted to get an apartment and share expenses. Once again Nikki agreed and they started looking.

A few nights later while at the club, Nikki looked up and saw Laura and she headed straight for Nikki. She said she still had her little girl, but had placed her two boys for adoption and pulled her life together. Nikki told her she was glad to hear she had gotten her life straight. It could have been the booze or the fact Nikki was lost, but they seemed to make up that night. Laura was looking for a new place too and Lynn told her they were going to look for an apartment and if they could find one big enough, she could move in and share bills. It would be all girls and a total blast. The next week they found a four-bedroom apartment on Third Avenue. Lynn had her room, Nikki had her room, and Laura shared her room with her little girl and Lynn's two girls shared the fourth room. It was one big happy family.

Nikki changed jobs again; she went to work for a convenience store, and there she met the assistant manager Renee and they hit it off well. She too became one of the girls at the local club with Nikki. Renee and Nikki got close and Nikki told her almost everything. They were almost like sisters. Nikki spent some time at Renee's Mom's house, Ms Canny and bonded with most everyone there as well. It was a house for wayward souls. Society's outcast, not bad people, just people that didn't fit in anywhere else, people that had few friends, but mostly ones with know family. So to Nikki she finally found a family.

Nikki started seeing the lead guitar player in the band where the girls hung out and he wanted to move to California where the action was and further his music career. Renee told Nikki she was making a big mistake and begged her to reconsider. Know one could talk Nikki out of anything once she made her mind up. She was sullen and stubborn, even to her own detriment, but she was determined to do what she wanted, her way. Nikki left with Dray for California she knew Kirsten and Ashley were there and hoped to rebuild her relationship with them.

When they got there Nikki found out who Dray really was. He snorted coke every chance he got and stole Nikki's gun and traded it for drugs, then stole Nikki's money from her purse. She was back in the zone she had been in with Todd. She told Dray she would through him out; she had already ended one relationship over drugs and she wasn't going though it with another one and he promised it wouldn't happen again.

The next night four o'clock rolled around and Dray still wasn't there. Nikki knew he didn't have any money on him, so she wondered what he did that time to get it and went to her room to search for anything missing. Everything seemed to be in place, so she though he might be broke down somewhere and felt guilty. Then Nikki thought about the necklace Desmond had given her. Nikki protected that necklace with her life. She couldn't wear it; because it hurt too much it was a constant reminder of the love she lost. Nikki would have killed over that necklace, because it was all she had left of Desmond. She placed it in a sock and hid it in her drawer under all the other socks. She ran to the dresser, jerked open the drawer and pulled out the socks searching through each one as she threw it across the room and reached for the next one. The necklace was gone. Nikki had never been so devastated in all her life; she was hysterical.

Nikki waited in the living room for Dray to get home. When he walked in the door Nikki attacked him like a caged animal. She told him, he had know idea what that necklace meant to her, it was the only airloom left of her relationship and she was going to kill his ass if he didn't take her to it right then. Dray told her he was sorry, but the necklace was gone. Nikki went to their roommate's bedroom and pulled out his gun. She went back in the living room and cocked the trigger and pointed the gun in Dray's face. She told him he was going to take her to the place he traded her necklace for drugs and she would buy it back; know matter how much they wanted.

Dray told Nikki he would take her there, but it might cost both of them their lives. Nikki told him without that necklace she would just as well be dead. The guys standing on the street told Dray to get the fuck out of there and reminded him that he was told; he would die if he returned. Dray pointed to Nikki holding the gun and told him that he had to come to buy back the necklace he traded that night. The guy laughed and told him the necklace was gone and so was he, if he wasn't out of there in ten seconds. Dray rolled the window up and backed the car up. Nikki started crying hysterically, she wanted to kill Dray, but she couldn't pull the trigger. She screamed,

"Stop the fucking car!"

Dray told her, they had to get out of there or they would die. Nikki put the gun to his head and screamed,

"If you don't stop the car, I'll blow you're fucking brains out!"

Dray stopped and Nikki told him to get out. He begged her not to leave him there, but Nikki made him open the door. As he opened the door, he begged, but Nikki placed her back on the passenger door and kicked him out on the ground with her feet. She told him if she ever laid eyes on him again she would kill him; that was if he was lucky to get out of there alive, he better wait until she was gone to work to get his things.

Nikki drove away with Dray chasing the car, but she never looked back. When Nikki got home she cried herself to sleep. It was hard to imagine that Nikki was so devastated over the loss of a necklace. Nikki would never trust again and refused to love anyone enough to make her cry if they were gone. When Nikki woke up she packed Dray's things in trash bags and sat it by the road. The next day was trash day, so if he didn't get it that morning before the trash came, it was gone. She went back inside took her shower and dressed for work. When she got home that night, Dray's things were gone and she Nikki never heard from him again. She stayed in California working at the club. She made killer money, bought a new car, and thought she was pulling it together. She didn't date, she was asked out, by customers in the club and was told how rich some were, but Nikki didn't care, if she couldn't have the man she wanted, know one else would do.

Nikki hung out and partied with the people she worked with. On Halloween the girls dressed up like playboy bunnies. They had a great time that night, and made killer money. Nikki walked out with fifteen hundred dollars after tipping the bar tenders. Nikki was content with her life, but after Halloween Nikki went to a local OBGYN for a pap smear. When he did a breast exam, he found several lumps in both Nikki's breast and said she needed surgery.

Nikki asked, if she had cancer, but the doctor told her he didn't know. He ordered a mammogram and a thermal study. They told Nikki they thought they were cyst, but needed to remove it before they could be sure. Nikki was referred to the best plastic surgeon in town for reconstructive surgery. When she went for the evaluation she walked out on the surgeon.

He was high on something when he walked in the room; Nikki was dressing trying to get out the door as the nurse was telling Nikki the doctor was just tired. Nikki laughed and said,

"Tired my ass. He is shit faced, I don't know what he is on, but he is on something and he is not touching me."

Nikki left the surgeons office and cried herself to sleep again, wondering what she was going to do. When Nikki woke up she called her old friend Renee in New Orleans. Renee was happy to here from Nikki and cried when she told her what was happening. Nikki said she had to go so she could get ready for work and Nikki was dressing for work when the phone rang again and Renee told Nikki to pack her things and come home, her and Ms Canny would see her through the surgery and if anything went wrong, she wouldn't be alone, so Nikki quit her job, loaded her car and left for Louisiana.

CHAPTER 19

When Nikki got back to New Orleans, she called her gynecologist Dr. Hawkins. He had her in his office the next day. After examining Nikki, he scheduled the same test. When the results were back, he agreed that her breast needed to be removed Nikki was only twenty-three. He referred her to a female doctor that he had worked with on a few cases. Dr. Hawkins called Dr. Leslie to get Nikki in to see her the next day. Nikki took all the x-rays and results from her tests to Dr. Leslie. She felt comfortable with her and scheduled surgery for the following Monday morning. Renee went with Nikki to the hospital and sat with her while she waited in pre-op. Nikki wasn't given any medication in pre-op so she was shaking. Nikki was scared and told Renee she didn't think she could go through with it. Then Dr. Leslie went to Nikki's bedside in pre-op to talk with her.

The anesthesiologist had already put the syringe of Versed in her IV, but Nikki wouldn't let him sedate her. Dr. Leslie told Nikki she really needed the surgery and promised her, she would be more than happy with the end results. Nikki asked, what to expect if it was a malignancy and Dr. Leslie told her they would do either radiation or Chemo, but because they scheduled the surgeries consecutively with a team in place to do a frozen sample prior to the reconstruction she felt pretty confident it was not cancerous. Dr. Leslie told Nikki to take some deep breaths and relax. She told Nikki she was going to give her just a little bump of the versed in her IV and assured Nikki it would just relax her and take the edge off. Nikki calmed down, but couldn't stop shaking. She agreed to let the doctor push a little of the medication to see how she would feel. When the medication hit Nikki she was in Margaretville. She would have consented to her legs being amputated at that point. She remembered Dr. Leslie asking her if she was ready and saying yes. The next thing she remembered was waking up after the surgery and being bound tightly around her chest.

She woke up slowly, as the nurses took vital signs and fussed with the covers and her position. They re-adjusted her bed and offered her ice chips. They sat her up in the bed and told her Dr. Leslie would come in and speak with her and let Renee in to sit with Nikki. Renee was incredible, she held Nikki's hand and helped her pull the covers off, because she was hot and gave her some sprite. Dr. Leslie arrived and told Nikki they removed all her breast tissue. She said she had a hundred and twenty-nine tiny tumors in her tissue, and that it looked like some were precancerous. They were sending them off to be studied and the results would be back in about four days to a week.

Nikki was numb to the news. She was still sedated. Dr. Leslie told her she could go home if she drank, peed, and had no vomiting. Nikki was sipping sprite while they were talking. The Dr. asked Nikki if she was in any pain and Nikki told her she couldn't feel anything. She was told they used a twelve-hour lidocaine to help with pain control. Nikki did what she had to and was discharged to home; she went to Ms Canny's and went to bed. When Nikki woke up that night, the lidocaine had worn off. It hurt to breath, Nikki thought she was going to die; she was in so much pain. Renee gave her pain medicine, but it didn't help. Nikki was hot all over and couldn't get cool. The ace wrap was tight and made Nikki feel like she was smothering. Her back was on fire and since the ace wrap was in place, Renee couldn't wipe her back down. She called the Dr. and told her she had to take the bandage off, because her back was on fire. Dr. Leslie told Nikki she was having a reaction to the drugs and not to touch the bandage, because she could hemorrhage. Nikki was miserable.

It was winter and cold outside, so Nikki stripped, put on a robe and went outside. She pulled the robe down to her hips to expose her upper body to the cold to try and cool off. Renee and Ms Canny ran out the door to get Nikki, but she refused to go back in, so they got their coats and sat in the backyard with Nikki for three hours before the burning sensation passed.

Nikki finally went back to bed and the rest of the house got some sleep too. The next morning Nikki could hardly move. She thought at least she could breath. It only hurt to move, so she limited her movement as much as possible. Three days later she went back to the doctor to have the bandages removed. When the Dr. entered the room she told Nikki she had gotten the preliminary report and it was positive. When Dr. Leslie removed the bandages, Nikki looked down at her breast and said,

"I must be really swollen, you think."

Dr. Leslie told Nikki she was still a little swollen, but that was her breast or pretty close to the breast size she would be when the rest of the swelling went away. Nikki asked her if she was kidding. The Dr. wasn't, Nikki thought they were way too big and she would look like Dolly Pardon when it was over and started to cry. When the Dr. asked what was wrong, Nikki told her she really messed up, Nikki just wanted to be normal and not look like a bimbo. Dr. Leslie assured Nikki that in the next week the swelling would subside and she would be pleased with the results. Nikki asked how long it would take for the bruises to go away and was told they would start to fade soon, but it could take up to three weeks. She was a solid bruise from the top of her shoulders to just above her belly button.

Nikki went home and waited for the swelling and bruises to subside before she made up her mind about how she felt about her breast. Then, Nikki had to endure 6 months of chemo and 24 radiation treatments. Dr Leslie then told Nikki to be careful about rapid changes in her weight, like gaining a lot of weight at once, because if she grew more breast tissue, she wasn't sure the tumors wouldn't return. Nikki was told they thought it was something genetic, but they didn't really know why it occurred. A few weeks later she started looking for work at the local clubs, because Renee and her sister Kirsty worked for a club in the center of the city and told Nikki to apply there. Nikki was hired and trained to be a bartender and was great at it. She danced behind the bar, joked with the customers and had fun while she worked and made killer money. Kirsty and Renee asked Nikki if she wanted to get a house and be roommates, so Nikki gladly accepted. They lived together, had parties and camped out on the couch watching movies, life was great.

Nikki met another guy named Daniel while bartending and gave him her number after a few weeks. He called her of course and spent almost every-night at the club with Nikki. After a while Nikki let him come to her house as long as one of her roommates was home. Nikki broke her rule when she promised herself she wouldn't fall in love again. Daniel worked in the plants, and traveled a lot. He told Nikki he was from Oklahoma City; he was a big old country boy. Daniel was a tall, blond hair, blue eye. He too was a dream to Nikki. She met the other two guys he lived and traveled with Moody and Lee. Moody dated the girl that lived across the hall named Andrea and Lee didn't date anyone, but spent a lot of time with Andrea and Nikki. Nikki and Andrea bonded like nails; it became a connection that was unspoken.

Andrea was a hairdresser and lived with another girl that was totally opposite of Andrea. Dawn was loose, wild and would bring home man after man. Andrea was laid back, easygoing and very private. Nikki and Andrea's tie became so tight that Andrea could call Nikki and Nikki would answer the phone with,

"Hey Andrea, what's going on."

Andrea freaked every time and asked Nikki how she knew it was her calling. Nikki told her, she couldn't explain it, she just knew when the phone rang it would be her on the other end and it was. Andrea and Nikki stayed at the pool during the summer, except for the weekend they spent in Florida at the beach. They rented jet skies and raced half the day up and down the coastline. The girls hung out on the beach and danced the night away in the lounge of the hotel they stayed in. They had a blast as always, Nikki in her bikini and Andrea as always in her one piece.

When the girls got home, it was Lee's birthday, so Nikki and Andrea thought Lee was sweet, because he was quite and didn't say much when the girls were around, but he adored Nikki and Andrea. Moody and Daniel were gone of course, so Nikki and Andrea decided to take Lee out on the town for his birthday and surprised him with cake and balloons. He took a shower and got dressed while Andrea and Nikki opened the bottle of champagne and drank a glass while waiting. They took him to the club where Nikki worked and danced the night away. Every song all three were on the dance floor kicking up their heels. Nikki spotted Lynn in the club and introduced her to Andrea and Lee. Lynn latched on to Lee, so Andrea and Nikki were left dancing alone, which didn't bother them in the least. The plan was to stay at Nikki's that night, because Kirsty and Renee were out of town. Lynn just invited herself home with them and before Nikki and Andrea knew it, Lynn and Lee had found them a room to crash in or other things. Andrea and Nikki slept together in Nikki's room. The next morning Nikki and Andrea got up and made coffee. They were sitting in the living room when Lynn came out the bedroom and put her shoes on and told Nikki she would call her later. Andrea and Nikki just stared at each other. Lee came out the room and sat on the sofa and Nikki handed him a cup of coffee, as he reached for the cup he said,

"Don't say a word, either of you, just don't say a word."

Nikki and Andrea looked at each other and busted out laughing. Lynn as sweet as she was; was not the most attractive woman in the world. She was somewhat over weight, bucked tooth, and rolls of wrinkles on her face and other places. Lee just leaned back on the couch and wanted to die, he was totally embarrassed. He asked if either of them had ever woke up with someone and when the lights were turned on, they wanted to scream. Nikki and Andrea laughed even harder. Lee asked the question again and said he was serious. Nikki said she had not personally experienced that yet in this lifetime, while Andrea agreed and they laughed even harder.

Nikki asked if they were hungry and wanted to go to Waffle-house for breakfast. Lee offered to buy, if they would stop laughing, so they muffed their laughs, twisted their hair up in clips and out the door they went.

When they ordered their breakfast, Lee asked again, if they were sure they had never had that experience, after confirming their answers again they died laughing. Lee thanked the girls for the night before, the cake and the club that is. He had never had anyone do anything like that for him before, especially two beautiful women like the two of them. Nikki told him, he was welcomed and Andrea said it was their pleasure. Lee said he wished his friends knew how lucky they were, that he would have given his eyeteeth for a chance with either one of them. Nikki told him he was sweet and assured him, that if he stayed just the way he was, he too would find happiness. Lee told the girls, he was just as big a snake as Moody and Daniel; then you could have heard a pin drop.

Nikki asked what he meant by that and Lee told them Moody was married with two kids at home and Daniel was engaged to be married in two months. Nikki and Andrea were silent with know response at all. They just sat there unable to move or speak. Lee told them he had wanted to tell them, but was sworn to secrecy. He apologized repeatedly for knowing and not saying anything. Andrea told him she wished he had spoken up before, but at least he came clean in the end. Nikki told Lee they would love him forever, but then he was going to keep his mouth shut that they knew. Andrea agreed. She said she was going to freak out Moody by telling him she was pregnant and moving to Oklahoma City. Nikki agreed and said she would tell Daniel that she was moving there too, to roommate with Andrea. Lee agreed to keep his mouth shut and agreed the two ass-holes needed a life lesson. He told Nikki she should tell Daniel she was pregnant too and watch the fire works really fly. They decided to do it together at dinner with all four of them together.

Moody and Daniel got back in town that night and called their sweethearts as soon as they got home. The girls told the guys, they wanted to go out to dinner the next night and said they were too tired for company that night. The following evening at dinner Andrea said,

"You guys, we are so excited about some news we have together. We couldn't believe it happened like it did, but we are so excited that we are going to experience it all together."

The guys were totally into the conversation, hanging on every word. The girls looked at each other and Nikki asked if she wanted to go first. Andrea said; know they should both go together since it was the same news. Nikki agreed and said on the count of three. One, two, three,

"Were Pregnant!!!!"

The guys almost choked on their beer. There was a million and one questions like, are you sure, and how far along are you. It was hard to answer with a straight face, because the sheer panic was written all over each of their faces. Andrea said it gets better. The guys could barely look at the girls.

"We're moving to Oklahoma City next month, so we can be near you."

Both said they traveled so much and were not home very often. Nikki couldn't take the site of Daniel anymore so she stood up and threw her drink in his face and told him he better never call or contact her again and walked out. Andrea did the same. Daniel sat there while Moody went after Andrea. She told him, she was not a violent person, but if he came near her she would induce bodily harm. She suggested he move out the apartment across the hall from her or his wife was going to get a call. As the girls were walking away, Daniel walked out and they heard Moody tell him,

"They know."

The girls kept walking and never looked back. Nikki quit working in the club and started a waitress job in a small sports bar during the day and started night school for computer programming. Nikki was working nights for six months when she walked to the bar to order drinks for her customers and saw an attractive older man sitting alone at the center of the bar. Nikki made a comment, that he was an attractive man and the waitress standing close by heard Nikki's comment and took it upon herself to deliver the message to him. Nikki got her drinks and went back to the restaurant side when the waitress told Nikki the gentleman said,

"Thank you for the compliment."

by that time Nikki had forgotten what she said, so the girl told Nikki she had told the gentleman in the bar what she said and he told her to tell Nikki,

"Thank you for the compliment."

Nikki was appalled, upset and embarrassed all at the same time. She called the bartender in the restaurant and told her to send the gentleman a drink and explain to him it was something said in passing and not meant for someone to deliver that message to him. Casey the bartender took Vincent a drink and explained what had happened. He sent Nikki another message, that he was impressed by the compliment coming from someone like her, but Nikki wouldn't go back on the bar side the rest of the night. At the end of the night Nikki was cleaning tables in the restaurant. When she looked up and saw Vincent standing there with his hand reached out as if to shake hands and introduced himself as Vincent Decody and asked if they could meet the right way.

Nikki laughed, shook his hand and said her name was Nikki. He asked her if he could buy her a drink when she got done working and talk for a few minutes. Nikki accepted, but told him she couldn't stay long because she had a test to study for.

Vincent asked her to have dinner one evening and she accepted, but told him she would meet him at the restaurant. Nikki had dinner with Vincent, but she thought he was on drugs because his eyes were red. When Nikki asked him what was wrong with his eyes, he told her, he had been on the river all day in a boat and the wind irritated his eyes. When dinner was finished Nikki said her goodbyes to Vincent at the restaurant. Vincent asked if he could see her again and Nikki told him to call her. When Nikki got home she called Andrea, she didn't think she was really interested in Vincent at the time. Andrea told Nikki, to give it some time and see if she really wasn't interested or if it was just all the other stuff from all the other relationships she was afraid of happening again. Nikki went out with Vincent several times to dinner and movies, but her feelings never changed, she could take it or leave it. When it was time to go home at the end of the date and Nikki knew Renee or Kirsty wouldn't be home, she called Andrea and made her go to her house and wait for her to get there. Andrea would be falling asleep on the end of the sofa, but Nikki wouldn't let her leave until Vincent was gone. Nikki didn't let Vincent stay the night with her for three months.

Vincent was soft spoken, centered, calm, and unemotional about everything. This was the attraction to him for Nikki to understand the life style. He introduced Nikki to his family, his mother Gina was sweet as could be, his brother Mike was an ass from the start and his brothers wife Candice was tiny like Nikki and they hit it off well. Vincent's sister

Ann was as cold as winter and she had a handicap child named Beth. Mike and Candice had two kids, both girls, Joanne and Roxie, spoiled rotten, but cute as could be.

Every Sunday was dinner at Vincent's Mom's house. Nikki was still hanging out at Ms Canny's every chance she got and made a knew friend there as well named Melissa. She was tall, blond, with bulging blue eyes. Melissa was way under weight for her height, but sweet as could be. Melissa also had a boyfriend named Tray and Nikki started spending more time with Melissa and Tray and less time with Vincent. On an average she saw Vincent about twice a week and Melissa and Tray three or four times a week. Andrea went to work for a traveling industrial company and left Louisiana all together.

Nikki missed Andrea terribly, but couldn't fault her for wanting more out of life and wanting a fresh start. Melissa and Nikki became as close as she was to Andrea with the same connection and bond. When the phone rang she would answer,

"Hey, Melissa, what's up?"

Melissa, just like Andrea wanted to know how she knew. Nikki couldn't explain it, she just knew. Melissa and her laid out in the sun in the back yard, bar-b-qued, and hung out watching movies and talking about their lives. Nikki trusted Melissa with her life. Then Melissa called Nikki and asked if she wanted to go mud riding with her and Tray. Nikki thought they were crazy, but decided to go. Nikki and Melissa sat in the back of the truck and got covered with mud before the night was over. They drank, laughed and joked around most of the evening. On the way home Nikki and Melissa argued over who was getting the shower first. Both argued passionately with the other and neither agreed to give in. When they got to Melissa's apartment, Tray was going to stay outside to rinse his truck off, so Nikki and Melissa tore off to the bathroom. Nikki was first up the stairs striping, trying to stay in front to beat Melissa to the bathroom. They both jumped in the shower together and fought over the water. Nikki was standing at the back of the shower with shampoo in her hair and her eyes closed when she felt her breast being caressed. She stepped under the water to rinse the soap out her eyes and felt the fingers follow her as she moved. Know words, just touch. When Nikki opened her eyes, Melissa was not in the shower with her, Tray was. Nikki got out the shower, got dressed and left. Nikki and Melissa tried to talk about the night on the phone, but neither one agreed with the other. Melissa thought Nikki wanted things to go that way and Nikki was adamant she didn't want it. It strained their friendship, so Nikki stopped calling and Melissa left Tray and moved back home with her mom.

Vincent's sister-in-law Candice called Nikki and asked her to lunch and to join her and her friends at the club that evening. Nikki met her a few times and spent a lot of time on the phone with her. Vincent wanted Nikki to move in with him, so he could see her more. Nikki wasn't sure, but Candice begged Nikki to try it out and give it six months. Nikki thought at that time she didn't have very much more to loose so why not, so she moved in with Vincent in his two-bedroom condo.

Life was calm and laid back for about a year, nothing special, but comfortable. Nikki took Vincent home to meet her Grandmother Breaux and the family stared of course, because they went home in jeans. Nikki wore her make up and jewelry; she was herself. You could have almost heard a pin drop when she walked in the house. Her Grandmother on the other hand was happy to see Nikki as always. Nikki had kept in touch with her Grandmother by writing mostly, but spoke to her on the phone from time to time. Nikki told her Grandmother she had moved in with Vincent and in time she may be coming to a wedding, but she had to know a few things first. Of course her family told her she was hell bound, but her Grandmother told her not to forget all she had been taught and to stay in touch with her.

Nikki and Vincent were great roommates. Nikki spent her time with Candice, family dinners on the weekends and worked during the week. She completed her studies in computer literacy at the Votec School she was in when she met Vincent and got a job with Leading Generations in tech-support and learned how to trouble shoot software on computers. She enjoyed her job and met too many people to count. She became close to one co-worker in particular named Kelly. They went out together, had lunch together and shared a lot with each other about their lives and experiences. Nikki told Kelly she was comfortable with Vincent, but not dying to go home after work. She could take it or leave it, but she felt secure with Vincent and that to Nikki meant more than anything else she had at the time.

Kelly told Nikki she should never settle; if she wasn't passionately in love with Vincent she should move on. That Summer Nikki left Vincent to see if she really would miss him. Nikki also called Desmond and went to see him. They shared an evening together, but the passion wasn't there that time for Nikki. He had just divorced Marcy, but something didn't feel right to her. Nikki was totally confused about her life, Vincent had asked Nikki to marry him before she left and it scared the hell out of her. It was the talks with Kelly that got Nikki thinking she should have more in a relationship than what she did with Vincent.

In the middle of the confusion Nikki picked up the phone and reached out to Desmond. He accepted and was glad to see Nikki again. They talked about their lives and how things were. Desmond told Nikki that Marcy was seeing another man and had returned to see him again on a few occasions. He said one night Marcy showed up at his house scared, because she had, had a fight with her boyfriend. While she was there, someone pulled up in the driveway and Marcy looked passed Desmond with shear terror in her eyes. Desmond said he jumped up and ran through the screen door to get to him. Nikki thought that was a sign to her that they would never have a life together without remembering how it started and Nikki always being reminded of Marcy some how. She no longer felt that bond she once shared, it was gone and replaced only by sexual desire at that time, but for Nikki she needed something more. The passion seemed to be there for Desmond as he made love to Nikki, but in the middle of making love to Desmond, Nikki started to cry. She was embarrassed, so she got up, got dressed and left. Nikki was lost. She knew she had to build her life elsewhere and she would not see him anymore.

When Candice called Nikki to tell her how miserable Vincent was without her, Nikki decided to go back to Vincent and make it work. She thought if he loved her, and she didn't have to worry about him chasing women, he offered stability and security; she would have everything she needed. Nikki returned, not with the intentions of marring Vincent then, but to give herself more time to adjust.

Unfortunately, Nikki had, had female problems since the birth of Tricia and when she saw her OB doctor, he told Nikki she had to try and have a baby, schedule a hysterectomy, or get another doctor, because she was placing him on a level of medical responsibility he couldn't allow anymore. He had told Nikki for years how bad things were and told her constantly to think about children if she wanted them. Nikki's periods were getting worse and the pain as well. Nikki knew she had backed herself into a corner, but promised she would go home and talk it over with Vincent and make a decision in the next month. Dr. Hawkins said, thirty days and no more.

When Nikki got home, she waited for Vincent to get in from work. She cooked dinner and had it waiting. After dinner Nikki told Vincent what Dr. Hawkins had told her. Vincent told Nikki, there was no question; they would be married and start their family. Nikki was hesitate, but she knew she wanted to experience a pregnancy in a normal way and she wanted more children. Nikki told herself, it was then or never, so she agreed to marry Vincent. Two weeks later, they said their, I do's with Kelly standing as her maid-of-honor. Right before the wedding Kelly asked Nikki, if she was making the right decision. Nikki told her she didn't know, that time would tell and that was all she had left. Kelly hugged her and told her she only wanted her to be happy and she would always be there for her.

Nikki told Kelly not to say another word, just to smile and look pretty. She told Kelly she needed her support just to get through the day. Kelly hugged Nikki and escorted her to the door. After the wedding Nikki and Vincent went to Dustin Florida for three days. In the honeymoon suite, Nikki stepped out the hot-tube on a half-carat diamond. Nikki hoped that was Gods way of telling her things would work out.

Nikki called the Breaux's to tell her Grandmother she had gotten married and was going to try and have another baby. Nikki's Grandmother was ecstatic, but she was also sick. When Nikki heard the news her Grandmother was ill, she returned home. She knew her Grandmother had suffered a stroke, because she was paralyzed on the left side of her body. Nikki also knew her Grandmother's religion wouldn't allow her to go to the doctor, so Nikki worked in her Grandmother's element to help her; the best she could. Nikki got squeeze balls and all kinds of exercise things to rebuild her Grandmother's strength. She went home on weekends to do physical therapy with her Grandmother and left her with instructions on what to practice during the week until she returned.

Her grandmother looked forward to Nikki's visits and Nikki lived for her time with her Grandmother as well. To Nikki her Grandmother had always been a rock and a solid foundation to lean on. Know matter when Nikki called, her Grandmother was home, know matter what Nikki needed she got. Nikki never really needed a thing, except to hear her Grandmother's voice most of the time and she knew everything would be all right.

Nikki was at work when her Aunt Gabrielle called to tell her, her Grandmother had slipped into a coma and wouldn't live the day. Nikki almost killed herself trying to get home. When she ran in the house, her Grandmother was sitting up in bed talking. Nikki fell in the chair beside her bed when her Grandmother asked why she was there in the middle of the week. Nikki told her she thought she was sick as several people from the church entered the room. The Christian's stared at Nikki once again, because she came home in jeans, makeup, and had rings on almost every finger.

Her Grandmother sensed the tension and told Nikki to come sit on the bed with her. When Nikki sat on the bed, her Grandmother took her hand and asked about the rings, Nikki told the story behind each ring, why she wore it or why she bought it. Her Grandmother looked at Nikki and asked her point plank,

"Nikki, do you believe in God?"

The talking in the room ceased, you could have heard a pin drop as Nikki looked back at her Grandmother and said,

"Yes Grandmother, I do believe in God, I just don't believe you have to live the life that you have chosen to get to heaven."

Her Grandmother looked in Nikki's eyes and told her,

"Nikki, I raised you and I taught you right from wrong, I know your heart and your soul, I want you to know that you turned out to be the best kid in your class with the most accomplishments. I know when you left; then Stacy behind you, the church said you both would not amount to anything, you would wind up as street walkers, dope heads or dead, but you and Stacy out did everyone here with your accomplishments. I want you to know how very proud I am of you and if you tell me you believe in God; that's good-enough for me."

Nikki fell on her Grandmothers chest and sobbed uncontrollably. She told her Grandmother how much she loved her and she didn't want her to ever leave. Her Grandmother told Nikki she knew all things had to end and her life was slowly ending, but she would live forever in Nikki's heart and she knew that Nikki knew that. Then her Grandfather walked in and told Nikki's Grandmother she looked really beautiful that day in her new peach gown. Nikki's Grandfather had never been a man of compliments in the past, so it kind of took Nikki by surprise to hear the words. Nikki turned to see her Grandfather when she heard her Grandmother tell him to get himself back in the yard; she was fine and didn't need all those people fussing over her. Nikki couldn't help, but laugh, because that was just like her Grandmother, strong to the end and refusing to be a burden on anyone; if she couldn't do it herself, it wouldn't get done.

She squeezed her Grandmother's hand and told her she loved her. Her Grandmother told her she knew she didn't need to miss work, so she needed to go home, go back to work and come the weekend. Nikki's Grandmother said Gabrielle was upset that morning, but she just needed a few extra winks, so she didn't want to wake up. Nikki told her she loved her again and assured her she would see her that weekend, but she had to double her exercises with her hand. Her Grandmother laughed and agreed she would.

Nikki returned home and back to work. The next day Gabrielle called again with the same news. Nikki again, told her she would be there soon and left work went home to pack and called Vincent to tell him she was leaving again. Nikki was calm as a cucumber, she told herself, when she got there it would be just like the time before. Her Grandmother would be sitting up in bed fussing over the attention, but when Nikki arrived and entered the house her Grandmother was already gone. Nikki asked where her Grandmother was and Gabrielle told her the funeral home had just left with her. Nikki said she didn't see a hearse, so there was know way they just left with her. Nikki's Aunt Janet told her they made the hearse take the long way around, because they didn't want Nikki to pass it on the road, because they were afraid she would wreck.

Nikki's Aunt Janet told her she prayed they had her Grandmother loaded and gone before Nikki got there. Nikki fell to the floor crying, both her Aunts tried to console her, but there was know consoling Nikki. She demanded to see her Grandmother, because she couldn't believe she was gone. Her Aunt Janet took Nikki to the funeral home and walked her to the back to see her Grandmother. Nikki saw her Grandmother lying on a cold hard steel slab in the holding-room. Nikki touched her Grandmother with trembling hands and burst into tears. Her aunt took Nikki in her arms and told Nikki to come with her, there was nothing more she could say or do at that point, but let them take care of her Grandmother.

Nikki went back to her Grandmother's house and waited for the family to come and make arrangements. She called Vincent, but he didn't want to attend, because the religion made him feel uncomfortable.

The funeral was difficult and Gabrielle told Nikki not to cry in front of her Grandfather. She said they all needed to be strong for him. Nikki tried, but she wasn't successful. Her Aunt Janet stayed by her side most of the time. Darwin was no-where to be found, he was in the bars drinking, except the day of the funeral. The preacher said some great things about Nikki's Grandmother during the funeral; then said in the end her Grandmother lost her religion, because she doubted God's will. Then Brother Jones said, he had to go pray for her Grandmother and she received a special anointing from God and said she was ready to go. It sounded to Nikki like he was portraying her Grandmother as a weak Christian and him being a hero. It was more than Nikki could stand; she bit her lip so she wouldn't stand up and curse him out right there in the church. Then it came time to pay their last respects. Nikki stood to follow in the precession and her Aunt Janet came up behind her. Nikki did really well until she got to the casket. Nikki realized that would be the last time she ever saw her Grandmother and lost her composure.

Nikki cried uncontrollably while her Aunt led her out the church with Nikki screaming,

'Don't let them take her away, please God don't take her away!"

Nikki couldn't understand at that moment; her Grandmother was already gone, she couldn't let go. Nikki stood in the bathroom with her Aunt trying to get herself together, while the pastor dismissed the church to go to the gravesite. Brother Jones waited for Nikki to express his condolences. When he called Nikki, she turned and saw red. Nikki screamed,

"How dare you ever think you were some hero to my Grandmother and you had to go pray, so she could receive an anointing from God, if there ever was a person on this earth that walked the walk and talked the talk of a true Christian it was her. She was dying; it was OK to have a fleeting moment in the end to hope or wonder if everything she believed all her life was true, it didn't make her a back slider or a non Christian!"

Bro Jones said he didn't mean it that way, but she did loose her faith for a fleeting moment. Nikki told him he had a lot of answering to do with God in the end and she prayed for his sake he had some dam good answers and if he wanted to talk about lost faith, they could talk about hers. He looked at Nikki and asked her what she meant. Nikki enlightened him to the fact, that she believed all he was, was a showpiece. She reminded him when she was pregnant and he called her to the alter to pray or God wouldn't give her another chance, she went to the alter and was praying from her heart for forgiveness for anything she could have done and he picked her head up off the alter and told her to pray for forgiveness, because she was sorry, not because she got caught. He looked at Nikki and told her he thought he remembered, but wasn't sure.

Nikki told him she would never forget it, because the child she carried was conceived from a rape, the secret her Grandmother just took to her grave, so she dam well knew his floor show was a fake, because God would have never sent her that message, because he too knew how that child was conceived. Bro Jones stood there speechless. Nikki told him to pray real hard, because from that exact moment on, her faith and trust in religion went to shit thanks to him and waked away.

Nikki got in her car and drove home, she couldn't go to the gravesite; she was pissed at the world for taking the only solid thing in her life away. She was left with nothing and she knew it. Nikki was angry with herself for not speaking the truth and speaking her true feelings. It took something huge to make her angry to express anything at all, the rest of the time she kept a plastered smile on her face, was well mannered and soft spoken, but dead inside. Nikki didn't feel a single emotion, not happiness, not sadness, she felt some anger, but she was a pro by that time of losing that emotion too. She knew she would never be able to trust another person like she trusted in her Grandmother, and she would never forgive another person that crossed her or hurt her again. She hated Vincent for making her go through that alone, but didn't have anywhere else to turn at the time, but to go back home.

Nikki returned to her life the best she could; she knew she would never be the same and that her family life was over. She talked to Kelly at work about a few feelings and resumed her life style as much as possible, which meant, Nikki and Kelly had lunch, and one or two nights a month out on the town.

Kelly was married to a great guy named Dean. He allowed Kelly to have as much freedom as she wanted within reason. Kelly was a sports fen and ran at least ten miles three times a week for exercise and one morning while out jogging Kelly was grabbed by two black men and beaten half to death and raped on the side of the street repeatedly. A woman getting up fixing coffee in the kitchen spotted the attack and called the police. When they heard the sirens coming they ran. Kelly couldn't identify the men, because she kept her hands up trying to block the blows to her face and eyes. She couldn't believe what was happening to her and didn't think to remember what her attackers looked like, so the lady that called the police gave a description of the two men.

The police department dispersed nine units to the scene and searched the area. They picked up two men fitting the description, but Kelly told the officers she couldn't identify them. The lady that called the police did identify the men as the attackers, so there were booked. One of the attackers had charges pending for sexually assaulting another woman and the other one had just been released from jail serving time for aggravated rape.

Kelly's whole life changed that day, the sweet faithful girl Nikki knew, left that day. Kelly started having affairs with several men she worked with including one of her bosses. She got a divorce and dated some really poor choices in men. Kelly didn't date and not sleep with the person she spent the evening with for quite a while. It wasn't unusual for Kelly to have four or five different partners in a week's time.

It put a strain on Nikki's relationship with Kelly, but Nikki knew her life was changing too at the time and needed to focus more on herself than what was going on with Kelly. Nikki thought Kelly didn't care or seem to be too concerned with what was going on in her own life, so if she didn't care about herself, know one could help her. Speaking from the past, Nikki couldn't judge Kelly for running, because she knew she had run her whole life too. What had happened to Kelly was a reminder of the un-godly thing she lived through and no matter what the cost; Nikki couldn't think of that then or ever, so Nikki moved on with her own life.

CHAPTER 20

Nikki called Dr Hawkins for an appointment as promised. She had never used birth control, so she knew she would have to do fertility drugs. Dr Hawkins referred Nikki to a specialist for an induction of fertility drugs as well as a magnitude of testing. They wanted to do a hystoscalpinggram and Nikki was told; it was no big deal. They would shoot some dye through her tubes and she would be back to work in an hour. When they shot the dye through her tubes, Nikki almost came off the table it hurt so bad. Her tubes were open, so she had a chance to conceive if they could get her to ovulate. Nikki went home after the test, not back to work. She barely made it to her car she was hurting so bad. When she got home, she called work, but could barely speak she was in so much pain. Her supervisor called Kelly and sent her to check on Nikki, because she sounded so bad. Kelly called Vincent and told him he needed to come home, because something obviously went wrong.

Nikki called the doctors office and was told her uterus was contracting trying to expel the dye. Nikki asked how long it would last and was told it could last up to twenty-four hours. Nikki hung up the phone and started crying. She told Vincent she couldn't stand the pain for twenty-four hours. Vincent sat on the end of the bed and asked Nikki what she wanted him to do. The tone in his voice pissed Nikki off, so she screamed at him to go the hell back to work and not worry about it. In that moment any and all feelings of security with Vincent left Nikki, she was left with nothing.

Nikki told herself if she got pregnant the baby would be her life and Vincent could live his. Nikki was placed on fertility drugs that made her moody, irritable, and almost homicidal at times. The doctors had to use the maximum dose allowable to stimulate Nikki's ovaries and harvest her eggs. Nikki just thought the pain from the hystoscalpinggram was bad, but on the fourth month, she got pregnant.

Dr. Hawkins called Nikki at work to tell her she was pregnant. She stood up, while on the phone with the doctor and said out loud,

"I'm pregnant, I'm really pregnant!"

The whole office cheered. Nikki thought more, because the bitchiness would be gone, than the fact she was pregnant, but she didn't care, she was pregnant. Then standing in the cafeteria one of the girls that worked in customer service went bouncing through the lounge all bubbly and happy. Kelly asked her why she was so happy, had she gotten laid the night before or what. She turned to Kelly and said Desmond Stewart had fucked her half the night. Nikki almost dropped her teeth. Kelly looked at Nikki and asked her if she was all right. Nikki said, she was fine and left the cafeteria. Nikki never wanted to hear Desmond's name again as long as she lived.

Nikki thought life would settle down after she got pregnant. She was glad she had done fertility drugs to conceive, because she didn't want Vincent to touch her. She and Vincent had settled into a life without sex and for Nikki she was content with just a roommate.

Nikki's pregnancy was difficult from conception. She had major side effects from the fertility drugs that were still in her system. The combination of the drugs and the pregnancy made Nikki sick as a dog. Nikki vomited from the time her feet hit the floor until she got in bed at night and slept with a trash can by her bed in case she woke up in the middle of the night. Nikki starting dropping weight and lost pound after pound, even with the doctors trying to stabilize Nikki she got sicker and sicker. She quit her job, because she couldn't function anymore. Nikki laid on the bathroom floor many days just crying. She told Vincent she had never ever considered terminating a pregnancy, but she didn't know how much more she could take.

Vincent saw how sick Nikki was and told her if she felt like that was something she needed to do, he would support her decision. Nikki tried to tough it out, but she just kept getting sicker and sicker. Things were getting worse not better. The doctors told Nikki she would not go to term with the pregnancy if things continued on the same path as they were. They did sonogram after sonogram to look for birth defects; there were none, all test came back normal. Nikki had a viable fetus, but her body was shutting down slowly, but surely. Then at the fifth month the nausea finally stopped. There was nothing left of Nikki except skin and bones. Nikki started eating and holding food down. She was discharged from the specialist back to her regular OB doctor. Dr. Hawkins saw her on a Friday afternoon and did another sonogram. He told Nikki all looked well, so she needed to go home and prepare to have a baby.

Nikki called Candice to tell her she could bring her maternity cloths over the next day and help her baby shop for the nursery. Candice said she would be there early the next morning and they would shop all day. The girls made plans for that Sunday, to bar-b-que and make the guys assemble everything. Saturday morning Nikki got up, got dressed, and headed to the baby store. She bought everything a person could imagine, a baby bed, changing table, stroller, high chair, walker, basinet, cloths, blankets, diapers and bottles. You name it; Nikki bought it. They were finished shopping by noon and Nikki called Vincent to have him meet her with a truck to bring the baby things home.

Vincent and Mike picked everything up at the store and Mike told Nikki they were going to go a head and bar-b-que that afternoon, and put everything together, so they could watch the game on TV the next day. Nikki laughed and agreed it would be a good idea. Candice washed all the maternity cloths and ironed them for Nikki. She finished dinner and demanded Nikki sit with her legs up and relax for the afternoon, so Nikki sat and watched TV while everyone else worked around her and supervised the nursery telling them where to put everything. Candice made the bed and put the baby cloths away. That night when everyone was gone, Nikki walked in the nursery and told her unborn child she carried inside her, she couldn't wait for it to see its little room. Nikki sat in the rocker and rocked thinking how complete she felt at that exact moment in time.

Nikki was tired, she had too much excitement for one day, so she told Vincent she was going to bed early. He kissed her on the cheek and told her he would be in later. Nikki went to bed and fell asleep before her head hit the pillow. Vincent woke her the next morning to tell her he was going to get a newspaper and donuts. He told Nikki to go back to sleep, he wouldn't be long, so Nikki rolled over and drifted off to sleep again. She wasn't sure how long Vincent had been gone when she woke up and felt sick to her stomach again and realized she was shaking. She thought she just needed some juice to feel better, so Nikki got out of bed and staggered to the Kitchen. She opened the refrigerator door and poured herself a glass of orange juice.

Nikki knew she felt weak and different from ever before, but just told herself to drink the orange juice and wake up. Nikki was drinking her juice when she felt something warm running down her legs, when she looked down, blood was everywhere. Nikki looked up and followed the trail of blood from the kitchen to the bedroom. She made it back to the bed and jerked the covers back; her side of the bed was coved with blood. Nikki reached for the phone to page her doctor. Dr. Hawkins called Nikki back immediately and told her, he already had an ambulance in route to her. Dr. Hawkins told her to lay down and not move until they got there. Nikki was crying when Dr. Hawkins told her to stay on the line with him until the ambulance got there. He asked Nikki where her husband was and Nikki told him he had gone to the store and should be back any minute. The ambulance was loading Nikki to take her to the hospital when Vincent got home.

When they arrived Dr. Hawkins was waiting for Nikki. On examination Nikki was told her cervix had opened and she had dilated 8 centimeters. Dr. Hawkins then told the nurse to go get a machine for a sonogram. When she returned Dr. Hawkins did the test; Nikki was watching the machine and asked were the heartbeat was. Dr. Hawkins told Nikki he was measuring the baby right then, he wasn't looking for a heartbeat, but Nikki knew on all the sonograms she had before, the heartbeat was the first visible thing they saw. Nikki turned to Vincent. He was sitting in the corner of the room like a zombie with know expression on his face, as if he wasn't there. She looked back at Dr. Hawkins just as he took her hand and said,

"I am sorry Nik, there is no heart beat."

Nikki started crying as Dr. Hawkins sat on the side of Nikki's bed holding her hand, when Nikki looked at him he had tears in his eyes as well and she asked what was going to happen to her. Dr. Hawkins said he did the test to determine if he needed to call the neonatal team in, but then he had to get the baby out. The problem, Nikki had drank orange juice, which would put her at risk during surgery. Nikki instantly sat up in bed and dried her tears, because she knew then her life was on the line. She looked at Vincent and saw that far away stare with no emotion and knew he would not get her through this ordeal.

Vincent finally stood and walked to Nikki's bedside, she thought to comfort her or tell her everything would be all right, but he walked up and said he was stepping out the room to call his mother. Dr. Hawkins looked at Vincent strange, as if he too expected more from him or at least some sort of a reaction.

Dr. Hawkins told Nikki he was going to pack her and place her in holding for surgery. He said she had to go six hours from the time she drank the orange juice and by his calculations they needed to hold her off at least four and a half more hours. Dr. Hawkins also said if they could not contain the bleeding with packing her, she would have to be rushed to surgery and the risk of complications would be higher. Nikki asked Dr. Hawkins, if she could use a phone, because she had to call someone she knew she could trust to help her through the ordeal. Dr. Hawkins told her as soon as he packed her and she was placed in holding, he would get her a phone.

Nikki was packed with sterile gauze and placed in holding; she was hurting pretty bad so they placed her on a monitor. When they put her on the monitor, they realized she was contracting. Dr. Hawkins brought Nikki the phone and told her, that her body was trying to deliver the baby. The afterbirth was still attached to the uterine wall, but was pulling away and causing the hemorrhaging. So she needed to get who ever she needed there quickly. Nikki called her friend Renee at Ms Canny's. They told Nikki they were on their way not to worry. Then Gina Vincent's mother walked in, just as Nikki was hanging up the phone. She looked at Nikki and told her she knew they should have never tried to conceive a child the way they did, because it wasn't Gods way. The nurse was standing at bedside with Nikki when Gina said those words and saw the effect it had on Nikki, so Gina was asked to leave the room. Vincent stood at the foot of the bed and stared off in space.

The social worker came in to talk to Nikki and Vincent about the baby and planning ahead. She told Nikki she needed to see the baby for a healthy mourning process. Vincent spoke up immediately and said he didn't think that was a good idea. He looked at Nikki and told her,

"Just let it go."

The social worker said, this was a child inside Nikki's body and it was important to deal with the issue and mourn the loss. Vincent told her to just dispose of the body however and let it be. The social worker told him, it wasn't that simple. This baby would be born weighing over the minimum grams and would be required by law to be named and buried. Vincent had a fit for the first time in their life, so the social worker told him there was one other option. They could donate the body to science and request they dispose of the body when they were finished with the remains. Vincent insisted that was how it should be handled. He told the social worker he didn't want to see the baby and didn't want to know the sex of it either.

The nurse asked Vincent to walk out in the hall to be with his mother while the nurse examined Nikki to see if the bleeding was under control.

When he was gone the social worker told Nikki she had choices in the decision too, if she wanted to handle things differently. Nikki asked if she would be awake when they took the baby. The nurse told Nikki she would be put to sleep, because of the likelihood of complications, but would wake up in recovery. Nikki told the social worker she wanted to see the baby just once to say goodbye. The social worker told Nikki they would bring her the baby in recovery, prior to bringing her out on the floor to her room.

The nurse examined Nikki and said she had to call the doctor, because the bandages were soaked in blood. As she was leaving Ms Canny, Renee, and Kristy walked through the door. Nikki started crying as soon as she saw them. Dr. Hawkins went in shortly after they got there to take a look at the bandages. He put the covers back down after examining Nikki and said he had to get her to surgery. He ordered a pre-op shot for Nikki, because she became so up-set. Vincent was trying to talk to Nikki telling her to calm down, but nothing was going to work, especially not him at that moment. Ms Canny told Vincent and Kirsty to step outside the room and let her talk to Nikki a minute. She wanted to get Vincent out of Nikki's site and Kristy, because she was crying. Ms Canny walked to Nikki's bedside and told her to let the nurse give her the shot. Nikki told her she couldn't, but Ms Canny touched Nikki's face and told her to look at her and said,

"Look at me baby, look at your mama and know, I won't let anything bad happen to you, just look at me and know my face will be the last one you see and the first one you'll see when you wake up."

Ms Canny pulled Nikki's face towards her and motioned for the nurse to give Nikki the shot. Nikki asked if it would hit her right away and the nurse said'

"Are you kidding?"

Nikki consented to the shot and stared at Ms Canny with tears streaming down her face. As soon as the nurse backed away from the bed the room started spinning, Nikki looked at the nurse and told her, she thought she said; it wouldn't hit her that soon. The nurse backed up against the wall in the room as Nikki looked back at Ms Canny. The last words Nikki spoke before losing consciousness was,

"Please don't let them take my baby."

Nikki didn't wake up in recovery; she woke up the next evening with Dr. Hawkins, the Anesthesiologist and a Nurse at her bedside. Dr. Hawkins told Nikki she gave them quite a scare. They had thought she was slipping into a coma from shock. Nikki had almost stopped breathing on them, because she didn't have enough of a certain enzyme in her body to breakdown the drugs given to her in surgery.

When Nikki could open her eyes she saw, Ms Canny standing there waiting. Vincent was in the hall with his Mom, and Renee was sleeping on the cot beside Nikki's bed. Gina walked in and told Nikki not to worry, because they were going to get her a baby. Dr. Hawkins told Nikki adoption was an incredible experience and one she should look into, in the near future. Nikki asked if she could try again to get pregnant, but. Dr. Hawkins took Nikki's hand again and told her she almost lost her life with that pregnancy and because of her history and the complications of the pregnancy he felt strongly, she should not attempt another pregnancy or it would cost her, her life. Gina hugged Nikki and told her, she scared the crap out of all of them, but she knew that Nikki would pull through somehow.

Then the social worker went in to talk to Nikki, when Nikki saw her; she asked if everyone would please let her be alone with the social worker. Vincent said he would stay, but Nikki looked at him and told him to go home, she wanted to be alone. The social worker asked everyone to please respect Nikki's request and allow her to call them if she needed anything. Vincent left with his Mother without a word. Ms Canny, Kristy and Renee hugged Nikki and told her they loved her and made her promise to call if she needed anything. Nikki told them she would and thanked Ms Canny for coming, because she wouldn't have gotten through it any other way.

When everyone was gone, the social worker told Nikki, because she didn't wake up in recovery, they held the baby. She asked Nikki if she still wanted the baby brought to her for viewing and Nikki said she did. The social worker told her, she would be back shortly with the baby and Nikki pulled herself up in bed and waited. She was trying to prepare to say goodbye to something she wanted more than breathing herself. Nikki didn't know how she would feel holding her dead baby in her arms and thought she might faint if it was stiff. Then Nikki started to cry. She refused to feel her pain and dried her tears. The thunder rolled inside her mind and the internal tornado brewing was a category ten, but Nikki pushed it aside once again.

The social worker walked in with the nurse pushing a basinet. The nurse picked the baby up from the basinet and handed it to Nikki. Nikki looked at the nurse and asked if it was a boy or a girl. The nurse told her, she had a girl and she weighed one pound and fourteen ounces. When Nikki took the baby from the nurse she was startled when she felt the baby was warm. Nikki asked the nurse how that was possible and the nurse told Nikki, because the baby was being donated to science she was held in the NICU area with fluids and kept under a warmer until they knew for sure Nikki did or didn't want to see her. Nikki turned back to the baby and asked if she could be alone with her, so the Nurse and the social worker left after they told Nikki they were placing a sign on the door not to disturb her. The nurse told Nikki to call when she was ready for them to take the baby and asked Nikki if she wanted a rocker brought in the room.

Nikki looked at the nurse with tears in her eyes and told her a rocker would be nice. When they left the room Nikki laid the baby on the bed with her and removed the blankets slowly. Nikki was scared to see any deformities, so she was pacing herself in viewing the body. The baby was perfect, just so tiny, her eyes were still fused shut, but other than that she was perfect, Nikki touched her tiny toes and counted all ten, she looked at her legs perfectly formed, she had a cute little butt, so Nikki told her she got her butt from her mommy. Nikki looked at her stomach, her umbilical cord still attached, her arms were perfect and she still had hair on her back and shoulders. She had a head full of blond hair. Her ears were perfect, her lips were perfect and her nose was beautiful. Nikki put the cloths they brought her in back on her and put her bonnet back on her head and wrapped her in her blanket. Nikki told her she looked like an angel and picked her up and held her close. Nikki tried to be strong, but the tears streamed down her face.

The nurse knocked on the door and asked if she could bring the rocking chair in and Nikki told her to place the rocker in front of the window. The nurse took the baby, so Nikki could get out of bed and settle in the chair. When Nikki stood the room started spinning and she told the nurse she was going to faint. The nurse told Nikki she would be weak the first time she tried to stand, but to take it slow. Nikki took a few steps towards the rocker and the blood trickled down her legs. She looked at the nurse and asked if the bleeding was ok or was she bleeding too much. The nurse told her, she would bleed a little heavy; because of how far along she was. She said for Nikki to take it easy, but she needed to move around some as well. Nikki made it to the chair and the nurse cleaned the blood off the floor and handed Nikki the call light to call when she was ready. Before she left she placed the baby in Nikki's arms again. Nikki rocked the baby and told her she would always and forever be an angel to her. She promised she would remember her like that always. Nikki kissed her on the cheek and called for the nurse.

The nurse came back to the room and asked Nikki if she wanted any photos or prints, like handprints or footprints, but Nikki declined the offer and asked her to please just take the baby away. The nurse placed the baby in the basinet and carried her away. Nikki didn't really want to donate the body to science, but she didn't think she could bare a funeral either, so she didn't protest Vincent's decision to have the baby's body donated.

Nikki was discharged the next day. When Vincent showed up to get her, he told Nikki they would never discuss the baby again. They would put it behind them and move on. Nikki looked at him like he had lost his mind, but didn't speak a word. Nikki knew for Vincent he would never discuss the baby again or talk about his feelings. Nikki knew for her, that child died inside her, so that made her feelings different. Nikki felt lost, empty, hurt, angry, disillusioned, and frustrated. Her emotions were like a whirlwind spinning all around her, a whirlwind she couldn't get out of. Not only was she faced with losing her baby, she also was faced with the fact her own health was in danger and she would never have another child of her own.

Nikki hated God and everything he represented. She wanted to know why or what she had done too loose the only three things she really cared about. She wanted to know why her innocence was stripped from her and why God's master plan allowed her to give birth to Tricia and lost her the way she did and wanted to know why she couldn't have another child of her own.

Nikki felt a rise, as if the tides were coming in and flooding out in her mind. She stood as if she was on a beech watching the ocean. Nikki knew there was a hurricane brewing inside her, one that would be a category ten on a reactor scale, but she turned her mind off and forced the door closed again. Nikki drifted back into a world of silence. Nikki tried to tell herself that it didn't matter and to move on with her life. She thought if she put it out of her mind and moved in another direction she would be all right. She decided to move into adoption and focus her attention there.

When Nikki got home, Dr. Hawkins had left some pamphlets on adoption for her to take with her from the hospital. She read through the pages and felt hope one last time. Vincent was ready to move straight into the adoption world and walked around as if nothing had happened, so Nikki did the same. They became people that existed in a room together; not quite strangers, but not quite friends either, they just existed. There was a big white elephant in the room that they didn't look at, didn't talk about or acknowledge the presence of.

Vincent called the adoption agencies to see how to start the process and they gave their requirements and stipulations for adoption. Most of the adoption agencies were into open adoptions at the time, where the adoptive parents knew the birth mother and the birth mother knew the adoptive parents. Nikki told Vincent without a doubt she wanted know part of any open adoption and if that was the only way they could adopt, she refused to be an active participate.

Then Vincent found, "Heaven's Arms," an adoption agency that was working with children from Russia. Most of the children there were handicapped in one form or another, but this agency was getting lucky in getting mostly healthy children, so Nikki agreed to start the process and see where it would lead.

They had to go through the home study process first. Nikki and Vincent were interviewed by social workers, therapist, had to have physicals, pass drug screens, local police clearance and a federal clearance with the FBI, because they would be adopting abroad. Their financial history was reviewed; their current and past employers were interviewed, as well as their neighbors. Nikki thought in was an unbelievable process before they were cleared for adoption.

Nikki began concentrating on the adoption more and more everyday. There was so much to do and get ready for the new baby. Then Nikki realized one morning, the door to the baby's room was closed when she got home from the hospital and had remained closed. She remembered all the baby things that were all over the house when she left to go to the hospital and she hadn't seen a single baby thing since she got home. Nikki stood outside the door to the baby's room with one hand on the door and the other on the doorknob. She hesitated almost holding her breath when she opened the door. She closed her eyes and walked in. When Nikki knew she should be in the center of the room she opened her eyes slowly. The room was empty; there wasn't a stitch of furniture or one diaper left in sight. Nikki was over taken by a rush of emotions and collapsed on the floor crying. Then she dried her eyes and told herself, it was better that way. She thought it really would be a fresh start, so she started planning another nursery.

Nikki was trying to plan a new life, eating and trying to stabilize her weight, but the pounds just kept falling off. Nikki was already so tiny before the pregnancy; she had weighed eighty-nine pounds. Even though Nikki only weighed eighty-nine pounds, she looked solid with her bone structure and looked healthy. Nikki wanted to stay at her pre-pregnancy weight, but her body had another thing in mind. She continued to shed the pounds know matter how much she ate. Nikki thought if she just went about her life and continued to eat, she would be all right eventually.

The adoption agency called to let Nikki know that she and Vincent were placed on the list to leave for Russia in two months. Nikki's heart skipped a beat when they told her the news and agreed that her and Vincent would go and choose their child when they got there. Nikki called Vincent at work to give him the news. He too seemed excited and told Nikki he had told her everything would work out. She called several of her friends to give them the news and everyone was excited about new arrival.

That afternoon Tom and Candy from next door wanted to bar-b-que, and celebrate. They had a two-year-old little girl named Morgan, tiny and cute as a bug in a rug. Morgan loved Nikki, she ran to hug Nikki every-time she saw her. The two couples had spent a lot of time together playing cards one night a week and a bar-b-que one-day on the weekend. One night Nikki was embarrassed while playing cards, when Tom asked when she was going to lay out again. Nikki asked how he knew she had laid out that day and Candy told Nikki she had to make Tom go inside when he spotted her through the fence. Nikki had been laying out topless in her backyard. She thought she was safe with the wood fence, but obviously not. Nikki apologized, but Candy laughed it off, so Nikki let it go, but she didn't lay out in her back yard again unless she knew Tom and Candy weren't at home.

That night at dinner, Candy told Nikki she was concerned because she looked really bad. Nikki said she was dropping weight and couldn't figure out why, so Candy told Nikki she needed to go back to see her doctor to make sure everything was all right, especially before she got on a plane. Nikki told Candy she had an appointment the next week to see Dr. Hawkins and not to worry.

When Nikki got to her appointment with Dr. Hawkins the nurse weighed Nikki in at sixty-one pounds and Dr. Hawkins had a fit and asked Nikki if she was mourning herself to death or what. Nikki told him she was eating and she was leaving for Russia in seven weeks to adopt a baby, but Dr. Hawkins told Nikki he was calling her husband, because she was going to the hospital. Dr. Hawkins wanted to run test, but told Nikki he thought she was anorexic. When Nikki asked what that was, Dr. Hawkins told her it was an eating disorder that some women had that made them starve themselves to death. Nikki laughed and told him he had lost his mind and she was going home, but Dr. Hawkins told Nikki she wasn't going anywhere, because he was getting a corners bond as they spoke to have Nikki committed.

Nikki asked,

"Committed to what?"

Dr. Hawkins, told her she was going to be placed in "Physicians Hospital," to address her eating disorder. Nikki wanted a simple answer as to what was wrong with her, so she thought

"It's just an eating disorder."

Nikki said she would go to the hospital, take care of the eating disorder and be fine, but Dr. Hawkins told her it wouldn't be that simple that there had to be several underlining issues that created the state and fixing it would take some time. Nikki told him he had seven weeks and not a day past that, because nothing was going to stop her from being a Mom. Dr. Hawkins called Vincent at work and told him to come to his office right away. He called the hospital, reserved a bed and spoke with the medical director Dr. Black to let him know Nikki was coming that day.

Nikki arrived at the hospital and met the staff. She was put threw several test to determine if she was stable physically and then went threw a series of psychological testing. After all the results were completed she was placed in the eating disorder program with the deadliest diagnosis of, "Anorexia with Bulimic Tendencies."

She was told her life was in jeopardy, but to Nikki it didn't sink in. She met the eating disorder team she would be working with. The head psychologist named Dr. Patricia Jean Martin and her assistant Sammy Dody whom was working on her masters. Both were females called by nicknames to be more personal in-group settings they became known to Nikki as PJ and Sam.

PJ was warm and personal, but a bitch at times. Nikki butted heads on a regular basis with Sam, because she was head strong and confronting. In-group settings, Sam called on Nikki repeatedly on issues she refused to discuss. When Nikki told them about the adoption both PJ and Sam were adamant she should wait. Nikki was adamant she wasn't going to wait. They told her she would die if she adopted a child then, but Nikki told them they had lost there minds and asked why they thought a child would kill her. PJ told Nikki she would wrap herself up in caring for the child and forget she was sick herself and die. Dr. Black didn't agree with PJ that Nikki had a true eating disorder, so her treatment team was divided and after the three day corners bond was up Nikki left the hospital against medical advice. She was home four days when the adoption agency called asking if she would consider a closed adoption of a handicap child in the states. Nikki told the agency she wanted a copy of the child's medical records and a photo, so the agency agreed she would have the information by noon the next day. When Nikki opened the package, she read the reports before she opened the envelope with the photo. The child was a male in stable condition, but diagnosed with,

"Downs Syndrome."

Nikki opened the envelope and saw the picture of the little man in a green suit smiling and something inside Nikki knew this child would be hers for the rest of her life. A child that really needed a Mommy and Mommy that really needed a child.

Nikki called Vincent and told him she got the package. Vincent asked Nikki what she thought, so she told him she wanted to accept the child and not go to Russia. Vincent went home to look at the paperwork and after he read all the papers and saw the photo Vincent agreed with Nikki this was the one and Vincent called his Mom. When she arrived, she told Vincent and Nikki they were making a mistake. Then, Vincent's sister showed up and threw a fit over bringing another handicapped child into the family on purpose. Nikki threw her out the house and told her not to come back. Vincent told Gina he wanted to be a Dad and because of his age that might be his only chance. He told Gina that the children in Russia were also handicapped and some would have far greater problems than this child, so Gina told Vincent and Nikki she would stand behind their decision if Nikki was well physically. Nikki assured Gina she was eating and she would be fine in a few weeks.

Nikki continued to try and eat and called the adoption agency to accept the baby and the paperwork was started for the adoption. Nikki put food in her mouth and swallowed, but it came back up without her trying to vomit. She could drink liquids, but she couldn't eat solid food so Nikki returned to the hospital and was admitted to the eating disorder program under Dr. Ashton. He was from India and soft spoken. After interviewing Nikki he told her he wanted her in the eating disorder program, but also wanted her in the sexual trauma program as well and would be starting Nikki on some medication. Nikki agreed, but thought the sexual trauma program would be a waist of time and was scared to death to take the medicine, but said she would trust him if he didn't drug her.

The sexual trauma program was not a waste of time, but put Nikki in touch with emotions she wasn't prepared for. She talked about the rape in the beginning with know emotion what so ever, just like she was telling a story. When Nikki started to process the rape she couldn't deal with the emotions it invoked so she refused to return to the group. Nikki took her medicine and was drugged out of her mind for three days again. Nikki couldn't function, but refused any more medicine. She stayed in the eating disorder program thinking if they could get her body to accept food again everything else would just fall in place.

Nikki told PJ and Sam about the baby on the way and showed them the picture of the baby so they decided if they couldn't talk her out of the adoption they would use it as a motivating factor to get Nikki to eat. PJ asked Nikki for the photo at lunch, so Nikki went to her room to get the picture. When she returned she gave the picture to PJ and she placed the picture in front of Nikki and told her to eat lunch while looking at the photo and decide how much she wanted the child. Nikki asked her what she meant by that, so PJ told her if she really wanted him she would eat her lunch and Nikki agreed. They brought Nikki red-beans and rice with sausage. PJ saw Nikki struggling, so she got Nikki talking about the baby while eating. Before Nikki realized what she had done, she had cleaned her plate. When she realized she ate everything, she had a panic attack. She jumped up and started pulling at her cloths, she couldn't breathe, she was full and the feeling was uncomfortable to her, she couldn't breath, PJ tried to talk Nikki down, but she was too far gone. The adrenalin was pumping, her heart racing and sweat was forming on Nikki's skin, she felt faint and nauseated, she told PJ she was going to through up, but PJ told her to breath and calm down. Nikki picked up her tray and threw it at PJ. When PJ stood, Nikki took off running down the hall looking for a bathroom. She heard PJ on her portable radio calling for back up as she got through the doors.

Nikki ran to every bathroom she could find, they were all locked. When she got to the last bathroom Nikki was running her fingers down her throat to make herself vomit and PJ was hot on her trail; Nikki was screaming she had to get it out, while PJ was trying to catch up with her. When Nikki made it to the last door it too was locked. Nikki turned just as PJ grabbed her. Nikki looked at PJ and told her if she let them put her in a straight jacket she would never eat again and would die and it would be her fault. PJ put Nikki up against the wall and told her if she threw up she was going in a straightjacket period. Nikki could feel the food at the back of her throat. She swallowed to keep herself from vomiting as the little men in white jackets approached. PJ stood there holding Nikki against the wall and Nikki burst into tears and slide to the floor. PJ called off the men in white, but Nikki looked up at her and told her she hated her and would never forgive her for tricking her. PJ told Nikki she would see that she would feel better after she calmed down and know she didn't die because she ate a fear food.

Nikki starting eating after that meal, one hundred percent of her meal plans. The baby was coming the next week, but PJ wasn't prepared to let Nikki out the hospital. As much as Nikki was eating she wasn't gaining weight as fast as they thought she should be, so they called her in and asked how and or when she was purging her food. Nikki got upset, because she wasn't purging. PJ told her that they were going to increase her meal plan again to see if that would help her. Nikki had a certain amount of pounds she had to gain prior to discharge and she wasn't close.

When Nikki checked in, she weighed sixty-one pounds and was told she had to gain fifteen pounds before she could be discharged. Nikki asked how much she weighed, but she was told that information was privileged. Nikki was weighed every morning with her back to the scale. PJ told her that even as much as she was eating she had only gained five pounds and Nikki started crying and told PJ she couldn't understand why she wasn't gaining weight, because she stayed stuffed all the time. PJ told her, she would be going threw some more test, but in the mean time they were increasing her intake. Nikki told her she couldn't eat anymore, but PJ told her this would be a true test of her stabilization prior to discharge.

Nikki's intake was increased and the baby came all at the same time. Gina took the baby until Nikki could be discharged, but Nikki was granted permission to leave the hospital for one night to get the baby at the airport and get him settled at her mother-in-law's before the next morning.

Nikki and Vincent went to the airport after Vincent picked her up at the hospital. They waited together for the arrival of their son coming into their lives. When the social worker stepped off the plane with the baby, Nikki met her at the door. She placed the baby in Nikki's arms while introducing her to her son. Nikki took him and said,

"Hello little man, I'm your Mommy and this is your Daddy. We'll be calling you Andy from now on."

Andy snuggled up to Nikki, but had know emotion on his face. His little hand extended and touched Nikki on the face. Nikki cried when Vincent spoke to Andy. It was a very emotional moment for Nikki. The social worker asked if she could bum a ride home, so Vincent told her they could drop her off on their way in. Nikki held Andy all the way home. As soon as they dropped the social worker off, Andy vomited all over Nikki in the car. She wiped Andy and herself off the best she could with the baby blanket, but he vomited again before they could get home and Nikki was up all night with Andy vomiting. She called Gina frantic at six' o'clock in the morning and Gina told her she would call the pediatrician the rest of the grandkids used to see if she could get Andy seen that morning.

When Nikki took Andy to the doctor with Vincent he was diagnosed with ear infections in both ears and an upper respiratory infection. The doctor said the ride in the plane aggravated the ear infection and threw his equilibrium off, so he gave him a shot and told Nikki he would be fine. Nikki told Vincent she didn't want to return to the hospital, because the baby was sick and needed her. Vincent told her she had to go back and not to worry, his Mother would take care of Andy and he would bring the baby to see her every night. Nikki told Vincent she would go back, but they had to go take their first family photo. After the picture was taken Nikki was dropped off at the hospital and Vincent took Andy to Gina.

Nikki ate one hundred percent of the meal plan they gave her and was assigned another tech to follow her for two hours after all meals. Since Nikki was eating every two-hours she lived with her tech. Even with the meal plan Nikki was given, she still only gained five more pounds at the same rate she had gained the last five pounds. PJ and the treatment team were startled. They knew with certainty she wasn't purging, but she wasn't gaining like she should either.

Nikki continued her groups and did as she was told, but she stopped gaining weight at seventy-four pounds. It didn't matter what she ate or how much she ate, IV calories, shakes, candy-bars, the list went on with her meal plan; she stopped gaining. Nikki had been in the hospital three months by then. Nikki was finally released to follow up with an internal medicine specialist and continue therapy in an outpatient day program were she would have all her meals at the hospital and go home at night.

When she got home it was baby shower after baby shower. Andy was better and everyone was accepting of the adoption. Andy's face started to light up. Everything about him began to change. Nikki had some more photos taken of Andy after she had, had him for four months and the two photos of Andy; the first day after they got him and the second four months later; he looked like a totally different child. He totally glowed in the second photo. Andy's second birthday was approaching, so Nikki planned his party at a local amusement park and Tom dressed up like a clown and the party was on. Morgan from next door played with Andy everyday and called him her,

"Little Poopsy."

It was too cute. Tom and Candy were heart broken when Nikki told them they were going to start looking for a house. Nikki thought things were looking up. Vincent wanted to buy a house close to his Mother and Nikki agreed and started looking.

PJ wanted Vincent to do family counseling to understand all that had happened and make sure he knew what to do and not to do at meal times, but mainly to talk about their relationship. Vincent agreed, but when PJ asked him how he felt about being in a sexless marriage, he said it didn't bother him, because he was not a sexual person and wasn't driven by sex. Then PJ asked Nikki how she felt about it. Nikki told PJ at the time she was all right with it, but knew it wouldn't be ok for the rest of her life.

Vincent was closed off during the counseling sessions and quite. Nikki was bouncing off the walls screaming and having fits, but he just sat there with know emotion. Nikki told Vincent she was a prostitute, had a drug problem and liked to fuck women. He sat there with no emotion and said it didn't matter. When Nikki screamed at him about the baby that died and told him he had a daughter. He told her he was not discussing that subject with her ever again. PJ told him he couldn't act like it never happened. Vincent told PJ that all the therapy was for Nikki not him, that Nikki was the one with the issues, he didn't have any, but PJ told him if his wife had issues, so did he and if he wanted his marriage he had better be willing to deal with those issues or they would destroy their marriage.

Vincent told PJ again that he didn't have any issues and didn't care what Nikki did in their marriage or before he married her. He would always be there and if Nikki got her shit straight their marriage would be fine. PJ told Vincent he was looking through rose colored glasses and needed to see things as they truly were, but Vincent continued to not show a single emotion. He remained on his path of the straight and narrow, but refused to acknowledge there were problems in the marriage. He told Nikki he wasn't going back to therapy, because it wasn't helping either of them and she needed to just get a grip and leave well enough alone. Nikki decided to leave therapy also and devote her life to her family and see what the future would hold. PJ told Nikki she was running from all her emotions and she was setting herself up for a fall that could and one day would take her sanity if she didn't deal with her issues and stop skating around them. PJ told her to plow through the middle and stop touching on them and closing the doors, because all those bottled up emotions would one day explode. Nikki told PJ she was crazy and told her of course, she didn't want her to leave therapy, because she was nothing, but a money machine for her. PJ told her she was sorry she saw it that way and wished her well, but also told her when she was really ready to deal, to call her, she would be there. Nikki left therapy, bought a house, found a new job, and started remodeling her home.

The next year, Nikki spent going room-to-room remodeling. She painted, hung wallpaper, re-finished cabinets and spent all her time with Andy. She and Vincent touched in the halls passing, but not in their bedroom. Nikki didn't care; she bought a new car every year, lived in a three thousand square foot house with a pool in the back yard, bought a hot tub and hung out with the neighbors. She became friends with the new neighbors, Bill and Perry Jackson and their two girls Lain and Leslie. Nikki introduced Vincent to the neighbors and Vincent spoke to Bill, but never really bonded with him. Nikki and Perry became really good friends. They talked about a lot in their lives and after a while they really got to know each other. Perry was a scaredy cat; she wouldn't go out after dark and was completely paranoid over her kid's safety. After a while, Nikki asked, what her problem was and Perry told Nikki she was raped in her home by a man that had came through a window of her parent's house when she was young and she had never gotten over it.

CHAPTER 21

Perry spent more and more time with Nikki who was free spirited and not afraid of anything. It must have rubbed off, because Perry started doing more and more after dark. At first she wouldn't go out alone, Nikki or one of the girls had to be with her. Then slowly she ventured out on her own. It was an amazing transformation for Nikki to watch.

Nikki and Perry shared cooking duties. Two nights a week Nikki cooked and two nights a week Perry cooked. The other times they ate at Gina's after work or had a sandwich. Nikki was back at work with another computer company doing tech-support and loving it. The house was finished, the landscaping complete, so it was time to reap the benefits of her work.

Then Nikki got a call from Desmond. The two talked like old friends and Nikki told Desmond how frustrated she got at times with Vincent and Desmond actually defended Vincent's honor. He laughed at Nikki's sense of humor when she told him about some arguments she had, had with Vincent and how sometimes she wanted to shake him to see if he reacted. Desmond told her to have patience with him and he would come around in time. Desmond wanted to see Nikki, but she knew her marriage wasn't strong enough for an encounter with Desmond, so the best thing she could do was to stay away from him and she did.

Nikki was happy to hear from Desmond, she thought of him from time to time and wondered sometimes about the; what could have beens or just how he was doing. The love in her heart still had a faint glow even though the flame had long been blown out. Nikki talked to Desmond about her sex life a little, not too much, just enough to say she didn't have one and didn't miss it either. Desmond told her, it was hard to imagine her in a sexless relationship, because she was always so sexual. Nikki told

Desmond, that sexual being had cost her a lot and she was content where she was, but she wasn't about to see Desmond to put it to the test either. The conversations got less frequent and stopped altogether, once again.

Then shortly after the phone calls with Desmond stopped, Nikki went to pick Andy up one afternoon from Gina's after work. When she saw Gina, she asked her how she was feeling. Gina told her she was fine, but Nikki told her that her color didn't look right, she couldn't put a finger on it, but her color was strange. Gina told her she had thought the same that morning, but she must have eaten something that changed her skin tone, but she was sure she was fine. Nikki took Andy home and told Vincent he needed to go check on his Mother. Vincent told Nikki she was just being paranoid, that Gina was fine, so Nikki let it go.

The next morning, the phone rang at six o'clock on a Saturday, it was Gina and she wanted to talk to Nikki. When Nikki got on the phone, she told Nikki to come to her house something was really wrong. Nikki asked her what the problem was and Gina told her, her skin was completely yellow. Nikki sat straight up in bed and said,

"Oh my God Gina, you've got hepatitis!" and told Gina she would be right there.

When Nikki got to Gina's, her skin was flaming yellow; even the whites of her eyes were yellow. Nikki told her she had to go to the hospital right away and get checked; especially if it was hepatitis, because the kids were exposed and would need treatment as well. Nikki called Vincent and told him to get out of bed and come to his Mothers, because he needed to take her to the hospital and Vincent said he would be right there.

Vincent took Gina to the hospital and Nikki stayed with Andy. She told Vincent to call her the minute he found out what was wrong. Nine hours later Vincent pulled up with Gina. Nikki asked what they found and was told they didn't know, but they did know it wasn't hepatitis. The emergency room doctor ran a series of test and found a tumor in Gina's pancreas. They referred her to a surgeon named, Dr. Cleo and made the appointment for that following Monday.

When Gina went to the surgeon he looked at the x-rays and cat scans and put Gina in the hospital to remove her pancreas. Gina checked in, got settled and waited for Dr. Cleo to make rounds. When Dr. Cleo got there, he had scheduled the surgery for the following day. He called it a: "Whipple," procedure and said it would take at least six hours to complete. Nikki asked if he knew what the tumor was or did he have any speculation on what it could be. Dr. Cleo was a very direct doctor and came right out and said he was ninety-nine point nine percent sure it was a malignancy. He said he wouldn't be one hundred percent until he biopsied it, but he was sure it was cancerous. Tears came to Nikki's eyes, but she fought them back. Vincent sat there again emotionless and Gina didn't shed a tear either. Nikki looked at her, squeezed her hand and told her know matter what everything would be all right. Gina told Nikki she knew she would be fine and not to worry. Nikki respected Gina's strength and composure at the time.

The whole family gathered that morning before they took Gina to surgery. Dr. Cleo went in again and told the family and Gina what to expect. He told her where she would wake up and the surroundings to expect. The family said their, I love you's and off to surgery Gina went.

Gina was in surgery three hours when the family was called to a side room by the surgeon. Vincent turned to Nikki and asked what she thought. Nikki told him the news would be really good or really bad, because Dr. Cleo had told them she would be in surgery at least six hours, maybe more if there were complications. Vincent took Nikki's hand and they walked to the room to wait for the surgeon. When Dr. Cleo walked in, he told the family Gina had an advanced malignancy. He said it started in the tail of the pancreases and had grown through to the head of the pancreases and attached itself to the wall of the main artery in her stomach. He said he had worked for the last two hours to remove it, but he could not detach it from the artery. Dr. Cleo said he did biopsied the tumor to identify the cell, but the family needed to know it didn't look good. Dr. Cleo said he gave her three to six months if she was lucky. Ann fell back on the couch and started crying uncontrollably. Vincent told Ann to get herself together while Mike and Candice stood at the door with their arms crossed without emotion. Nikki hugged Ann and told her she had to be strong for Gina. Ann hugged Nikki and told her, she didn't know what she was going to do without her mother. Nikki told her she was sorry, but they had to hold it together for Gina's sake.

Vincent asked the surgeon where things would go from there and Dr. Cleo said he would do chemotherapy for palliative measures, but it wouldn't treat the cancer, because it was too advanced; his partner was closing Gina as he spoke and they would transfer her back to her room. Nikki told him that when Gina woke up she would not be in the setting he had prepared her for and would know right away that something had gone wrong and the surgeon said he would be at the nurse's station if she needed anything. Then Nikki asked when he was going to tell Gina about the cancer, but he thought it might be easier coming from one of them.

Then they all started talking, arguing about who had to tell Gina, because none of them wanted to.

Dr. Cleo said when Gina woke up, have the nurse page him and he would talk with Gina. When they brought her to her room none of her children wanted to wait with her until she woke up. They all went down stairs and Nikki sat at Gina's bedside until she woke up. When she did wake up she saw Nikki and told her she knew it was worse than they had thought. Nikki called the nurse to let her know Gina was awake and told Gina the doctor was coming to see her.

Dr. Cleo walked in and sat by Gina, he told her it was a very advanced malignancy and he couldn't remove it and had to close. Gina asked how long she could expect to live and he gave her three to six months. Gina asked if there was any treatment for it, but Dr. Cleo told her it was too far advanced and because of her age the chemo would kill her sooner. He offered to do the treatment, if that was how she wanted to pursue it, but Gina told him know, she would put her affairs in order.

When he left the room, Nikki was fighting back the tears. Gina asked where her kids were and Nikki told her they had gone down stairs to eat, but she would go let them know she was awake and wanted to see them. When she entered the cafeteria she saw them sitting at a corner table. When she got close enough she could hear their discussion, they were already planning to put Gina in a nursing home. Nikki bit her lip and told them Gina was awake and asking for them. She told them the doctor had spoken to Gina and she knew her prognosis so they headed to Gina's room.

Everyone left to go home that night including Vincent, but Nikki stayed with Gina the first three nights. On the fourth day, Gina told Nikki her bed was wet, so Nikki pulled the covers back to check her and found a foul odor and a lot of drainage. Her stomach was swollen twice its normal size, so Nikki called the nurse, who in turn called the surgeon. Dr. Cleo went in the room and called for a surgical blade. He lanced the incision in the room before Nikki's eyes. The fluid ran out of Gina's stomach on the bed on the floor, everywhere. Dr. Cleo said she had abscessed from the surgery and air hitting the cancer and told Gina the wound would have to heal from the inside out.

He was telling Gina, her family had approached him about a nursing home, so he would make a referral and transfer her in the next week. The next day when Mike and Candice came to visit they told Gina how hard it was to come with three kids and working full time jobs. They thought Gina would understand and she said, she was sorry for being a problem and she didn't want to complicate their lives. Nikki was ferrous, but again bit her tongue to keep her mouth shut. The hospital stay became an extended one due to complications. Ann was in and out and Vincent the same. Nikki went home three nights out of the three-week hospital stay.

Nikki told Vincent that she in good conscious could not see Gina die in a nursing home. She told him how upset she was at the whole situation and knowing how much Gina had given to him and his siblings. She told Vincent he didn't have a clue how lucky he was to have had a Mother like Gina that had done so much for them and the whole family. Gina had kept Andy while Nikki worked, kept all three of Mike and Candice's kids and Ann never took Beth home, she lived with Gina. Nikki said she cooked dinner every night for them and bathed their kids, put them in their pajamas and washed their cloths. Nikki said,

"Now Gina is sick and all you kids can talk about is putting her in a nursing home."

Vincent told Nikki he didn't want to see his Mother go to a nursing home, but he knew he couldn't care for her and thought it would be too much to ask her to do. Nikki told him the doctors said someone would have to stay with her in the nursing home because of her wound and she was volunteering her time so she could sleep at night when this was over. The family was in the room when Nikki and Vincent got to the hospital. They were telling Gina why they thought it was a good idea for her to go to the nursing home when Nikki walked up to her bedside and took her hand. She told Gina there wouldn't be any nursing home; she was going to go home with her and Vincent.

Gina asked Nikki if she was sure, because she didn't want to be a burden. Nikki told her she would never be a burden and it wasn't a subject for discussion, she was going with her. Gina squeezed her hand and thanked her. Mike, Candice and Ann didn't say a word, but the tension was so thick you could cut it with a knife.

Gina went home with Nikki and Vincent and Nikki gave her resignation at her job, but they didn't want to see her go, so they offered to buy a computer and Nikki could work by modem at home. Nikki said she would try it, but didn't know how long or how much she could work. Nikki's boss told her, he didn't care as long as she stayed working for them. Nikki agreed to try it out and see how it would work. She turned the dining room into an office. Had the modem installed and the computer set up. Her desk was brought in, filing cabinets set up, and her carrier service put in place. The service would pick up in the evenings and deliver the next morning.

Things worked well for the first month Nikki was at home with Gina, but Gina kept getting sicker and weaker. It got to the point that Gina didn't want Nikki out her site. Nikki stayed with Gina night and day. Andy was home and played in his room most of the time with a fence placed at his bedroom door, so he couldn't get out, because if he cried it upset Gina.

Nikki was spending less and less time working or with Andy and more, and more time caring for Gina. Nikki resigned from her job and told her boss if he wanted her to call when the situation was over, she would. Her boss told her to take care of herself and call if she needed anything. He assured Nikki she would always have a position to return to when she was ready.

Andy cried for his Mommy to hold him, but as soon as Nikki picked him up, Gina screamed for her attention. Nikki thought some of Gina's behavior was deliberate, but she never treated her with any form of disrespect.

Nikki bathed Gina and cleaned her gaping wound every morning and packed it with gauze. Gina's immune system was weakening with every passing day. Nikki sat and played cards with Gina, board games, and talked about anything she wanted to talk about. When visitors came Nikki welcomed them, offered something to eat or drink and would graciously excuse herself to allow Gina her privacy. Nikki told the whole family they could visit anytime they wanted, just be careful if they were sick.

Everyone came and went as they pleased and Mike called one afternoon to say him, Candice, and the two girls were dropping by. Roxie was sick, running fever and coughing up a storm. Nikki told Candice, she knew she should not have brought her there, because a simple cold could wipe Gina out. Nikki reminded Mike and Candice about the doctor's orders and things Gina had to avoid. Candice told Nikki she would do what she wanted to, when she wanted to, and how she wanted. Nikki told her, she could, but with a stomped ass in her house. Nikki told Mike and Candice to get the hell out her house and not come back while Vincent sat there like a bump on a log, not saying a word.

Mike told Nikki she wasn't big enough to put him out, but Nikki told Mike he was leaving one way or another. Mike asked why it would matter to Nikki if Gina caught a cold or not and Nikki told him, that him and his so-called wife went home every night to their own lives as if nothing had changed except for the fact they had to raise their own kids. Nikki was the one sleeping two or three hours a night, because Gina was afraid of the dark. Nikki told him if he thought for one minute she was going to allow him or anyone else to make it harder than it already was; he had another thing coming.

Mike told her, he would take his Mother to his house, but before he could finish his statement, Nikki told him to take her. Give her the word and she would pack Gina's things and have her ready to go, then when Gina was in his home he could call the shots.

Candice told Mike she couldn't take care of Gina at the time and Nikki looked at Candice and said,

"What, oh, I'm sorry I forgot; it would interfere with your nights out on the town."

Nikki told Mike, that as long as Gina resided in her home whither Vincent backed her or not she wasn't getting ran over anymore. He would respect the rules that everybody else abided by and was posted at the door for all to see, or he could take his Mother to his house and do as he pleased. Mike told Gina he would just leave and not come back to see her at all. Nikki looked at him and told him not to let the door hit him in the ass on his way out, so Candice gathered their children and they left.

When they were gone, Nikki cursed Vincent out. She told him that his family and him were totally selfish and self-centered. She said she was the only one that had sacrificed anything for Gina; everyone else's life was unaffected. She demanded their help taking care of their Mother, because she and Andy were entitled to a life too. Nikki hadn't left the house in four months; she hadn't had a single uninterrupted conversation with Perry or anyone. She hadn't even spent one afternoon alone with her son. She had slept on the couch with a nursery monitor for the last four months getting only two to three hours sleep a night, if she was lucky. She told Vincent all he did was, get up go to work, come home, expect dinner to be waiting, played with Andy for thirty minutes, sat like a zombie when people came and went, let his family run over her and then just went to bed. Nikki told him that every night he slept and she was exhausted. Nikki was more upset that, she even had to say the words; she felt he should have known.

Nikki had told Vincent, she would care for Gina until the end, but when the end got there Gina would have to be taken back to the hospital, because she could not die in Nikki's house, or Nikki thought she would never sleep there again. Vincent had agreed to those terms up-front. Vincent asked Nikki what she wanted him to do and she told him he was sleeping on the couch that night with the monitor and every night from then on if he didn't, want to share that responsibility with his family. Vincent then asked Nikki if she expected him to call his brother and sister and tell them they had to stay with Gina a couple nights a week so she could sleep. Nikki looked at Vincent and told him, she didn't expect him to do one dam thing, he hadn't to date, so he didn't need to start then, but Nikki reminded Vincent that Dr. Cleo had told the family, that even if she was placed in a Nursing Home, someone would have had to stay with her at all times, because of her wound. So Nikki felt the family could stay with Gina there or at their own house, but she had already sacrificed as much as she could.

Nikki turned on her heels, picked up her son, went to her bedroom and closed the door. Nikki slept for the first time in four months. Andy cuddled up with his Mommy and didn't move the whole night either. When Nikki woke up she went to the living room to find Vincent sitting on the edge of the sofa. He looked up and told Nikki he was exhausted, he had only gotten an hour of sleep and Nikki told him welcome to her world. Perry came over to have coffee with Nikki that morning. When she walked in she could feel the tension and asked Nikki if everything was alright, so Nikki said,

"Hell know everything is not alright."

Nikki told her what had happen the night before and thought Perry would tell her how selfish she was being, but Perry told her she wondered how long she would keep putting up with all the shit she had encountered with Vincent's family and wondered why they weren't helping.

Nikki burst into tears and told Perry her heart bleed for Gina and she could almost die herself when she thought about what she must be thinking, but she had to have sometime to herself. She said it was like she had become a safety net to Gina and Gina was smothering Nikki to death. She told Perry if she didn't breath she was afraid of what might happen. Perry told her; to tell Vincent he could sit that night or get someone else to sit, because she was taking Nikki out to dinner. Nikki agreed that maybe that was what she needed, just a night away.

Vincent said he would stay with Gina that night, so Nikki took Andy and went to dinner, after dinner they went to a movie and Nikki enjoyed herself for the first time in four months. When she walked in the door Vincent was sitting on the couch waiting. Gina told Nikki she was gone too long and Nikki asked if she enjoyed spending the evening with her son, when Vincent chimed in to say his Mother lost control of her bowels and he had to clean her up. Gina told Nikki she should have been there to clean her up and had know business staying out and going to a movie. Nikki looked at Perry and thanked her for the dinner and the movie. Perry's eyebrows were raised, but she didn't say a word, except goodnight. Nikki picked Andy up and went to bed. Vincent went to her room and asked if she was going to stay with Gina that night, so he could sleep. Nikki told him she wasn't if he wanted to rest he could call his family to take their turn, she had her turn for four months straight and a month before that in the hospital.

Vincent told Nikki his family was selfish and self-centered and they wouldn't help even if he begged. Nikki told Vincent she didn't realize the magnitude of the responsibility and she couldn't do it anymore without help and rest of her own. Vincent told her he knew how much she gave of herself, but he needed to sleep because he worked. Nikki told him she would go back to work the next day and he could stay and care for his Mother. Vincent told Nikki she was being unreasonable, but Nikki told him the only thing unreasonable was the fact she even had to speak up for her self at all. He knew all along this was coming to a head and ignored it like he did everything else, like it didn't exist or it didn't happen, or it wasn't happening. Nikki told Vincent, that this was one situation he couldn't wish away and he was going to have to deal with it.

Vincent left the room and called Mike to come spend the night with their mother, so he could rest. In the middle of the night Nikki heard Gina screaming. She jumped out of bed and ran to her room. Gina wanted a glass of water and the channel changed. Nikki stumbled to the living room to find Mike past out on the couch with the nursery monitor turned off. Vincent was on her heels looking for Mike. Nikki went in the kitchen to get Gina her water and Vincent woke Mike up to ask him why he turned off the monitor. Mike told Vincent he needed to sleep and Gina was calling wanting something every fifteen minutes and he was exhausted. Mike and Vincent had words over the fact he was to stay up with Gina that night so he and Nikki could rest, but Mike told Vincent he couldn't physically do what Gina needed, so he wouldn't be coming back to stay the night anymore and left.

Ann had to take care of her handicapped daughter, so she too was unable to take her turn. Candice told Mike, Gina was not her responsibility, so she wasn't staying either. Vincent and Nikki were the only ones left to take care of Gina. Nikki had resigned herself that she was in the situation for the long haul and would be the only person standing to care for Gina. Vincent had to work and needed his rest, but Nikki was exhausted emotionally and physically. Nikki had never quite recovered from the miscarriage and was still trying to stabilize her weight. Nikki continued to bleed three weeks out the month, so her physical health was failing fast as well.

Nikki had another follow-up appointment with Dr. Hawkins due to her excessive bleeding and on that appointment her wanted Nikki to check into the hospital for a laser surgery to see if that would stop the bleeding. Nikki scheduled the surgery on the following Thursday.

Nikki told Vincent he would have to make arrangements for help because she would not be able to lift for two weeks. Nikki said they could contact a sitter service for part-time sitters until she recovered. Vincent had already been placed as Gina's power of attorney and could disburse her funds as needed, so Vincent told Mike and Ann that he was hiring the agency for sitters, so Nikki could recover from surgery.

That was a problem for both Vincent's siblings, because what money was spent on sitters, meant less they would receive when Gina passed away, so they decided they would help take care of Gina the next two weeks. Candice took off a week to spend the days with Gina and Ann and Mike could split the nights. Nikki agreed, but told Vincent she wouldn't be able to get up every-thirty minutes with Gina if they turned off the monitor, so they could sleep, but if he wanted to handle it that way he could, but he was the one that would have to pick up his siblings slack. Vincent told Nikki he would handle it somehow, so Nikki had her surgery.

Candice and Nikki had drifted apart, mainly because Nikki couldn't accept the terms of her marriage and didn't want to live the life Candice did to stay in her marriage. Nikki did at one time meet Candice out on a few occasions, to find Candice had taken off her wedding ring and locked it in the glove compartment of her car. She told Nikki that sometimes, she just had to blow it out her system or loose her sanity, so her nights out, was her time to do what ever she wanted. Candice also told Nikki that when she met Mike she didn't know who she was there to date Mike or Vincent, because they both were making plays for her. Candice had a way of making herself appear so much more than she was and stretched stories beyond belief.

Nikki stopped going out with Candice and stayed at home more. She didn't call Candice on the phone, but would talk to her if she called Nikki. The conversations were limited and the scope of discussion was of family matters. Candice told Nikki if she really wanted to hurt her she could, but warned her not to. Nikki was appalled at her accusation and asked her what the hell she meant by her statement. Candice told Nikki she knew too much about her life outside her marriage and if she told Vincent, he would tell Mike and there would be hell to pay. Nikki laughed and told her to get a grip. She didn't give a shit what she did and as far as her talking to Vincent about anything anymore, she could rest assure her little secret life was safe, but told her not to call her anymore and live her life as she chose.

While Nikki was recovering from surgery, Gina had, had some Demerol tablets that were prescribed for her for pain. When Nikki had given one to

Gina she responded in the total opposite manner expected. She was wired to the hilt and nervous, instead of being calm and sleepy. Gina told Nikki she didn't want to take the Demerol anymore, so Nikki just left the bottle in the kitchen cabinet. While Candice was staying there during the day, Perry from next door called and invited Nikki to come to her house for lunch. When Nikki returned, Gina asked Nikki for the Demerol tablets. Nikki told her they were in the kitchen cabinet, but Candice screamed from the kitchen they weren't there.

Nikki told her they were in the cabinet where they had always been and asked Gina why she would even want them. Gina told Nikki she didn't want them that Candice did. Nikki asked why Candice wanted Demerol and Gina said Candice had an earache and wanted some painkillers to help ease the pain. Nikki said Demerol wouldn't do much for an earache, but she would get the pills for Candice. When Nikki went to the kitchen to search for the medicine Candice got in her car and left without saying goodbye or anything. The pills were gone, so Nikki called Candice and asked her where they were, because she knew what medications were in her home for Gina. Candice told Nikki she didn't see the medicine and didn't know where it was, but Nikki asked Candice how she knew to ask for the Demerol if she never saw the bottle. Candice told her she wasn't discussing the subject with her anymore and hung up.

Nikki called Vincent at work to tell him what was going on at the house. Vincent wanted to know why Candice left, so Nikki told him she didn't offer an explanation, she just got in her car and left when Nikki went to look for the medicine. Vincent told Nikki he had seen the Demerol in the cabinet and he too knew it was there. Nikki told him it wasn't anymore, so Vincent called Mike and told him he had to go to the house. Vincent went home; then Mike arrived about ten minutes later. Vincent told Mike he wanted him to go with him to Mike's house to look for the pills. Mike told Nikki she had lost her fucking mind, because Candice wouldn't do anything like that. Vincent told Mike to prove Nikki wrong, by going and look for the medicine. When Mike and Vincent got to Mike's house, Candice was sleeping on the sofa. Mike searched Candice's car before they went in the house. He went to the kitchen and bathroom looking while Vincent waited for Mike in the living room.

They didn't find the meds and Mike woke Candice up, but she was buzzing too much to talk. Mike didn't know what to say, so Vincent left of course without saying another word. That night, Mike called Vincent to tell him; Candice got sick at Nikki's, but she thought Nikki had accused her of taking the medicine to start some shit with her. Vincent told Mike he didn't know his wife like he thought he did, but Mike totally defended Candice and hung up the phone. When Vincent told Nikki what Mike said, she was ferrous. She told him to ask Gina what she remembered about the situation, but he refused. He told Nikki to drop it and let it go. She told him to go fuck himself and if Candice drove her ass back down her driveway, surgery or not she was going to kick her ass. Nikki picked up the phone, called Candice and told her what she just told Vincent. Vincent was pissed at Nikki and told her it wasn't a big deal to let it go, but Nikki had taken all she could at that point. Mike called Vincent and told him that he was coming to get Gina for the weekend instead of staying at his house with her. Vincent asked Nikki if she could have Gina ready to go in about thirty minutes and Nikki told him she would be packed in fifteen.

Nikki gathered her things and got her medicines together and sat her stuff in the living room. Nikki took Andy and went to her room when Mike got there to get Gina. When Gina got to Mike's house she ate dinner with them and got sick. She vomited all over herself, so Candice cleaned her up and called Nikki to tell her she was bringing her home. Nikki told her if she showed up at her house she had an ass-whipping coming, so bring her home and hung up the phone. Mike brought Gina home and argued with Vincent in the driveway.

When Vincent went in the house, he told Nikki she had to keep her mouth shut and let Mike and Candice come and go as they pleased. If she didn't Mike would take Gina to his house and Nikki wouldn't be able to see her anymore either. Nikki told Vincent she would have all Gina's things packed within the hour, so he could call Mike and tell him to bring his ass right back and take his Mother with him. She also told Vincent; while she was packing his Mothers things he could pack his. Nikki said she had put up with this situation as much as she was going to and she wanted his ass out of her life too.

Nikki packed Gina's belongings, sat them in the living room, picked her son up and went next door to Perry's and waited until everyone was gone. Perry and Bill told Nikki, that way too much was placed on her shoulders with know help. Bill said Vincent was a wimp for allowing his family to run over Nikki like they had and told her she lasted longer in that situation than anyone in their right mind would have. Nikki cried and told Perry she just couldn't take another day, another hour or another second and Perry told her she did the right thing. Bill watched as they loaded Gina's hospital bed and belongings in the back of Mike's truck.

After everyone left he told Nikki they were gone. When Nikki went back to her house Vincent was still there. He asked Nikki to reconsider asking him to go, but Nikki told him she had to have time alone to think things through. He told her he was going to stay at Ann's house and she could reach him there if she needed anything.

Nikki spent the next few days taking care of Andy and trying to pull herself together. Perry sent her daughter Lain to stay with Nikki to help with Andy, because Nikki wasn't suppose to be lifting. The next Sunday night Ann called Nikki to come to her house, because Gina wanted to talk to her. Nikki asked Ann why Gina was at her house and was told Mike had taken her that Friday night, then Saturday morning Mike loaded all Gina's things and brought her to Ann's, because they couldn't take care of Gina. Nikki agreed to come and speak with Gina, but told Ann she really didn't have anything to say on the matter. Ann told her to just come and see what Gina had to say.

When Nikki got to Ann's, she was waiting under the carport. She told Nikki she wanted to thank her for all she had done for her Mother, she knew the sacrifices Nikki made and how difficult it was and wanted Nikki to know she appreciated everything she did. She also told Nikki that Mike had been spoiled all his life and this situation was know different. Ann said she had taken a medical leave from work to stay home with Gina until she passed away and then she would return to work.

Ann was scared and hoped she could take care of Gina and meet all her needs. Nikki told her she was sure she would do fine, but if she needed help she could call her and she would do what she could to help. Ann hugged Nikki and told her she was hoping she would say that, because she knew she too would need help, because it was just her and Sandra her partner.

Nikki went to Gina's bedside and Gina asked her to listen to her and wait until she was finished speaking before she spoke. Gina told Nikki she had spent her life taking care of her children's Dad; then when he died, Beth was born; then Beth became her life. Gina said she lived for her kids and putting out fires to keep the peace in the family and trying to hold her children together. She told Nikki she couldn't bare the thought of leaving knowing that her children would be scattered three sheets to the wind, so she needed Nikki's help to bring her family back together. She said she knew Mike and Candice would never admit they were wrong about anything. Gina told Nikki they would never apologize for a thing, but she knew Nikki's heart and knew she would apologize to make peace and was begging her to do so for the sake of her family.

Nikki listened with tears streaming down her face. Gina told her, her heart was warm and loving, that Nikki was filled with compassion and had the ability to give peace in situations were peace wasn't possible. Gina told Nikki when she was scared, Nikki made her feel safe, when she felt alone Nikki made her feel like she had a friend and when she vomited or had an accident on herself, Nikki kept her dignity intact. Gina told Nikki that she had become her safe haven in the mist of her final and most crucial storm. She wanted Nikki to promise her she would bring her family back together.

Nikki promised Gina she would know matter how difficult it would be. She would do her best to make the situation right and that she didn't want Gina to worry about a thing. Gina told Nikki if Nikki gave her, her word that was good enough for her. The last thing Gina needed was for Nikki to start with Nikki's home first and let Vincent return home. Even though in Nikki's heart she didn't want Vincent back, she wasn't going to deny Gina her death wish either.

Vincent moved home that night, but Nikki told him he would have the guest bedroom until she figured out what to do about their marriage. Vincent agreed and moved in the guest room. Nikki then asked Vincent to call Mike and see if they were willing to talk. Mike said for them to come over and see what happened. When they got there, Nikki told both Candice and Mike she knew they had, had a strained relationship for quite sometime. She asked them to put the past behind them and get along for Gina's sake and continue to be a family, which was what Gina wanted. Everyone agreed except Candice, she told Nikki she didn't want any part of anything anymore. Nikki told her that was her decision if that was how she wanted to handle things, but she needed to tell Gina she couldn't grant her, her final wish and stop putting all the blame on her. Candice told Nikki she wasn't going to have a conversation with Gina about a dam thing and her wish was of no concern to her, when Mike jumped up and screamed,

"Know concern of yours, that's my Mother we're talking about and by God you will do what ever it takes to settle this shit. Nikki came here only, because my Mother asked her to and dam it; you are going to put this shit aside."

Candice looked at Mike, but never spoke a word, he turned to Nikki and told her they would put the past behind them for his Mothers sake and make her final days as peaceful as they could. Nikki told Mike she couldn't ask for anything more and told Vincent she was ready to go.

Ann called Nikki on a few occasions in the middle of the night for Nikki's help, because Gina's pain became uncontrollable. Gina had been vomiting most days and couldn't keep her pain medication down and Ann was frantic and instead of calling the hospice nurse she called Nikki. Nikki went and gave Gina her pain medication rectally. She told Ann to let her stomach rest for six hours, then start her on clear liquids, and give her, her pain medicine rectally for the next twenty-four hours. Nikki was like the doctor, she knew how to take care of Gina and Ann knew Nikki would know what to do.

The next couple weeks the family got together at Ann's for bar-b-ques and movies. Gina looked better than ever and was getting around better as well and Nikki went shopping with Perry one Saturday morning and when she got home Vincent left a note for her to call him at Ann's. When Nikki called, he told her that Gina was really bad off and said the whole family was there, but Gina was asking for her. Nikki told Vincent she would be right there and took Andy to Perry's house. When she got there, everyone except Ann was outside under the carport laughing and carrying on. When Nikki got out her car, she asked if Gina had turned around and was better, but Vincent told her, Gina was inside and there had been no change and the priest had just left after administering Gina's last rites.

Nikki went to Gina's bedside and told her she was there. Ann was standing on the other side of the bed and Vincent sat down in the kitchen that over looked the living room. Gina's hospital bed was by the French doors in the living room, because she liked to look outside. Nikki told Gina again she was there and took her hand. Gina opened her eyes and asked Nikki if she remembered her promise. Nikki told her she did and told her not to worry about a thing that everything was and would be fine. Gina said she was so tired and Nikki told her she had fought a long hard battle and it was OK to let go. Gina smiled at Nikki and took a deep breath and exhaled. Her breathing pattern changed immediately. Ann looked at Nikki and asked what was happening. Nikki told Ann with tears in her eyes she was going. Vincent ran to his Mother's bedside and Ann hugged her Mother and told her she loved her, Sandra ran outside to get Mike, but by the time he got to her bedside, Gina had already taken her last breath.

They called the hospice nurse to come take care of the final arrangements. Gina was taken back to her hometown in Louisville, Kentucky. Gina had told Ann about her funeral arrangements, she requested a lady in Louisville that had done Gina's hair when she lived there to do her hair one last time. She told Ann she didn't want a stranger to do her hair the last time she wanted someone that knew her. Ann and Nikki made the arrangements for the funeral and the lady that did Gina's hair was out of town, so Ann was distrait. She too wanted to grant her Mothers last wish, but was at a loss on how to do it.

Nikki told Ann she would go to the funeral home and do Gina's hair, she said she had bathed Gina and set her hair in curlers more times than she could count and knew how Gina liked her hair. She said she wasn't a stranger so, in essence, Ann would be granting Gina her last wish. Ann told Nikki, she couldn't go in the back of the funeral home, but would be grateful for her doing Gina's hair.

Nikki went to the funeral home with her curl-n-iron, brush, comb, and hair spray and the manager escorted Nikki to the morgue. Nikki went in the holding-room with four other bodies besides Gina's. Nikki turned the stretcher around so she could only see Gina and went to work. The smell in the room was so strong it almost took Nikki's breath. Nikki worked with her tools and was grateful the funeral home had already bathed Gina and washed her hair. Nikki fixed Gina hair, kissed her on the cheek and told her she was beautiful. Nikki left the funeral home and went back to the hotel and assured Ann everything went well. Then Nikki took her shower, got dressed and went to the wake.

Candice tried everything in her power to upset Nikki at the funeral home. She put on a floorshow on what she did and how she did things and how upset she was that Gina was gone. Nikki just left the room and thought, how stupid she was, because everyone in the room never saw Candice. After the funeral, Nikki and Vincent went home, they saw very little of Mike and Candice, but at least there wasn't any more feuds and Nikki slept knowing she did her best for Gina.

CHAPTER 22

The next month Nikki registered for a couple general courses at Louisiana State University in New Orleans. She started in the pass program, which allowed her to take up to twenty-four credit hours before applying for formal acceptance. She got her GED in the first semester, sat for the SAT exam and after two semesters, she was accepted full time in law school. Nikki was ecstatic, she didn't think she had it in her and Vincent thought it would be something Nikki would start, but not finish, but Nikki was determined to finish, she made up her mind that nothing was going to stop her from finishing school, because then she could support herself and her son.

During the first summer of college, Perry and Bill were taking their girls to the river in New Orleans for the annual fire works. They invited Nikki and Vincent to go with them so they tagged along. They were standing on the bank of the river watching the fire works with: Nikki and Perry standing behind Bill and Vincent. Vincent had Andy on his hip with the two girls standing in front of Bill and Vincent. The fire works was almost over when they shot a cannon off on the ship. It made a horrendously loud bang and scared everyone on the riverbank. Andy was in his father's arms and he turned and jumped on Nikki when Leslie and Lain grabbed their Dad around the legs. When they realized what had happened they were laughing and Bill made the comment he could see who Andy felt more secure with. Vincent laughed it off by saying Nikki weighed eighty pounds soaking wet; like she could have done something more than him if she needed to, but Nikki looked at Perry and walked up the bank with Andy in her arms. Nikki thought to herself, Andy as young as he was and with his handicap, he too knew he was safe with his Mommy, but didn't feel safe, even in his father's arms.

Nikki was focused on school and wanted something more out of school or life. She knew she wasn't working and even though she took out enough in student loads to pay her car note and insurance, she knew she couldn't support Andy yet and felt trapped. She returned to school that fall as planned and in her English class she met a girl named Tess. She was friendly, beautiful and funny. Nikki and her became friends and started hanging out together and Nikki met her roommate that turned out to be her old friend Melissa, it was a small world.

Nikki was as attracted to Tess, as Tess was to her and before long, Tess called Nikki and she would go to the house to pick up Tess for dinners or movies. Melissa and Nikki didn't reconnect at the time, but Melissa did warn Nikki to be careful with Tess, because she liked to play head games, but Nikki told Melissa she was a big girl not to worry.

Nikki and Tess decided to spend the weekend together at Tess's boyfriend's condo while he was out of town. Nikki had Andy with her, because Vincent had gone fishing. Nikki was honest with Vincent in telling him she was seeing Tess and she thought it could lead somewhere. Vincent told her to do what made her happy at the time, so she did. That night at the condo after a drink or two Nikki told Tess about Desmond and Tess wanted to call and invite him to the condo. Nikki agreed and thought it would be nice to reconnect or see how she felt when she saw him again and felt pretty secure with Tess being there. When he got there, they blew some grass, had a few drinks and Nikki went to the store for more alcohol.

Andy was asleep upstairs and when Nikki returned, Desmond and Tess were in the bathroom. Tess was in the bathtub with Desmond standing in the bathroom, looking too comfortable for Nikki. Desmond left the bathroom and told Nikki his heart was beating too fast. He thought he was reacting to the weed he smoked, because it had happened to him the last time he tried it. Nikki told him to take some deep breaths and relax, he would be fine. Nikki went to the front of the condo and Desmond returned to Tess. Tess kept going to get Nikki, but she told Tess to go have fun, it was obvious that's what they both wanted.

Nikki sat in the living room for a while; then she walked to the bedroom in time to see Desmond pushing Tess on the bed and she just kept walking. She went upstairs, picked up her son and left. They tried to call Nikki on her cell phone, but she wouldn't answer. When Nikki got home she was crying hysterically and Vincent came out the guest bedroom to find out what was wrong, but Nikki told him to leave her alone. She put Andy to bed and went to her room.

Tess called and called that weekend as did Desmond, but Nikki wouldn't talk to either one of them. Tess left the message she had Andy's frog that he liked to sleep with and would bring it to class that Monday. Nikki thought she would quit school before she would see her again. Vincent begged Nikki to tell him what had her so upset, so she finally broke down and told him. Vincent told Nikki, he was sorry, but she should have known, all Desmond was looking for was a good time and she never meant anything to him, if she had, he wouldn't have done what he did. Vincent begged Nikki to give him another chance for their marriage and she would see; he would give her the moon if she would let him. Nikki told Vincent she didn't ever want to be touched again by anyone. She just wanted to be left alone. He asked her if she was going to talk to Desmond and she told him when hell froze over.

That Sunday Tess called from her boyfriend's house, it was a number Nikki didn't recognize, so she answered the phone. Tess begged her not to hang up, to please talk to her. Nikki told her, she didn't want to talk about a dam thing; she just wanted Tess to leave her alone. Tess said she would if Nikki agreed to get Andy's frog and give her five minutes. After arguing on the phone, Nikki agreed and went to Tess's house to get Andy's frog.

Tess told Nikki she was confused and had thought Desmond and Nikki did that sort of thing. Nikki told Tess that Desmond had always been intrigued by her sexuality, but she had never shared that with him. Tess said she totally understood how Nikki felt and was cursing Desmond for messing up her chance for something real with Nikki. Tess tried to talk to Nikki about what happen, but Nikki told her not to say anymore. Tess told her no, she wasn't going to hide anything from her, because she was in-love with her and would not have done what she did, if she had known the whole story. Tess told Nikki, she should have told her how far things had gone with them and laid down some ground rules for her before Desmond had gotten there. Nikki said, she didn't think ground rules were necessary. Tess said she was sorry and said when he called her she would tell him to fuck off and Nikki said,

"When he calls you, how the hell would he know how to reach you?"

Tess had given Desmond her number, because he wanted Tess's help, to talk to Nikki. Nikki told her she wasn't going to talk to him ever again or her either and picked up Andy's toy and walked out.

Desmond called Nikki's house and Vincent answered the phone. Desmond told Vincent who he was and that he needed to talk to Nikki.

Vincent brought Nikki the phone and told her it was Desmond. Nikki got on the phone and told Desmond he had lost his mind calling her house. Desmond said he was confused and had started therapy and had gotten a girl pregnant and his therapist said he shouldn't close the door to Nikki and should try and say he was sorry. Nikki told him he said it, be a good daddy and fuck off forever. She told him she never wanted to speak to him again as long as she lived and hung the phone up before he finished speaking.

Nikki went back to school and was determined; know-one was standing in the way of her future, because that was her way out. Tess followed her out the classroom every day until Nikki finally talked to her. They agreed to go away for the weekend to talk about the issues and see if they could put it behind them and move forward.

That weekend, Tess told Nikki, Desmond called her repeatedly and asked if she had talked to Nikki. She said she kept the conversations limited and told him she saw Nikki at school, but she wouldn't talk to her either. Nikki told her she didn't want to talk about the situation anymore, she had put it behind her and she wanted to let it go. Tess agreed and asked Nikki to sleep with her and just let her hold her, but Nikki refused. That night, Tess went to Nikki's room, crawled in bed with Nikki and snuggled up close to her and they went to sleep without anything sexual between them.

The next morning Nikki woke up and went to the living room to build a fire. She ordered breakfast and woke Tess when breakfast arrived. Nikki was fighting a battle within herself wondering if she was bi-sexual anymore or was what she had in the past with Lisa just a phase she was going through. She decided that day she would get her answers. When Nikki woke Tess, they ate breakfast. Tess feed Nikki strawberries with cream as well as other fruits that were brought on the breakfast tray. Tess leaned in to kiss Nikki and Nikki responded. The kiss was warm and soft just as Nikki remembered from her past. Tess touched Nikki, but Nikki pushed her away. This wasn't about Nikki's pleasure from being touched; it was about Nikki finding out if this was part of her anymore.

Nikki kissed Tess softly, caressed her breast, ran her fingers over her skin and slid her tongue between Tess's legs. Tess moaned with pleasure as Nikki moved her tongue over her body softly. Nikki explored Tess's body, every square inch. Nikki touched with her tongue and fingers and embraced the sensation and feeling from touching Tess. Touching, caressing, licking, and kissing Tess. Nikki was stimulated audibly, the louder Tess moaned the more Nikki devoured her, until she climaxed.

Nikki kissed Tess softly on the lips and laid beside her. She lit a cigarette and watched the roaring fire in the fireplace. Tess drifted off to sleep again, so Nikki laid there in the silence and listened to the roaring fire. Nikki knew in her mind, she no longer had to wonder if her sexuality was a phase or not, she knew she was bi-sexual. Nikki got her answers, but wondered how much or how little she should invest in her relationship with Tess. Nikki couldn't afford any more complications in her life at that time. She had a one-track mind and that was on finishing school. Nikki wanted a way out and she would have sacrificed anything and or anyone to get there.

Nikki wondered if she would ever be able to look at Tess and not be reminded of Desmond. She wanted to forget Desmond ever existed, but he came to visit her in her dreams. Nikki wanted to push him as far out her mind as she could push him, but his presence was over whelming at times. The harder Nikki tried to forget him the stronger his memory burned. Something inside Nikki knew he would return in the future and she saw darkness consume her. Nikki denied the knowledge and told herself she was focused on the present and the future would just have to take care of itself.

Nikki decided to let time tell where her relationship with Tess would go, but the situation with Tess was getting more and more complicated for Nikki, because Nikki was growing to love her. Vincent spent his weekends away with his friends, so Nikki spent a couple with Tess at her house, mostly studying, but entertaining as well. Nikki cooked dinner one evening and invited Kelly to come join her and Tess. The evening went well; the girls cooked together, cleaned the kitchen and watched a movie. When the movie was over, they sat in front of the fireplace drinking wine and talking. After a while Kelly said her goodbyes. When Kelly left, Tess got on the phone arguing with her boyfriend over his car being stolen while in Tess's possession. Nikki said her goodnights, kissed Tess on the check and went to bed.

Nikki thought things could have possibly worked out with Tess, but she couldn't leave well enough alone. Nikki was trying to put Desmond out her mind, but every time Nikki turned around, Tess was bringing him up. Tess told Nikki repeatedly, that Desmond called her and starting asking if they could get together again. It made Nikki angry and at times it hurt as well. Nikki told Tess to drop the subject and not tell her when and if he called again, but Tess always found a way to work it into their conversations. Nikki couldn't figure out if Tess really was telling the truth or trying to use the subject to make her jealous. Either way, Nikki got tired after a month of trying to figure it out. She decided the semester was ending and her class with Tess would be over as well. Nikki had completed her prerecs and applied to Law School that semester, but had to wait until she had the grades turned in from the current semester before they would let her know if she was accepted or not.

Nikki was accepted in Law School and knew there wouldn't be any chances she would be registered for any more classes with Tess, so Nikki broke all ties with her.

Nikki decided the only way she was going to finish what she started was to totally devote herself to school and break all ties to anyone with any information about Desmond. Nikki knew she would have to work twice as hard to finish law school as the next person, because she already had strikes against her. First she had not finished high school. Second, she had a police record, a record that had been expunged to the public of course, but the record existed, so Nikki devoted her life to school and making the right kinds of friends to get her though school.

Tess however, was determined to stay in Nikki's life; she called repeatedly, wrote letters, and even left messages with some of Nikki's professors. Nikki told them to keep any future messages to themselves, because she didn't want to hear from Tess anymore. Tess had told one of Nikki's professors, she was leaving messages with Vincent and she didn't think he was giving Nikki the messages, because he was jealous of her relationship with Nikki. Nikki laughed when her professor gave her the message and told her teacher that Vincent had given her every message Tess had left and if she wanted to talk to Tess she would, but she was finished with that friendship, because her life was moving in a new direction. Her professor respected Nikki's answer, so finally, Nikki stopped getting messages through her professors and the phone stopped ringing as well.

Then, just when Nikki thought Tess had moved on, she called again and left a voice mail telling Nikki she was moving to Europe. Tess said she would be leaving in a few weeks and just wanted to get together to say goodbye and pleaded for Nikki to call her before she left, but Nikki didn't return her call. Nikki erased the message and moved on with her life.

CHAPTER 23

Vincent asked Nikki if she would consider adopting another baby. Nikki thought she would try another adoption, but she refused to adopt another handicap child thinking the process of adopting a healthy child would take years. Nikki only needed two years to graduate, so if it took at least that long she would have graduated and be in a better frame of mind to make that kind of a decision.

Nikki and Vincent watched a television program about children in orphanages in foreign countries. They showed the little girls lined up in high chairs waiting for a caregiver to come down the line and feed them. They sat in chairs with a whole cut out in the bottom of the chair so they could potty and not require diaper changes. Nikki had tears running down her face at the end of the program. Nikki wrote the agency that was sponsoring foreign adoptions for the program and started the process of adoption again. They were told it would take two to four years for the adoption process to be completed. So, Nikki agreed to start the process and see where it would lead.

The home study process was more intensive, because adopting internationally had more rules and stipulations than when they did their first home study. After six months Vincent and Nikki were cleared once again to leave the states and adopt abroad.

Nikki concentrated on school solely, night and day. She thought law school had to be worse than boot camp, but she stuck it out. There were many days Nikki went home crying thinking she wouldn't return the next day, but she hung in. During the times Nikki doubted her abilities; Vincent encouraged her to quit. The more he encouraged her to just give it up, the more determined Nikki became to finish.

Then, in the first semester of Nikki's senior year she had gone to Dr. Hawkins for her yearly check-up. He told Nikki he wanted to do a bone scan, because of her weight and medical history and the bone scan came back positive for a degenerative bone disease. He referred Nikki to the American Women's Hospital director. The hospital had just received a grant to study degenerative bone disorders to see if they could rebuild bone mass. When the director looked at Nikki's records, she was told her disease process was too far advanced and she could not participate in the program safely.

Nikki asked how bad the disease was at that point and was told she had the bone mass of a ninety-year old woman. When Nikki asked what that meant, she was told, she could fracture her bones just by walking across the living room, or with a position change while in bed. Nikki was told her life would be cut short by the disease and if they had to guess, she probably would suffer a massive fracture in the near future and because of the possibility of throwing a clot with a fracture she could die within the year.

Nikki sat in the chair as if she was in another world, hearing the words again, but not hearing the words. She couldn't believe her ears; her mind was in complete shutdown, total denial. She asked what she could do to stop the process and was told, there was nothing that could be done. Nikki went home and told Vincent what the doctors said and went to bed. Nikki became afraid to breath. She moved around very carefully and didn't make any sudden moves; her life was over. Nikki sank into a major depression and stopped living life at all.

Her professors called to find out why Nikki hadn't been in class because she had always been so diligent in attending classes; she never missed. Nikki told her professors that she had been diagnosed with a degenerative bone disease and said she was resigning from school. Her professors made the announcement in class to let Nikki's class mates know why she wouldn't be returning. In the mean time, Dr. Hawkins called Nikki to see how the program was going and what she thought of it. Nikki told him the director had told her she was too far advanced and he wouldn't let her participate in the program, because of how serious her condition was at the time. Dr. Hawkins was livid. He referred Nikki to an Internal Medicine specialist and an Endocrinologist. He told Nikki, he would have her, an appointment with both those specialist within the week and if they cleared her, he intended to demand she be put in the study.

Nikki went to see Dr. Babin the internal medicine doctor and he agreed to be Nikki's primary doctor for medical treatments in the future, but wanted her to see Dr. Gilva the Endocrinologist as well. After Dr. Gilva reviewed Nikki's medical history and examined her, he told Nikki he thought her condition was much worse when she lost her baby than it was then. He told her not to mistake his findings, she was a real sick lady, but he felt she had potential for recovery or at least stabilization. Dr. Hawkins called the hospital director and insisted Nikki be entered in the program, even if they had to assign her a one on one tech to get her through the initial set up.

Needless to say, Nikki started the diet and exercise program through the research center at the hospital. She was assigned a tech to remain with her during all exercises and meal times and Nikki kept every appointment. Nikki had not returned to school, but her study mates visited. Nikki didn't realize how much she had missed Jena and Ryan until she saw them. She cried, they cried, then they dried their eyes and told Nikki they were not going to let her quit school. Ryan told Nikki if he had to come drag her little ass out of bed everyday for class, he would, but she couldn't give up so close to the end. Jena told Nikki that medicine changed everyday and they could cure the problem, then she would be stuck in the same situation she wanted out of, if she didn't finish school. They reminded Nikki all she had already survived and reminded her she was a fighter not a quitter.

Nikki had gotten close to Jena and Ryan in the last year. They studied together, hung out together, and ate all their meals together. Jena's kids played with Andy while Ryan, Nikki and Jena studied. They worked on all school projects together and did more group projects than they cared to remember. All the while their friendships grew stronger everyday. Nikki told Jena she didn't think she could pass the semester, because she had missed so much work. Jena and Ryan told Nikki they would copy their notes and work extra projects to help her pass if she would just agree to give it another try. They both went with Nikki to the Dean to discuss the possibility of Nikki returning to school. The Dean told Nikki if her doctors put in writing her diagnosis and the need for her absence she would excuse the absences, but because Nikki had not taken the tests already administered, her final, would count for eighty percent of her grade.

Nikki accepted the terms for her to return to school. Her doctors placed in writing Nikki's diagnosis and her absence due to stress of the diagnosis and then treatment at the Hospital's Women Center. Nikki worked on the projects assigned in both her classes. She did her projects at night to catch up and completed her mandatory hours for both her classes. She had four days to prepare for finals in both her classes. Nikki, Jena and Ryan rented a hotel suite to study. Ryan and Jena drilled Nikki on the topics and lectures until Nikki wanted to scream. She was frustrated and scared out her mind she would never make it. Just knowing the weight of the final would be enough to discourage anyone, but Ryan and Jena wouldn't let Nikki give up. They pushed her until she didn't think she could go any further; then they pushed her more.

The night before the final, Jena and Ryan told Nikki they were all ordering dinner and a movie, the books would be closed and they would relax and enjoy the evening. Nikki told them they had lost their minds to waste the night before the final. Ryan and Jena assured Nikki she knew the content, she could spit out the answers to their drill questions in her sleep.

Nikki ate dinner and enjoyed the movie with her friends. Ryan passed out on the floor, so Nikki covered him up with a blanket. Jena fell asleep on the other bed, so Nikki curled up in her bed and read her notes one more time before she turned the lights out. The next morning, they had one final review, hugged each other and out the door they went to take the first final.

When the test was over Nikki, knew she had one more the next day to get threw. They met up at the hotel and reviewed the information for the last final until three in the morning, slept for four hours, got up ate breakfast, reviewed notes one last time and headed out for the exam. When the scores were posted, Nikki passed both courses with flying colors, she completed the first exam with an A and the second with a B. Ryan and Jena had B's in both courses. Nikki laughed until she almost cried at the looks on their face when they got their grades. Then Nikki did cry. She hugged them both and told them she would love them until the end of time. She wanted them to know the only reason she was still there, was because of their persistence and support. She also told them she would have never passed those courses had it not been for their help.

They had lunch together and promised to keep in touch between semesters and Nikki went home to finish her program through the hospital hoping something was working. She wouldn't know until her next scan in three months. Nikki had the summer off with only one semester left to go before she graduated and the adoption agency called to tell Nikki and Vincent they had been assigned a child and would need to be on a plane in four days. Nikki was blown out the water. Nikki told Vincent she didn't think that was the right time to adopt another child, but Vincent told Nikki she would never pass another physical and that might be there last chance to adopt a healthy child. Nikki agreed to go to Romania and decide there if she could complete the process.

When they arrived in Romania, Nikki and Vincent flew all over the continent. In one city they started the process of the adoption and in the next city they got the baby. Nikki was told she wouldn't have to go to the orphanage before she went to Romania, but the government changed the rules when they got there. Nikki and Vincent got on a bus with six other parents that were also from the United States adopting a child and had an interpreter to take them to the orphanage.

As they drove through the gate of the orphanage, Nikki saw all the children in the fields working and a building that looked like a school. Nikki told the interpreter, it was nice the government put the orphanage behind the school and the interpreter said; there was no school that was the orphanage. Nikki asked how many children were in the orphanage and was told more than ten thousand. Nikki knew the history of Romania from the program she watched, but it was different to see something on TV than it was, to see it in person.

Nikki knew the government determined how many children a family was allowed to have. If the family lived in the city and had money or middle class, so to speak, they were allowed two children. If the family was poor and lived on the countryside, they were allowed one child.

The poor people that were allowed only one child wanted boys to carry on the family names. If the baby born was not a boy, the family would abandon the girls, for the government to find and place in an orphanage or they would kill them. The woman heed during their pregnancy, so if they killed their baby or abandoned them, know one would know they were pregnant, so they would not be prosecuted. The woman of Romania also induced self-imposed abortions as a form of birth control, to control when they did or didn't give birth. It was a horrifying reality of a way of life many humans to had to endure. When Nikki and Vincent went to the orphanage, they were told not to take any photographs or videos. Nikki still walked with her camera at her side snapping photos as she walked passed the doors of the orphanage. They saw baby's, two to a bassinet, children tied to cribs and chairs or sitting rocking silently. The families were taken to a room, so the workers of the orphanage could bring in the children to be adopted.

One by one they brought in these babies and called the parents name of the adoptee. Nikki watched, as these dishrag children came through the door with know emotion what so ever when they were placed in the adopting parents arms. Nikki leaned over and told Vincent they were in trouble, she told Vincent to look, none of the babies were crying.

Then they brought Mia in the room and called Vincent and Nikki. As soon as Nikki took her, she started screaming and looked over Nikki's shoulder and saw Vincent. Mia had never seen a man before and was mesmerized by Vincent. He had a beard and mustache she couldn't stop touching. Mia just sat and stared at Vincent for the longest time. Nikki was worried about a baby that might be a zombie or non-responsive, but Mia defiantly wasn't either. She scream at the top of her lungs to get her way, She threw fits, she had temper tantrums, you name it, Mia did it.

Nikki didn't bond with Mia; she sat and stared at her from across the room. Nikki told Vincent she did not want to complete the adoption process. She told Vincent her health was failing and she could die. She asked him if he really wanted the responsibility of raising two kids alone, but Vincent was adamant he was not leaving without Mia. Nikki just shut her mouth and stopped speaking like she always did, when she became frustrated. The two-week trip to Romania turned into five weeks, every time they went to another step in the adoption process; the government wanted expiating fees to complete the process. A twenty five thousand dollar adoption turned into fifty thousand dollars before they got out of Romania.

The last stop was the worst. Nikki had remained silent; she just wanted to go home. The adoption was finalized at that point and the only thing they needed was Mia's Visa to leave the country. The government said they would issue the Visa, but it would take ten days to do a criminal background check on Mia before they could complete the paperwork. Nikki screamed,

"What the hell do you think this kid could have done, climbed out her crib, slide out the door, crawled under a fence, knocked over one of your stores, crawled back under the fence, slide back in the orphanage and climbed back in her crib, give me a break!"

Vincent was trying to get Nikki to shut up, but Nikki had, had all she could endure with their process. The officer of course said, for expatiating fee he could finish the paperwork that afternoon. Nikki told Vincent to give him the money and get her on the next plane out of Romania, or she was leaving on the next plain with or without him and Mia. The interpreter then informed Nikki if she tried to leave the country without completing the process, she could be charged with abandonment.

Nikki was trapped and she felt like she was suffocating. All she wanted to do was get the hell out of Romania. She would kiss American soil and swore she would never leave the United States again if she could just get home. Nikki had lost eight pounds while in Romania, because the food was not what she had imagined. Nikki remembered, when the plane landed in Romania, the pilot let everyone except the Americans off. Then he made the announcement, to be careful about the food and not drink the water and never eat food from the local venders on the street. They were told if they got sick to go to the American Embassy, not to seek treatment in the local hospitals, because they didn't have modern medicine. Nikki thought they should have told them the ground rules before the plane took off rather than when it landed.

They completed Mia's passport and visa that afternoon, so Nikki and Vincent were cleared to depart Romania the next morning. Nikki packed their things and spent the night at the airport waiting to leave on the red-eye at five o'clock the next morning. The flight home was twenty-three hours. Nikki and Mia slept, while Vincent watched movies, then Nikki stayed awake while Vincent slept.

When they got home, Nikki and Vincent had to file a petition for America to recognize the foreign adoption as legal in the United States and Mia's name was changed to Jessie Renee. The process was completed in three days in America. Nikki thought America was too good to be true and the rest of her life she swore she would tell anybody that was unhappy in America to take their ass to Romania, then they would be grateful just like her and kiss American soil when they returned.

CHAPTER 24

Nikki had no respect left for Vincent and he knew it. Vincent told Nikki she wasn't going back to school for her last semester, because she should stay home and be a Mom. Nikki made it clear she was going back to school and if he thought Jessie needed a full time parent he could stay home with her. Nikki had a medical program to complete for her health and one semester left to go before she finished college. Vincent made it clear when the semester started if she went back, he would leave and offer no financial support while she completed her last semester. Nikki told him school started in two weeks, so he had better start looking for a place to go.

At that time, Nikki had two dogs called Trip and Tujack when she adopted Jessie. When they walked in the door the night they got home with Jessie the dogs ran to Nikki. Jessie had never seen a dog before and was mortified, screaming and clinging to Vincent. Know matter what Nikki did Jessie wanted no part of the dogs, so Nikki had to find other homes for the two dogs. The next weekend, Nikki was going to the stables to take care of her horses named Holy Smoke and Ransom. Vincent had plans to go fishing and Nikki needed to check on the horses, buy hay and feed, but Vincent told Nikki he was going fishing anyway, so they fought.

Nikki told Vincent to think about Jessie's reaction when she saw the two dogs, could he imagine her reaction when she saw two monster horses. He laughed and told Nikki, she would figure something out and walked out the door. Nikki loaded the kids in the jeep and headed to the barn. When she got there, she pulled the jeep up to the barn so she would be able to see the truck and rolled the windows down. Jessie was hanging out the window when Nikki got out, so Nikki told her to stay in the car. Nikki pulled Ransom out his stall and tied him up outside the door, then went to get Holy Smoke, but the ranch hand had already turned him out. Nikki went in to clean Ransom's stall and heard the kids laughing. She thought the sound was too close for comfort and threw down the rake and ran to see where they were. Andy was standing at the barn entrance, but Jessie was under Ransom with her arms wrapped around his leg.

Nikki was speechless. She walked over to Jessie and asked if she liked the horse, Jessie just smiled at Nikki, so Nikki saddled Ransom and took Jessie for a ride. Jessie loved it and Nikki almost had to kill her to get her off Ransom that night. Everyday Jessie's favorite pass time was going to the stables to ride Ransom. Nikki could put Jessie on Ransom bareback and Ransom just walked around with her. It was unbelievable to Nikki that Ransom knew Jessie was a baby. Ransom knew he had to walk know matter what she did, but he was the most incredible horse ever anyway. He was black with a white blaze stripe across his nose; Ransom was a thoroughbred show horse and was what one would call a flashy horse. He was a registered racehorse and had won the Evangeline Downs race the year before. He was the only race horse Nikki had ever known that could be put on a race track, ran wide open and then put a kid on his back and he would walk.

Jessie looked so cute at the stables with her cowboy hat, T-shirt, diaper and rain boots. That get up, was Jessie's favorite, even when she was home she had her boots and hat on.

Life with Nikki and Vincent was only going from bad to worse as the semester approached. Vincent told Nikki again he would leave and not support her in her senior semester, so she didn't have a choice, but to stay home. Nikki told him to pack and go, if she had to live in a garbage can to finish the last four months of school she was going, so Vincent packed his things and moved in with his friend.

Nikki was struggling to make it, but the day after Vincent left, Nikki went to the bank and cleaned out the account. Vincent had checks bounce and was pissed, but Nikki didn't care. She meant she was finishing school know matter what the cost.

Nikki still had not totally bonded with Jessie; she was just a little lost soul in the room with Nikki. Jessie spent most of her time with Andy and the two kids adored each other. Andy was protective of Jessie and rocked her to sleep during the day for naptime. Nikki would find Andy passed out on his beanbag chair with Jessie passed out on top of him. They were so cute together, but Nikki couldn't shake the uncomfortable feeling she had in the pit of her stomach.

Nikki bathed with Jessie everyday and after Nikki finished with Jessie she let her run through the house naked until she finished her bath, then she would dress Jessie. One morning Nikki bathed Jessie as always and turned her loose in the house. When Nikki finished her bath, she realized Jessie was too quite. That always meant trouble, so Nikki went to look for Jessie. She wasn't in her room, so Nikki proceeded down the hall to the living room. When Nikki entered the living room, she was startled. Jessie had climbed on top of the couch and had her hand in the fish tank trying to catch the fish. Jessie was leaning over the fish tank with her knees on the edge of the tank. Nikki took a deep breath; when Jessie heard her she turned, fell and hit the fish tank with her head, then hit the table with her head and hit the floor with her head. Nikki stood there for a second or two waiting for the blood-curling scream one would expect, but it didn't come.

Nikki ran to Jessie and picked her up and told Jessie to look at her, but Jessie's eyes were glassed over, like she couldn't see her. Nikki started pacing the floor talking to Jessie. Nikki begged Jessie to look at her, but she didn't. Nikki shook Jessie to get her to snap out of it, but Jessie bowed her back and had a seizure on Nikki, then stopped breathing. Nikki was begging her to snap out of it, but realized she wasn't breathing when she started turning blue. Nikki dialed 911, she was hysterical. Nikki screamed for help and told the person on the other end the baby wasn't breathing and turning blue. Nikki thought Jessie was going to die before they could get there. The operator told Nikki she was dispatching an ambulance and putting her through to another operator.

When the other operator got on the line, Nikki was still hysterical. The operator asked Nikki if she knew CPR and in that instant Nikki calmed down enough to remember she did. She threw the phone down and ran to Jessie and started CPR. Nikki screamed for help, she was crying and trying to breath for Jessie and begged the ambulance to get there. They arrived within five minutes, but it seemed like a year to Nikki. They got Jessie breathing and transported her to the hospital. Nikki told the Nurse she felt helpless and the nurse told her she was in, "Mommy mode," and commended her on her CRP efforts.

Jessie had a sub-dural hematoma, a bleed on the outside portion of the brain. One minute she was going to surgery; then the Neurosurgeon said he was going to watch Jessie for twenty-four hours and see what happened. Jessie came to, off and on, but she was sluggish. The next day she was weak on the right side of her body, because the bleed was on the left side of her brain. The Neurosurgeon told Nikki it was expected and her strength should start returning in the next day or two as the clot was reabsorbed by her body.

Jessie was discharged to go home after two days and while in the hospital Nikki never left Jessie's side. She rocked her day and night. Needless to say, that little act from God forced the bonding between Nikki and Jessie and from that moment on, Nikki had a daughter she would kill for. Nikki took Jessie home with her and picked up Andy from Perry's next door and took her children home. Nikki didn't know what kind of life they would or wouldn't have, but she vowed they would stay together and they would have each other know matter what.

When Nikki got home her pager went off and she didn't recognize the number, so she called it to see who it was. It was Desmond. When he answered the phone he asked Nikki if she ever returned pages and she told Desmond she had put her pager away for a while and had just pulled it out and started using it again. Nikki told Desmond she was sick and the doctors didn't know if they could or couldn't treat the disease. Desmond told Nikki the doctors would treat it and be successful, because he couldn't think any other way. Nikki was touched by his concern and wanted to see Desmond, but knew she couldn't for her sake. They spoke briefly about the situation with Tess, but Nikki told Desmond life was too short and she didn't want to talk about it. Nikki thought, Desmond thought, it was behind them, but the truth was it wasn't. Nikki would never let him know how much it had hurt her and Nikki decided she wasn't going to deal with Desmond. Nikki had to focus on a way to finish school and her treatment without anyone's help and she did.

Nikki took out the maximum amount in student loans that semester and lived on her credit cards, she went back to work in the DA's office as a clerk for the experience and the money. Jena worked with Nikki and Ryan spent his time keeping the kids while Nikki worked. Then two weeks before graduation, Vincent moved his things back in the house while Nikki was at school. Nikki was pissed when she got home, but Vincent told her he wasn't leaving his home, she could go, but he wasn't leaving. Nikki finished her classes, but failed her comprehensive exam, so she wasn't going to graduate. Ryan had failed also, but Jena had passed by the skin of her teeth. Nikki was devastated. The university posted another test date, but the grades would not be available until the day before graduation.

Nikki and Ryan retook their comprehensive exam and passed. It was nerve racking not knowing if she would graduate or not until the day before graduation, but Nikki sucked it up and made it through.

Nikki graduated on her birthday, to her; it was the best birthday present she ever gave herself. She went to work in the DA's office. She worked the evening shift and did her research at night so Vincent could keep the kids. They didn't have a life together anyway, so the less she saw of him the better. Nikki napped when she got home until the kids woke up, then again when they took their nap during the day. When Vincent got home she got dressed and went to work. Nikki worked six days on, seven days off. It was the perfect schedule for her life and the kids. When she wasn't working she was gone to Florida or the Mississippi coast. She almost never stayed home unless Vincent left for one of his fishing trips.

CHAPTER 25

Nikki decided the time had come to tell Tricia the truth. When Nikki's half sister, Kirsten came back in her life years before, Nikki had found out where Tricia was. She lived in Colorado with Kevin's sister. Nikki went there after speaking to one of Tricia's Aunt's on the phone. June had told Nikki if she came, she would help her meet Tricia; then the rest was up to her, so Nikki went to tell Tricia the truth about how Kevin and Michelle had stole her.

When Nikki got to Colorado, June greeted Nikki warmly. She asked Nikki for the truth surrounding the circumstances and how Kevin got Tricia to begin with. Nikki told June what had happened and told her where to go to get the records to verify the truth. June told Nikki she didn't need the records, but Tricia might want them some day.

That night Nikki stayed at June's house. The plan was to go to the school the next day to talk to Tricia, so the next morning Nikki got up, got dressed and waited for June. Nikki went with June to the school to find Tricia. Nikki's heart was pounding in her chest as she walked the halls. They searched the school, but couldn't find Tricia anywhere and Nikki's heart rate slowed down when they decided to leave, because they thought she had not gone to school that day.

As they headed out the school, Nikki was passing the door to the gym and Tricia came barreling out the door and ran straight into Nikki. She almost knocked Nikki down. Tricia apologized to Nikki and told her, she had just taken her school picture and she couldn't see a thing without her glasses. Nikki offered to help her get her glasses, but Tricia looked in Nikki's eyes and told her she had to go. Nikki asked her again if she could help her get her glasses, but Tricia was steadily backing away;

looking at Nikki as if she knew her. Nikki could see the fear in Tricia's eyes, so Nikki stood there and watched her daughter run down the hall to her classroom.

June asked Nikki why she didn't stop her and tell her who she was, but Nikki said the time wasn't right. She said Tricia was too young and wasn't ready for the truth, but she would come back when she thought Tricia was.

Nikki left Colorado and returned home. She waited patiently for Tricia's eighteenth birthday and on that day; Nikki sat down and wrote Tricia a letter. In the letter Nikki told Tricia the truth about her life and how she was stolen from her. She told her she knew she was told that Nikki was strung out on drugs and abused her, but that wasn't the truth. Nikki told Tricia in the letter where to go to find her hospital records and the records for the child protection department that handled the case. Nikki told her, how they tricked her into signing adoption papers and then disappeared with her, leaving Nikki walking the streets at the age of fourteen.

Nikki sealed the letter in an envelope and bought a CD by, "The Kinleys.'"

Nikki packed her bags and called June to tell her she was on her way. June said she was expecting her call any day and the time was right, because Tricia had started asking a lot of questions about her life. Nikki called her family to let them know where she was going and much to her surprise, Darwin offered to go with her, but Nikki told him she needed to go on her own. Nikki also called her girlfriend Renee whom was also an attorney, who in turn called a Federal Judge; that asked Nikki to come to his chambers before she left. After telling the judge what had happened and what she was going to do, he asked Nikki to give him until that afternoon and come back to his chambers before she left. When Nikki returned the judge had pulled all the records Nikki told him about and said he could have both Kevin and Michelle prosecuted if Nikki wanted to pursue it. Nikki told him she was going to meet her daughter and wanted to wait and see how things went before she decided where and how to handle the situation. He told Nikki if she had any problems while she was there to call him and to report in as soon as she returned home.

Nikki then left for Colorado and arrived at June's house. June told Nikki they would wait for Tricia at the grocery store where she worked the next morning. That day, Nikki waited at the front of the store; her heart again started beating out of her chest. When Tricia walked in, Nikki knew her on sight. Tricia was still a spitting image of Nikki.

Nikki followed Tricia down an isle in the grocery store and called her name. Tricia turned to Nikki with her boyfriend by her side and Nikki asked her if she could speak to her for a moment. Tricia looked at Nikki and said,

"You're my Mother aren't you?"

Nikki said,

"Yes, Tricia I am."

Tricia blinked her eyes and told Nikki to get away from her; she didn't want a dam thing to do with her. Nikki told her she would go, but she handed her the letter and the CD. She asked Tricia to listen to the song, "Please," on the CD, because it spoke from her heart and to read the letter or through it away, but she had to know that at least once in this life time she had placed the truth in her hands and how she decided to deal with it was up to her.

Nikki told Tricia she was going back to June's house for the night and if she wanted to talk to her, that's where she would be. She said if she had not heard from her by the morning she would leave Colorado and never return. Tricia took the letter and the CD from Nikki and walked away. Nikki went to the car where June was waiting and told her what had happened in the store. June told her, it was in God's hands then, so they went back to her house.

Within the hour, Kevin burst through the door at June's. He was angry and told Nikki she was leaving and not going to tell Tricia a thing. Kevin told Nikki his father was the Mayor of the city and his brother was chief of police and she would disappear if she didn't leave. Nikki told Kevin a Federal Judge in the state of Louisiana knew where she was and if anything at all happened to her while she was there with her children, it wouldn't matter if his father was the President of the United States, his ass was going down.

Kevin told Nikki he would die before he let her talk to Tricia and tell her anything, but Nikki told him it was too late for that, because she had already written a letter with the truth in it and told Tricia where to go on her own for the proof. Kevin told her, he was an up-standing citizen in the community and he wouldn't let her destroy his family, even if he had to die for it. Nikki screamed,

"Up-standing citizen my ass, let me tell you what you are, you son-of-a-bitch. You stole my kid and left me walking the streets at the age of fourteen, that is what kind of person you are and if you thought for one dam minute you could do that and it never would come back to haunt you, you got another thing coming, because I am not fourteen anymore and I am far from being stupid. If that kid tells me to leave and she doesn't contact me by the morning I'll leave, but if she decides she wants to be a part of my life, I'll fight your ass every step of the way and you know the only reason you're not in prison now, is because of my age then and I didn't know what to do, but I do now!"

Kevin jumped over the coffee table and attacked Nikki. He was choking her when June and her daughter jumped in and pulled him off Nikki who had kicked Kevin in is private parts and brought him to his knees. June screamed at Kevin to get out her house. He looked at Nikki, but she told him again she wasn't afraid of him anymore, because she had already survived his ass once and told him the question then would be, if he would survive her.

Kevin left and called his brother the chief of police, which happened to be the house Nikki, was staying in. He went home and asked what the hell was going on, so June told Kevin's brother that Nikki comforted Kevin with everything she had already told them. She told her husband, that if those things were a lie Nikki would have never confronted Kevin with it, but she did and he went ballistic.

He asked Nikki if she was all right and said he was told Nikki didn't come without a Federal Judge and her family knowing where she was. Then asked if Nikki wanted to press charges against Kevin, because he wasn't placing his ass on the line, but Nikki told him she didn't at that point.

Then the phone rang, it was Tricia. She wanted Nikki to meet her at a restaurant in the city, so June and Nikki loaded up the kids and went to have dinner with Tricia and her boyfriend. Tricia told Nikki she read the letter just before Kevin burst through the door to get it. She told him she had already read it and his actions alone were enough to let her know, what was written was true, but she was going to Louisiana to pull the records for herself. She said Kevin fell to the floor crying, saying how sorry he was, but Tricia walked out on him to call Nikki.

They sat in the restaurant talking for hours; it was almost as if they had an unspoken, unbroken bond. Nikki was devastated when she found out that Tricia had a hard life and was raised by someone she detested. Nikki told Tricia that the time had passed for her to be her Mother, but she would settle for being her friend, if that was possible. Tricia told Nikki she had a lot of questions, but needed time to absorb all the information she had gotten. Nikki told her she would not contact her, but gave Tricia her phone number and address. She told Tricia when she was ready, she could call her and they would see where life would lead them.

When Nikki got home she called the judge to let him know she was home and how things went. He was ready to start the criminal prosecution and issue a warrant for Michelle and Kevin for leaving the state before the adoption process was finished and presenting false testimony to a court to adopt a child, but Nikki asked him to hold off for a while. He told Nikki to give him the word and he would see to it that Kevin and Michelle paid for their behavior.

At that point and time, it wasn't about vengeance for Nikki, it was about salvaging what ever relationship she could with a child she delivered and thought about almost everyday of her life. Nikki then called her family to let them know she went and she would wait and see if Tricia called. Darwin was totally pissed when he heard what Kevin did and wanted a phone number to him or he was going to Colorado himself.

Nikki gave Darwin the number, so he called Kevin and told him father Mayor or know father Mayor, if he ever laid another hand on his daughter by the time he finished with him, his father the Mayor wouldn't be able to recognize him. He told Kevin he was possibly facing a prison term if Nikki decided to pursue it, so he had best cool his jets or he and his family would have a hell of a lot to worry about in the future. Kevin tried to tell Darwin he lost his cool and was fighting for his daughter, but there was know explanation Darwin was willing to hear. Darwin told Kevin what he and Michelle had done was wrong and had come back to bite him on the ass and if Tricia wanted Nikki in her life she was going to get it, if he had to go with Nikki every time she went to visit, so be it. Then he told Kevin he would only have to make one trip, because after that, there wouldn't be a need for a second one.

Kevin said he understood and promised there wouldn't be anything physical with Nikki again. Darwin's last words to Kevin were, if he didn't like things the way they were for him to bring it to the court system himself and see where it would end, but Kevin didn't think that was necessary. Darwin said he thought not on his part, but that would be Nikki's family's next step if it went any further.

Two weeks after Nikki's visit to Tricia, she called Nikki and wanted to visit Louisiana and meet her family. Nikki told her she would arrange it and gave her directions to get there. Nikki called Gabrielle to let her know Tricia was coming and they planned a family fish fry for the reunion and it turned out to be a great experience for them all. Tricia was welcomed back in the family with open arms. She cried, Nikki cried and the family cried; the family bond was for life. Tricia was told, she did belong in their family and if she ever needed any thing, all she had to do was ask.

Nikki threw a party at her house with all her friends to meet Tricia as well. It was a busy week for Tricia meeting people, seeing the city and spending time talking to Nikki. Tricia had put an album together for Nikki of her life and wrote a poem to tell Nikki how she felt. Nikki read:

"Emotions by Tricia:"

"To have something deep inside, you can't quite understand, but you can't quite put aside.

A feeling of being scared, and of love, but somehow feels as if they are joined as one.

Never understanding, but wanting to know why.

Words of wisdom could have helped me deal, but instead I found myself beside my bed ready to kneel.

Thanking God for each and every day, but still begging him to show me the way.

And to my amazement, I looked up, and was faced with something I knew would happen one day.

A stroll of emotions took over my heart, but that was after we were already apart.

I read your letter that very day and it made some of my fears go away.

Then I sat with you and had a talk and I realized some things were not true that I had been taught.

Meeting you made me realize, that I have found something I don't want to do without, for the rest of our lives.

Scared and a little fragile, yes I was, but now I just hope we can grow together forever in love."

Nikki hugged Tricia and knew that was their beginning. Tricia went back to Colorado, but her and Nikki talked on the phone, wrote letters and became close in the process of getting to know each other and again Nikki felt the return of a spiritual connection to Tricia. Nikki called Tricia one day and in the conversation Nikki told Tricia her right knee was killing her for some reason and was told Tricia had fallen at work the day before and hurt her right knee. They had several little encounters like that over the next few months. It was as if Nikki knew when something was wrong with Tricia or she needed to talk. Nikki called Tricia on several occasions just as she was getting ready to call her, or Nikki would be getting ready to call Tricia when the phone rang.

Something was happening with Nikki in the process of all this as well. When Nikki was pregnant with Tricia, the only prayer she prayed was for the baby to look like her. Tricia was a spitting image of Nikki, every curve of her face, her eyes, lips, chin, nose, and hair. The reunion was all Nikki ever wanted and Nikki didn't understand why she became afraid to be alone again, afraid of the dark and afraid to breath. She had no understanding at the time what was happening, but she was terrified of the unknown. Nikki once again tried to stuff her feelings and ignore them, thinking they would just pass.

Nikki would bury herself in something to run from her emotions, so she enrolled in an advanced law course that would last two weeks. Then Nikki got out of class early on the last day and went home. When she got home, there was a card on the kitchen table from Andy's Godfather Larry. Nikki opened the card and read,

> "I miss the days when you and I would sit and talk
> about what we would become and what we would never
> become and I miss you."

Nikki was reading the card again when Vincent walked in and asked if she thought it was a nice card from Larry. Nikki looked up at Vincent and told him he made her sick. When he asked her why, she told him, he was a liar. Nikki had told Vincent the truth about her sexuality; she didn't lie about Tess or anything. Nikki said another man doesn't write to another man in that manner, unless there was something going on. Nikki had thought something was wrong with her. She felt Vincent was gay and she was just a cover up, so people in his industry wouldn't know about his life style.

Vincent told Nikki she was wrong, but Nikki knew she was right, she knew Larry was bi-sexual by his own admittance. She remembered all the weekends Vincent left and spent with Larry. She knew Larry was uncomfortable around Nikki after Andy was adopted, and she saw all the feminine qualities in Vincent she had so blindly overlooked. Nikki told Vincent he was leaving, but Vincent said he wasn't going anywhere. Nikki said he was leaving the house that night one way or another, he could pack his belongings and go or he would leave in a body bag and to her, it didn't matter which.

Vincent stood there as Nikki walked in the dinning room looking out the window. She told him again to leave while staring out the window, but he refused again. Nikki turned on a dime and picked up the kitchen table and flipped it upside down. She told Vincent he was next if he didn't get the hell out of the house, so Vincent packed his things and move in with Larry.

Nikki went the next three months without speaking to anyone, except Ryan, Jena and Perry from next door. After three months she called Desmond to talk and they started seeing each other again, but he seemed distant to Nikki. Something didn't feel right. Then Vincent called and told Nikki he lost his job and was thinking about suicide if Nikki didn't let him come home, he said Nikki owed him that much. Vincent wanted to move back in the guest room until he got a job, then they could settle everything else. Nikki reluctantly agreed, but she agreed.

Desmond was furious with Nikki. Nikki told Desmond that Vincent had told her she owed him something, but Desmond told Nikki she didn't owe Vincent anything. Nikki decided to see what would happen in the next couple days. Vincent sat around and didn't go look for another job and that infuriated Nikki. She told him he had to leave and she didn't care where he went, but he couldn't stay there, because she couldn't look at him anymore. Nikki didn't know what she wanted, but she knew she didn't want Vincent in her life any more.

Nikki told Vincent he could see the kids anytime he wanted, she would never use the kids against him, but if he ever did anything that would hurt them or if they got hurt when he had them, he had better hope he died too. Vincent agreed, but said all he got out the marriage was debt up to his ass and responsibility for two kids that weren't even his. Nikki charged after Vincent who turned and ran. He locked himself in his room, but Nikki told him threw the door he was getting the hell out the house one way or another and as far as his dept up to his ass, Vincent had never paid one dam car note for Nikki, not even when she was in school or her insurance. Nikki bought all the groceries and wanted to know how the hell he put a second mortgage on the house and where the hell the money for the loan went.

Needless to say the divorce got messy. Vincent didn't have anything to do with the kids and didn't pay child support. He filed bankruptcy-leaving Nikki holding everything. Nikki had to file bankruptcy as well, but she kept the house, the furniture, her car, and her credit card. She sued Vincent for a divorce and requested an immediate hearing on the child support issue. Nikki won the child support. Vincent told the judge he wanted to surrender his rights as a parent and forfeit any visitation in the future. Nikki was upset, but kept her mouth shut. The judge told Vincent, it didn't work like that, he could forfeit his visitation rights, but if he didn't pay his child support on time he would rote in jail.

When they walked out the courtroom Vincent asked Nikki if she felt like she won. Nikki looked at him and told him she didn't adopt those kids alone and was forced into the second adoption. She said she might not be able to force him to be a parent, but she sure as hell could make him pay child support and dared him to miss one payment and see where he would wind up. Before he could respond Nikki turned and walked away.

Nikki fought with Desmond over the settlement, because Vincent got nothing and Nikki got it all, plus child support. Nikki couldn't explain all she had been through because; Desmond either wouldn't or couldn't hear her, so she stopped trying to talk to him to make him understand. Nikki decided she did what she had to, to protect her future and the future of her children. She also decided that Vincent walked away, filed bankruptcy and left her with the responsibility of paying for it all, so why should she have to give him any thing she was making the notes on. Nikki did pack Vincent's family air-looms and his Dad's guns, his Mom's dishes and what-knots she left to them when she died and returned those things. Nikki felt Vincent did deserve to have the things his family left him.

Nikki wondered if her and Desmond were meant to be and she had always wondered about the, "what if's," and she wanted an answer to that unresolved question and a final ending to their story. Nikki knew she couldn't or wouldn't be able to move on completely, until that answer was given to her in this lifetime, so Nikki ignored Ryan's warning that Desmond would be the death of her and continued to see Desmond. Desmond had his issues and did a little disappearing act on multiple occasions and Nikki thought if he wasn't spending his time with her, who was he spending it with. Ryan on the other hand was always there for Nikki. She could call him in the middle of the night or anytime and he would answer the phone. If she needed him, he would be there; he had already proven that time and time again throughout their friendship.

Ryan tried to tell Nikki he had been in-love with her for quite sometime, but didn't know how to tell her. Ryan swore he would do anything to have

Nikki in his life as his, but Nikki didn't feel the same way, she was in-love with an ass-hole, she would admit, but she was in-love with him period.

When Desmond returned, the tension was intense. The walls in Nikki's life were starting to close in on her and she didn't understand this distant thunder that rolled and echoed in her mind constantly know matter what she did to silence it. Nikki's past techniques weren't working anymore.

Nikki wanted to cling to Desmond and expected him to rescue her, from what Nikki wasn't sure, but she always thought Desmond was her Knight in shining armor. Nikki had placed Desmond in her mind as her hero, the one that could fix all and heal all, but the more she tried to cling to Desmond, the more she felt him slipping away. Nikki felt this empty hole or bottomless pit in her life. She wanted to fill it with something, anything, but the void was still there leaving Nikki more and more in despair.

Nikki's life began spinning further and further out of control, the harder she tried to maintain control the harder it got to keep it together, the nightmares about the kidnapping and rape returned and Nikki was petrified to be alone. She would wake up with blood-curling screams, and shaking uncontrollably. She tried to hide it from Desmond, because she didn't know what was happening, but Desmond was watching TV one night when Nikki was tired and retired early.

When Nikki screamed, Desmond ran in the room and found Nikki shaking. He held her and asked what was wrong, but Nikki told him she was fine and pushed him away. All Nikki wanted him to see, was someone strong and independent, because he didn't like clingy needy individuals. Desmond stayed with Nikki that night. The next morning he said he knew something was wrong and insisted she talk to him. He told Nikki the scream made the hair on the back of his neck stand up. It was a scream of shear terror, not just a scared scream.

Nikki admitted the dreams about the kidnapping and rape had returned and was getting worse. She wasn't sleeping anymore and was tired all the time, because she was afraid to close her eyes. She knew the dreams would come and she would relive the attack over and over again. Desmond said he would help her get though it, if she would agree to see someone to help her. He promised he would stay and do what he could to support her, so Nikki went back to see PJ again.

PJ told Nikki that even though she didn't think about the kidnapping and rape when she saw Tricia. It was an unresolved factor in her life she had never dealt with and bringing Tricia back in her life reopened an area in her mind she had fought so desperately to forget. She told Nikki she needed an antidepressant to help make things easier, but Nikki had developed a fear of all medications, she wouldn't even take a Tylenol for a headache. Nikki tried to take the medicine, but she couldn't. When she tried she had panic attacks so bad, she couldn't breathe, she got hot all over, ripped her cloths off, screamed and ran to the bathroom to through cold water in her face to stop her from fainting. After a couple of those episodes Nikki told PJ she wasn't coming back, she would deal with the issue on her own.

PJ told Nikki she was setting herself up for a major fall. She told Nikki she had spent her whole life running and she had filled the volcano up to the point of eruption. PJ told Nikki she was numb inside, because she could know longer tell if she was stuffing good emotions or bad emotions. Nikki told PJ she was crazy and reminded PJ she said not to adopt Andy, it would kill her, but it didn't. PJ admitted she was wrong about that situation, but this one, was a totally different matter. Nikki told her, she just wanted her there for the money and she didn't need her help anymore and left.

Nikki told Desmond she finished therapy and was fine, she was selling the house and giving herself a fresh start. Desmond agreed and told Nikki he didn't want to be in a house she shared with another man; then they talked about getting married. Nikki decided, that was the answer to her prayers and placed her house on the market. Much to Nikki's surprise the house sold within two weeks. Nikki and Desmond had looked at some houses, but had not agreed on what to buy. They found a house they fell in-love with, but it was sold and when Nikki talked to the builder about building the house again on another lot. He agreed, but told Nikki it would take four to six months to complete.

Nikki asked Desmond about putting her things in storage and staying at his condo until the house was built. Desmond agreed, but told Nikki they would be really cramped in his two-bedroom condo. Nikki took it, as him saying, he really didn't want her and the kids to stay there with him, so Nikki decided she needed a house soon, because she was closing on her home and had to get out. Nikki told Desmond she had two houses she had found, but Desmond wasn't happy with either one, but said he liked the first one they had looked at, but Nikki liked the second one instead. Nikki told him she needed to sign a purchase agreement, but Desmond wanted to think about it. Nikki needed a home for her and the kids, so she signed the agreement and bought the house. Needless to say, Desmond was not happy with the house or Nikki's decision to buy the house without his input.

Nikki knew she was moving out the house and was looking forward to a new beginning. Her own home and to her she didn't care if Desmond was part of it or not. Desmond was still staying with Nikki during the night, so Nikki was sleeping a little better, but Desmond hardly ever slept. Much too Nikki's surprise she found out what Desmond was doing while she was sleeping. Desmond was sitting up ordering porn flick after porn flick. Nikki's final satellite bill was nine hundred ninety dollars and Nikki was livid, but Desmond told her not to worry about it, he would pay it.

Nikki hired the movers to help her move and closed on both houses. The movers didn't show up, so Nikki got a U-Haul truck and asked the teenagers in the neighborhood for their help. They were eager to run to her rescue and Desmond helped with the move also, but he wasn't happy about it. Nikki and Desmond argued throughout the day off and on. That night in the middle of an argument over what to eat, Desmond slapped Nikki; she was taken back. To Desmond it was a love tap, but to Nikki it was the end of her hero period and something changed. The darkness started creeping out the cracks and Nikki started descending.

Nikki's kids started going to the sitters every weekend, because Desmond introduced Nikki to strip clubs and she liked them a little too much. She was embarrassed to walk up to the stage and tip the girls, so Desmond did, but she enjoyed going and watching. On a few occasions they took a stripper to the private rooms for private dances and that became their favorite pass-time.

A few months later Nikki got a letter from a collection agency for the satellite bill that Desmond never paid not even a portion of it. Nikki went to her room, laid on the bed and cried. Desmond got upset with her for being so emotional over the bill, but money didn't grow on trees for Nikki. She put the bill on one of her credit card so she wouldn't be turned into the credit bureau. Desmond told Nikki he would pay her back, but she never saw a penny.

Nikki was living paycheck to pay check and Desmond was at her house every night, eating her groceries, watching her TV and using her home as if it was his. He never offered Nikki money for bills or groceries. He knew she was struggling, because Nikki tried to tell him, but he didn't want to hear it. He could walk in a strip club and drop five hundred dollars for a five-minute song in a private VIP room, but he wouldn't help with the house expenses.

His life with Nikki was separate from any and everything. If they met someone Desmond knew in a restaurant, he would go to their table, but he wouldn't introduce Nikki. She never met his family, never met his friends, in fact Nikki couldn't name one person that Desmond had any form of a relationship with. When Nikki got enough nerve to say something, she told Desmond she was going to the grocery store and needed money. He handed her a hundred dollars and paid the cable bill when he ordered porn and Nikki demanded he pay it. Their existence together became more twisted by the day, but for some reason Nikki didn't let go.

Nikki made friends in almost every strip club she entered. She was small, attractive and a magnet to those girls. Life became one big party on the weekends and Nikki tasted the forbidden fruit of passion, eroticism and she liked it too much. In the first club they went to, Nikki and Desmond met the waitress Connie. She didn't dance, but she openly admitted to being bi-sexual. She was a little over weight and not Nikki's type, but Nikki really liked her, mainly because of her personality. Every time they went to the club, they sat in her section and she took care of them, as well as partied with them. Connie introduced them to the girls and they never had a bad time when they went there. They played pool with the girls, drank and had their private showings in the back room. For the most part those private dances were just dances; then it moved to another level.

Nikki and Desmond went to another club for Varity and met a dancer called Angel. She was totally attracted to Nikki and Nikki to her. Nikki had sex with her in the Private showroom that night, then went home and tore Desmond apart. Desmond and Nikki's sex life went to another level as well; it was more passionate than ever and much more aggressive.

They returned to the first club and partied again with Connie and she introduced them to Raven and Page. They were wild women and loved to party. They were stoned out their heads on drugs and in the mood for a good time, just like Nikki and Desmond. Nikki had just bought a Mustang and showed Connie her new convertible that night. They drank, laughed and wound up in the private show room as always, but that night, Nikki danced in the private room for the girls and Desmond. Connie and Raven were throwing their money on the table mesmerized by Nikki's moves and her body and Nikki sank deeper in a world where nothing was forbidden.

Connie wanted to see Nikki, but not with Desmond. Nikki told her that would never be possible, because that was their agreement between the two of them. After that, Connie partied a few times with them, but she was never the same, so Nikki and Desmond changed clubs and met Hunter, Katelyn, Cat, and Nikki spotted Angel again. This club then became the place to be. Hunter and Katelyn became friends with Nikki and Desmond and partied with them every time they showed up, Angel was standoffish at first, but Nikki didn't care. At that time Cat mesmerized her. Cat could dance and draw you into her world with her eyes. She wasn't bi-sexual, but told Desmond she had to stay away from Nikki, because she could be, with Nikki. She was a biker chick and beautiful. Cat was looking for a way out of dancing and left the club to move in with a police officer and planned her wedding and prepared to raise her kid with her new man.

Nikki was upset when they told her Cat was gone, but she moved on to the next one. Hunter was a tease in Nikki's mind; she didn't like Desmond, but didn't say why she didn't like him either. She just told Nikki that Desmond was too pushy for her. Angel warmed up to Nikki again and went to the VIP room with Nikki and Desmond again after she told Nikki she had a new boyfriend that didn't care if she slept with woman and she couldn't stay away from Nikki any longer. That night in the VIP room, Nikki had sex with Angel again, it wasn't totally erotic, but it was all right Nikki thought.

Then Angel called Nikki to tell her that Desmond was trying to have sex with her on the side. Then Hunter called Nikki and told her the same thing. At that point Desmond was having business dinners telling Nikki he was working, but these two girls were telling Nikki he was in the club trying to arrange something with them and swearing them to secrecy. He told them not to tell Nikki they had seen him.

Nikki had her engagement ring from Desmond and they were planning their wedding, Desmond had placed his condo on the market and moved in with Nikki. As the date approached both Nikki and Desmond agreed to move the date because they were not sure what kind of wedding they wanted and Nikki had more questions than answers.

Nikki still had not met a single friend of Desmond's or his family for that matter. She knew something was wrong, but she didn't acknowledge it either. In the mist of everything happening, the phone calls started and Nikki asked Hunter why she called; why then, did she decide to tell Nikki that Desmond was trying to have an affair with her. Hunter said Nikki had helped her and she liked her and thought she deserved someone better than Desmond. Nikki asked how she had helped her and Hunter reminded Nikki when she had a lump in her breast, Nikki had told her where to go to get free medical attention. She had thanked her, for her help and thought she was a good person with a good heart and didn't deserve to have someone like Desmond in her life. She told Nikki she was beautiful and deserved better than what he was giving her. She told Nikki she was going back home and wouldn't be dancing anymore, but she couldn't leave without answering Nikki's question. Hunter thought Nikki deserved that much. Nikki asked her why the call then again and Hunter told her, because she wouldn't have to see Desmond anymore and before that, she was afraid of him, and said Nikki should be too. Nikki laughed and told her, thanks for the call and good luck wherever it was she was going.

Angel on the other hand kept calling Nikki. The phone rang on the nights Desmond was suppose to be having dinner meetings, with Angel on the other end telling Nikki, her boyfriend just walked in the door. Nikki told her to prove he was trying to fuck her or leave her alone, so she told Nikki to come to her trailer the next day and she would show Nikki the calls on her caller ID box and call Desmond. Nikki went to the trailer and saw the calls on her caller ID box and when Angel called Desmond at work, he told her he was busy at the moment, but they would set something up real soon and he would call her back. Angel told Nikki that Desmond wanted her to move in with him in his condo and said; he had planned to blow Nikki off.

Nikki left there knowing that what these girls said was the truth and she meant Desmond would pay for using her the way he did, but Nikki wanted the truth in front of her no more wondering or guessing. Nikki told Desmond she was leaving town to go to her fathers for a family emergency and she borrowed a friend's, truck to followed Desmond. He stayed at her house that night, but he went to the strip-club for about an hour.

Nikki wondered why Desmond didn't stay with Angel that night, then figured he would expect her to call him, but she didn't. Nikki went to the house and looked through the curtains to find him sitting on the couch, watching a football game, so she went back to Shelly and Keith's house and slept on the couch.

The next night she confronted Desmond with the girl's conversations, as well as the caller ID. Desmond told Nikki he never had a thing to do with Hunter and he was trying to rent his condo to Angel, so he could stop paying the mortgage and contribute more to their bills and said he didn't tell her because Angel asked him to keep it a secret for a little while. Nikki wanted to tear him apart, but she froze like always and stuffed her feelings. Nikki had a problem with conflict and she was not good at confrontation, so she tried to swallow his story, because she couldn't prove anything otherwise. She did tell him he had no business-keeping secrets with strippers and he invited her in their lives to start problems. Angel knew she had the opportunity to destroy them and she took it.

If there was any trust at all in her heart for Desmond it wasn't there anymore. Katelyn was the only stripper left Nikki was talking to at that point and Katelyn told Nikki that Angel had been saying she was getting her a condo on Fifth Avenue and would be moving in with this guy. It took some time, but Katelyn finally figured out she was talking about Desmond and told Nikki that Desmond had been in the club without her to see Angel, but she didn't want to confront him. Nikki told Katelyn she could and would beat Desmond at his own game if it killed her. Nikki thought the way to do so was to be more erotic than ever and asked Katelyn to share an evening with them. They agreed to have this evening in the private suite at the new club Katelyn was dancing in that night or the night after.

Nikki told Desmond that Katelyn started dancing at another club in New Orleans and she wanted to go check it out and he was all too eager to go. Desmond and Nikki had a few drinks, but Nikki spotted a tiny petite blond like herself and fell in lust. Her name was Alicia. They took her to the private VIP room and Nikki devoured her as Desmond stood in the door. Desmond was blown away, how Nikki was turned on by this girl and couldn't believe his eyes or his ears. They left the club and pulled over on the interstate to have sex before they got home, because he couldn't wait to have Nikki.

While in the mist of an erotic night in the back seat of the Mustang, Nikki opened her eyes to see red lights parked behind them. The windows were fogged up and Nikki was scared out her mind. All she could see was bars and the charge of indecent exposure. Desmond told her to get dressed and just sit in the back seat. She got her cloths on just as the officer knocked on the window. Desmond told him they were tired and stopped to get some rest before they finished driving home. The officer stuck his head in the car to ask Nikki if everything was all right and she told him she was fine, just tired and he left without giving them a ticket or a warning.

Nikki and Desmond drove home and started stripping in the garage before the door could close. They had sex on top of the hood of the car before Desmond picked Nikki up to take her inside to the bedroom. Nikki passed out in the bedroom after Desmond was finished with her and Katelyn knocked on the door that night when she got off work. She had been spending a few days with Nikki and was considering moving in to share expenses. When she knocked on the door Desmond opened the door in the nude. He told her he was tired and Katelyn went to bed. The next day Katelyn told Nikki she was moving away and Nikki should get Desmond out her life.

CHAPTER 26

A few weeks later Desmond approached Nikki about her girlfriend Kelly. There was a computer programming position available in the company he was working for and Kelly was one of the best in her field. Kelly and Desmond had not had a good history for quite some time. Kelly had, had many dilemmas and obstacles in her life to over come and she didn't like Desmond when she met him. Some people just take an instant disliking to some people when they meet and this was one of those times.

A while back when Nikki was starting therapy, Desmond had called Kelly to ask her to be a friend and call Nikki, because he was sure that Nikki would have issues to talk about that she wouldn't want to discuss with him. Kelly told him she would, but called Nikki and told Nikki she was upset that Desmond would call her and tell her she needed to call and Nikki told Kelly, Desmond was just concerned for her well being at the time.

Kelly told Nikki she felt like Desmond was too pushy for her taste and she felt like he was coming on to her more than being concerned for Nikki. Nikki almost fell over when Kelly told her she didn't appreciate Desmond calling her. She told Nikki she was her friend not his and she didn't want him calling her anymore. When Nikki told Desmond not to call Kelly he was livid. He said all he was trying to do, was have a friend over for dinner and help Nikki through a tough time and he didn't want anything else to do with Kelly. Then unfortunately, Nikki had to have surgery, because she was bleeding too much and the pain with her periods had become unbearable. Dr. Hawkins told Nikki she had to have a hysterectomy to stop the bleeding and end the pain, so Nikki checked in for surgery. At the time Nikki didn't fell like she could count on Desmond, because he told Nikki he needed to work and she didn't fell close to him either, so Nikki called Kelly to be there and asked Mona from her job as well.

Nikki was nervous that morning and had given all the contact phone numbers to Mona if anything happened to her and made Mona promise not to let anyone give her pain medicine that would knock her out. Mona and Kelly told Nikki not to worry about a thing, they would see that she was well taken care of and nothing would go wrong. Nikki didn't have a pre-op shot before surgery, so when they came to get her she was awake, but all right at the time.

When she got to the operating room she was transferred to the operating table. Nikki told the nurse she couldn't do the surgery, so the nurse called Dr. Hawkins. He broke sterile technique to go in and talk to Nikki. He told her it wasn't exactly an elective surgery and she needed to get it over with so she could go on with her life. Nikki told Dr. Hawkins he needed to just knock her out or she would never consent or say it was ok to proceed. Dr. Hawkins looked at the Anesthesiologist when Nikki realized what she said; then the room started spinning.

The next thing Nikki knew, she woke up in recovery with Dr. Hawkins by her side. He told her everything went well and he would be moving her to her room soon. Nikki told him the catheter was burning and wanted it taken out. Dr. Hawkins said he spoke to her boyfriend and he said he couldn't stay and Mona was to return after she checked in at the office. Dr. Hawkins told Nikki he was going to give her another shot so she could rest and transferred her to her room. He promised to leave an order that when someone was at bedside to help Nikki to the bathroom, they would remove the catheter.

When Nikki got to her room she was hot all over, her face was beat red; her body was thrown into menopause immediately after the removal of her uterus. The hot flashes were incredibly intense. They draped cold wet towels on Nikki's chest, under her throat and on her forehead. Dr. Hawkins pushed his medicine through Nikki's IV and she was out like a light again. When Nikki woke up she was alone in her room. She called the nurse to remove the catheter, but was told someone had to be with her to help her to the bathroom before they could take it out, so Nikki asked the nurse to get her a phone and she called Kelly.

Kelly told her not to worry she was on her way. When Kelly got there, the nurse took the catheter out. Nikki cried, because it burned so bad, but the nurse told her after she went to the bathroom a couple times it would get better. Kelly asked Nikki why Desmond didn't stay with her and Nikki told her he had to go back to work, but Kelly was ferrous and said Desmond could disappear from work to take his ass anywhere he wanted to go when he wanted, but he couldn't take off to stay with her; but he was suppose to be in-love with her. Nikki was crying and told Kelly not to start about Desmond, she couldn't take it then. Kelly sat on the side of Nikki's bed and washed her face, she put cold wet towels soaked in ice water on Nikki's back, but nothing seemed to stop the hot flashes. Nikki's blood pressure also elevated, but was stable.

Kelly stayed with her the rest of the day and Nikki tried to pee on a bedpan, but couldn't. She had to urinate so badly, but couldn't. Nikki had to be re-cauterized and was told it had to stay in for at least twelve hours. Mona got back that afternoon and they bathed Nikki and kept ice water at her bedside with cold wet towels on her, but Nikki was miserable and tearful. Dr. Hawkins made rounds and told Nikki she was doing well, but Nikki was crying and told him she felt like she was losing her mind. Dr. Hawkins told Nikki her body was thrown into immediate menopause and her hormones would be messed up for at least six months to a year before the process would complete itself. Nikki said she couldn't take six months or a year of hot flashes like she was having and Dr. Hawkins said the hot flashes would go away in about a week or two, but her body had to adjust to not having a uterus anymore.

Mona told Nikki her boss Bridget would be coming to see her the next day. Nikki wasn't too excited about seeing her bible thumping boss. Nikki was tired and hungry, but didn't want the hospital food, so Kelly left to get Nikki something to eat while Mona stayed with her. When Kelly got back, Mona left for the night. Nikki ate her dinner, while Kelly surfed channels. Desmond got there about eight o'clock that night and said he had a business dinner he couldn't miss. Kelly just looked at him and told Nikki she had to go. She kissed Nikki on the check and told her if she needed anything, to call her and she would be there. Nikki thanked her for coming and told her she would see her the next day.

That night, Desmond was tired and irritable. Nikki was moody and irritable too. She was crying because the catheter was burning and having hot flashes and needed cold wet towels. Desmond told Nikki she was too needy and she needed to stop acting like a baby and Nikki turned her head and cried herself to sleep. When she needed anything in the middle of the night she called the nurse, instead of asking Desmond. At five o'clock the next morning, Nikki woke up with a warm sensation running out of her.

She thought the catheter was leaking, so she called the nurse. When the nurse responded, Nikki told her something warm was coming out of her and asked the nurse to check the catheter. It wasn't the catheter; Nikki was bleeding. The nurse told Nikki to say in bed, she was calling the doctor and they would probably just watch the bleeding, but if it got worse she would have to go back to surgery. Desmond got up and told Nikki he was going home to shower and for her to call him if she needed him. He kissed her on the forehead and walked out the door.

Nikki was shaking when Desmond left. She was terrified of going back to surgery again. Nikki needed Desmond, but she didn't want to be a burden either. Nikki was crying when the nurse came back in the room and asked if her husband went to get coffee, but the question only made Nikki cry more. Nikki told her that Desmond wasn't her husband, he left to go home and take a shower and get ready for work, but the nurse told Nikki she shouldn't be alone and if she had to go back to surgery someone had to be there with her, so Nikki called Mona and Kelly to tell them she was bleeding and needed someone to stay with her in case she had to go back to surgery. Mona told Nikki she was on her way and could stay until noon. Kelly was fine with the hours Mona could stay, because she could clear her desk and stay from noon until whenever.

Bridget, Nikki's boss showed up to visit while Mona was there and told her to stay with Nikki as long as she needed her. Nikki spent most of the day in the trendelinberg position, which was head down, feet up. Dr. Hawkins saw Nikki and told her he was going to give her some medicine to thicken her blood to see if that would help stop the bleeding. Then said; if the medicine didn't stop the bleeding in the next two hours, Nikki was going back to surgery.

Nikki's blood pressure continued rising, from stress and being scared wasn't helping the situation either, but Kelly and Mona started telling jokes to make Nikki laugh. It helped take her mind off the situation and allowed the medicine to work. Nikki's blood pressure came down, but Nikki's bleeding didn't stop, but it slowed down enough, that Nikki wasn't facing another surgery. Kelly stayed again, until almost nine o'clock that night before Desmond showed up. Kelly was upset again, but kept her mouth shut and left.

So, with all that history, between the two, Nikki was shocked when Desmond actually wanted to bring Kelly to the place he worked. Nikki called Kelly like Desmond asked her to, but Kelly said she wasn't interested. Then Kelly was approached by her priest about the job, because his friend

Rachael had asked if he knew of any computer people to talk with about the job. Rachael happened to work in the same office with Desmond, so Kelly agreed to the interview through Rachael.

There was a problem during the interview process that Nikki didn't understand and Desmond wasn't talking about, but she knew Desmond was upset about it. He said he could pull the plug on Kelly getting the job, but Nikki told him to leave it alone. Nikki told Desmond he started the process knowing how Kelly felt about him and he should have known from the start what he was getting into. She said for Desmond to do what he wanted, but he would have to deal with it in his way, but she wasn't getting involved in the situation anymore.

Kelly started working for the same company and started building her relationships in the office as all new employees do. She hated Desmond from the start. Desmond had always blamed Nikki for the way Kelly felt about him, because Nikki talked to her about their personal lives. Little did he know; Kelly felt that way about him from the moment she met him. Yes, the discussions with Nikki didn't help, but his actions when Nikki had surgery were the icing on the cake for that relationship; Kelly got her information first hand.

Kelly told Nikki that Desmond was pushing her at work and told her to keep her mouth shut about things she may hear about him. Needless to say, Kelly didn't take the threat too well. She called Nikki and told her she wasn't putting up with Desmond's crap and she had better tell her boyfriend to back away from her and leave her alone. Nikki told Kelly she was on her own with that situation and if she wanted Desmond to know something she should tell him herself. The next thing Nikki knew, Desmond was terminated, because Kelly went to her supervisor Rachael and told her that Desmond was a liar first of all and was engaged to her best friend and she had ate crap from Desmond since she started. Kelly said he demanded that she should be more grateful for her job, than she was willing to be and she was resigning her position. Rachael was appalled when she found out Desmond was engaged, knowing the life he lead around the office. Kelly told Rachael she wasn't lying to her friend Nikki about Desmond and she wasn't taking any more crap from him either.

Kelly made it clear the only reason she accepted the interview in the first place was because her Priest asked her to go. Rachael agreed with Kelly and assured her Desmond had nothing to do with her getting the job, and she would have never interviewed her based on Desmond's recommendation in the first place. Rachael told Kelly she was not resigning and took her to the President of the company. Kelly told the President what happened between Desmond and her. She made it clear, she would not tolerate anymore of his behavior, as well as telling him she would resign. The President told Kelly he would take care of the situation, but he would not accept her resignation. The President called Desmond to his office and terminated his services. Nikki still got the blame for Kelly's actions, as far as Desmond was concerned. He screamed at Nikki if she had not discussed their personal lives with Kelly, she wouldn't feel the way about him she felt.

Desmond also said Kelly was not as true of a friend as Nikki had thought she was and Nikki asked him to explain that accusation, but he refused. Nikki wasn't sure what had happened after Desmond left the company, but supposedly, Desmond had a conversation with someone and Kelly's name came up. Desmond wasn't kind in regards to some comments made and those comments got back to Kelly, which upset her. Kelly called Nikki and told her that every time something negative came in her direction, from Desmond, she was going to pick up the phone and call Nikki to tell her one of his betrayals she knew about. Nikki asked her what the hell she was talking about, so Kelly told her, next time she spoke to her boyfriend to ask him about the blond he took to the Christmas party that wasn't Nikki.

Nikki's heart sank to her knees; it was like Kelly took a knife and slashed her heart wide open and poured salt on it. Nikki was beside herself. She went to Desmond's to ask him about the party. He denied it happened, but when Nikki left she heard him scream and curse behind the door as she walked away. That night as Nikki slept, she tossed and turned, but when she woke up, she knew with one hundred percent certainty it was the truth and she meant she dam well wasn't letting another thing go. She called Desmond and told him it was time to come clean and he agreed to meet Nikki at his condo to talk. He told Nikki he took a girl in a time frame that she was being a bitch, his Mother had died and he was confused. Nikki screamed at him that she was wearing his engagement ring at that time. Nikki told Desmond she was done with him and she had had enough of his shit. She left boiling over with rage; this was the beginning of an eruption of the volcano of emotions that PJ told Nikki would come one day.

Nikki stuffed her feelings again, but it was getting harder and harder to maintain her peace. She was moody, irritable and disgusted. Nikki sat out for the truth and talked to anybody willing to talk to her. She spoke to a girl in Desmond's office, because she found a Victoria's Secret magazine with her name on it in Desmond's condo. Nikki called the girl and asked her why she would bring something like that to work and more importantly, how the hell did Desmond wind up with it. She told Nikki he took it off her desk. The girl said Desmond was seeing other women and had met her and the receptionist out on several occasions for parties. She didn't know who Nikki was and sure didn't know Desmond was engaged.

Nikki called Kelly and demanded to know anything else she had found out about Desmond. She told Nikki she didn't have any more information, but Rachael wanted to talk to her, so Nikki called Rachael as well. Rachael told Nikki she was the reason Desmond was hired on at the company in the first place. She said there were many women that called Desmond at work and she had seen him at football games over the last year with a few different women as well. The way she spoke and the tone in her voice, Nikki asked her, if she had sex with Desmond and Rachael said,

"Not in a million years."

Nikki told her she spoke of Desmond, not as a colleague, but as someone that was more personal. Rachel told Nikki she had invited Desmond to their company bar-b-que and they went together, and she introduced him around at the party. Nikki asked her, if it was a date and Rachael said it was and said Desmond tried to date her even after he started working at the company, but she could spot his type a mile away. She told Nikki he was a moocher, he was always mooching off people in the office for lunches, dinner and the President picked up the bill for his nightly entertainment.

Nikki told Rachael she knew, Desmond couldn't stand her and wanted to know what happened to sour their relationship. Rachel said that Desmond was jealous of her position in the company and her level of freedom. She said she had been with the company for a long time and had earned extra privileges that Desmond thought he should have when he entered the door. She said he kissed up to the President and hung out with him, thinking that put him on another playing field, but it didn't and Desmond resented it.

Nikki asked if it was a requirement that Desmond entertain clients in strip clubs and Rachael burst out laughing and said Desmond was sick and needed help. He spent most of his time surfing the internet looking for porn and his e-mails were enough to gag a maggot and he had almost crashed their company computer system, from opening porn that contained viruses. Rachael said Desmond had a golden opportunity there and his actions alone did him in. Nikki asked what actions in particular she was referring to, so Rachael told her the situation with Kelly was the icing on the cake, but Desmond thought he could go to work when he wanted, disappear when he wanted and he thought he didn't owe anyone an explanation of his time. He told the President he had appointments when he didn't and they started tracking him. They knew of several days; hours and hours of his time were unaccounted for. He would go in the office, take the newspaper to his office, kick his feet up on his desk and read the paper every morning.

Rachel said the whole office was upset and more than one person went to the President and complained as well as demanded he do something with Desmond. Rachael said the President liked Desmond and tried to give him a chance, but Desmond was impossible to work with. She also made it clear she wasn't tolerating anymore with Kelly when they talked with the President, so the decision was made to let him go. She asked Nikki to keep their conversation in confidence, because she thought Desmond could be dangerous and told Nikki she needed to get him out her life. She told Nikki he would only drag her down and was appalled when she found out Desmond was suppose to be engaged and acting the way he did. She told Nikki he not only lied to her, but he lied to every one of them too.

Rachael called names that Nikki had heard in the past, like Holly, and Mandy. She couldn't remember the girl's name at the Christmas party, but she did see her and said she could probably find out who she was if she needed too. She also told Nikki that Desmond was sending flowers to a girl at another contracting business and talked about a girl in the office he was infatuated with and her name wasn't Nikki. She called Desmond a snake in the grass and told Nikki again for her own sake and the sake of her children, she needed to get away from him and cut him out her life or he would cost her, her sanity.

Then Nikki talked to the girls that lived next door to Desmond in his condo. She was told on Sundays Desmond was out at the pool with them bar-b-queing, hanging out and drinking. Desmond bought them dinner, met them out and told them he was seeing several other people. Desmond promised one of the girls he could get her a job working with him and when they saw Nikki and asked Desmond who she was, they were told Nikki was just an old friend.

Nikki confronted Desmond with all the things she was told. He said he had told the girls, he saw other people, because he didn't want them in his personal business. He said he only lit the bar-b-que pit for them one day, but didn't have dinner with them. Then said he was out by the pool one Sunday and bought dinner for everyone there not just them. Nikki told him, he was just the perfect party boy and then asked where she was when he was partying by the pool with his college girlfriends. He didn't answer her, so she said she was sitting at home with her children waiting on him as always. He swore the relationships between him and the girls were exaggerated on their part, but Nikki had enough and told Desmond to move back to his party life at his condo and leave her alone.

Desmond moved out and Nikki thought maybe her life would settle down and she could put the insanity behind her. She had moved along in her career and money was no longer a problem for Nikki. Nikki decided the end had come for her and Desmond and she felt she could move on without, "the what if's," anymore. A few weeks pasts and Desmond started calling Nikki at work, when they would fight and Nikki would hang up on him he would call back repeatedly until Nikki would answer. Nikki tried to tell the secretary to tell him she was in a meeting, but Desmond would demand the secretary go get her because it was an emergency. He drove by the house several times a day and when Nikki was taking groceries out the car Jessie looked up and said,

"Mommy look, its Mr. Desmond."

Nikki looked up and again Desmond would be driving by. He called in the middle of the night to ask who Nikki had sleeping beside her and the encounters with Desmond became more than Nikki could bear.

Then Nikki and Desmond had a fight on the phone one evening as always and this time when Nikki finally started giving it back to Desmond, he hung up on her and wouldn't answer the phone, so Nikki went to his condo. He wasn't there, but the girls next door were sitting out front smoking and invited Nikki to have a smoke with them. She waited for almost two hours, but Desmond had not returned. Nikki was determined to put his ass in his place once and for all and figured he had to come home sooner or later and she would be there. What Nikki didn't know, was he was gone with the girl across the hall to get a pizza. While Nikki was sitting there, they called on their cell phone and was told Nikki was there, so they parked in the parking lot beside the condo waiting for Nikki to leave. When she got in her car to go the girls called them to say Nikki was leaving.

When Nikki pulled out, she turned in the opposite direction she usually did. When she got to the side parking lot she spotted Desmond's truck and she pulled in the parking lot as they were pulling out, when Nikki saw the girl next door driving his truck. Nikki turned around to

follow them and they turned on the next street by Desmond's condo, so
Nikki went down the street looking for them. She was turning around
when they passed her again. Little Miss Next Door Girl thought she could
out run Nikki, she was wrong. Nikki chased them down and they pulled
in a parking lot by a police officer; when Nikki saw who was in the truck
with Desmond, she was livid. Desmond told her she misunderstood what
she saw and the police officer told Nikki she couldn't drive like a maniac
and told her to leave and not follow them.

They pulled out one way and Nikki went another, straight to Desmond's
condo. When he pulled up Nikki was waiting. The girl ran in her condo
and locked the door, but when Desmond stepped out the truck with
his warm little pizza Nikki slapped it out his hand. She cursed him for
everything he was worth. Desmond was drunk and upset all at the same
time, but Nikki had had enough. She was too upset to care. She wasn't
going to be treated like that anymore and if he thought he was going to pull
all the shit he pulled and get away with it, he had another thing coming.
Desmond started pushing Nikki in the parking lot, but Nikki wouldn't
stop screaming at him. The girls next door watched with their eyes wide
open. Desmond started choking Nikki in the parking lot and told her he
would kill her. Nikki told him he was going to have to and she kneed him
in the groin and dropped him to his knees. The little lady next door saw
Desmond choking Nikki and called the police. When Nikki was walking
to her car to leave the police pulled in. They were going to take Desmond
to jail and the Police Officer asked Nikki if Desmond touched her and
she said he did.

Desmond went in his condo and slammed the door in the officer's face,
which pissed the officer off. They were calling for back up to take him in,
when Nikki got in her car and left.

When she left Desmond called her and asked if she was happy with
the scene she caused. Nikki was angry as hell and reminded him about
the scenes he caused. When they talked about what happened with the
girl next door. Desmond told Nikki he was drunk and asked her to drive
him to get something to eat, but denied sitting in the parking lot with the
girl waiting for Nikki to leave. The more he denied it, the angrier Nikki
became. She had been forced all her life as a child to say things were
different than they were, but she would die before she would say it was
different anymore. She saw him with her own eyes. He tried to tell Nikki,
it wasn't him, he didn't realize he was digging his grave deeper everyday.
Nikki finally realized Desmond would never admit the truth to her about

sitting in the parking lot with the girl, even though the neighbors admitted they knew they were there and called them to let them know Nikki was leaving, so she just hung up the phone and kept driving home.

Nikki thought in her mind there were too many lies on Desmond's part for there not to be something going on and she sure as hell didn't understand his friendships he lied about either. According to Desmond, everybody, but him was lying. Nikki knew too many people had the same story, different versions, but the same story. The only different story was Desmond's version.

CHAPTER 27

Nikki at that point was addicted to the so called underworld and strip clubs was the door to that world. She saw Desmond out and had already had a few drinks so that night was another of many ones spent in the heat of passion and Desmond thought that opened another door for him. Then Desmond wanted to give something to Nikki in return for all she had given him. He begged Nikki for forgiveness and told her he loved her and he couldn't live his life without her. Desmond said he wanted to share something sacred with her. He wanted to allow himself to become vulnerable in Nikki's eyes to open up to her. Nikki told him the nights with other women were done and if he thought that was going to happen with them again he was wasting his time. He told Nikki he wanted to share his inner most secret to show her he loved her. When Nikki said OK, Desmond said he wanted to have sex with a man, but he didn't want to do it alone. Nikki couldn't believe her ears and she thought this was just another one of his head games because he was so anti-gay. Nikki thought ok if she backed out that time that would be his way to say she didn't want to share in this so called twisted sex life so she went along with it knowing Desmond would not go through with it in a million years then the subject would be closed. Desmond called an escort service and ordered Tate. He was tall slender, in shape, gay, but not flashy gay and Desmond like him. Nikki watched Desmond touch Tate with his lips, mouth and fingers. She stayed in the room, when Tate took Desmond from behind. Nikki sat in shock as Desmond had intercourse with Tate.

The next morning, Nikki didn't know what she felt. Nikki had been numb for so long the only emotion strong enough to penetrate her was anger. If she wasn't angry, she was dead. She felt nothing for know one.

Desmond cried and held Nikki that morning and begged her to forgive him and put their lives together in a healthy way, but Nikki's heart had turned to stone and she couldn't fell any compassion or forgiveness for him. Nikki then understood Desmond's secret life and she too was locked in a dark place that she couldn't seem to find the surface of or a way out at the time.

Nikki became consumed with anger. She could know longer hide it or make it go away. The only time Nikki was calm, was when she was sleeping from pure exhaustion. The more Desmond begged for forgiveness the angrier Nikki became. Desmond continued to beg Nikki to forgive him and let the past go, to start a new future. He told her, he would do anything, give anything and she could have anything her heart desired, if she would just let the past go and know he had learned from his mistakes.

Desmond told Nikki he acknowledge the things he did to her were unspeakable, low down and dishonorable. He swore he would never do anything without considering her feelings or talking with her. He promised to never lie again and to be true to their relationship. Nikki heard his words, but she couldn't let go. Nikki had stuffed a lifetime of horror and betrayals. Unfortunately for Desmond, he was the one that set the eruption in motion.

Just as Nikki had been warned that one day those wheels would be set in motion and when it went off, she would be along for the ride until it was over. For Nikki the ride had just begun. Nikki was moody; she couldn't stand herself or anyone else for that matter. Desmond was trying to make things right and wanted Nikki to acknowledge his effort, but Nikki felt when Desmond took out the trash; he wanted a dam medal for it.

Nikki called Tate the guy Desmond and her had seen together, just to see if Desmond had called him; he had. Nikki went over the deep end. When Nikki confronted Desmond he denied it, but Nikki knew he was lying, so she went to the city to see Tate. When she got there Tate introduced her to the ladies that ran the agency called Choices. He told Nikki all her money problems could be over in a few months if she wanted she could be debt free. He said if the ladies liked her, they would work her, if not they would tell her she wasn't their type.

When Nikki met the ladies they were quite impressed with Nikki. When she walked in, they asked if she had ever worked for an agency before. Nikki told them she hadn't, so Angie the owner told her she was just what they were looking for. They said they had an elite clientele that wanted beautiful attractive women to party with. Angie told Nikki that the females were the only ones getting action in most settings usually, because the men were so wasted on snow they couldn't get it up if they had to.

Angie saw a certain set of people and since she was engaged, she agreed not to see any more clients, so she was looking for her replacement. She told Nikki they were big spenders and big tippers if they liked the girl, but they were only in town infrequently. She had a few local clients on her call list and thought Nikki could fit in well. Nikki agreed that she would go on an appointment and see what happened. Nikki's phone didn't ring for two weeks; then Angie called her to say one of her clients was looking to party. Angie said he usually liked several girls and a guy or two, but he wanted to keep it low keyed, because he wanted to introduce his wife to the scene.

Nikki agreed to call him and spoke with Jack the husband of CeCe. He told Nikki he would have a gentleman there for his pleasure, but wanted her to entertain his wife and invited Nikki to the city to join them that night. He told Nikki he would pay her ten thousand dollars for four hours of her time, so. Nikki agreed to go. When Nikki arrived she met Cece, which turned out to be a friend and much to Nikki's surprise, in walked Tate. He hugged Nikki and asked her how she was doing. Nikki said she was fine and it was nice to see a familiar face. Tate told Nikki she didn't have a thing to worry about, because Jack was as tame as a pussycat. He couldn't get an erection if his life depended on it. They offered Nikki a drink after the introductions and went to the kitchen to mix their pleasure. Jack was snorting coke every two seconds and Tate reminded Jack he needed to take care of the fees up front. He laughed and said he knew the drill.

Then he pulled out his checkbook and wrote a check to Tate and two checks to Nikki; one for five thousand dollars to the agency and another to Nikki for Ten thousand dollars. Nikki called the service to ask if Jack could write a check and Angie told Nikki his checks were signed in fourteen-carat gold, not to worry about a thing. Then said she would call Nikki out in four hours.

Jack and Tate had gone outside to the pool and CeCe never left the plate of coke. They snorted cocaine until it was gone while Nikki sat on the chair and talked with CeCe about what she had and hadn't done in the past. She told Nikki she had a couple nights with Jack like that one and knew Jack liked men. She told Nikki Jack wanted her to join him desperately on the partying scene, but she just wasn't sure that was what she wanted at that point and time in her life.

Nikki asked her if she had ever been with a woman before and she admitted she had kissed a woman, but that was as far as she had taken it, but was intrigued by the thought at times. Nikki asked her when she said,

"Join him on the partying scene," what she meant. She said she hug out with Jack while several other people were having sex, but she was enjoying her time, on the drugs she had done. She said her favorite drug in the world was ecstasy, but she had to leave it alone, because she liked it too much. Then Jack and Tate walked in from the pool, because Jack wanted more coke, but it was gone. He thought he had brought his stash at home; then decided to head back to the city for more snow. Jack said he was getting a suite at a hotel in the quarter, while CeCe went to get their blow at home. Nikki agreed she would meet them there shortly. Jack said they only had another eight ball and knew he would need more snow to last him the night, so Tate said he could go get more blow and meet them at the hotel.

When Nikki got to the hotel, she waited outside for Tate to arrive. When he pulled up he had another girl with him called Sissy. She had long blond hair and was quite attractive to Nikki. Tate had called Jack on his cell phone to get the room number and when they walked in everyone snorted several lines while Nikki fixed drinks for everyone at the bar. CeCe sat on the sofa, but she seemed different to Nikki. Nikki asked her if she was all right and CeCe told Nikki she took some ecstasy and was fine. She seemed to be in her own world, so Nikki talked to Sissy. Jack and Tate went to the bedroom and closed the door.

Sissy walked over to Nikki and kissed her, then walked to the window and turned to look at Nikki. Nikki walked over to her and kissed her passionately as Sissy leaned against the wall. She had on a mini skirt, so Nikki kissed her and stroked her leg. She responded with a moan and Nikki kissed her again and pushed her on the chair by the balcony and pulled her shirt off and caressed her breast, as she kissed her nipples. She reached for Nikki's breast, but Nikki pushed her away. Nikki pulled Sissy's skirt up and tore her panties away from her. Sissy laughed, but stopped when Nikki's tongue touched her skin. Nikki lit a cigarette and noticed they had forgotten CeCe was even in the room. CeCe was in the room all right, but Nikki didn't think CeCe knew she was in the room. Tate and Jack were still in the bedroom, when Nikki's phone rang to say her time was up. They asked Nikki if she was staying longer, but she told Angie she was leaving, so Angie told her to drop off their check on her way out the city.

When Nikki dropped the check off Angie asked her how it went, Nikki told her it was ok, nothing spectacular, but not as bad as she thought it might be either. She told Nikki she would call her when anything else came up, so Nikki drove home and told herself she could pay off her two credit cards and would be in a much better place financially than she already was. She told herself if she did it a couple more times, she could pay off her outstanding debt and she could see herself free and clear of all debt in the near future. Nikki also told herself she would be more relaxed if she weren't financially drained and she found another way to feed the darkness she survived in.

CeCe called for Nikki about a week later. When Nikki called her back, she told Nikki she wanted Nikki to meet her. When Nikki asked her what she had in mind, CeCe told Nikki she was going to give her a check for ten-thousand dollars and all she had to do was tell Jack if he called, that she spent the night with her and she was getting more comfortable with things. Nikki said,

"You're going to meet me and give me a check for ten-thousand dollars and I don't have to stay with you, just lie for you."

CeCe said,

"If you want to put that way then, yes that is exactly what I am saying."

Nikki asked her where she wanted to meet and drove to the city and met her at a restaurant. She handed Nikki two checks as before, one for five thousand to the agency and one for ten thousand made out to her. CeCe said Jack was pushing too hard since the night they were together and asked CeCe what happened while he was in the other room, she told him Nikki was great and she could probably get pretty comfortable with things if she spent more time with Nikki. Needless to say he wanted her to spend more time with Nikki. Nikki took the checks and left. She called the agency after an hour and dropped off their check and went home. Nikki was then debt free.

Desmond continued to call begging for forgiveness; Nikki decided to give Desmond a taste of all he had given her through the years. Everything he had done, she did right back to him. Nikki called Desmond on his job, showed up on his job and made her presence known. She sat in his office talking until she was ready to leave.

He quit his job and went to work at another company, but Nikki didn't care. She tried to calm down, but couldn't. She tried to stop, but couldn't, she needed a dumping ground and found it. Nikki meant she would kill Desmond for everything she went through. She hated him with a deep seeded hatred and made him the object of her attention. If she was investing her energy in making his life a living hell, then she didn't have to look at herself and deal with who she had become.

Desmond was six feet tall, two hundred forty pounds, and solid muscle. Nikki was barely five feet tall weighing eighty pounds soaking wet. Desmond could have snapped Nikki in-two if he wanted, but Nikki was no longer afraid of him or anything else for that matter. Even in the mist of everything, he begged Nikki for forgiveness and told her he loved her. This only made her hate him more.

There were moments she calmed down and Desmond and her would spend the night together and make love. After they made love Nikki and Desmond would talk like they did in the past, but the anger was still there mounting. The periods of quietness or peace with Nikki only lasted a day or two if Desmond was lucky. Desmond didn't know if he was coming or going.

Nikki betrayed Desmond in a way she had never before, just as he had her. Desmond thought their sex life was complete and trusted in Nikki to keep that part of their lives sacred. He thought even that part of their lives had become a lie as well, but to Nikki it had been a lie for quite some time. Nikki thought he could only understand the destruction he induced if he had it returned and she sat out to return it.

Nikki wanted to gain control of her life, but for some reason the harder she tried the more out of control it spun. Her thoughts continued spinning and whaling out of control. Nikki was so angry with Desmond she could have taken his life and at times wanted to. There were times when Desmond asked Nikki what was wrong with her and she answered him by saying,

"You breathe."

Nikki wanted him to die. She thought she could breathe if he wasn't breathing. She meant to end his life, if she couldn't find a way out of the darkness that consumed her, because to Nikki he was the one that set it off. He was the one that pushed her into the abyss and she couldn't find her way out because of him.

CHAPTER 28

Nikki took a year break from the world to try and get herself together, then Desmond called again to talk. Nikki didn't know how she felt and didn't think their relationship could be salvaged, but she knew she didn't want to be angry with him anymore. They sat and talked for a while and spent the night together. Nikki felt his fingers on her skin and fell asleep beside him. She woke up during the night to watch him sleep. For such a long time, all Nikki could remember was the bad and the ugly. At that moment, Nikki remembered the good, how his touch felt and how tender he could be. She thought about, how it felt to be in his arms and she missed him. The next morning she left after she told Desmond she had to complete what she started and she had to close her journal once and for all. She told him he could call her if he needed, but she wasn't going to call him until she was finished with everything she was doing to complete the person she was becoming.

Desmond told her he loved her and was proud of the work she had done to that point and encouraged her to continue. He called her a few times to ask more questions about the past and Nikki struggled with his questions and accusations, so again they fought when Desmond continued to bring up her faults in the past. Nikki could not forget what Desmond had done; his betrayals and was ferrous that he actually thought he was more wronged than she was. Desmond told Nikki he was at a party and a girl thought she was going home with him. Nikki felt Desmond was still only trying to pour salt in her wounds so she told him to leave her alone.

Desmond told Nikki she shouldn't react to what some bitch at a party said to him, but Nikki told Desmond not to call the girl a bitch for her benefit, because she wasn't a bitch when he was talking to her or when he was walking around the party thinking he could take her home and screw her. Although they had words, the intensity of the fight wasn't as it had been, but more importantly, Nikki didn't let the topic consume her life as it did in the past. Nikki ended all contact with Desmond for six months. She agreed to meet him at a restaurant for dinner and talk about what could or could not be salvaged, but she felt they needed time apart with no contact. Desmond reluctantly agreed, he said thirty days, but Nikki stood her ground on the six months.

Six months later, they met for dinner to talk about a few issues and Desmond's questions were more than Nikki could handle, but she tried to answer them. It didn't go very well, but Nikki was finished running and being scared too. She told Desmond if he wanted the truth to come to her house and she would tell him what ever he wanted to know, but he acted like an arrogant ass and left. When she turned in her driveway, she got out and went inside. Desmond called her again, when she answered. He asked her to look outside; he was sitting in her driveway. He told her she could sit down and they could talk on the phone or she could walk out the door and talk in person. She walked outside and they talked a few minutes. Nikki tried to tell Desmond she had worked too hard to get where she was. She couldn't afford to go back and wouldn't let anything, not even him take her there again. Desmond told her, she didn't have anything to fear from him, he was hurt, angry and trying to work through his issues and it was unfair of Nikki to think he should process all the crap she dumped on him and it just be ok. Nikki told him she was well aware things weren't ok, because he never wasted a breath to tell her. Nikki told him they destroyed each other.

Nikki and Desmond talked a couple more times in the process of finishing her project which turned out to be counseling and Nikki asked Desmond what he wanted from her. He told Nikki he really needed three things from her. First he needed her to forgive herself for all that she had done and what had happened. Second, he needed her to forgive him for all he had done and what had happened. Third, he needed to hear and fell Nikki was truly sorry for her betrayals and acts of treason toward him and their relationship.

Nikki was angry that Desmond still expected her to say she was the ultimate problem in their relationship. Desmond was responsible for his betrayals, but that wasn't a subject open for discussion with him. Just when Nikki thought it was over, the anger returned and it kept getting worse.

He and Nikki needed to find their own place to heal and Nikki came to realize that relationships could leave you stronger, weaker, more vulnerable and less venerable depending on the depth of the feelings and commitment to the relationship. She also realized, how healthy the core of the relationship was, would play a major role in the outcome of every situation and tragedy. Nikki had said before, a warm heart and true love could move mountains, just as a strong faith could. She also said reckless hearts cleared paths wider than a hurricane's aftermath.

Nikki also come to realize she got caught up in the should's of life. She should, this, she should that. She came to the conclusion, the only should she should have to live up to, was to just live her life and be herself. Nikki knew her teenage years were ripped away from her not by choice, by force. All the time she should have gone crazy and experimented was gone. It was as if Nikki started living her teenage years in her thirties and like everyone has to; she too had to grow up. She had to experience growing pains and come face to face with the person she was.

In the process she came to terms with the woman she was. There were nights she screamed at the top of her lungs, because the emptiness was too hard to bare. The quietness was almost enough to drive her mad. Nikki came to grips with the fact she had always felt tainted, dirty, undeserving and unlovable. She felt that people could see through her very soul. When she was in a crowded room, she felt strangers, somehow could see she was tainted. Nikki couldn't look at herself and see the beauty within or on the outside. She sought reassurance from others, because she couldn't give it to herself. She stayed in sick twisted relationships, because they were an addiction, she had gotten use to the pain and anything else didn't feel right. She dressed quickly in the morning, because she didn't like mirrors.

By the time Nikki finished her program, she smiled more than she had in years, she thought she was an attractive woman, and for the first time in her life truly felt that any person sharing their life with her would be as lucky as she would be. Nikki was sad, because others couldn't forgive her past, it made it more difficult to forgive herself, but she managed, because she realized she was a person with a conscious after all and that in itself was more than some people had. She couldn't betray or hurt another and live with a lie all her life. She wasn't afraid to face the truth anymore. As painful and heart breaking as it was, she stood face to face with the person she was and told herself she loved her, she loved her.

In the end Nikki told herself, she was just as good as the next person, no matter where she came from or what she did. Just because Nikki grew up poor on the banks of a bayou didn't make her a bad person, it made her real. That family gave her survival roots and grounded her in reality of how hard the world could be. Her Grandmother Breaux offered her sanctuary and she would always and forever love and respect her. There were times after her Grandmother's death she didn't pray, because she knew her Grandmother was ashamed of her and the things she was doing or had done. Finally, Nikki could see the smile on the face of her Grandmother, because she worked the program, utilized the tools and as pain staking as it was, she peeled away the layers to her very soul.

Nikki made a promise to herself. To live life in a way, she would never have to apologize for her actions. She thought, that God was right when he wrote,

"Not one, has not sinned and come short of the glory of God." she agreed with that statement, not to justify anything in her past, because she know longer felt she had to justify anything. She lived her life, she made some grave mistakes, she paid some heavy prices, she lost some dear relationships, she grew up and had to move on.

Nikki like a few others, walked on top of the earth, under the earth and through the earth. Everything that happened to her made her the person she became. When she cleaned her act up, she knew she had to become someone totally knew, because being the person she was, also got her where she was.

Nikki learned not to judge. That people are free to live their life as they see fit, because the only person anyone really had to live with was themselves. A person's own conscious can be a remarkable thing, if one is just willing to let go and let God take care of business. As far as Nikki's tainted life, Nikki felt like everyone had skeletons in their closets. She thought true survivors of the skeletons were the ones willing to face theirs and not spend a lifetime running from them, because she also realized the past would always catch up with her at some point.

Nikki looked forward to her future and thought sometimes it felt strange not to be afraid of anything anymore. She didn't cringe when the phone rang, or when she opened the mailbox. She slept well in her own bed at night and forgot at times to set the house alarm. Nikki decided that no one was sin free and if there was someone out there that was, let him or her be the one to cast the first stone in her direction.

Nikki knew life was full of little acts of treason, some intentional, some accidental. She knew she couldn't expect a life that know one would hurt her again, but she also realized the damage she caused in taking matters in her own hands to make some pay for their transgressions. She came to realize that God took care of things in his own time and sometimes that may or may not be in her time frame, just as she had to grow up in her own time frame. It wasn't convenient for several people in Nikki's life at the time, but she had to experience her own growth, at her pace and in its own time. Nikki was sorry that she took away with her more from the relationship with Desmond, than Desmond did. It wasn't until the storm passed that she could see the rainbow and all that that relationship had to teach her. Nikki came to realize people are all born with two lives; one they are given the other one they made. People may not be able to chose their family, or their childhood, but they can chose their adult life and decide whether the past will make or break them.

Nikki wanted to die for an ending; she had no hope left. Then she realized that in life there is hope for miracles and miracles were never ending. The thunder of silence was unexpressed emotions that remained silent for decades in Nikki's life. It started like a faint thunder one hears in the distance, then the thunder gets louder and louder. She could fell the storm approaching, getting closer and closer, until it became a rolling thunder in the pit of a raging storm.

A storm out of control that shook the very core of an individual all the way to their soul. She prayed for the storm to pass, but the thunder raged on and on and on. Just when she thought it was over, the worst was yet to come. She finally surrendered her soul to God in seeking shelter from the storm, but no shelter from the storm could be found there either. She finally realized this raging thunder was the expression of all her silent emotions. She knew she had stepped on the ride by accident, but one she couldn't get off until the ride was over.

As the ride was finishing, Nikki wondered if the end was really coming and braced for the next whirlwind. Then she finally fell asleep from pure exhaustion and being scared during the storm. She dreamed beautiful dreams and then woke up. The storm had really passed. There was no sound. It was quite for the first time in Nikki's life. There was no sound, not even the faint sound of a distant thunder, Nikki had become so accustomed to living with. Nikki developed the skill of floating through the difficult moments in life and realized her opportunities were endless. She saw the good in people and in her past, not just the bad. The moments with some individuals in her life had passed and Nikki remembered how good certain things felt. Like sipping tea with her Grandmother, skipping rocks on the bayou, her cat purring in her ear while she slept beside him.

Andy and Jessie when they smiled and how proud she was the day she graduated from law school. How it felt to hold Tricia's hand both times before she delivered Nikki's two grand children and how it felt each time when they laid her grandchildren in her arms. Where she was and where she ended the ride.

Nikki realized the dreams she had were hopes for her future and sat out one step at a time in finding the beautiful things in life. She grew up and vowed to communicate her feelings know matter how difficult they may be.

Nikki's advice to all that walked in the path she treaded for many years of her life became to know that love is patient and kind. Love should not have to hurt. It should be comforting and supporting. To know that some doors in life have to be closed and in closing that door another one does open. New beginnings are scary and sometimes even frightening, but some new beginnings are rewarding and a blessing in disguise. Know ones-self and know their limitations, trust in ones-self, to get yourself through anything. But most importantly, be stronger than anything that scares you, because the only thing that a person has to fear is fear itself.

Embrace the fear and let it teach you, because there is a lesson to be learned. If one runs from it, it will chase you, but if one stops and looks at it, it will change its form. There is a sixth sense in us all that guides us. The hardest thing one will ever have to do is to learn to trust it and live by it. Also, keep in mind, the hardest lessons some of us will ever have to learn, is the ones we must teach ourselves. So embrace your inner voice, it will keep you safe, embrace life, trust yourself, believe in yourself and carry on.

The night Nikki finished her journal there was a raging storm. The wind was blowing, the thunder rolling and lightening flashing. Nikki felt exhilarated, because she had completed the last obstacle to her future. She went to the kitchen, opened a bottle of wine and poured her a glass. She ran out in the rain by her pool in the back yard. She stood with her arms stretched out as if to embrace the storm. She twirled in the rain. The wind blew all around Nikki and the rain stung as it hit her face. Nikki realized that more importantly, than anything else she had learned, she learned to respect the true sound of thunder, because it would always be a reminder of where she was and where she will never be again. She lifted her glass and toasted to the four winds,

"This is to the well being of all that has come and gone and to the things yet to come in this lifetime, Amen."

Nikki brought her children home and rebuilt a life with them and healed the emotional scares she placed on their life the best she could. Her children had lived in a world of silence as well. Nikki wasn't aware of their silence, until the scares in her life healed and her children returned home. In time, their laughter echoed throughout the house as they healed as a family. Nikki smiled when she listened to them play.

After she completed her journal, she called Desmond and gave him a copy. She told him she wanted to give him understanding to the reasons she couldn't let her guard down and why she always appeared to be running. Nikki had made amends to all the people she had the ability to do so with, but saved Desmond for last, because he would be the hardest. Desmond took Nikki's journal and read the story page by page. It answered some questions for him and created different ones as well. It hurt Desmond to read the truth and he had to deal with his own whirlwind of emotions. Nikki didn't give Desmond the journal to hurt him, but to set him free. Nikki thought she owed him that much in this lifetime. Nikki took her journey in this life at her own pace. She knew that tomorrow, different challenges would follow, but for the first time, she thought she could handle whatever came her way. PJ cautioned Nikki and told her, her work was astonishing and her recovery had just begun, she cautioned her on relationships and encouraged her to concentrate on her family at that point in her life.

Nikki had multiple readings from mediums in her life that told her she was blessed with a special gift from God and if she learned to trust in it, the gift would not forsake her and would give her comfort. She was told that she and Desmond had shared many lifetimes together and in this lifetime they found each other to let go of the turmoil in past lives. In the first life Desmond was a King's advisor and in love with the Queen, which was Nikki. Nikki too was in love with Desmond, but was bound to the king. She craved Desmond and made love to him. Desmond was beheaded because of her and she mourned herself to death. They spent lifetimes searching for each other, but the turmoil of the first lifetime was never resolved. Nikki wanted to resolve the turmoil and understood the connection, but never thought they would reconnect again.

Just as Nikki closed the door on Desmond, She looked up to him standing at her door. He told Nikki he loved her more than breathing and wanted to share his life with her and her alone. He was willing to offer her anything her heart desired, within reason and would stand beside her all the days of her life, if she would have him. Nikki Grabbed Desmond and held him as tight as she could. They cried together and talked about what they had hoped their future could be.

They agreed to see where it would lead and have faith and trust in the core of their relationship and promised to never take for granted the opportunity they had been given or the lessons they had learned. They were different in this world yet the same and willing to accept that in the other without judgment or being condescending. They shared their lives and each other with boundaries and set limitations. They talked with open hearts and made their relationship their priority and built a core strong enough to withstand anything. PJ was not supportive of the reunion with Desmond and told Nikki that it could be detrimental to her recovery, but Nikki didn't listen.

Six months later, Nikki and Desmond were to be married on the edge of a cliff in Acapulco. On her wedding day Nikki called the states to speak to Desmond's boss. As a wedding present Nikki was going to fly Desmond to Vegas so he would need a few more days off work, but in the course of making their arrangements Nikki was told Desmond was in New York on business by the secretary and would not be returning for two weeks. Nikki asked what kind of business and was told all she knew was Desmond told the office he had family business to take care of in New York. Nikki thought as always know-one knew the truth about Desmond and once again he was taking her for another ride, one she wouldn't survive.

Nikki's hopes and dreams were a lie, once again, Nikki was a secret and know-one knew about the most important day of their lives, the betrayal once again, was more than Nikki could bare. Then, they stood on the cliff, down the beach from their hotel with their private pool, flowers and champagne waiting. Nikki stood side by side, hand in hand with Desmond looking out across the ocean. Desmond took Nikki in his arms and said he loved her. Nikki looked at Desmond, smiled and said,

"If our life ends today, right now, in this moment, all my dreams came true in one moment."

When Desmond whispered,

"Me Too."

Nikki walked behind him and pushed Desmond to his death, off the very same cliff, she said her vows on that very same morning, then turned and walked away. As Nikki walked away there was no emotion only the thoughts of who she was, all her dreams, hopes, desires and fantasies was gone, vanished in the blink of an eye. Nikki thought everyone had a breaking point, in an instant someone says enough, no more, end this.

Pushing Desmond off the cliff in that moment was like pulling the knife out her side that stabbed her repeatedly and she bleed until there was nothing left; nothing, but the dark black hole that had been like a drain sucking her in all her life; the dark side where something evil waited. Something waiting, wanting, but wait a minute, Nikki was blinking her eyes. The air around her moved as if it was leaving her. Her chest was crushing, something was wrong, nothing was right. Her vision cleared just as Desmond walked up beside her and placed his hand in hers to walk her down the aisle. Nikki turned to him and realized she was in a trance and saw a vision of the things to come. She dropped the phone in her hand and acknowledged the phone call to his boss was real. When she looked at him, she couldn't see him, only the faces of her children and the life she would through away if she stayed. The price was simply, just too high.

In that moment she acknowledged her gift or thing that lived inside her from birth. She respected it, agreed to live with it, grow with it, learn from it and find understanding of it. Nikki then, simply turned and walked away. She knew there was a darkness that had and wanted to consume her all her life that she never understood or accepted. She lived her life always on the edge just circling the drain. She also knew there was a light inside her that continued to pull her back and wouldn't allow her to cross over.

www.ingramcontent.com/pod-product-compliance
Lightning Source LLC
Chambersburg PA
CBHW031108030726
47496CB00002BA/439